ᴴᵉ Cartoon Chronicles of America

FIGHT FOR FREEDOM

ALSO BY STAN MACK AND SUSAN CHAMPLIN

The Cartoon Chronicles of America

ROAD TO REVOLUTION!

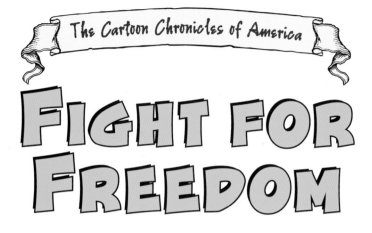

The Cartoon Chronicles of America

FIGHT FOR FREEDOM

Stan Mack and Susan Champlin

BLOOMSBURY

NEW YORK BERLIN LONDON SYDNEY

First published in the United States of America in July 2012
by Bloomsbury Books for Young Readers
www.bloomsburykids.com

For information about permission to reproduce selections from this book, write to
Permissions, Bloomsbury BFYR, 175 Fifth Avenue, New York, New York 10010

Library of Congress Cataloging-in-Publication Data
Mack, Stanley.
Fight for freedom / by Stan Mack and Susan Champlin. — 1st U.S. ed.
p.   cm. — (The cartoon chronicles of America)
Summary: In 1861, a young slave named Sam escapes to search for his father, who has been conscripted
into the Confederate Army, and makes his way to a northern city, while back at the Virginia plantation where
Sam was raised, Annabelle, the owner's daughter, struggles to run things after her father's death.
ISBN 978-1-59990-835-9 (paperback) · ISBN 978-1-59990-014-8 (hardcover)
1. Graphic novels. [1. Graphic novels. 2. Slavery—Fiction. 3. Plantation life—Virginia—Fiction.
4. Virginia—History—Civil War, 1861–1865—Fiction. 5. United States—History—Civil War,
1861–1865—Fiction.] I. Champlin, Susan. II. Title.
PZ7.7.M33Fig 2012   741.5′973—dc23   2011040481

Typeset in CCFaceFont
Art created with Pigma Micron pen and Pelikan watercolor on 1-ply Strathmore paper
Book design by Stan Mack, Susan Champlin, and Yelena Safronova

Printed in China by Hung Hing Printing (China) Co., Ltd., Shenzhen, Guangdong
2 4 6 8 10 9 7 5 3 1 (paperback)
2 4 6 8 10 9 7 5 3 1 (hardcover)

All papers used by Bloomsbury Publishing, Inc., are natural, recyclable products
made from wood grown in well-managed forests. The manufacturing processes
conform to the environmental regulations of the country of origin.

For Susan's parents: Peggy Champlin, PhD, for her enthusiastic and scholarly support of our books, and Charles Champlin, for his brilliant insights into the art and craft of writing

The Cartoon Chronicles of America

FIGHT FOR FREEDOM

PROLOGUE

IN WHICH WE LEARN HOW WE GOT HERE

Of all the issues that led to the Civil War, one overshadowed every other: slavery.

Slavery was nothing new in the 1800s. In fact, slavery had existed throughout history, including in ancient Greece and Egypt. And when traders brought the first shipload of Africans to Virginia in the early 1600s, slavery took hold in the new colonies.

The Declaration of Independence claimed that "all men are created equal"— but several Founding Fathers owned slaves. The signers of the Constitution meant to form "a more perfect Union"—but accepted slavery as a fact of life.

By the early 1800s, the North and South were very different places. The North had bustling cities, busy factories, and many people, white and black, who believed that slavery was immoral and must be "abolished" (gotten rid of). These people were called "abolitionists."

The South was largely rural and agricultural, with a smaller population. Using slave labor allowed plantation owners to enjoy wealth and leisure. Citizens of Southern states believed they had a constitutional right to keep slaves and hated outsiders telling them what they could and couldn't do.

As the country expanded West, new territories meant new battlegrounds over slavery. A series of events inflamed the issue. These included the Fugitive Slave Act (which said that citizens were required to help capture and return escaped slaves) and the Supreme Court's Dred Scott decision, which said that people of African descent could never be citizens (and therefore had no legal rights) and said that the federal government did not have the power to prohibit slavery in the territories.

Abolitionists were outraged. Many helped slaves run away through the Underground Railroad, a secret network of escape routes to the free states and Canada. The issue of slavery now divided the country: North versus South, abolitionist versus slave owner, states' righters versus those who believed in federal government control. Some were even demanding the country's breakup.

In 1860, Abraham Lincoln was elected president of the United States. Although he said he would not interfere with slavery in the states in which it already existed, Southerners believed that he meant to abolish slavery.

On December 20, 1860, South Carolina left the union—or "seceded"— soon followed by Mississippi, Florida, Alabama, Georgia, Louisiana, and Texas. Together they formed the Confederate States of America.

Lincoln declared that no state on its own could choose to leave the union. On April 12, 1861, the Confederate states bombarded Fort Sumter, the federal fort in the port of Charleston, South Carolina. The troops in the fort surrendered. The Civil War had officially begun.

Four days later, Virginia, Arkansas, North Carolina, and Tennessee seceded. Northerners and Southerners rushed into uniform—each side believing the war would be short-lived.

The first important battle took place at Manassas Junction, Virginia, in July 1861, twenty-five miles southwest of Washington City (now called Washington, DC). The Rebels sent the Yanks running, but it was clear that both sides needed organizing, training, and discipline.

The federals devised a two-part plan. In the West, the goal was to gain control of the Mississippi River. In the East, it was to capture Richmond, Virginia, the capital of the Confederacy. During the course of the war, more fighting would take place in Virginia than in any other state.

In the spring of 1862, the Union Army of the Potomac began pushing toward Richmond from the coast, only to be stopped by a smaller Confederate force, led by the man who would become the South's greatest general: Robert E. Lee. The war then moved from the outskirts of Richmond to northern Virginia.

Our story opens at Twin Oaks, a small plantation just south of Fredericksburg, Virginia. It is July 1862, and the war is coming ever closer to Twin Oaks's doorstep...

In this book, you'll meet fictional characters who get caught up with real-life people and events. After reading our story, please turn to the epilogue, in the back. There, you'll find out what's fact and what's fiction.

THE MAIN CHARACTERS

ABRAHAM LINCOLN

President of the United States during the Civil War.

JOHNNY REB & BILLY YANK

Nicknames for Confederate and Union soldiers.

EZEKIEL "ZEKE" JEFFERSON

An African American reporter covering the war for the North.

CAROLINE & BEAUMONT "BEAU" BEAUREGARD

Mistress and master of Twin Oaks Plantation.

MAE & JOSEPH

Mae is Caroline's personal slave. Joseph is a field slave at Twin Oaks.

MR. TWIST

The Twin Oaks overseer.

SAM

Young house slave at Twin Oaks Plantation. Son of Mae and Joseph. Sam is the same age as Annabelle Beauregard.

ANNABELLE BEAUREGARD

Daughter of Caroline and Beau. As a young child, Annabelle was cared for by Mae and played with Sam. But their worlds are changing.

TWIN OAKS PLANTATION

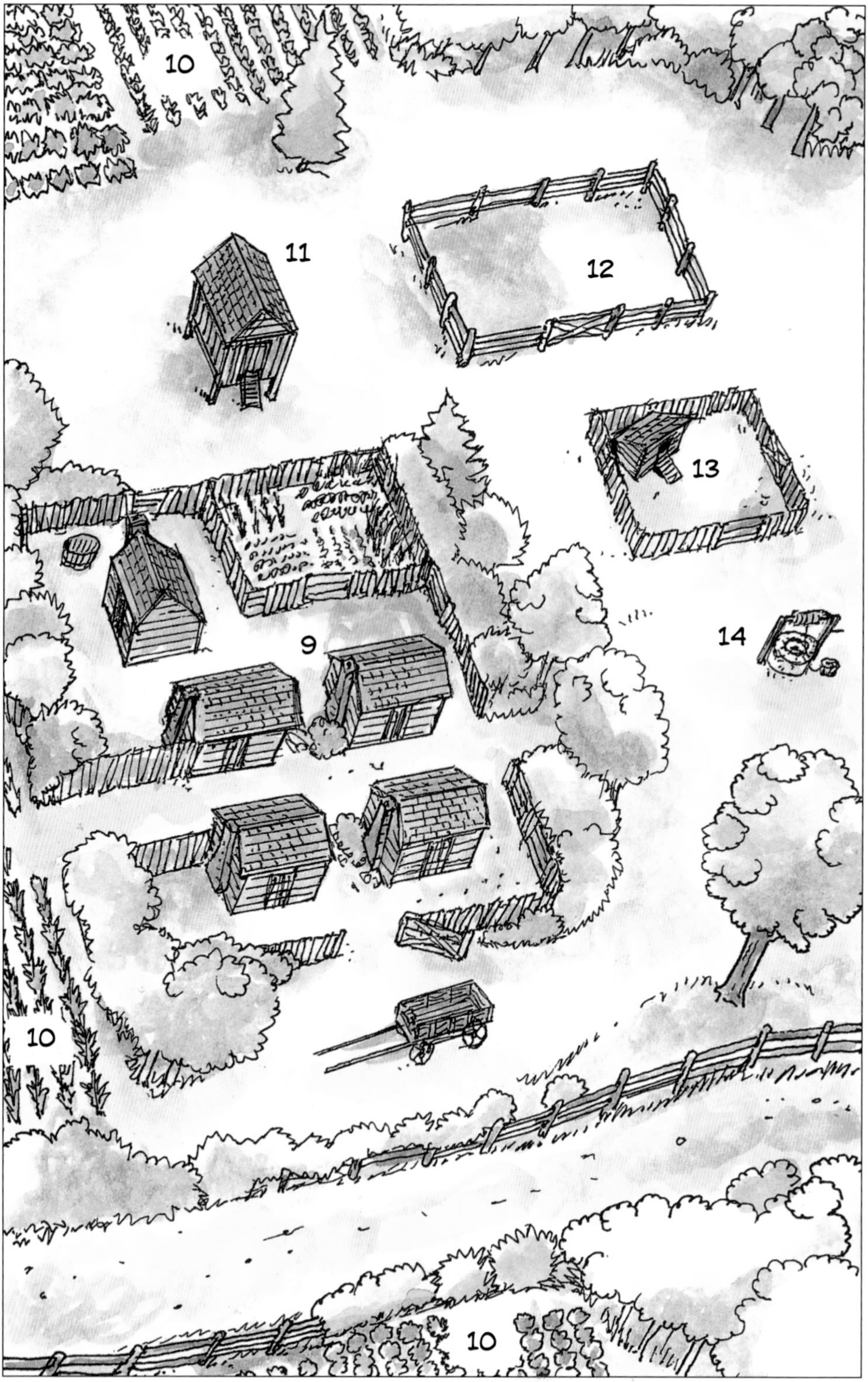
10
11
12
13
9
14
10
10

1. MAIN HOUSE	8. CARRIAGE HOUSE
2. KITCHEN	9. SLAVE QUARTERS
3. SMOKEHOUSE	10. THE FIELDS
4. GARDEN	11. CORNCRIB
5. SPRINGHOUSE	12. SHEEP PEN
6. CORRAL	13. HENHOUSE
7. BARN	14. WELL

VIRGINIA & WASHINGTON CITY, 1862

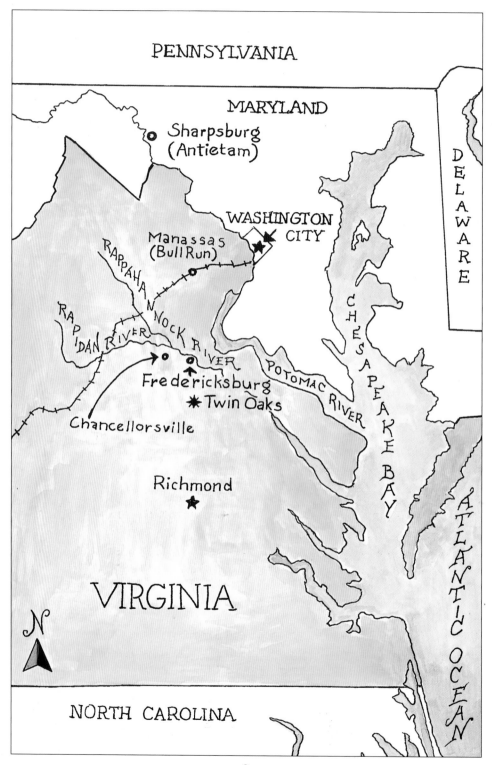

PENNSYLVANIA

MARYLAND

Sharpsburg
(Antietam)

WASHINGTON CITY

Manassas
(Bull Run)

RAPPAHANNOCK RIVER

RAPIDAN RIVER

POTOMAC RIVER

Fredericksburg

Twin Oaks

Chancellorsville

Richmond

VIRGINIA

N

DELAWARE

CHESAPEAKE BAY

ATLANTIC OCEAN

NORTH CAROLINA

CHAPTER 1

The Confederate Army, commanded by General Robert E. Lee, has beaten back every attack into Virginia by the Union forces. Each new assault serves only to inspire more devotion in the South.

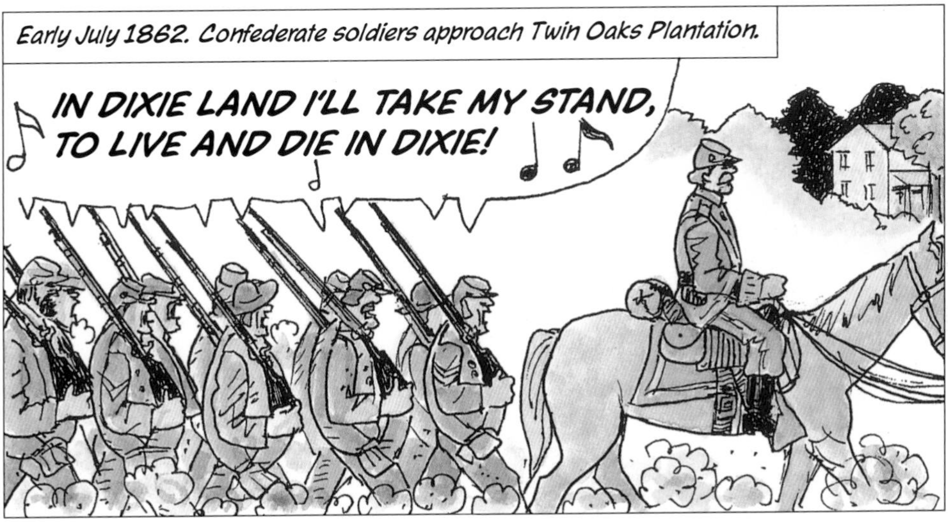

Early July 1862. Confederate soldiers approach Twin Oaks Plantation.
IN DIXIE LAND I'LL TAKE MY STAND, TO LIVE AND DIE IN DIXIE!

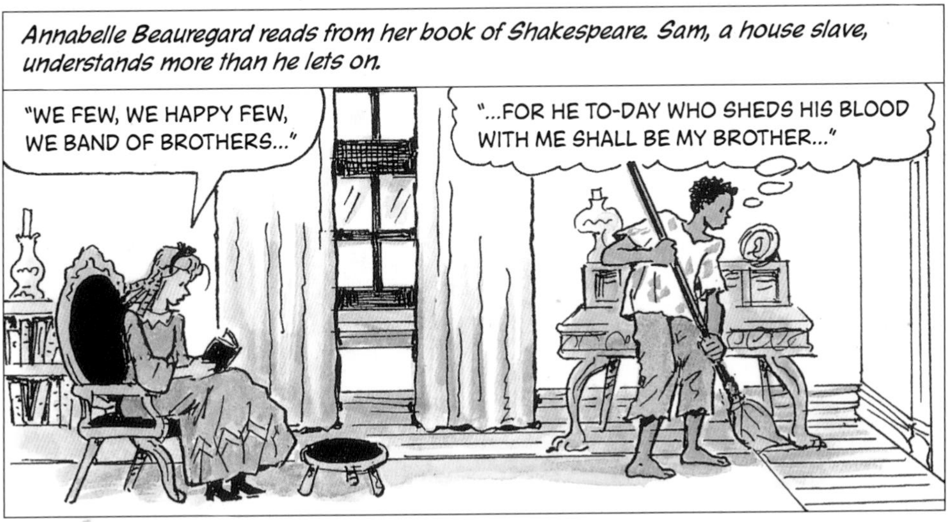

Annabelle Beauregard reads from her book of Shakespeare. Sam, a house slave, understands more than he lets on.
"WE FEW, WE HAPPY FEW, WE BAND OF BROTHERS..."
"...FOR HE TO-DAY WHO SHEDS HIS BLOOD WITH ME SHALL BE MY BROTHER..."

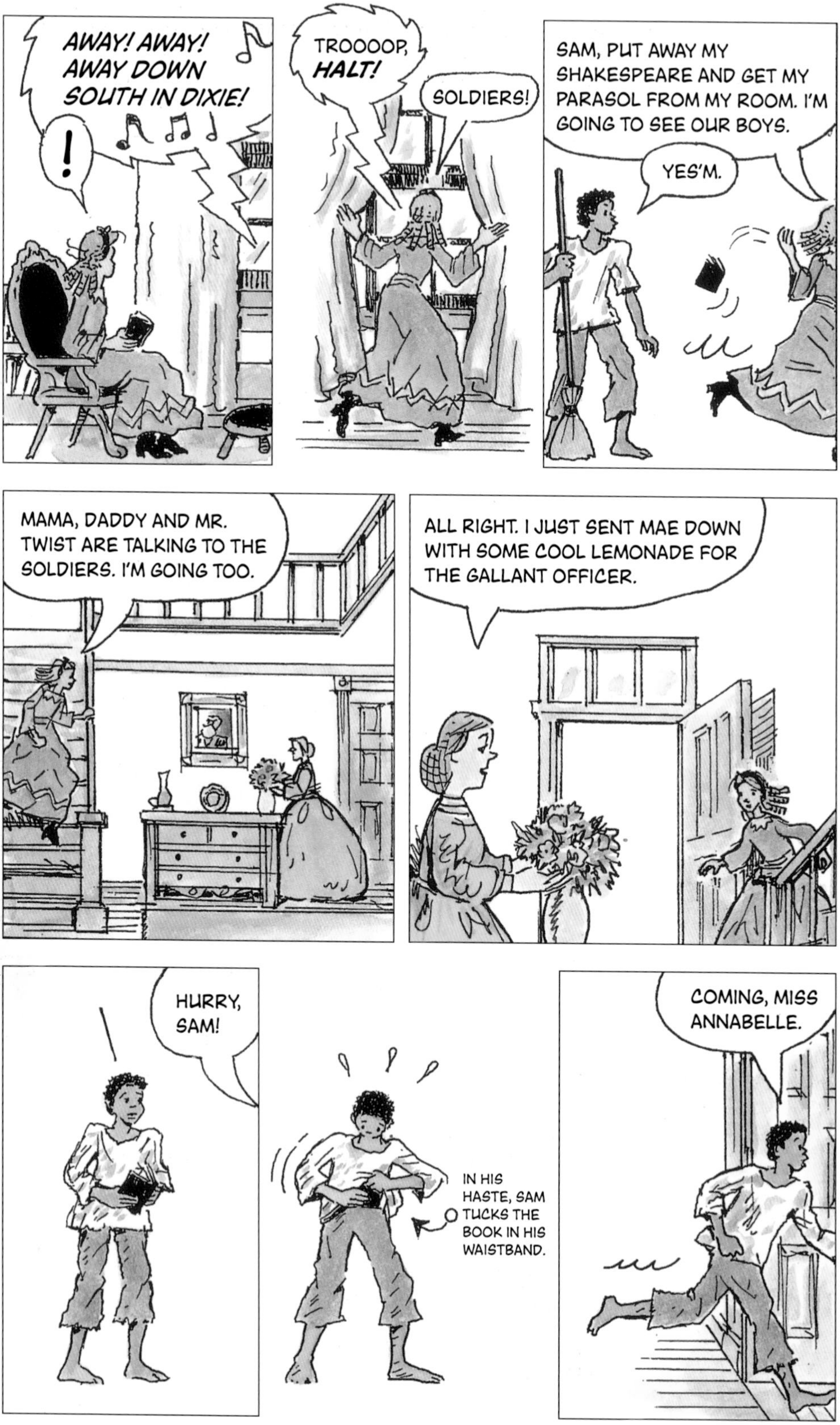
AWAY! AWAY! AWAY DOWN SOUTH IN DIXIE!
!
TROOOOP, HALT!
SOLDIERS!
SAM, PUT AWAY MY SHAKESPEARE AND GET MY PARASOL FROM MY ROOM. I'M GOING TO SEE OUR BOYS.
YES'M.
MAMA, DADDY AND MR. TWIST ARE TALKING TO THE SOLDIERS. I'M GOING TOO.
ALL RIGHT. I JUST SENT MAE DOWN WITH SOME COOL LEMONADE FOR THE GALLANT OFFICER.
HURRY, SAM!
IN HIS HASTE, SAM TUCKS THE BOOK IN HIS WAISTBAND.
COMING, MISS ANNABELLE.

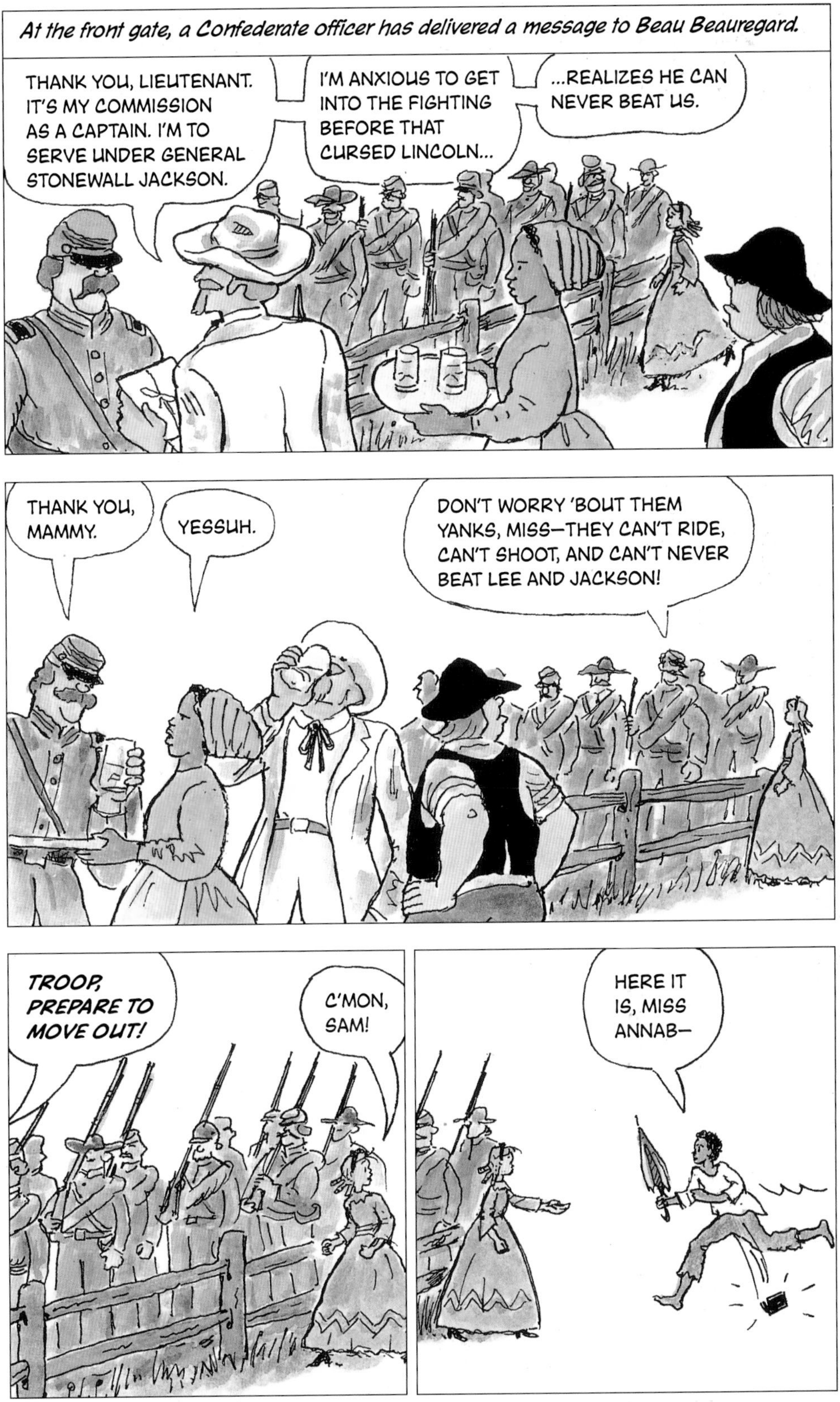
At the front gate, a Confederate officer has delivered a message to Beau Beauregard.
THANK YOU, LIEUTENANT. IT'S MY COMMISSION AS A CAPTAIN. I'M TO SERVE UNDER GENERAL STONEWALL JACKSON.
I'M ANXIOUS TO GET INTO THE FIGHTING BEFORE THAT CURSED LINCOLN...
...REALIZES HE CAN NEVER BEAT US.
THANK YOU, MAMMY.
YESSUH.
DON'T WORRY 'BOUT THEM YANKS, MISS—THEY CAN'T RIDE, CAN'T SHOOT, AND CAN'T NEVER BEAT LEE AND JACKSON!
TROOP, PREPARE TO MOVE OUT!
C'MON, SAM!
HERE IT IS, MISS ANNAB—

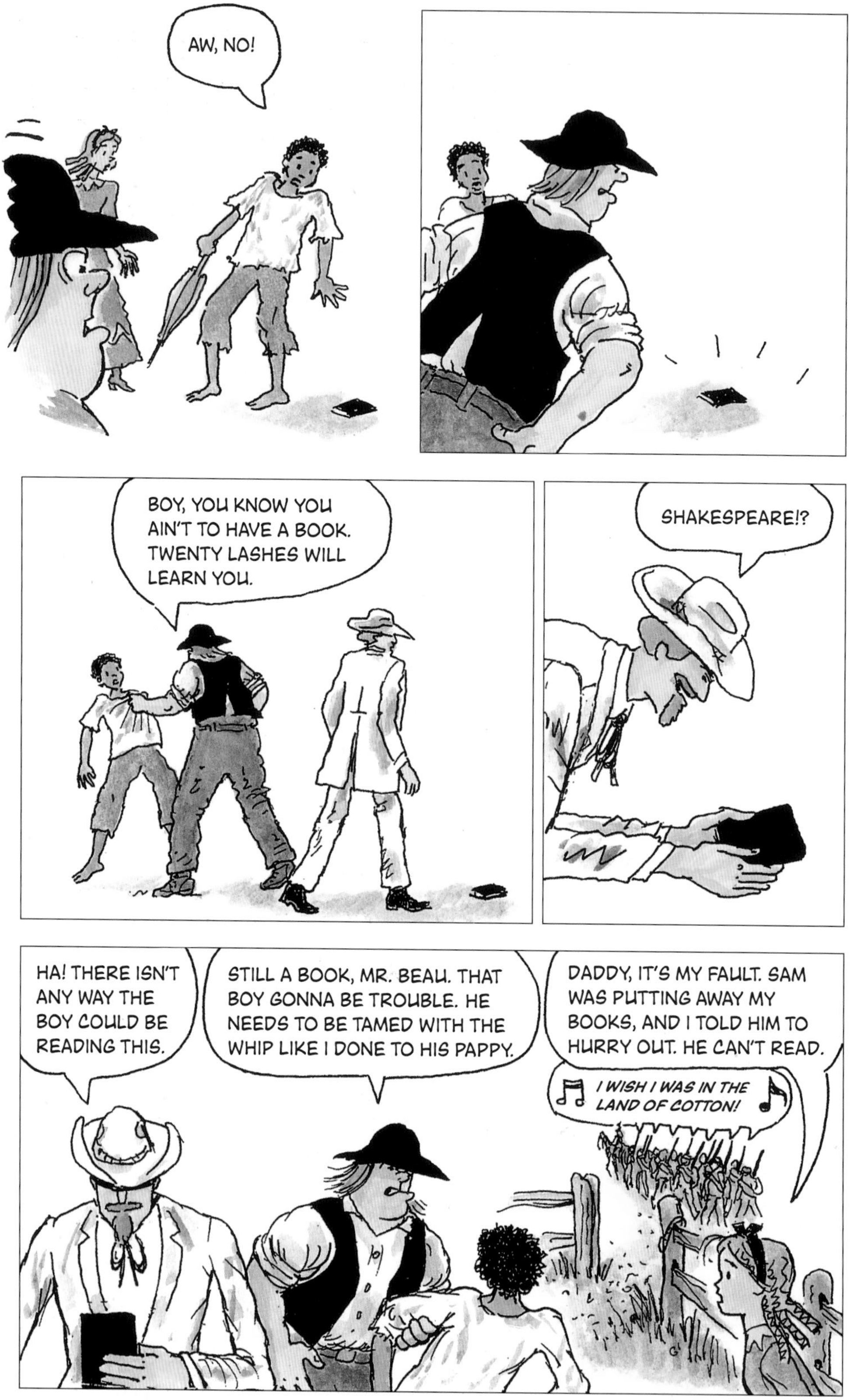
AW, NO!
BOY, YOU KNOW YOU AIN'T TO HAVE A BOOK. TWENTY LASHES WILL LEARN YOU.
SHAKESPEARE!?
HA! THERE ISN'T ANY WAY THE BOY COULD BE READING THIS.
STILL A BOOK, MR. BEAU. THAT BOY GONNA BE TROUBLE. HE NEEDS TO BE TAMED WITH THE WHIP LIKE I DONE TO HIS PAPPY.
DADDY, IT'S MY FAULT. SAM WAS PUTTING AWAY MY BOOKS, AND I TOLD HIM TO HURRY OUT. HE CAN'T READ.
I WISH I WAS IN THE LAND OF COTTON!

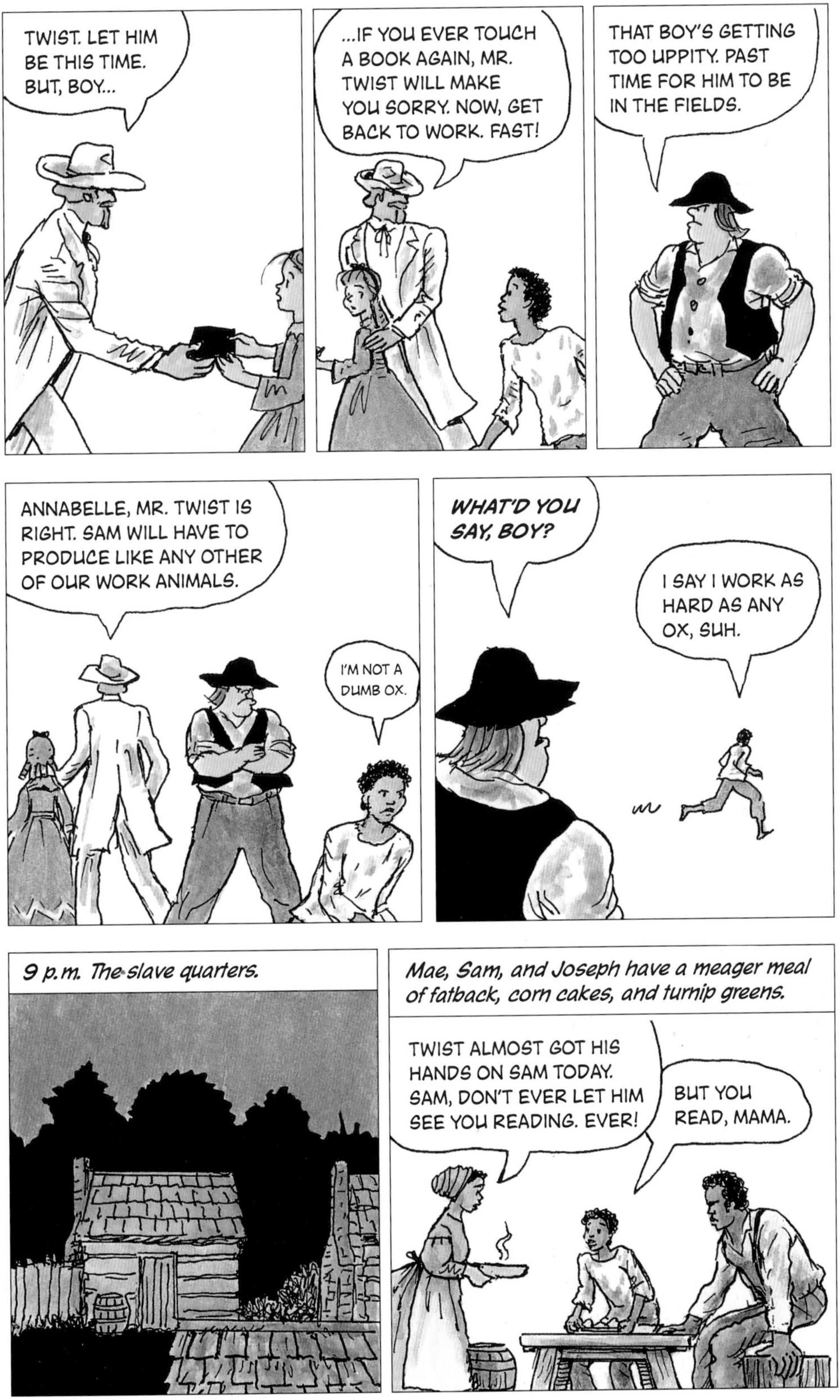
TWIST. LET HIM BE THIS TIME. BUT, BOY...
...IF YOU EVER TOUCH A BOOK AGAIN, MR. TWIST WILL MAKE YOU SORRY. NOW, GET BACK TO WORK. FAST!
THAT BOY'S GETTING TOO UPPITY. PAST TIME FOR HIM TO BE IN THE FIELDS.
ANNABELLE, MR. TWIST IS RIGHT. SAM WILL HAVE TO PRODUCE LIKE ANY OTHER OF OUR WORK ANIMALS.
I'M NOT A DUMB OX.
WHAT'D YOU SAY, BOY?
I SAY I WORK AS HARD AS ANY OX, SUH.
9 p.m. The slave quarters.
Mae, Sam, and Joseph have a meager meal of fatback, corn cakes, and turnip greens.
TWIST ALMOST GOT HIS HANDS ON SAM TODAY. SAM, DON'T EVER LET HIM SEE YOU READING. EVER!
BUT YOU READ, MAMA.

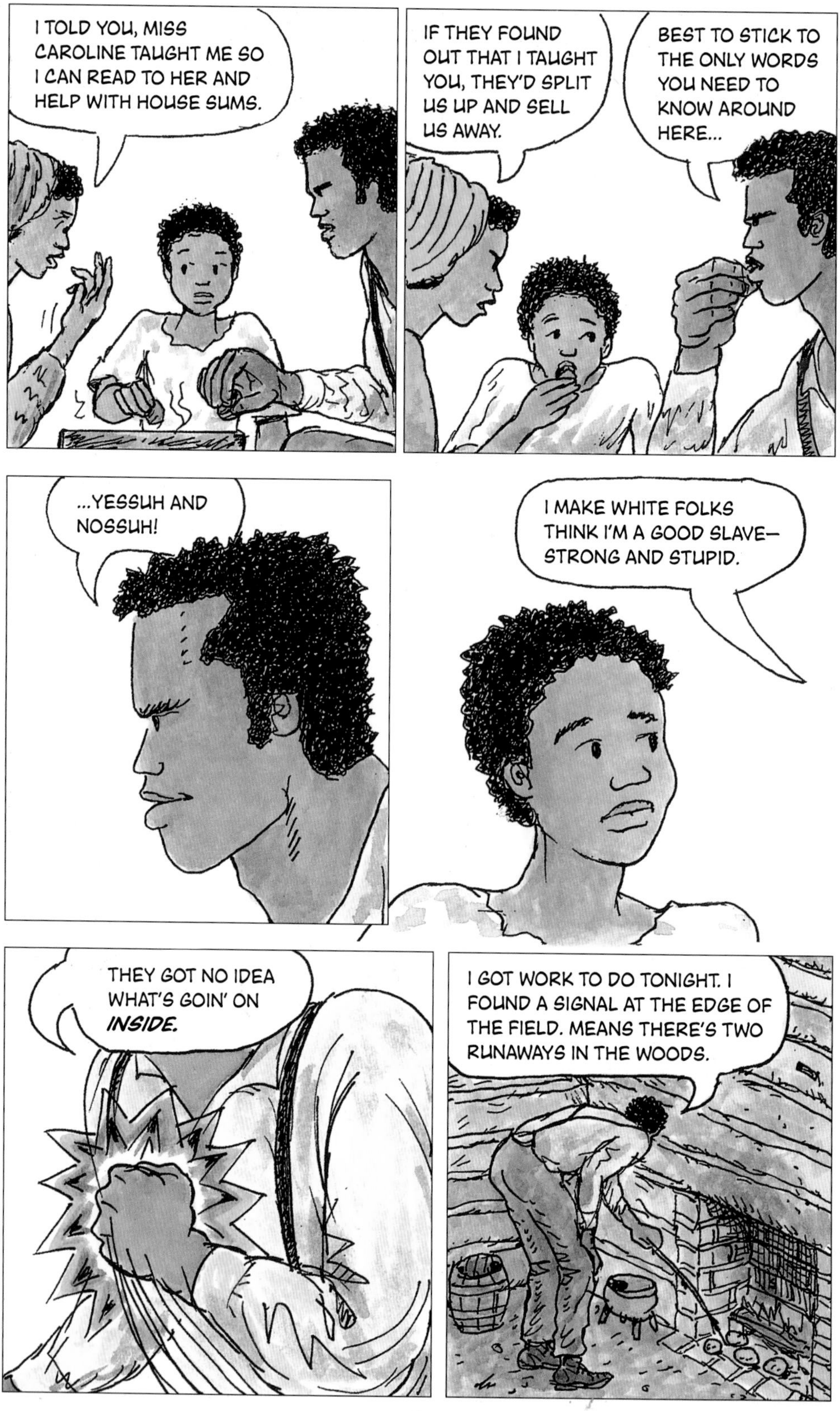
I TOLD YOU, MISS CAROLINE TAUGHT ME SO I CAN READ TO HER AND HELP WITH HOUSE SUMS.
IF THEY FOUND OUT THAT I TAUGHT YOU, THEY'D SPLIT US UP AND SELL US AWAY.
BEST TO STICK TO THE ONLY WORDS YOU NEED TO KNOW AROUND HERE...
...YESSUH AND NOSSUH!
I MAKE WHITE FOLKS THINK I'M A GOOD SLAVE— STRONG AND STUPID.
THEY GOT NO IDEA WHAT'S GOIN' ON *INSIDE.*
I GOT WORK TO DO TONIGHT. I FOUND A SIGNAL AT THE EDGE OF THE FIELD. MEANS THERE'S TWO RUNAWAYS IN THE WOODS.

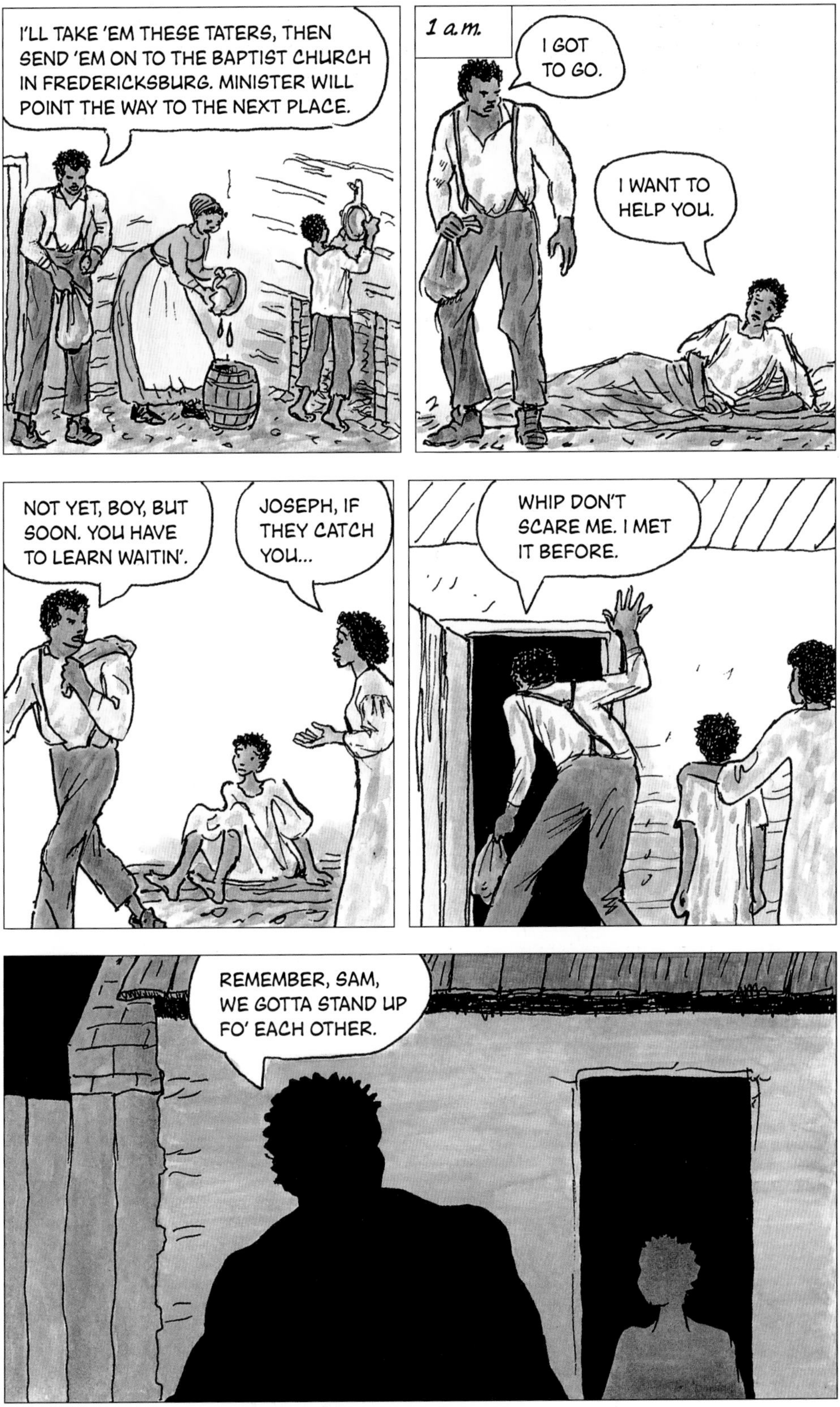
I'LL TAKE 'EM THESE TATERS, THEN SEND 'EM ON TO THE BAPTIST CHURCH IN FREDERICKSBURG. MINISTER WILL POINT THE WAY TO THE NEXT PLACE.
1 a.m.
I GOT TO GO.
I WANT TO HELP YOU.
NOT YET, BOY, BUT SOON. YOU HAVE TO LEARN WAITIN'.
JOSEPH, IF THEY CATCH YOU...
WHIP DON'T SCARE ME. I MET IT BEFORE.
REMEMBER, SAM, WE GOTTA STAND UP FO' EACH OTHER.

CHAPTER 2

As the Confederates continue to succeed on the Virginia battlefields, plantation owners are confident they can hold on to their privileged way of life—and the slaves who make it possible.

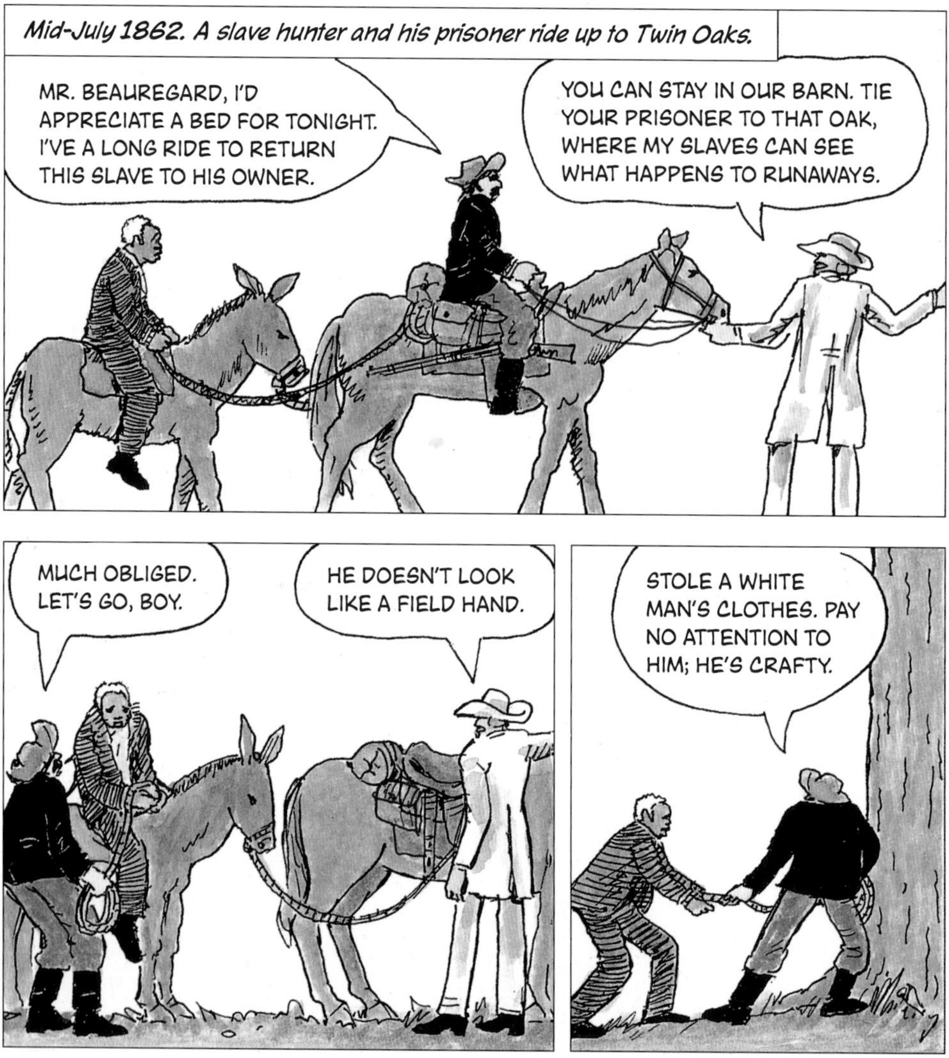
Mid-July 1862. A slave hunter and his prisoner ride up to Twin Oaks.
MR. BEAUREGARD, I'D APPRECIATE A BED FOR TONIGHT. I'VE A LONG RIDE TO RETURN THIS SLAVE TO HIS OWNER.
YOU CAN STAY IN OUR BARN. TIE YOUR PRISONER TO THAT OAK, WHERE MY SLAVES CAN SEE WHAT HAPPENS TO RUNAWAYS.
MUCH OBLIGED. LET'S GO, BOY.
HE DOESN'T LOOK LIKE A FIELD HAND.
STOLE A WHITE MAN'S CLOTHES. PAY NO ATTENTION TO HIM; HE'S CRAFTY.

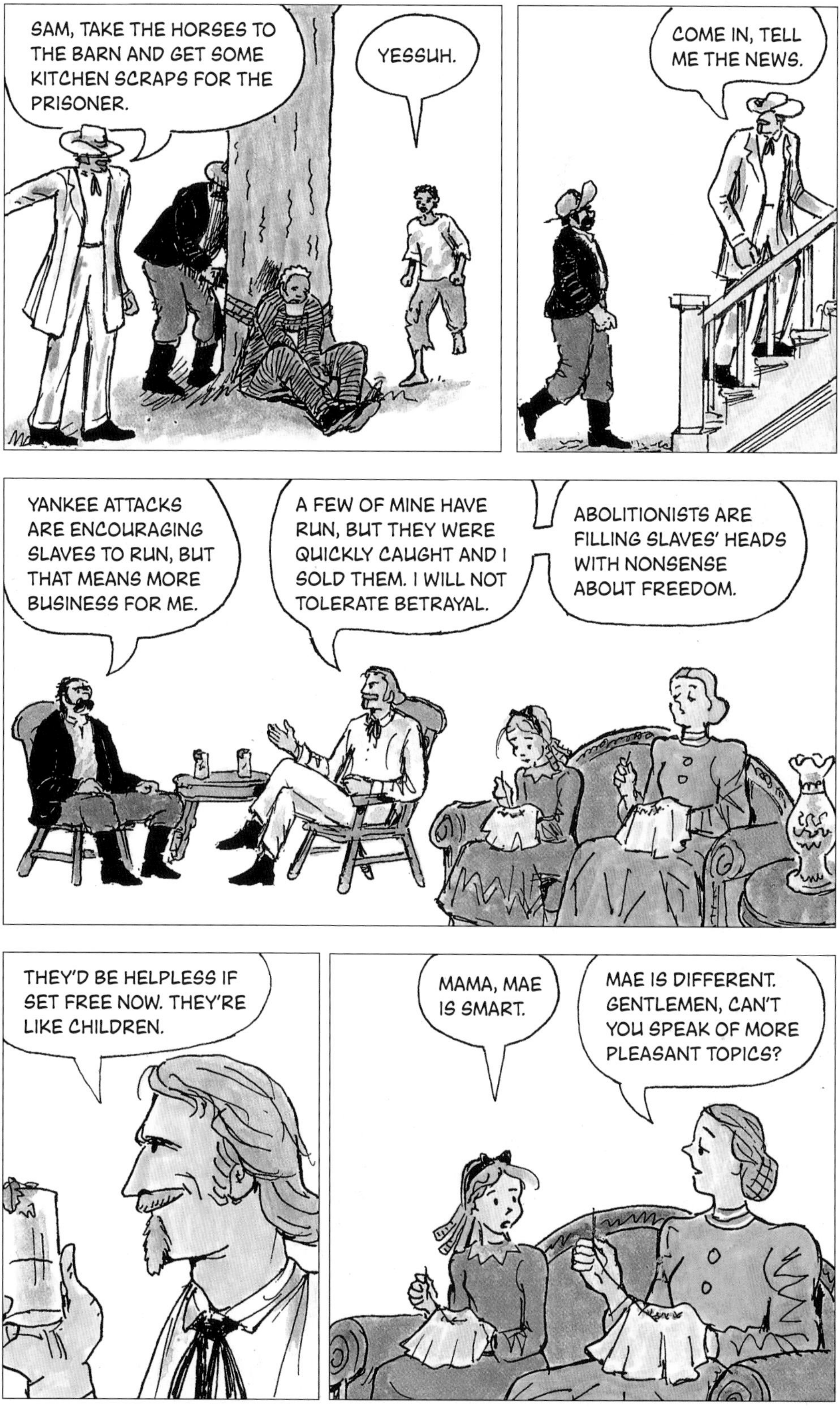
SAM, TAKE THE HORSES TO THE BARN AND GET SOME KITCHEN SCRAPS FOR THE PRISONER.
YESSUH.
COME IN, TELL ME THE NEWS.
YANKEE ATTACKS ARE ENCOURAGING SLAVES TO RUN, BUT THAT MEANS MORE BUSINESS FOR ME.
A FEW OF MINE HAVE RUN, BUT THEY WERE QUICKLY CAUGHT AND I SOLD THEM. I WILL NOT TOLERATE BETRAYAL.
ABOLITIONISTS ARE FILLING SLAVES' HEADS WITH NONSENSE ABOUT FREEDOM.
THEY'D BE HELPLESS IF SET FREE NOW. THEY'RE LIKE CHILDREN.
MAMA, MAE IS SMART.
MAE IS DIFFERENT. GENTLEMEN, CAN'T YOU SPEAK OF MORE PLEASANT TOPICS?

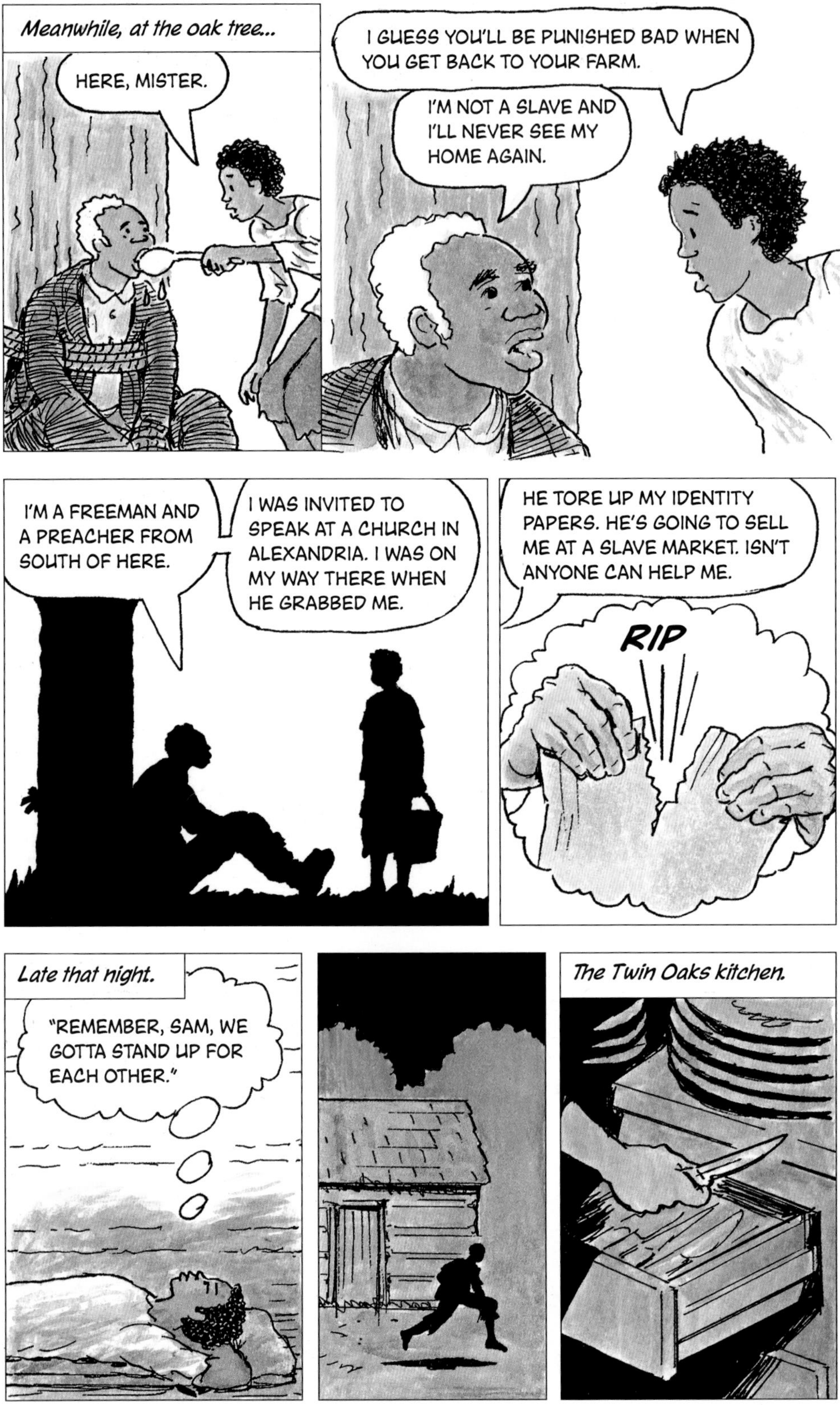
Meanwhile, at the oak tree...
HERE, MISTER.
I GUESS YOU'LL BE PUNISHED BAD WHEN YOU GET BACK TO YOUR FARM.
I'M NOT A SLAVE AND I'LL NEVER SEE MY HOME AGAIN.
I'M A FREEMAN AND A PREACHER FROM SOUTH OF HERE.
I WAS INVITED TO SPEAK AT A CHURCH IN ALEXANDRIA. I WAS ON MY WAY THERE WHEN HE GRABBED ME.
HE TORE UP MY IDENTITY PAPERS. HE'S GOING TO SELL ME AT A SLAVE MARKET. ISN'T ANYONE CAN HELP ME.
RIP
Late that night.
"REMEMBER, SAM, WE GOTTA STAND UP FOR EACH OTHER."
The Twin Oaks kitchen.

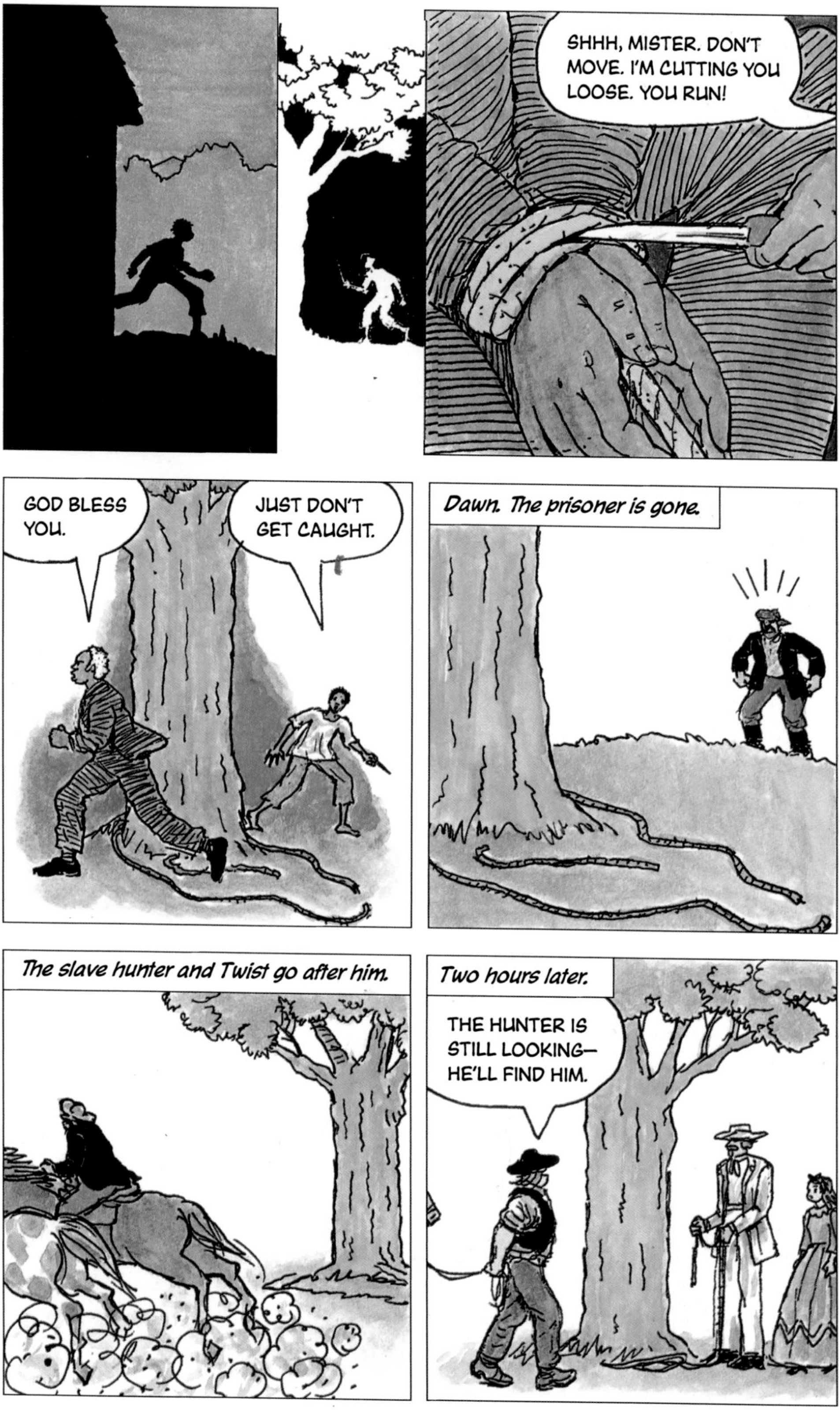
SHHH, MISTER. DON'T MOVE. I'M CUTTING YOU LOOSE. YOU RUN!
GOD BLESS YOU.
JUST DON'T GET CAUGHT.
Dawn. The prisoner is gone.
The slave hunter and Twist go after him.
Two hours later.
THE HUNTER IS STILL LOOKING— HE'LL FIND HIM.

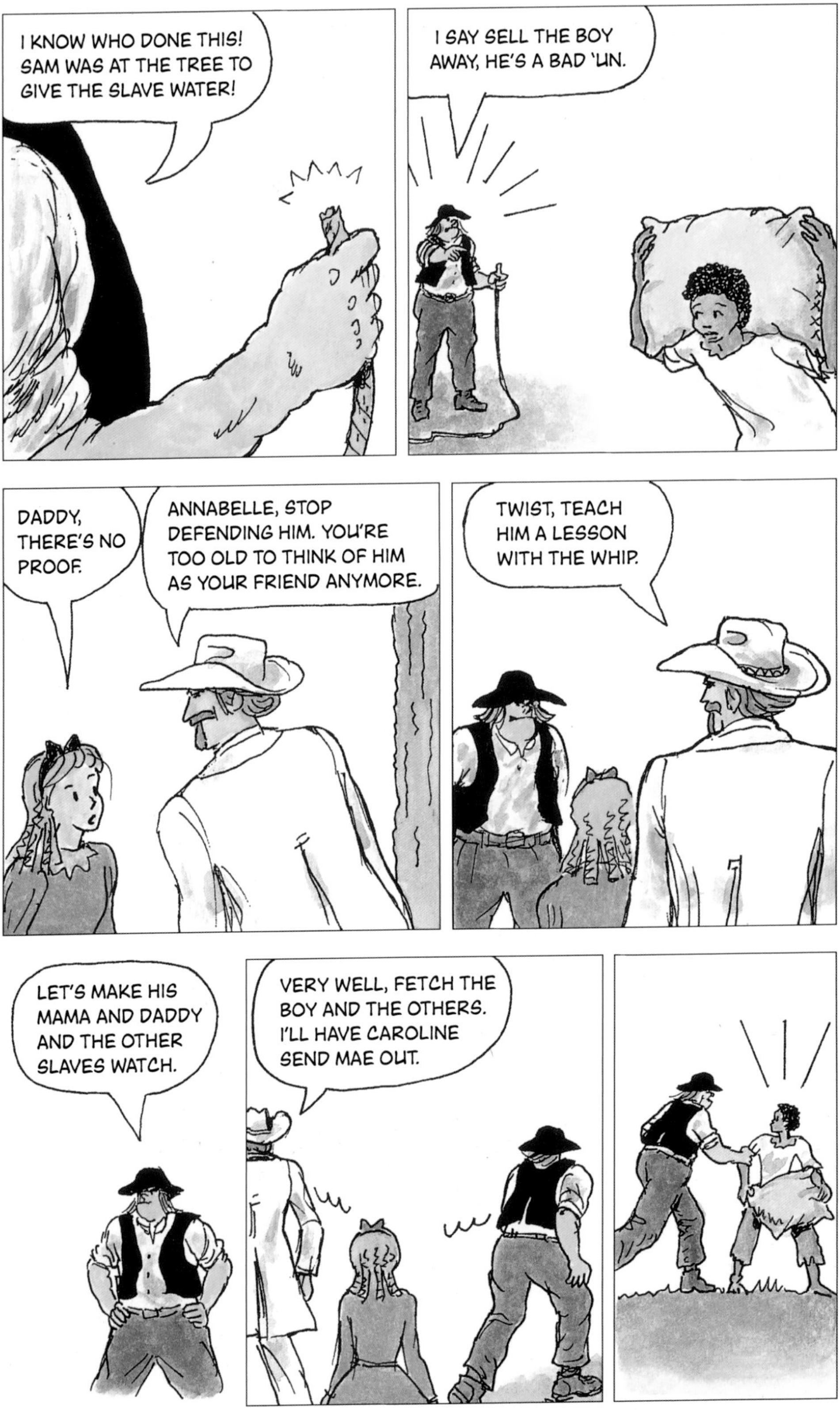
I KNOW WHO DONE THIS! SAM WAS AT THE TREE TO GIVE THE SLAVE WATER!
I SAY SELL THE BOY AWAY, HE'S A BAD 'UN.
DADDY, THERE'S NO PROOF.
ANNABELLE, STOP DEFENDING HIM. YOU'RE TOO OLD TO THINK OF HIM AS YOUR FRIEND ANYMORE.
TWIST, TEACH HIM A LESSON WITH THE WHIP.
LET'S MAKE HIS MAMA AND DADDY AND THE OTHER SLAVES WATCH.
VERY WELL, FETCH THE BOY AND THE OTHERS. I'LL HAVE CAROLINE SEND MAE OUT.

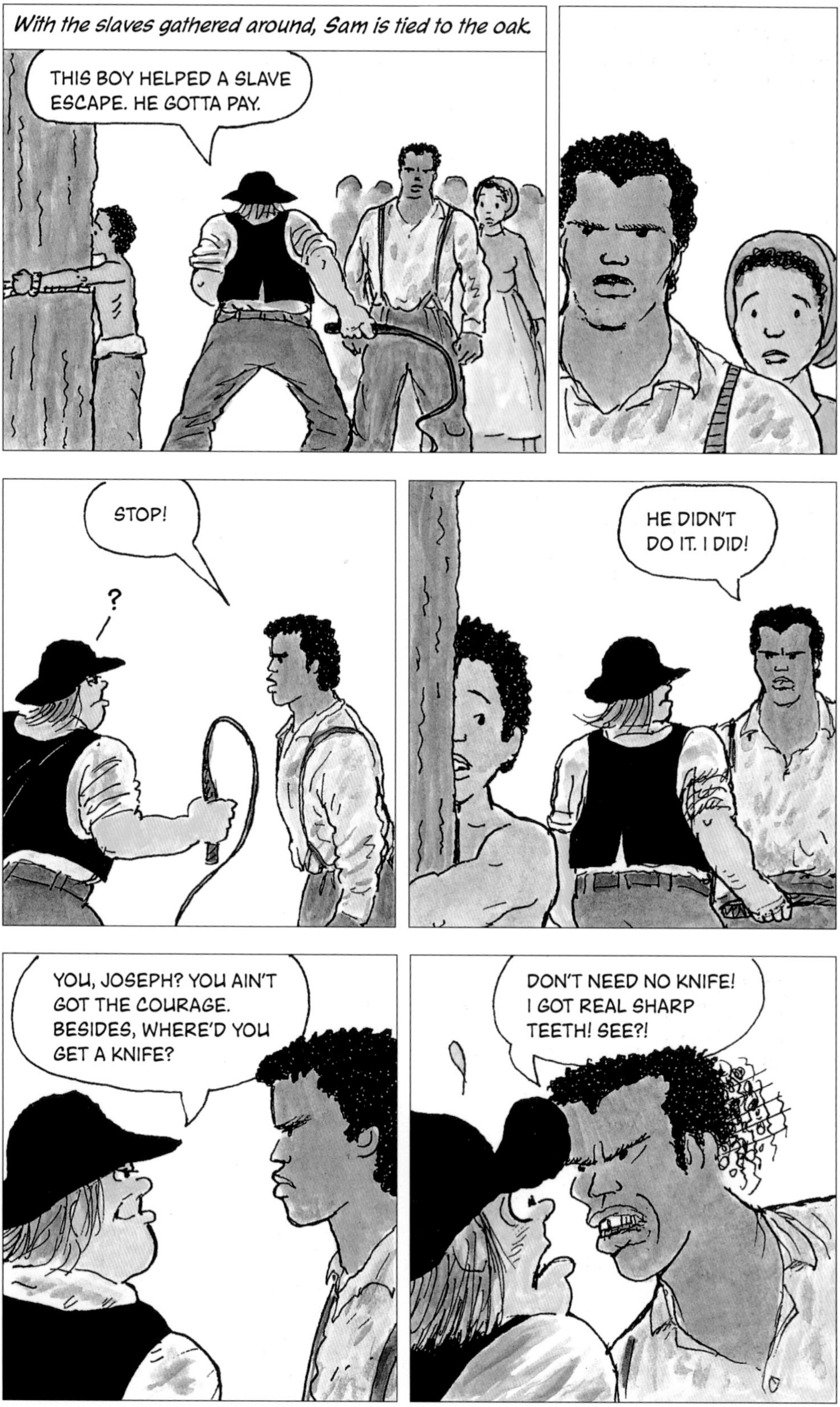
With the slaves gathered around, Sam is tied to the oak.
THIS BOY HELPED A SLAVE ESCAPE. HE GOTTA PAY.
STOP!
?
HE DIDN'T DO IT. I DID!
YOU, JOSEPH? YOU AIN'T GOT THE COURAGE. BESIDES, WHERE'D YOU GET A KNIFE?
DON'T NEED NO KNIFE! I GOT REAL SHARP TEETH! SEE?!

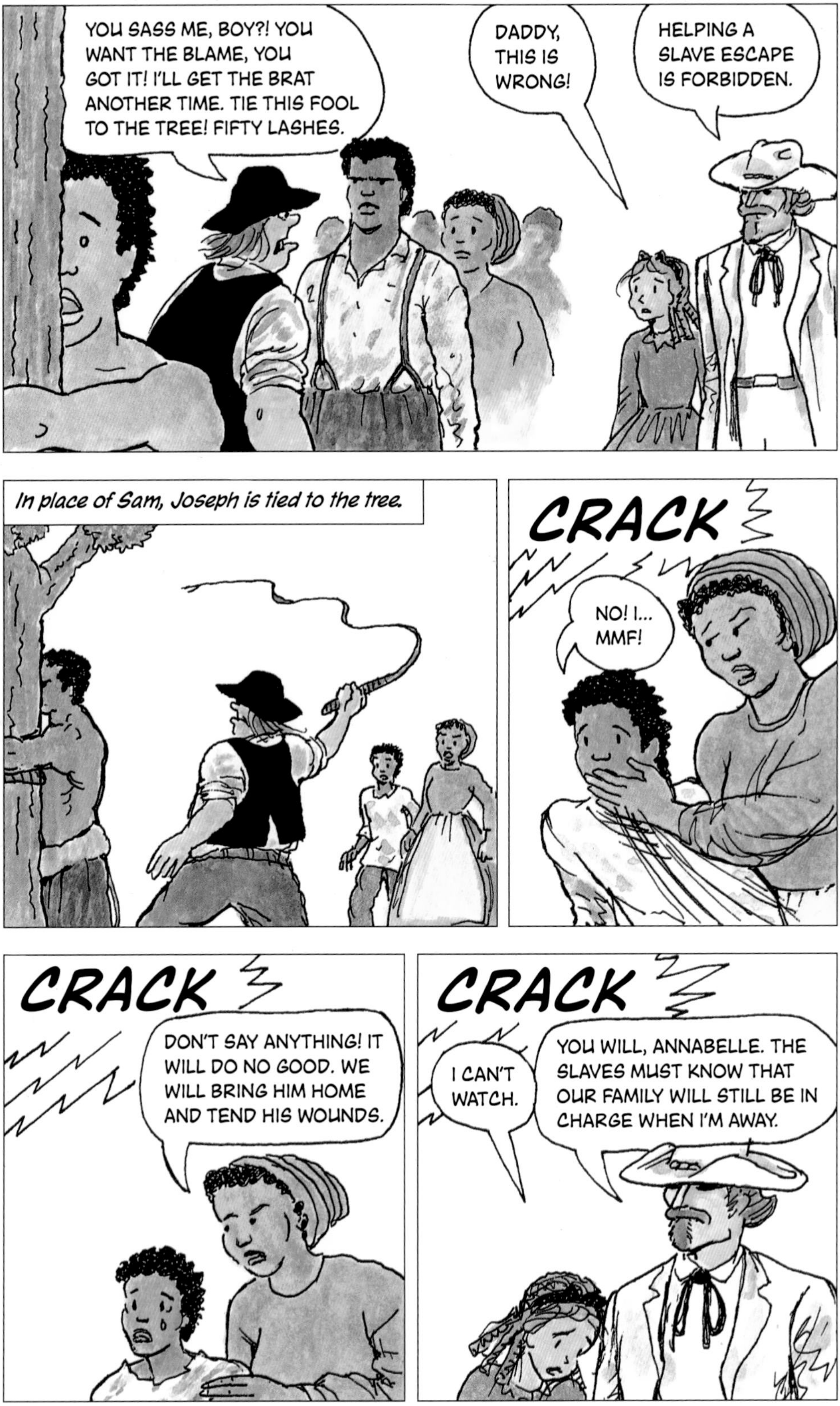
YOU SASS ME, BOY?! YOU WANT THE BLAME, YOU GOT IT! I'LL GET THE BRAT ANOTHER TIME. TIE THIS FOOL TO THE TREE! FIFTY LASHES.
DADDY, THIS IS WRONG!
HELPING A SLAVE ESCAPE IS FORBIDDEN.
In place of Sam, Joseph is tied to the tree.
CRACK
NO! I... MMF!
CRACK
DON'T SAY ANYTHING! IT WILL DO NO GOOD. WE WILL BRING HIM HOME AND TEND HIS WOUNDS.
CRACK
I CAN'T WATCH.
YOU WILL, ANNABELLE. THE SLAVES MUST KNOW THAT OUR FAMILY WILL STILL BE IN CHARGE WHEN I'M AWAY.

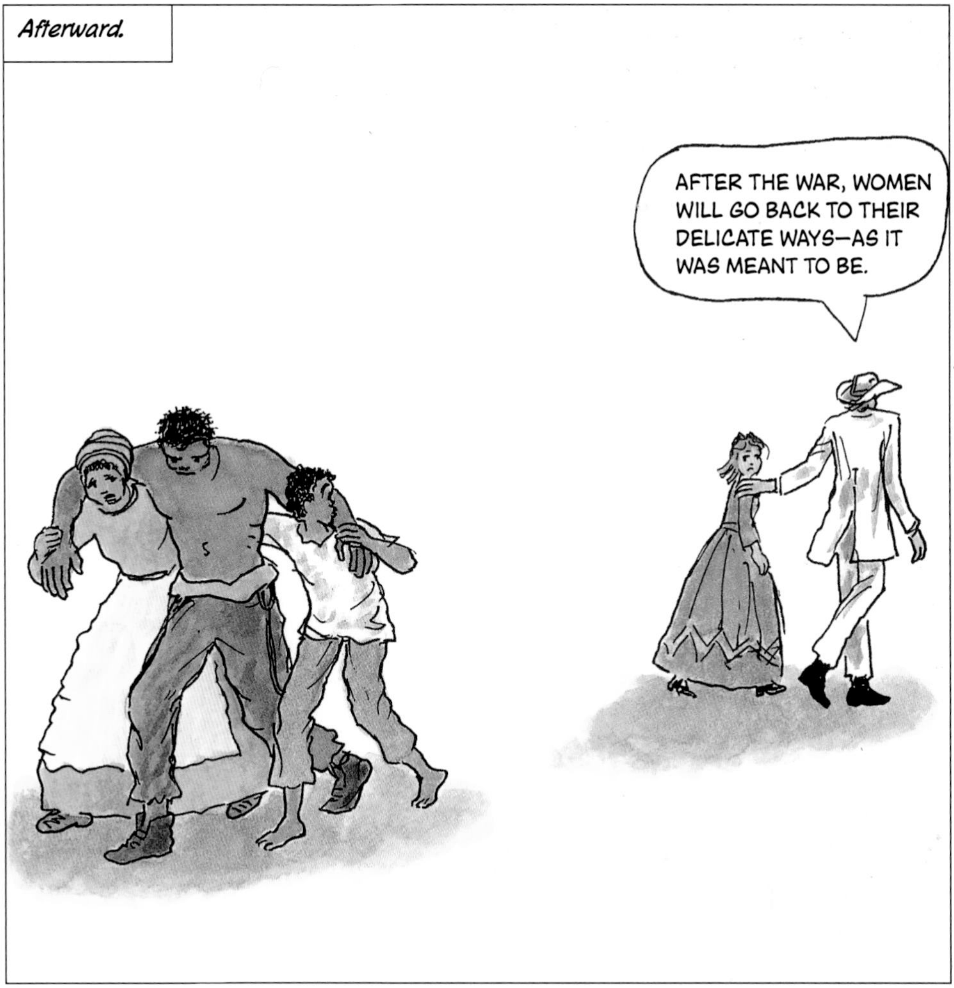
Afterward.
AFTER THE WAR, WOMEN WILL GO BACK TO THEIR DELICATE WAYS—AS IT WAS MEANT TO BE.

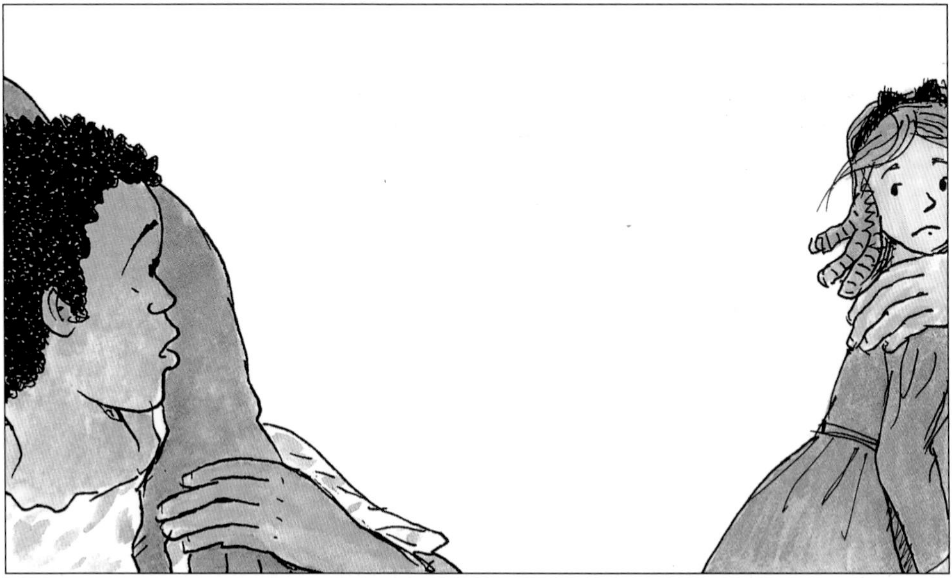

CHAPTER 3

On July 17, 1862, Lincoln signs the Second Confiscation Act. It says that slaves from Confederate states who reach Union lines will be considered captives of war and "free of their servitude."

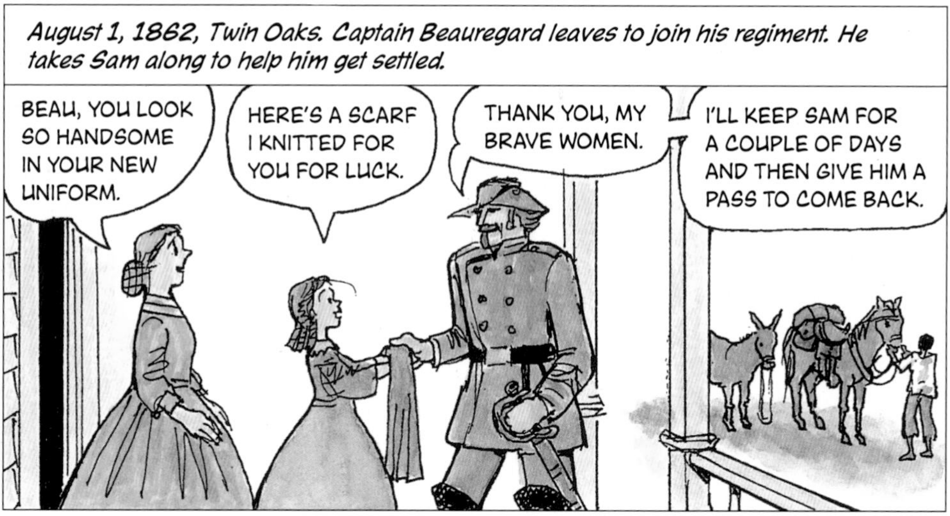
August 1, 1862, Twin Oaks. Captain Beauregard leaves to join his regiment. He takes Sam along to help him get settled.
BEAU, YOU LOOK SO HANDSOME IN YOUR NEW UNIFORM.
HERE'S A SCARF I KNITTED FOR YOU FOR LUCK.
THANK YOU, MY BRAVE WOMEN.
I'LL KEEP SAM FOR A COUPLE OF DAYS AND THEN GIVE HIM A PASS TO COME BACK.

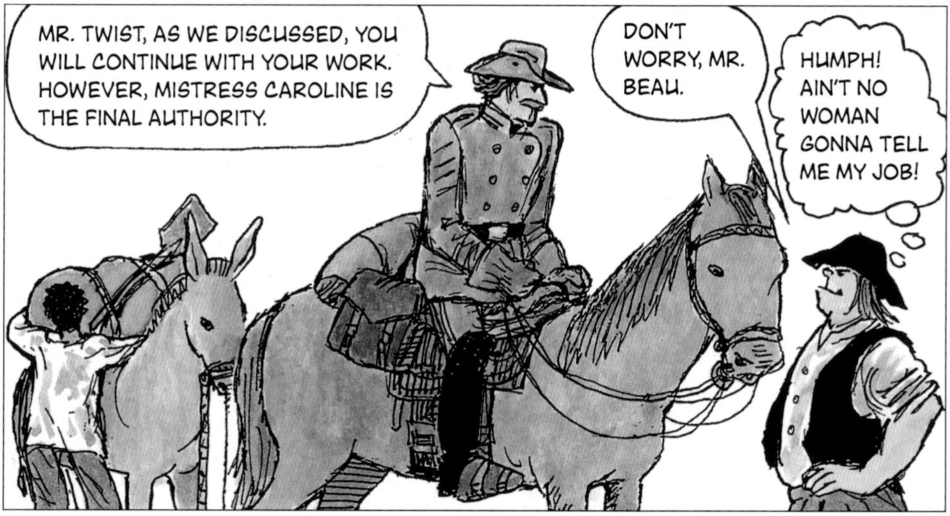
MR. TWIST, AS WE DISCUSSED, YOU WILL CONTINUE WITH YOUR WORK. HOWEVER, MISTRESS CAROLINE IS THE FINAL AUTHORITY.
DON'T WORRY, MR. BEAU.
HUMPH! AIN'T NO WOMAN GONNA TELL ME MY JOB!

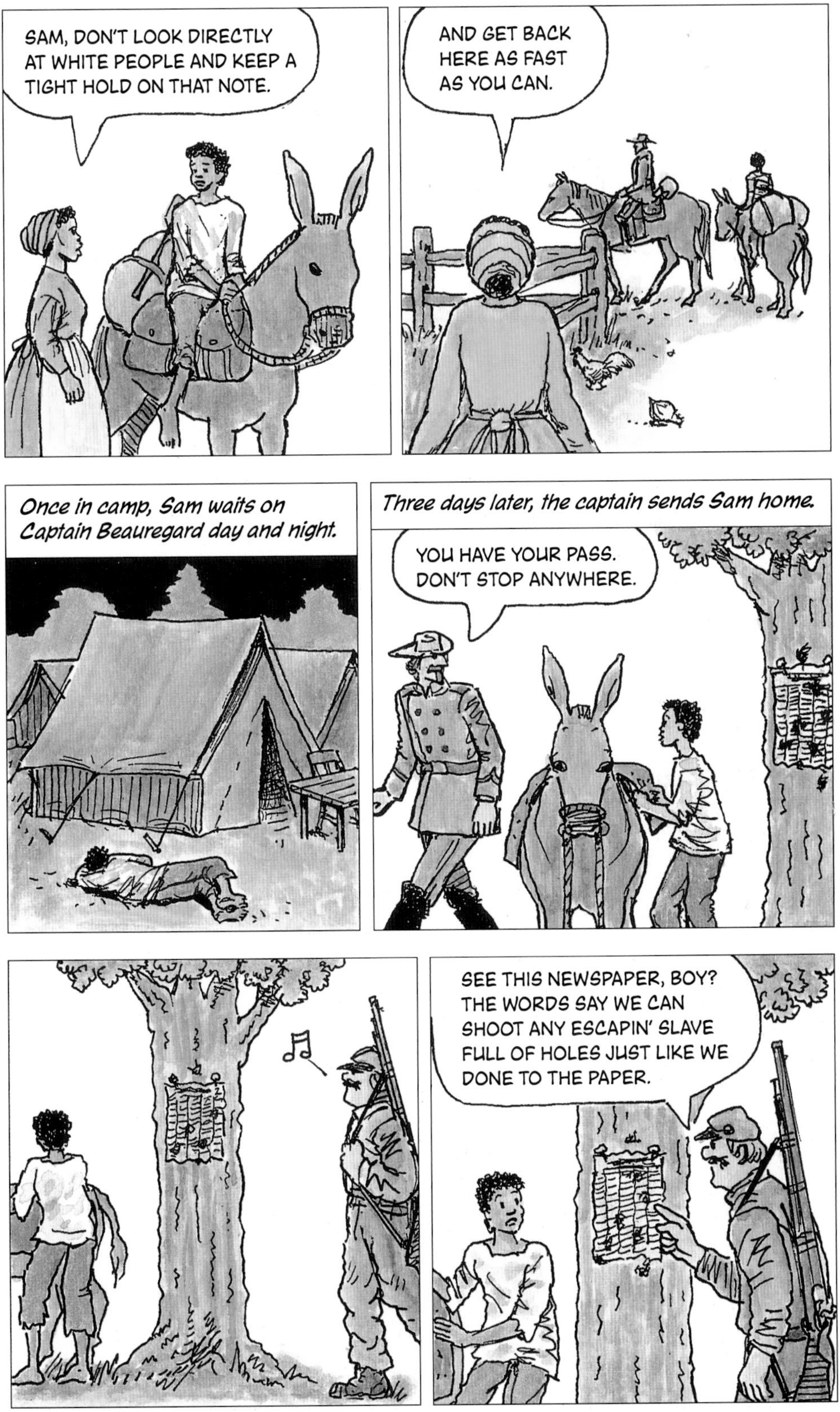
SAM, DON'T LOOK DIRECTLY AT WHITE PEOPLE AND KEEP A TIGHT HOLD ON THAT NOTE.
AND GET BACK HERE AS FAST AS YOU CAN.
Once in camp, Sam waits on Captain Beauregard day and night.
Three days later, the captain sends Sam home.
YOU HAVE YOUR PASS. DON'T STOP ANYWHERE.
SEE THIS NEWSPAPER, BOY? THE WORDS SAY WE CAN SHOOT ANY ESCAPIN' SLAVE FULL OF HOLES JUST LIKE WE DONE TO THE PAPER.

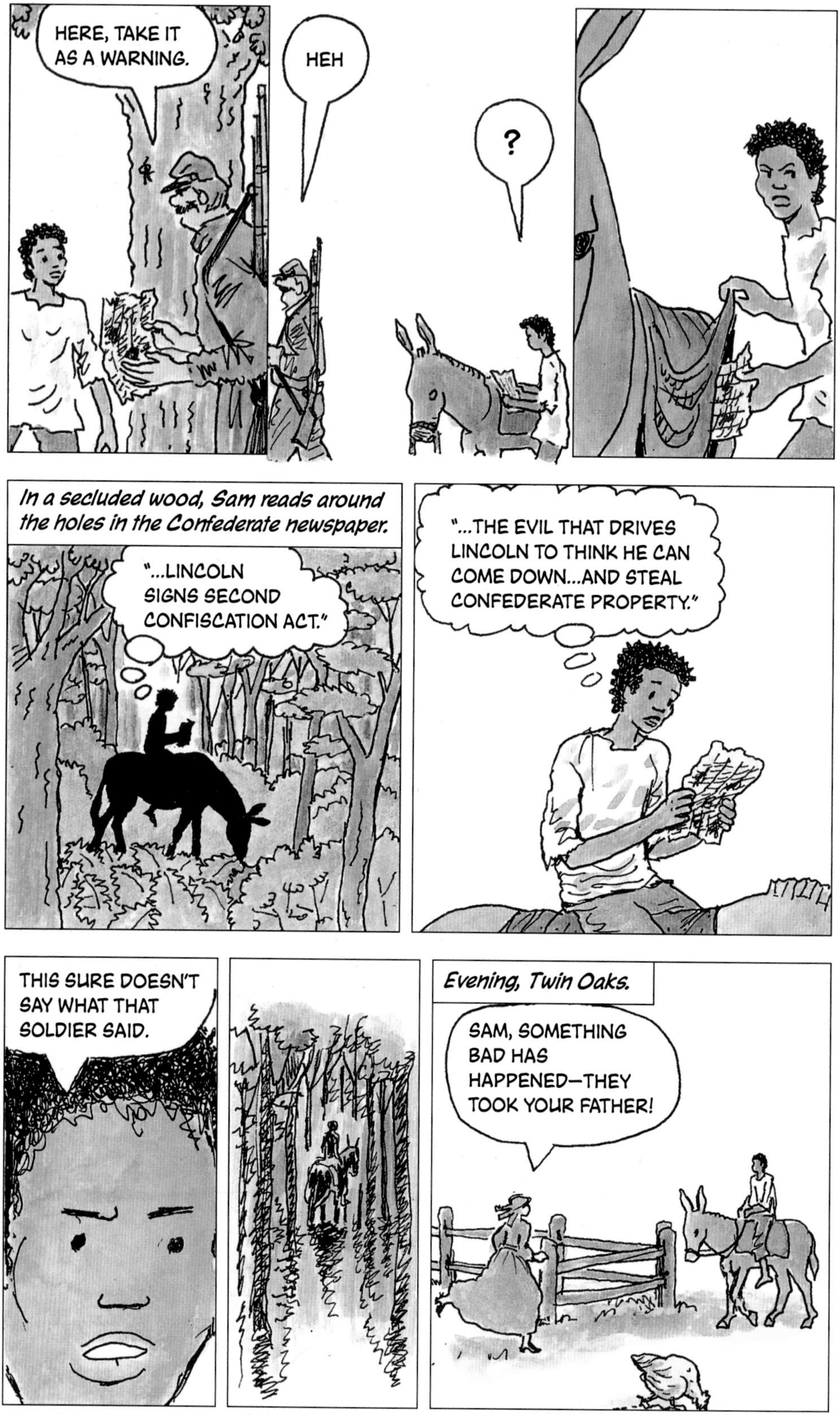
HERE, TAKE IT AS A WARNING.
HEH
?
In a secluded wood, Sam reads around the holes in the Confederate newspaper.
"...LINCOLN SIGNS SECOND CONFISCATION ACT."
"...THE EVIL THAT DRIVES LINCOLN TO THINK HE CAN COME DOWN...AND STEAL CONFEDERATE PROPERTY."
THIS SURE DOESN'T SAY WHAT THAT SOLDIER SAID.
Evening, Twin Oaks.
SAM, SOMETHING BAD HAS HAPPENED—THEY TOOK YOUR FATHER!

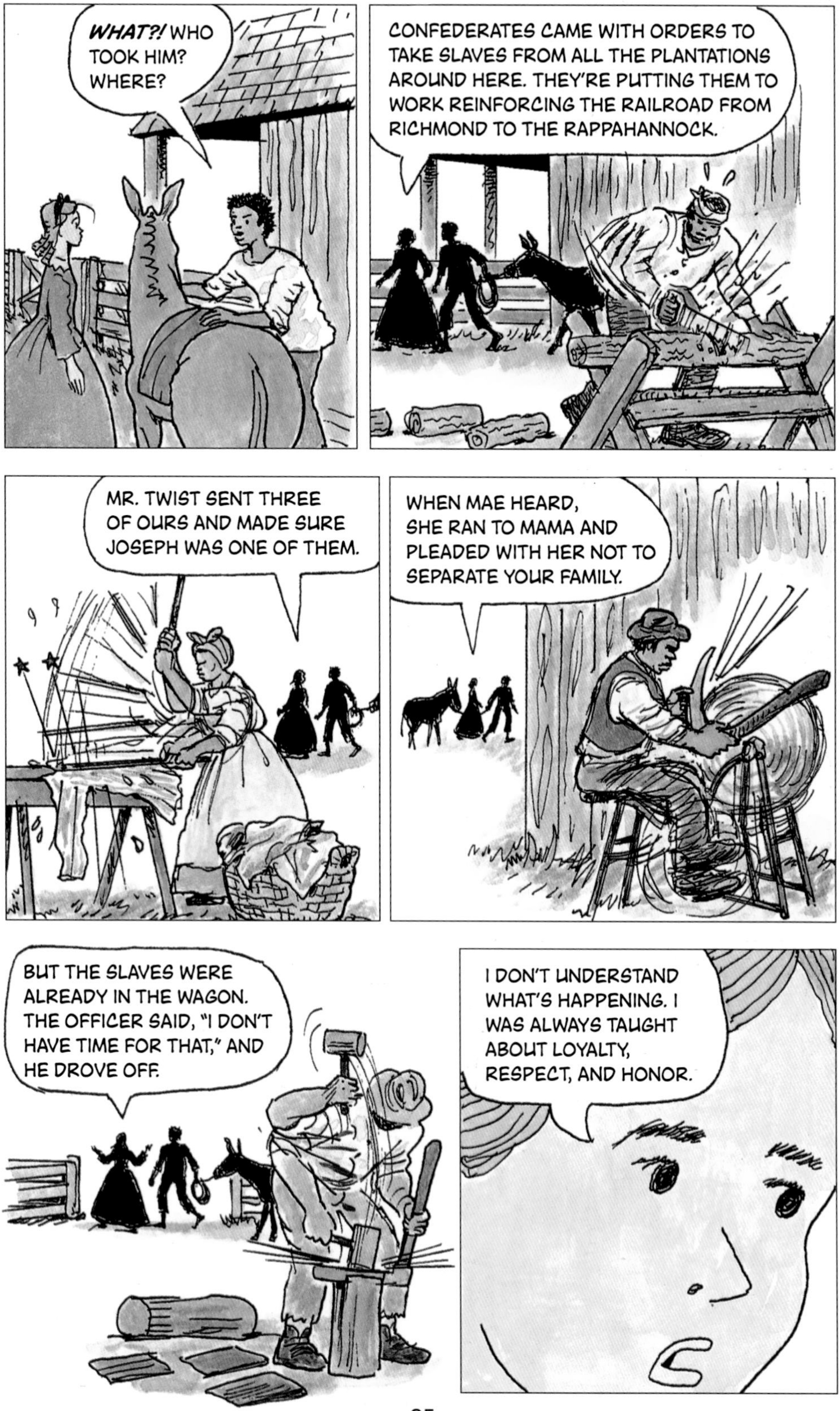
WHAT?! WHO TOOK HIM? WHERE?
CONFEDERATES CAME WITH ORDERS TO TAKE SLAVES FROM ALL THE PLANTATIONS AROUND HERE. THEY'RE PUTTING THEM TO WORK REINFORCING THE RAILROAD FROM RICHMOND TO THE RAPPAHANNOCK.
MR. TWIST SENT THREE OF OURS AND MADE SURE JOSEPH WAS ONE OF THEM.
WHEN MAE HEARD, SHE RAN TO MAMA AND PLEADED WITH HER NOT TO SEPARATE YOUR FAMILY.
BUT THE SLAVES WERE ALREADY IN THE WAGON. THE OFFICER SAID, "I DON'T HAVE TIME FOR THAT," AND HE DROVE OFF.
I DON'T UNDERSTAND WHAT'S HAPPENING. I WAS ALWAYS TAUGHT ABOUT LOYALTY, RESPECT, AND HONOR.

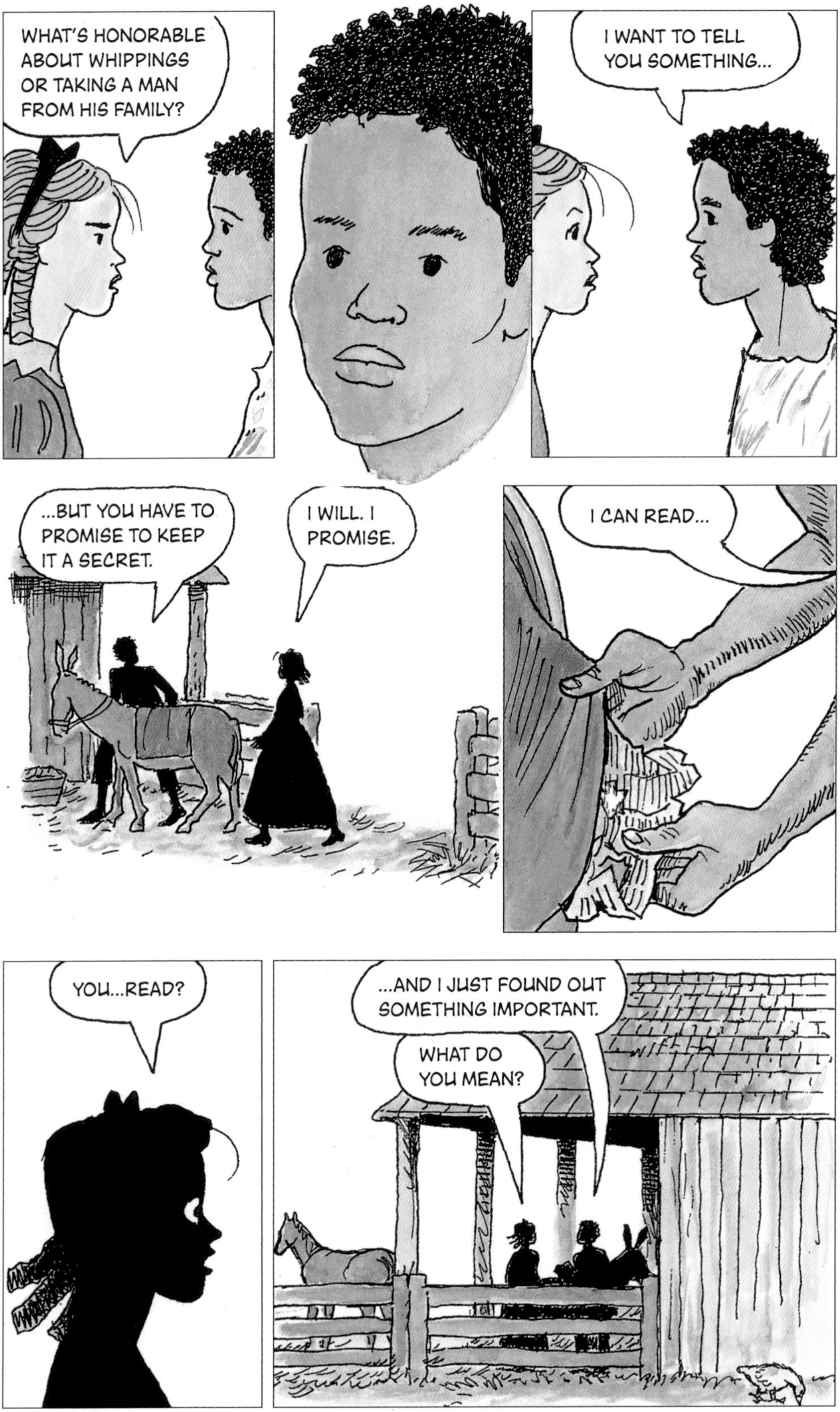
WHAT'S HONORABLE ABOUT WHIPPINGS OR TAKING A MAN FROM HIS FAMILY?
I WANT TO TELL YOU SOMETHING...
...BUT YOU HAVE TO PROMISE TO KEEP IT A SECRET.
I WILL. I PROMISE.
I CAN READ...
YOU...READ?
...AND I JUST FOUND OUT SOMETHING IMPORTANT.
WHAT DO YOU MEAN?

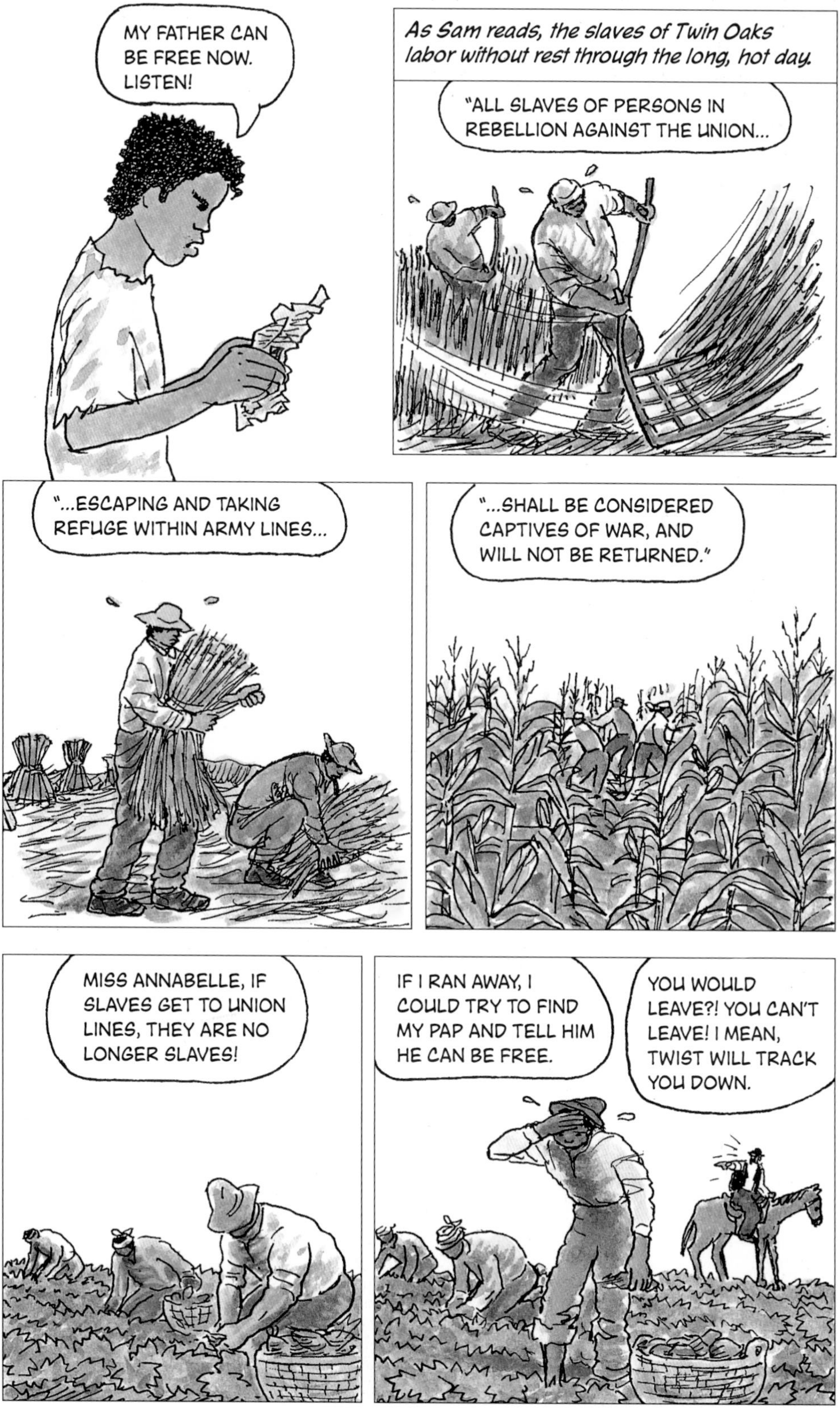
MY FATHER CAN BE FREE NOW. LISTEN!
As Sam reads, the slaves of Twin Oaks labor without rest through the long, hot day.
"ALL SLAVES OF PERSONS IN REBELLION AGAINST THE UNION...
"...ESCAPING AND TAKING REFUGE WITHIN ARMY LINES...
"...SHALL BE CONSIDERED CAPTIVES OF WAR, AND WILL NOT BE RETURNED."
MISS ANNABELLE, IF SLAVES GET TO UNION LINES, THEY ARE NO LONGER SLAVES!
IF I RAN AWAY, I COULD TRY TO FIND MY PAP AND TELL HIM HE CAN BE FREE.
YOU WOULD LEAVE?! YOU CAN'T LEAVE! I MEAN, TWIST WILL TRACK YOU DOWN.

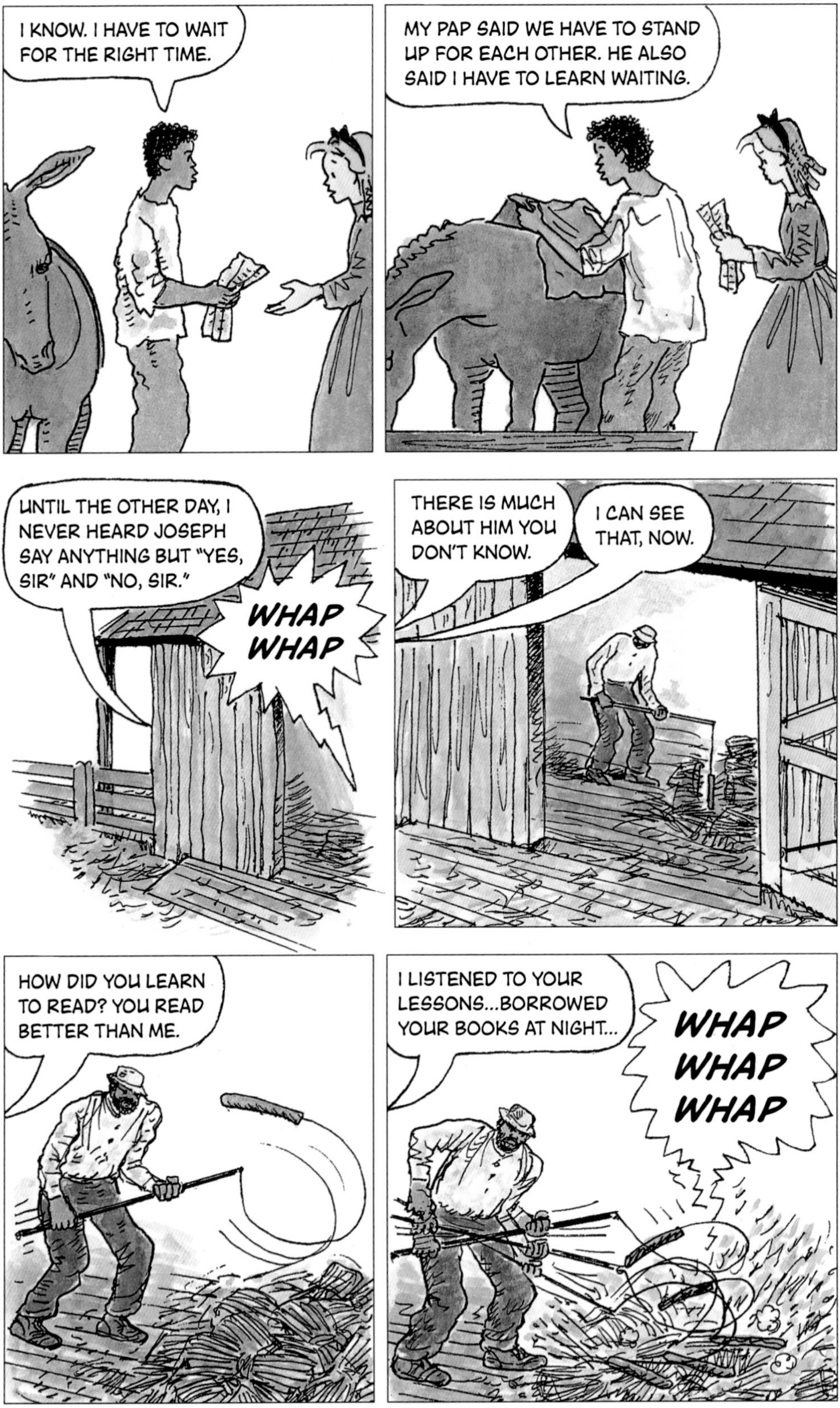
I KNOW. I HAVE TO WAIT FOR THE RIGHT TIME.
MY PAP SAID WE HAVE TO STAND UP FOR EACH OTHER. HE ALSO SAID I HAVE TO LEARN WAITING.
UNTIL THE OTHER DAY, I NEVER HEARD JOSEPH SAY ANYTHING BUT "YES, SIR" AND "NO, SIR."
WHAP WHAP
THERE IS MUCH ABOUT HIM YOU DON'T KNOW.
I CAN SEE THAT, NOW.
HOW DID YOU LEARN TO READ? YOU READ BETTER THAN ME.
I LISTENED TO YOUR LESSONS...BORROWED YOUR BOOKS AT NIGHT...
WHAP WHAP WHAP

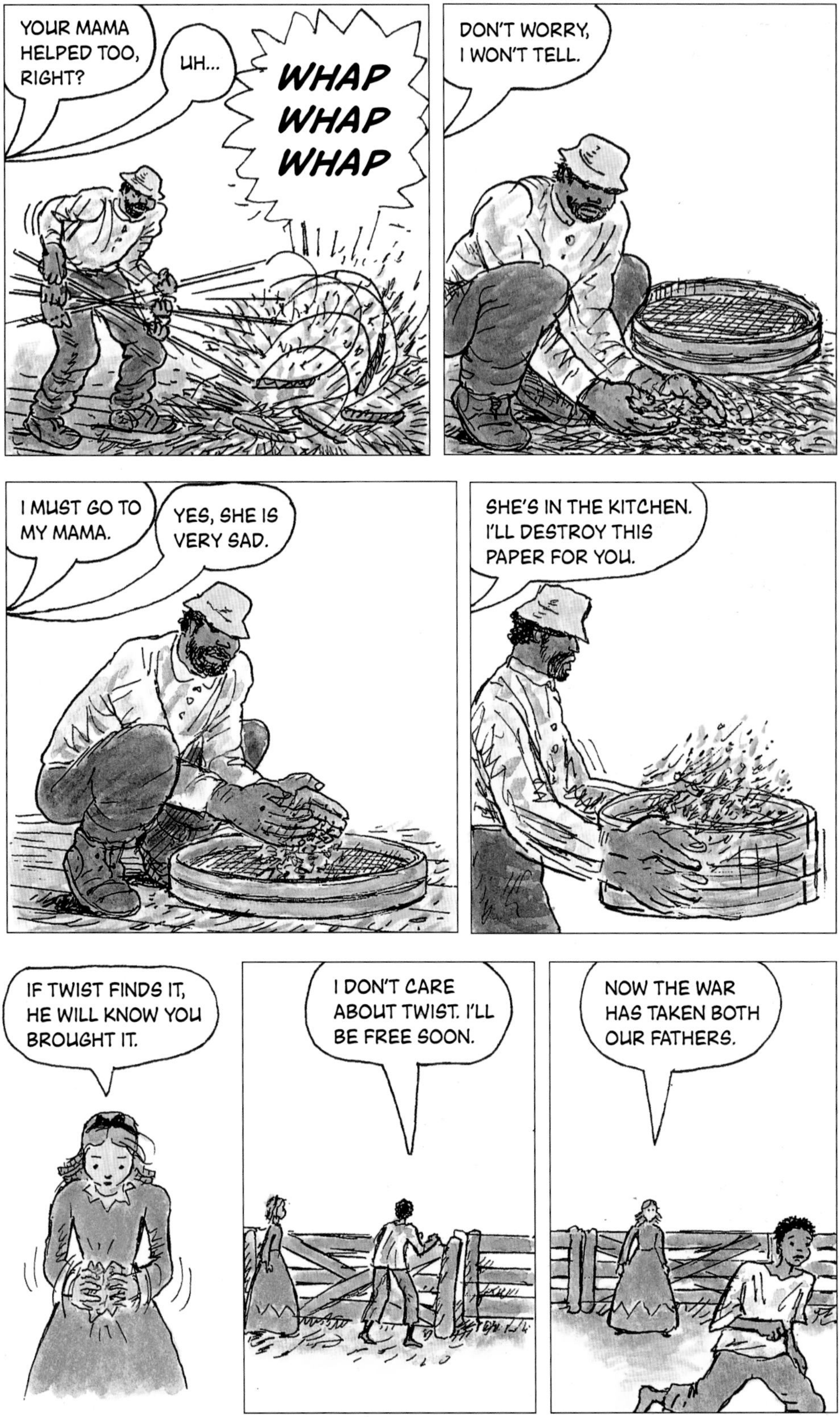
YOUR MAMA HELPED TOO, RIGHT?
UH...
WHAP WHAP WHAP
DON'T WORRY, I WON'T TELL.
I MUST GO TO MY MAMA.
YES, SHE IS VERY SAD.
SHE'S IN THE KITCHEN. I'LL DESTROY THIS PAPER FOR YOU.
IF TWIST FINDS IT, HE WILL KNOW YOU BROUGHT IT.
I DON'T CARE ABOUT TWIST. I'LL BE FREE SOON.
NOW THE WAR HAS TAKEN BOTH OUR FATHERS.

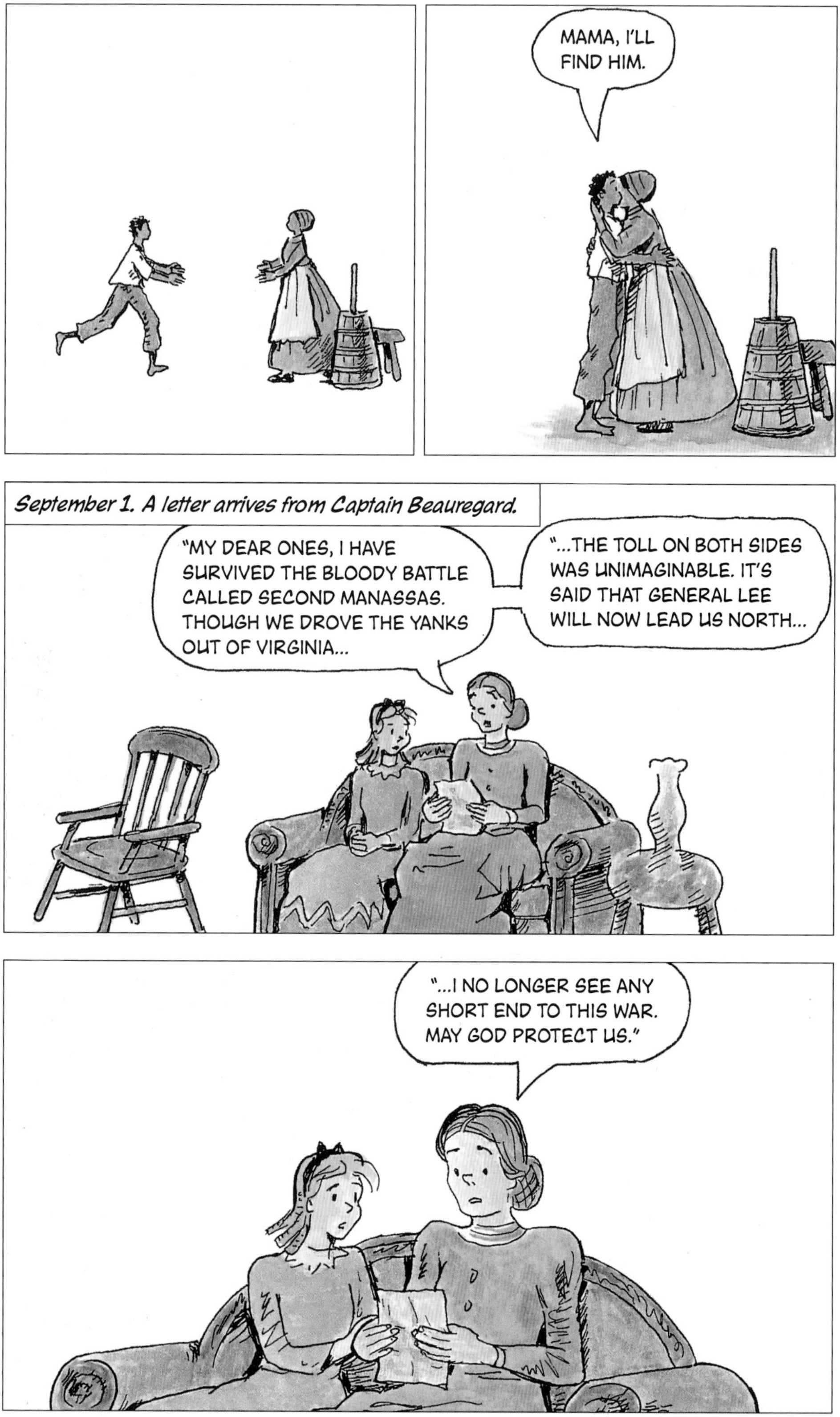
MAMA, I'LL FIND HIM.
September 1. A letter arrives from Captain Beauregard.
"MY DEAR ONES, I HAVE SURVIVED THE BLOODY BATTLE CALLED SECOND MANASSAS. THOUGH WE DROVE THE YANKS OUT OF VIRGINIA...
"...THE TOLL ON BOTH SIDES WAS UNIMAGINABLE. IT'S SAID THAT GENERAL LEE WILL NOW LEAD US NORTH...
"...I NO LONGER SEE ANY SHORT END TO THIS WAR. MAY GOD PROTECT US."

CHAPTER 4

A confident Lee attempts to move the fighting north but is stopped on September 17, 1862, at Antietam Creek, Maryland. The battle is known as Antietam by the North, Sharpsburg by the South. There's no clear-cut victory in what is called the bloodiest one-day battle in U.S. history. Lee retreats to Virginia.

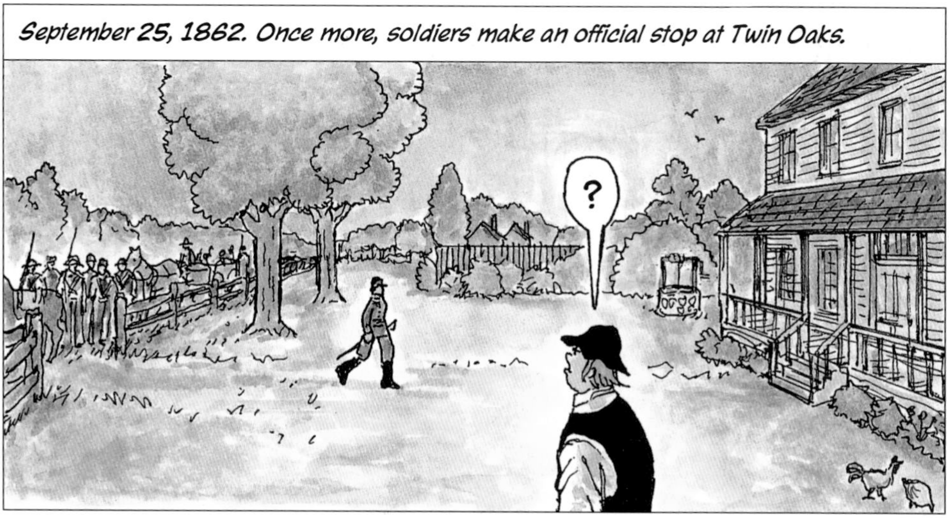
September 25, 1862. Once more, soldiers make an official stop at Twin Oaks.
?

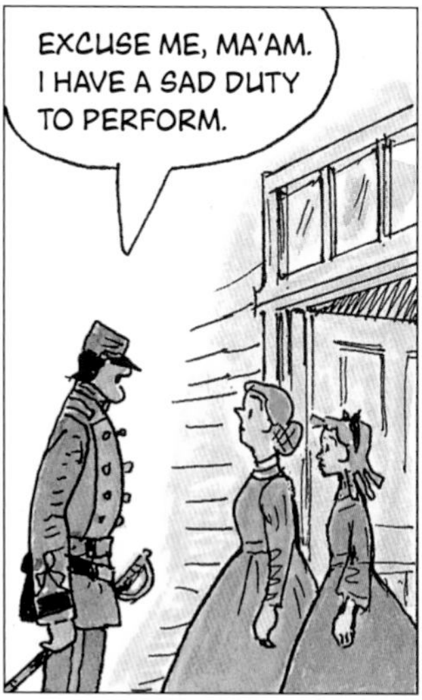
EXCUSE ME, MA'AM. I HAVE A SAD DUTY TO PERFORM.

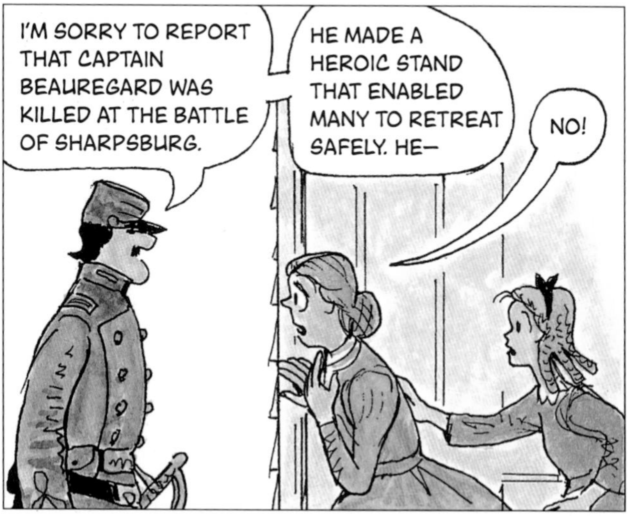
I'M SORRY TO REPORT THAT CAPTAIN BEAUREGARD WAS KILLED AT THE BATTLE OF SHARPSBURG.
HE MADE A HEROIC STAND THAT ENABLED MANY TO RETREAT SAFELY. HE—
NO!

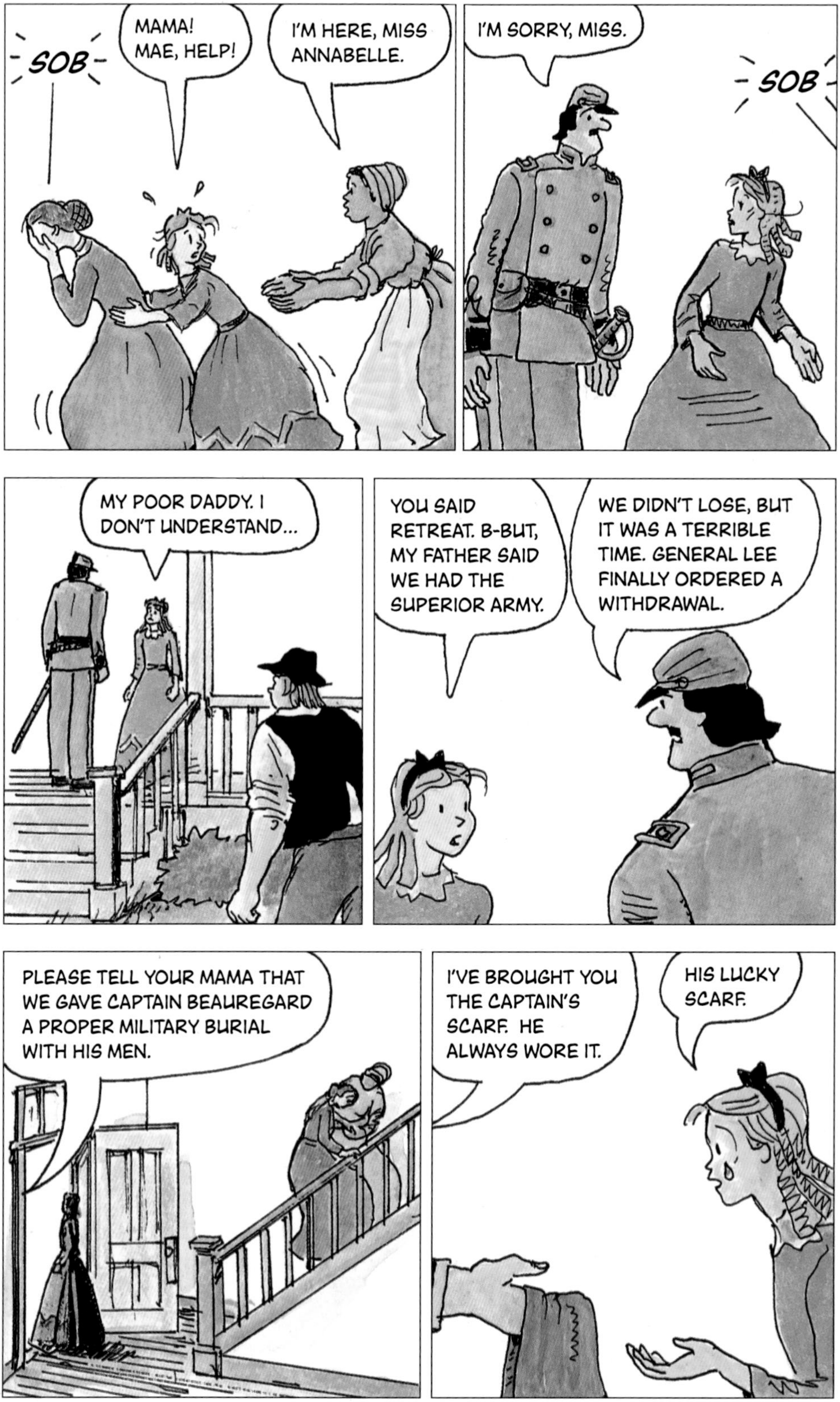
SOB
MAMA! MAE, HELP!
I'M HERE, MISS ANNABELLE.
I'M SORRY, MISS.
SOB
MY POOR DADDY. I DON'T UNDERSTAND...
YOU SAID RETREAT. B-BUT, MY FATHER SAID WE HAD THE SUPERIOR ARMY.
WE DIDN'T LOSE, BUT IT WAS A TERRIBLE TIME. GENERAL LEE FINALLY ORDERED A WITHDRAWAL.
PLEASE TELL YOUR MAMA THAT WE GAVE CAPTAIN BEAUREGARD A PROPER MILITARY BURIAL WITH HIS MEN.
I'VE BROUGHT YOU THE CAPTAIN'S SCARF. HE ALWAYS WORE IT.
HIS LUCKY SCARF.

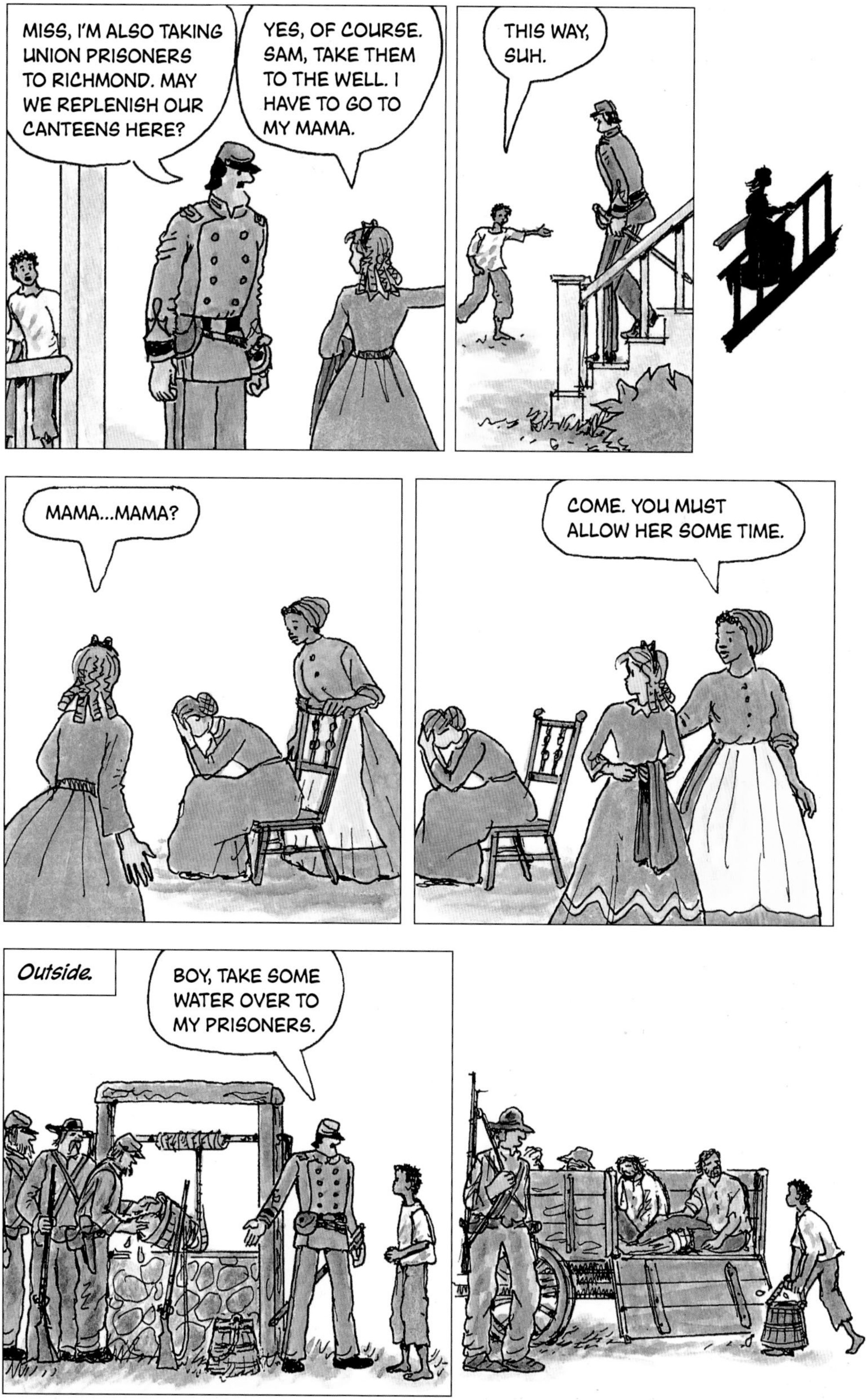
MISS, I'M ALSO TAKING UNION PRISONERS TO RICHMOND. MAY WE REPLENISH OUR CANTEENS HERE?
YES, OF COURSE. SAM, TAKE THEM TO THE WELL. I HAVE TO GO TO MY MAMA.
THIS WAY, SUH.
MAMA...MAMA?
COME. YOU MUST ALLOW HER SOME TIME.
Outside.
BOY, TAKE SOME WATER OVER TO MY PRISONERS.

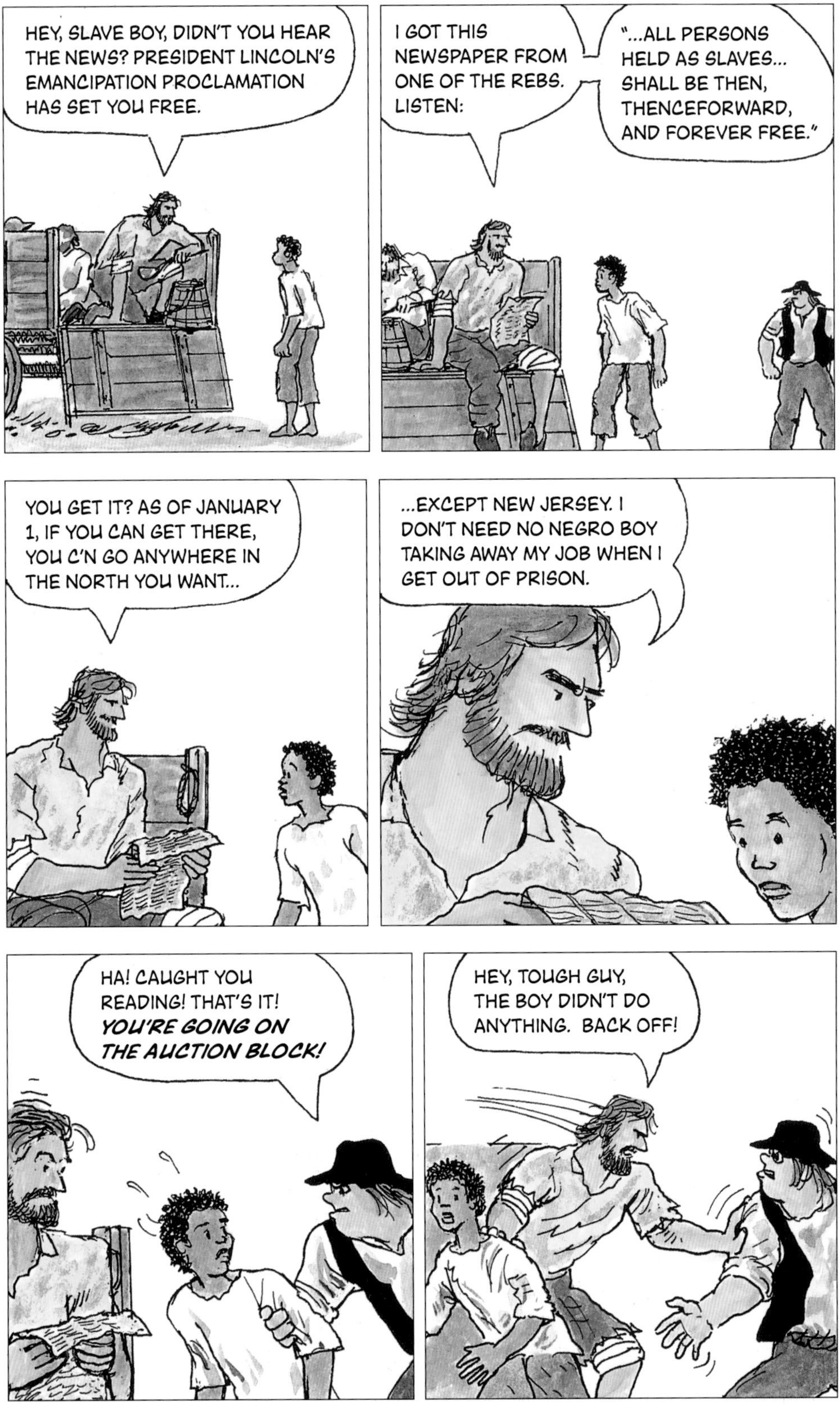
HEY, SLAVE BOY, DIDN'T YOU HEAR THE NEWS? PRESIDENT LINCOLN'S EMANCIPATION PROCLAMATION HAS SET YOU FREE.
I GOT THIS NEWSPAPER FROM ONE OF THE REBS. LISTEN:
"...ALL PERSONS HELD AS SLAVES... SHALL BE THEN, THENCEFORWARD, AND FOREVER FREE."
YOU GET IT? AS OF JANUARY 1, IF YOU CAN GET THERE, YOU C'N GO ANYWHERE IN THE NORTH YOU WANT...
...EXCEPT NEW JERSEY. I DON'T NEED NO NEGRO BOY TAKING AWAY MY JOB WHEN I GET OUT OF PRISON.
HA! CAUGHT YOU READING! THAT'S IT! *YOU'RE GOING ON THE AUCTION BLOCK!*
HEY, TOUGH GUY, THE BOY DIDN'T DO ANYTHING. BACK OFF!

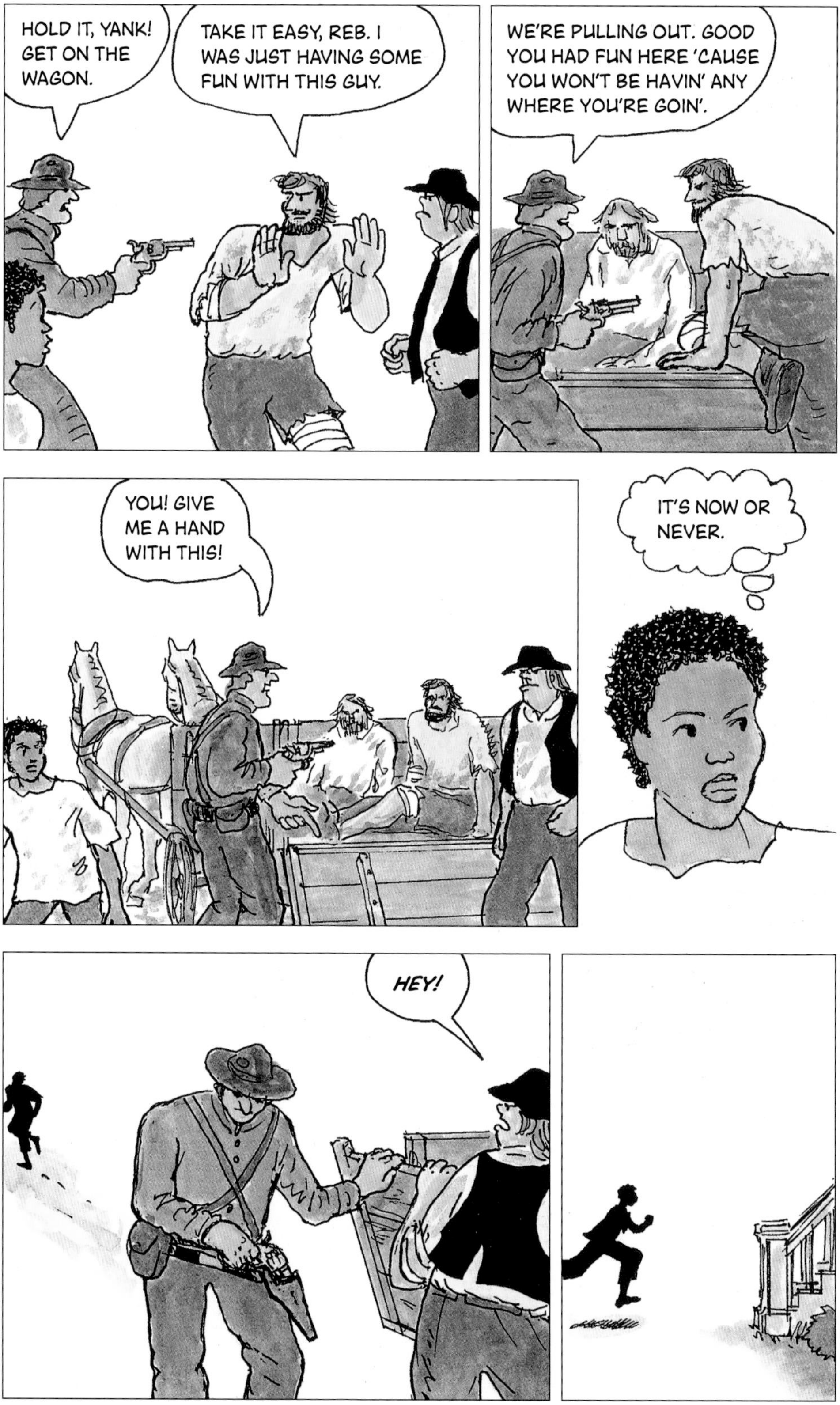
HOLD IT, YANK! GET ON THE WAGON.
TAKE IT EASY, REB. I WAS JUST HAVING SOME FUN WITH THIS GUY.
WE'RE PULLING OUT. GOOD YOU HAD FUN HERE 'CAUSE YOU WON'T BE HAVIN' ANY WHERE YOU'RE GOIN'.
YOU! GIVE ME A HAND WITH THIS!
IT'S NOW OR NEVER.
HEY!

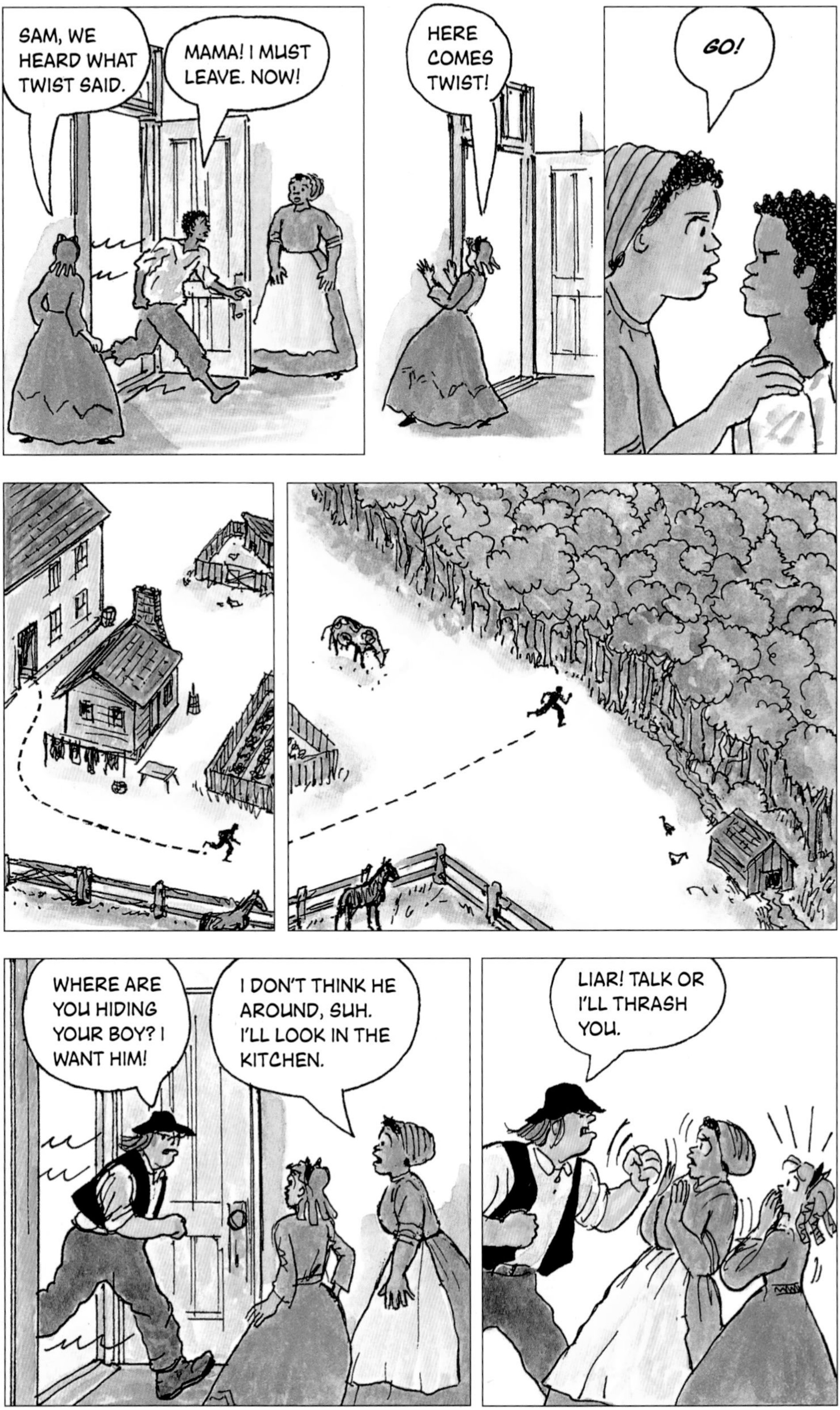
SAM, WE HEARD WHAT TWIST SAID.
MAMA! I MUST LEAVE. NOW!
HERE COMES TWIST!
GO!
WHERE ARE YOU HIDING YOUR BOY? I WANT HIM!
I DON'T THINK HE AROUND, SUH. I'LL LOOK IN THE KITCHEN.
LIAR! TALK OR I'LL THRASH YOU.

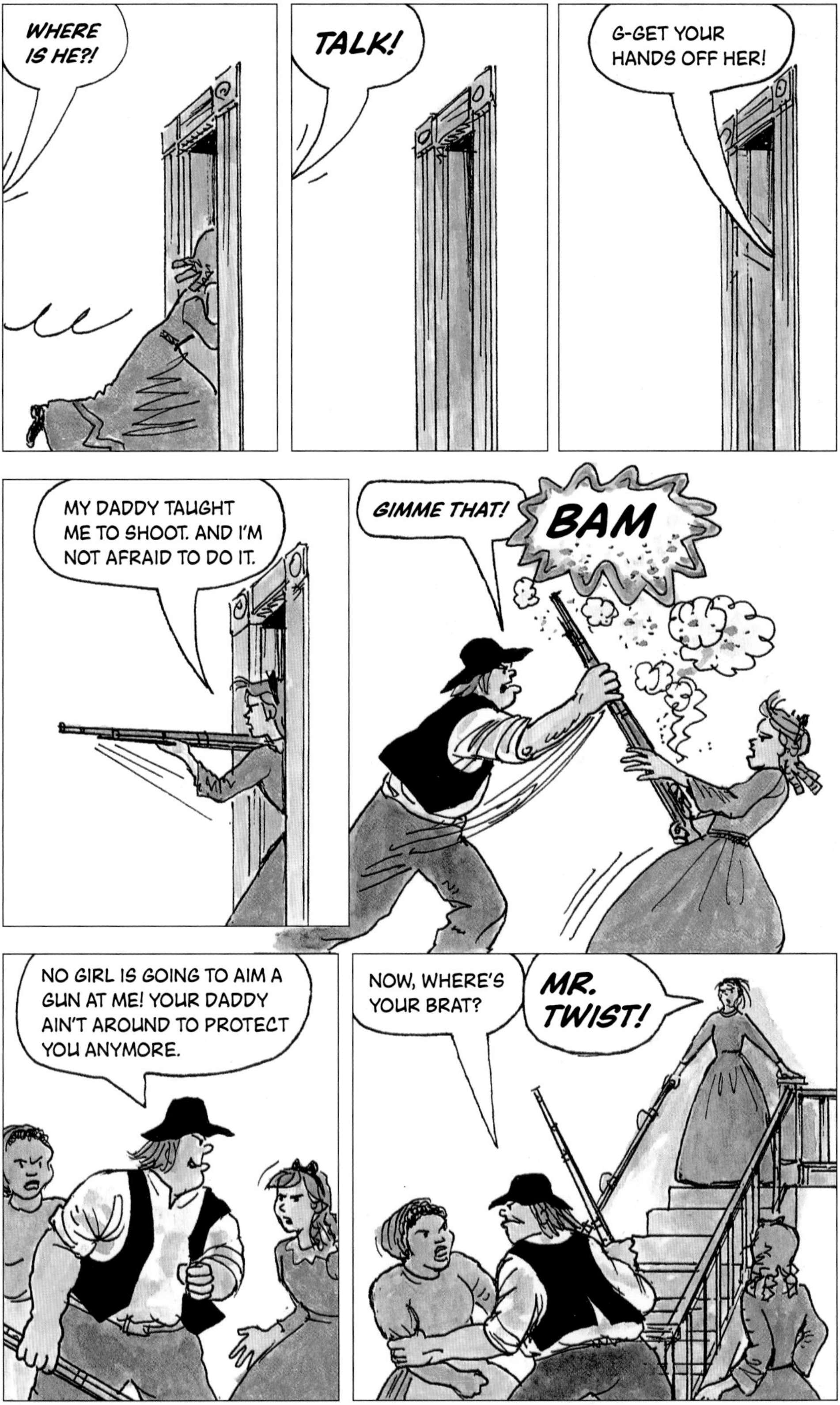
WHERE IS HE?!
TALK!
G-GET YOUR HANDS OFF HER!
MY DADDY TAUGHT ME TO SHOOT. AND I'M NOT AFRAID TO DO IT.
GIMME THAT!
BAM
NO GIRL IS GOING TO AIM A GUN AT ME! YOUR DADDY AIN'T AROUND TO PROTECT YOU ANYMORE.
NOW, WHERE'S YOUR BRAT?
MR. TWIST!

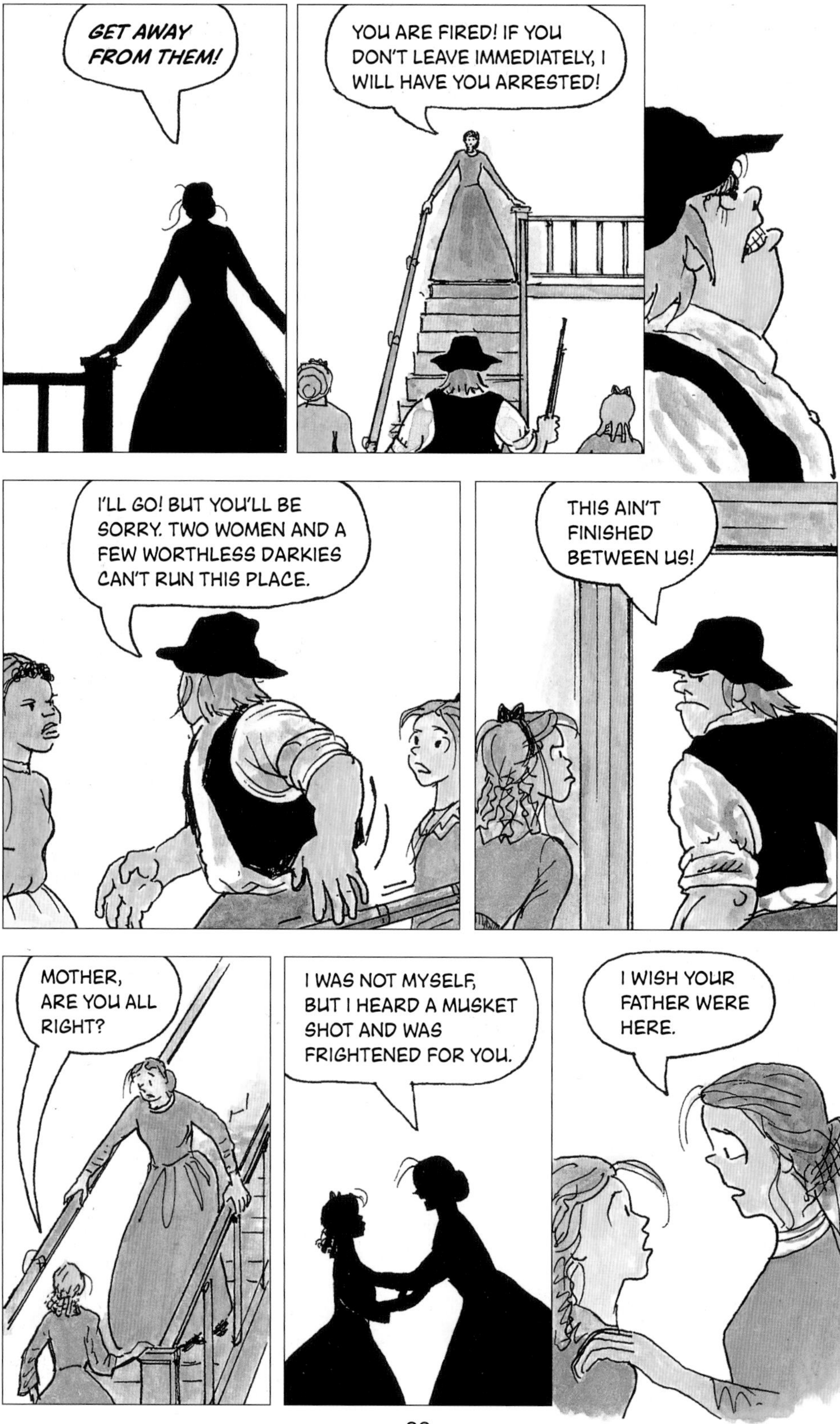
GET AWAY FROM THEM!
YOU ARE FIRED! IF YOU DON'T LEAVE IMMEDIATELY, I WILL HAVE YOU ARRESTED!
I'LL GO! BUT YOU'LL BE SORRY. TWO WOMEN AND A FEW WORTHLESS DARKIES CAN'T RUN THIS PLACE.
THIS AIN'T FINISHED BETWEEN US!
MOTHER, ARE YOU ALL RIGHT?
I WAS NOT MYSELF, BUT I HEARD A MUSKET SHOT AND WAS FRIGHTENED FOR YOU.
I WISH YOUR FATHER WERE HERE.

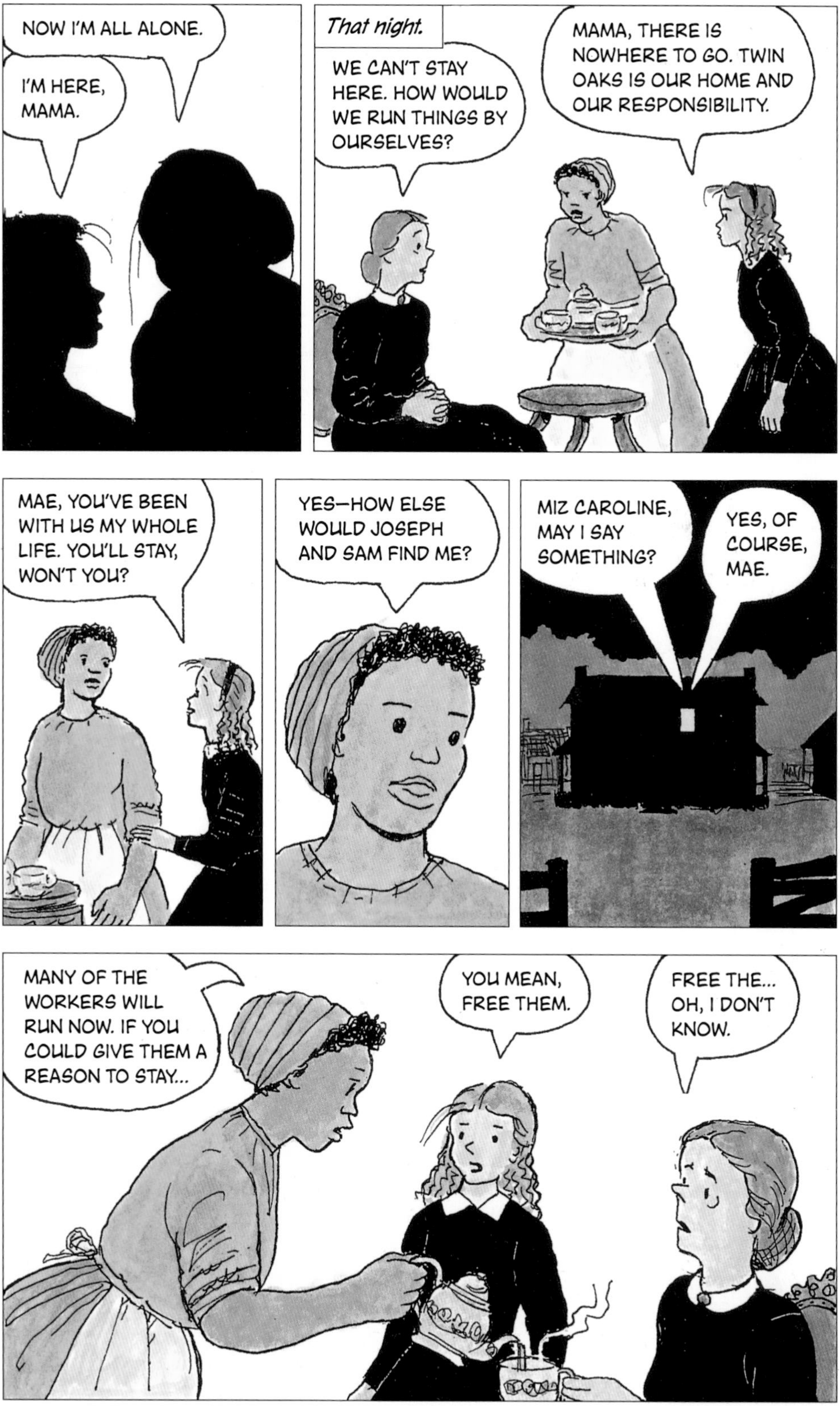
NOW I'M ALL ALONE.
I'M HERE, MAMA.
That night.
WE CAN'T STAY HERE. HOW WOULD WE RUN THINGS BY OURSELVES?
MAMA, THERE IS NOWHERE TO GO. TWIN OAKS IS OUR HOME AND OUR RESPONSIBILITY.
MAE, YOU'VE BEEN WITH US MY WHOLE LIFE. YOU'LL STAY, WON'T YOU?
YES—HOW ELSE WOULD JOSEPH AND SAM FIND ME?
MIZ CAROLINE, MAY I SAY SOMETHING?
YES, OF COURSE, MAE.
MANY OF THE WORKERS WILL RUN NOW. IF YOU COULD GIVE THEM A REASON TO STAY...
YOU MEAN, FREE THEM.
FREE THE... OH, I DON'T KNOW.

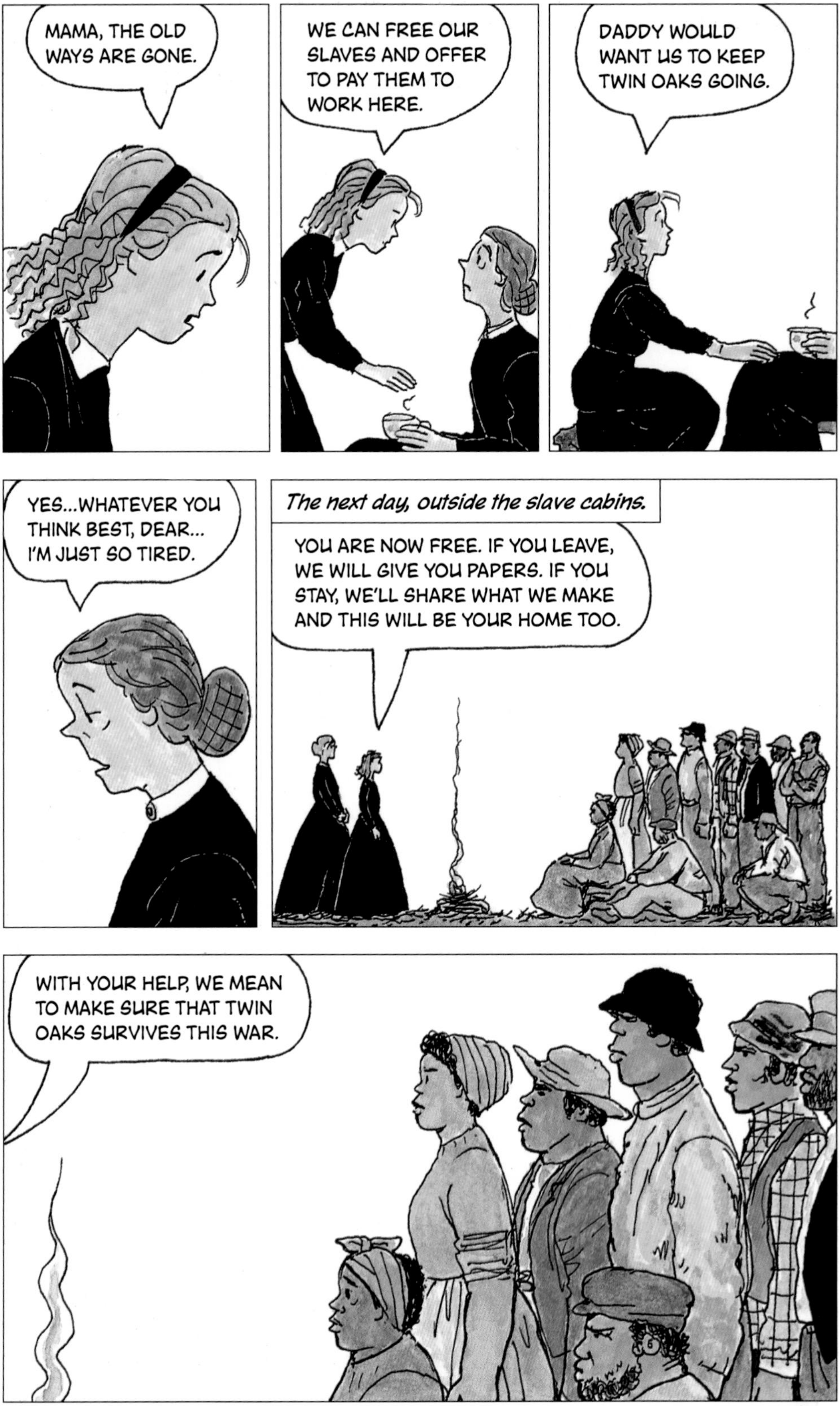
MAMA, THE OLD WAYS ARE GONE.
WE CAN FREE OUR SLAVES AND OFFER TO PAY THEM TO WORK HERE.
DADDY WOULD WANT US TO KEEP TWIN OAKS GOING.
YES...WHATEVER YOU THINK BEST, DEAR... I'M JUST SO TIRED.
The next day, outside the slave cabins.
YOU ARE NOW FREE. IF YOU LEAVE, WE WILL GIVE YOU PAPERS. IF YOU STAY, WE'LL SHARE WHAT WE MAKE AND THIS WILL BE YOUR HOME TOO.
WITH YOUR HELP, WE MEAN TO MAKE SURE THAT TWIN OAKS SURVIVES THIS WAR.

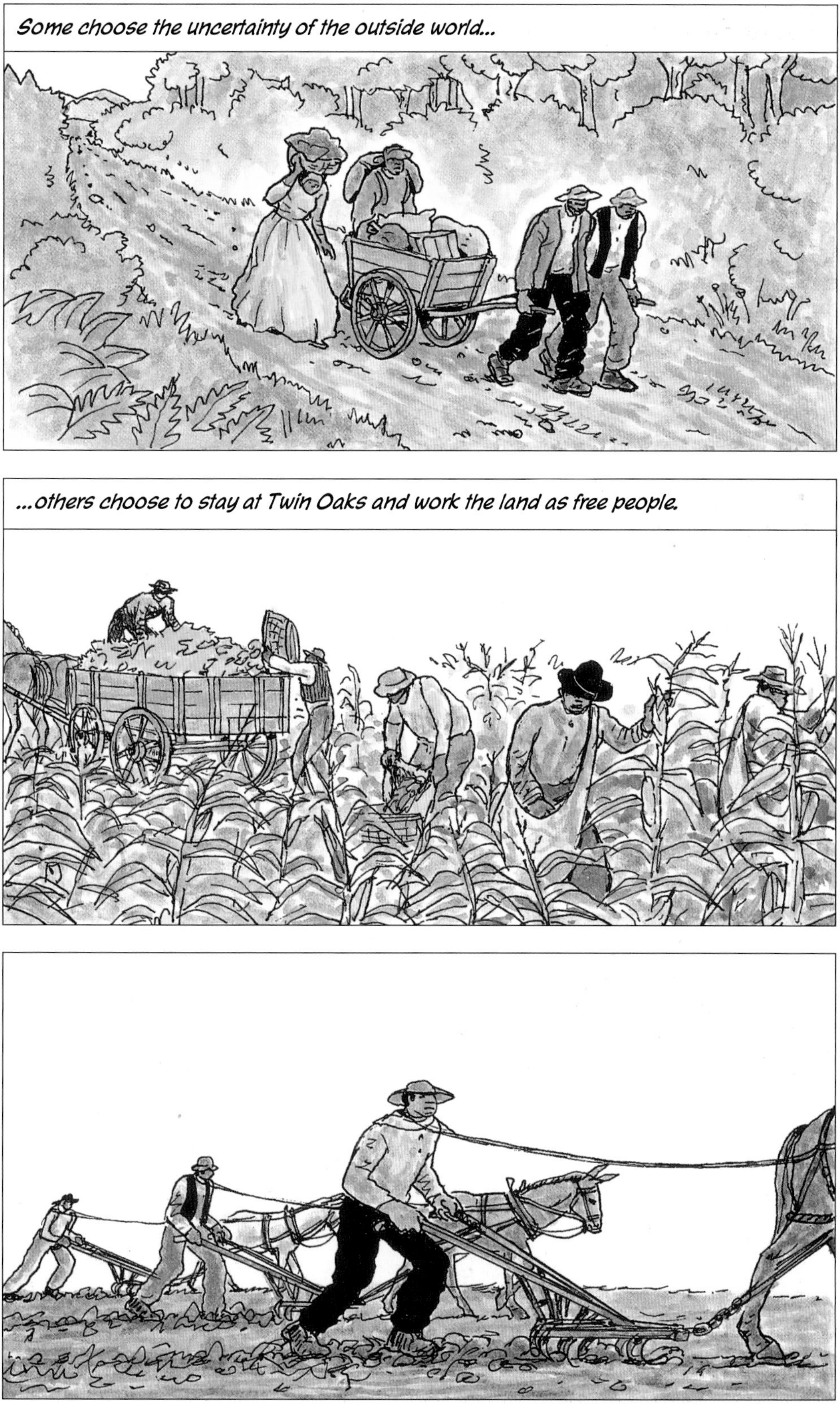
Some choose the uncertainty of the outside world...
...others choose to stay at Twin Oaks and work the land as free people.

CHAPTER 5

Runaway slaves, seeking refuge, begin to overwhelm Union Army outposts. The government and aid groups step in to provide assistance to men, women, and children who have never known anything but bondage.

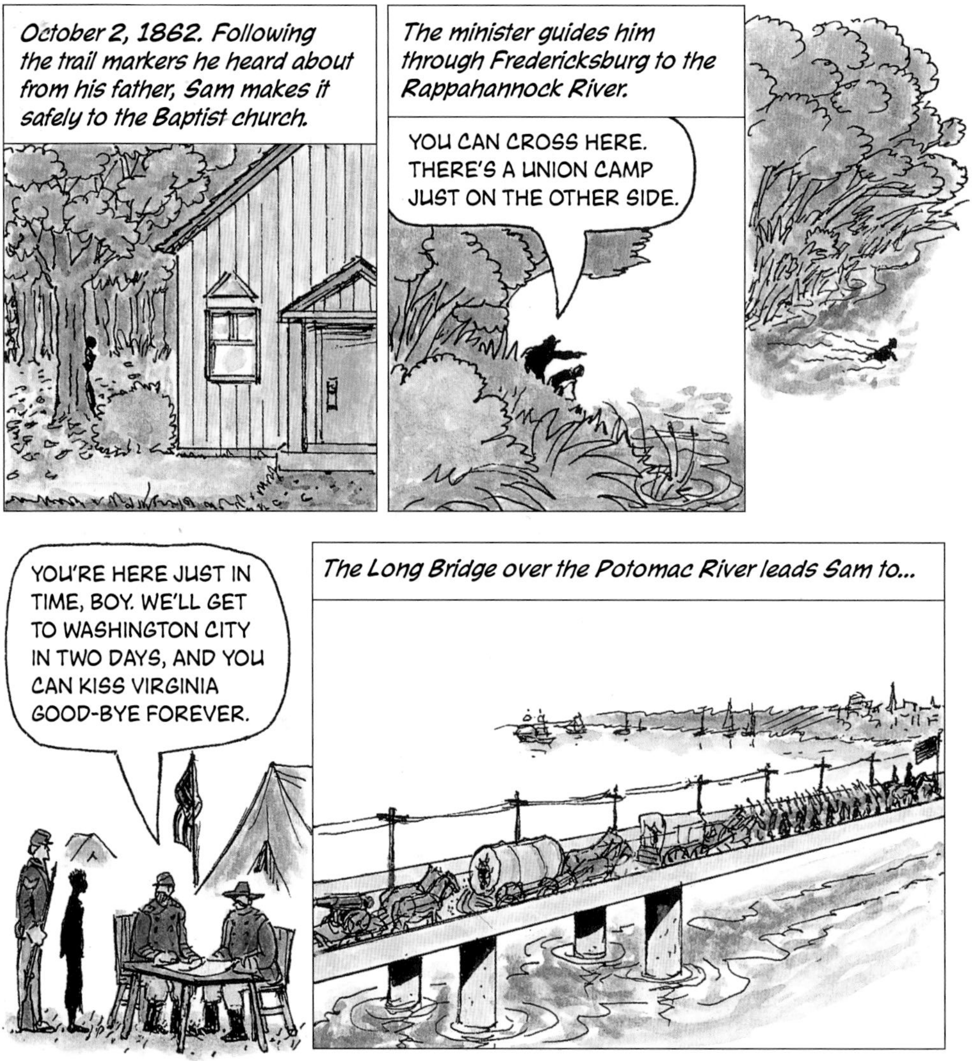
October 2, 1862. Following the trail markers he heard about from his father, Sam makes it safely to the Baptist church.
The minister guides him through Fredericksburg to the Rappahannock River.
YOU CAN CROSS HERE. THERE'S A UNION CAMP JUST ON THE OTHER SIDE.
YOU'RE HERE JUST IN TIME, BOY. WE'LL GET TO WASHINGTON CITY IN TWO DAYS, AND YOU CAN KISS VIRGINIA GOOD-BYE FOREVER.
The Long Bridge over the Potomac River leads Sam to...

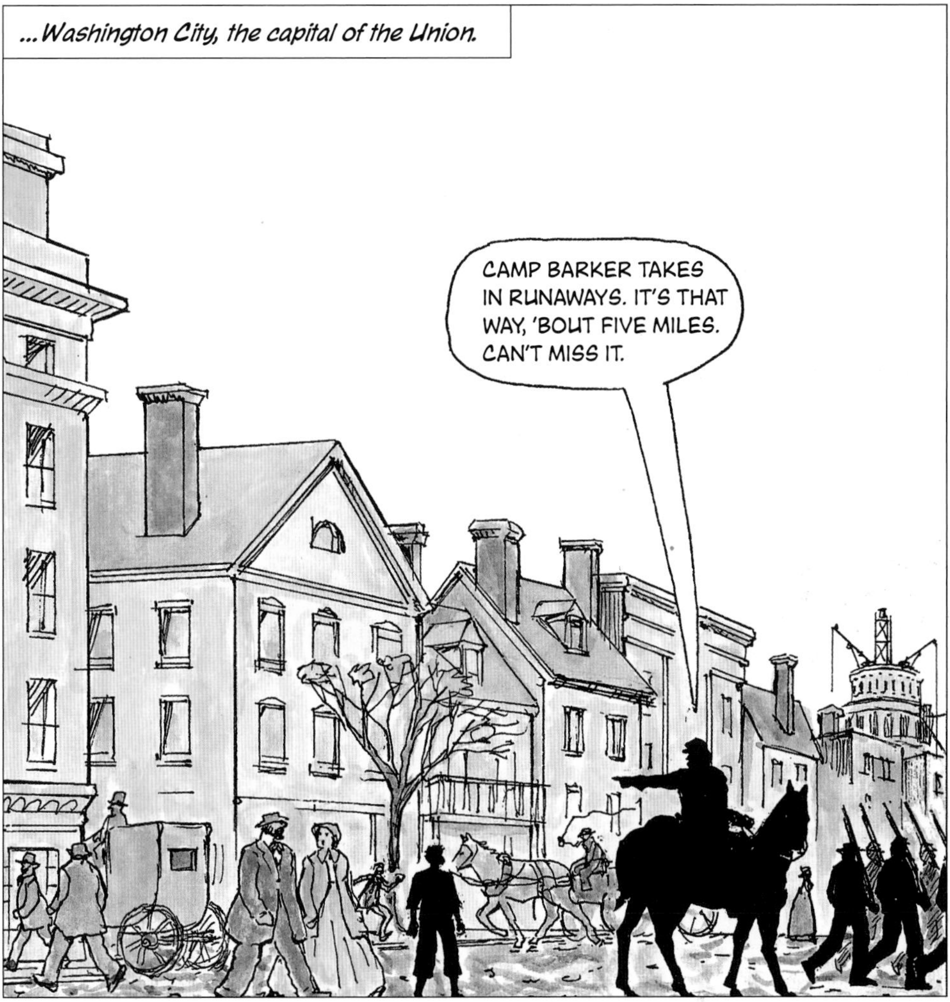
...Washington City, the capital of the Union.
CAMP BARKER TAKES IN RUNAWAYS. IT'S THAT WAY, 'BOUT FIVE MILES. CAN'T MISS IT.

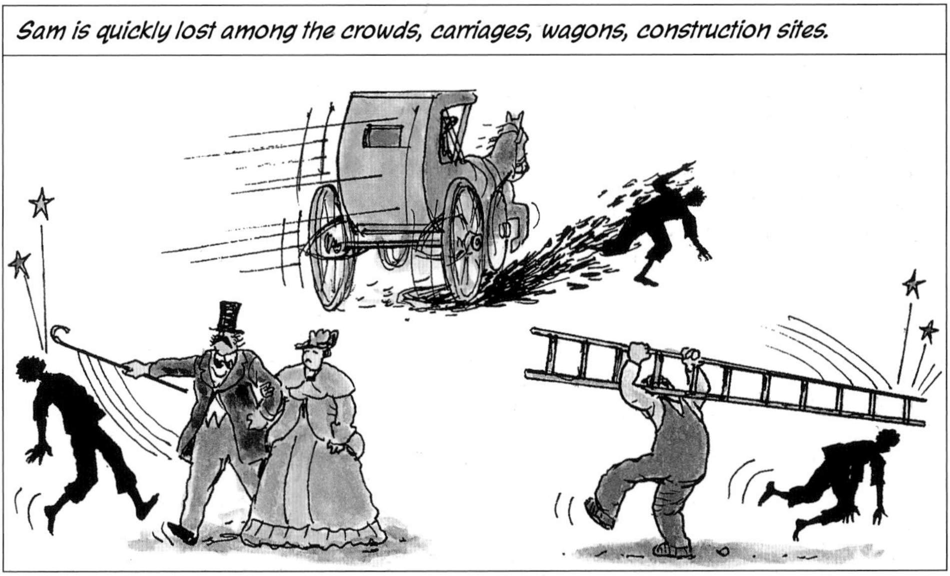
Sam is quickly lost among the crowds, carriages, wagons, construction sites.

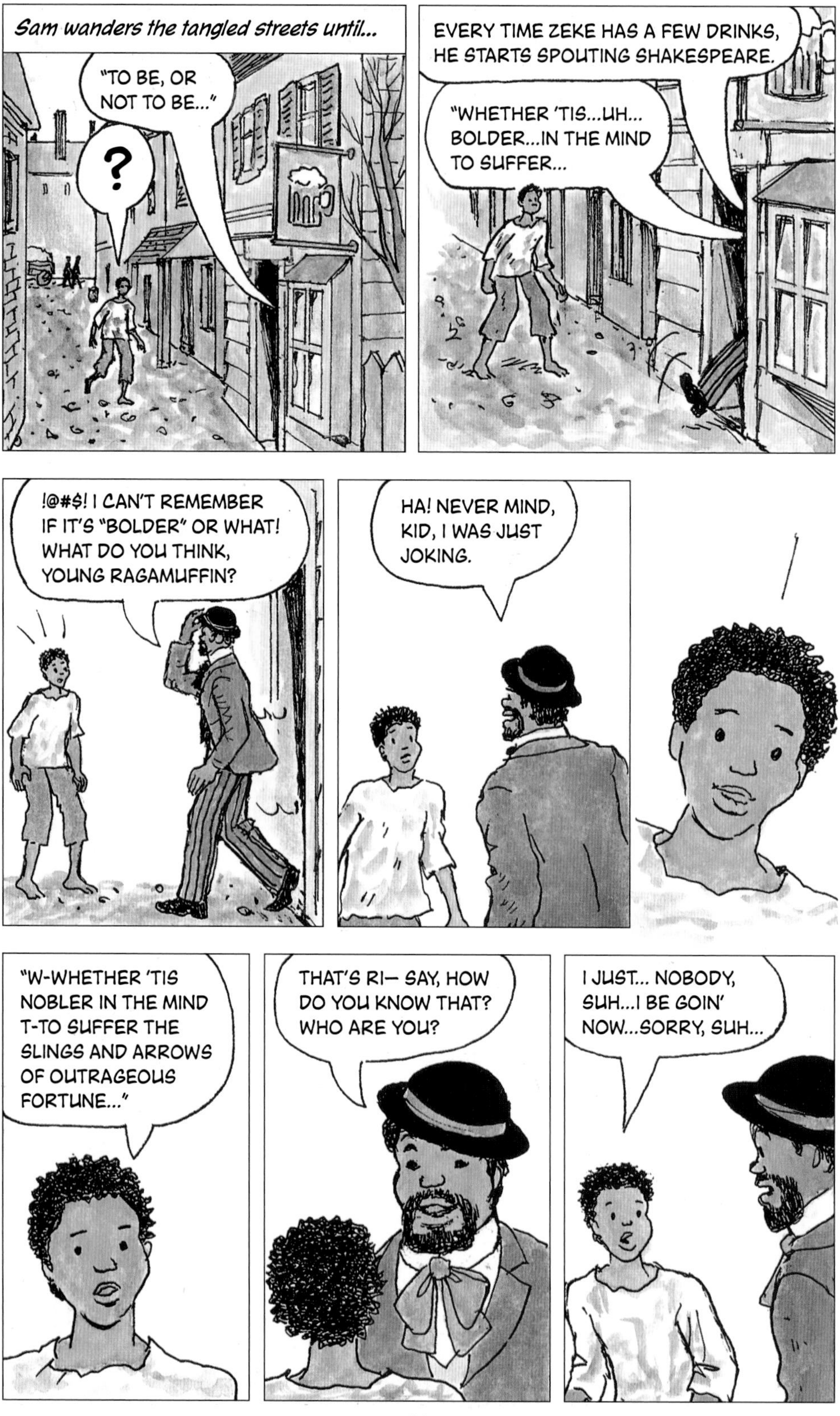
Sam wanders the tangled streets until...
"TO BE, OR NOT TO BE..."
?
EVERY TIME ZEKE HAS A FEW DRINKS, HE STARTS SPOUTING SHAKESPEARE.
"WHETHER 'TIS...UH... BOLDER...IN THE MIND TO SUFFER...
!@#$! I CAN'T REMEMBER IF IT'S "BOLDER" OR WHAT! WHAT DO YOU THINK, YOUNG RAGAMUFFIN?
HA! NEVER MIND, KID, I WAS JUST JOKING.
"W-WHETHER 'TIS NOBLER IN THE MIND T-TO SUFFER THE SLINGS AND ARROWS OF OUTRAGEOUS FORTUNE..."
THAT'S RI— SAY, HOW DO YOU KNOW THAT? WHO ARE YOU?
I JUST... NOBODY, SUH...I BE GOIN' NOW...SORRY, SUH...

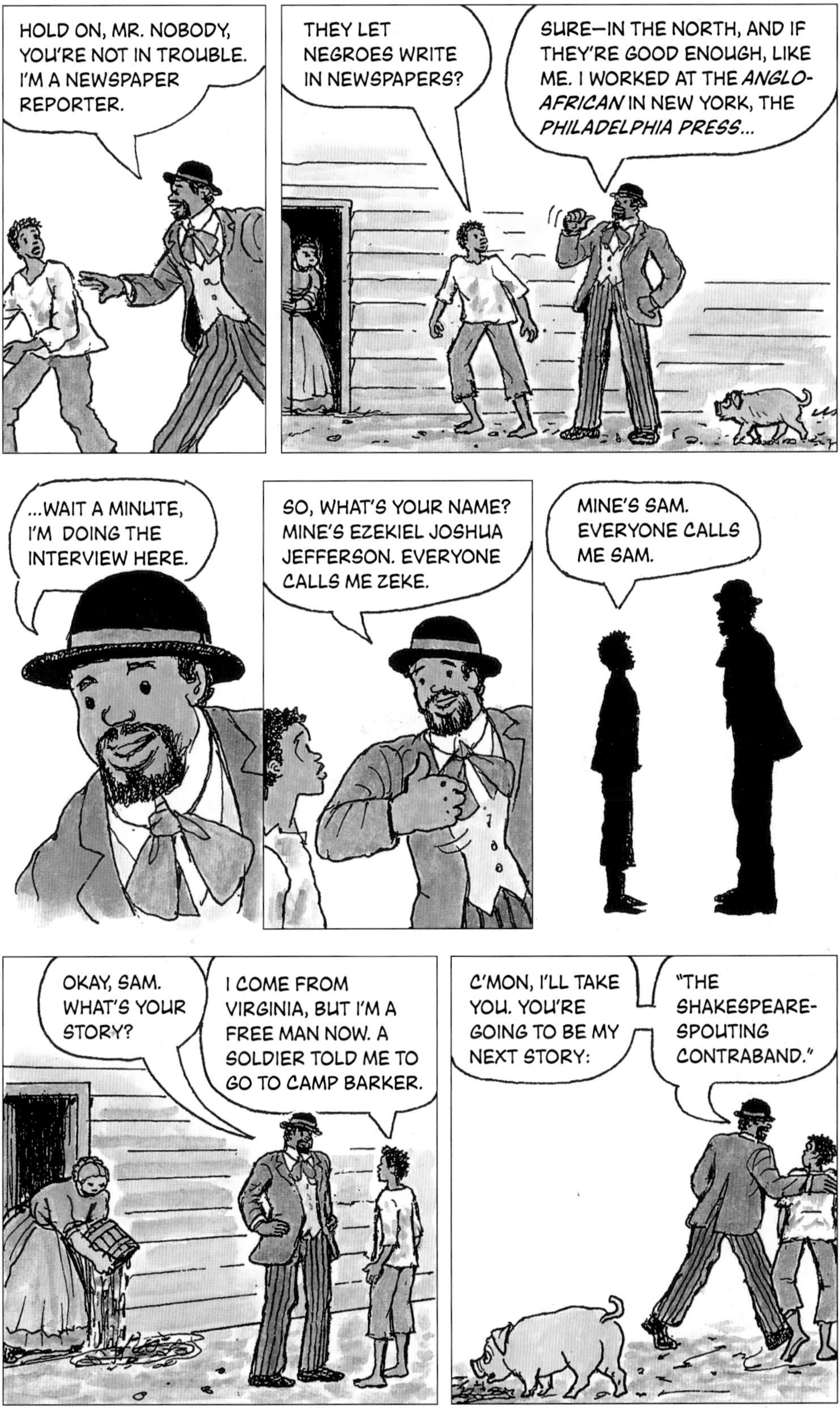
HOLD ON, MR. NOBODY, YOU'RE NOT IN TROUBLE. I'M A NEWSPAPER REPORTER.
THEY LET NEGROES WRITE IN NEWSPAPERS?
SURE—IN THE NORTH, AND IF THEY'RE GOOD ENOUGH, LIKE ME. I WORKED AT THE *ANGLO-AFRICAN* IN NEW YORK, THE *PHILADELPHIA PRESS*...
...WAIT A MINUTE, I'M DOING THE INTERVIEW HERE.
SO, WHAT'S YOUR NAME? MINE'S EZEKIEL JOSHUA JEFFERSON. EVERYONE CALLS ME ZEKE.
MINE'S SAM. EVERYONE CALLS ME SAM.
OKAY, SAM. WHAT'S YOUR STORY?
I COME FROM VIRGINIA, BUT I'M A FREE MAN NOW. A SOLDIER TOLD ME TO GO TO CAMP BARKER.
C'MON, I'LL TAKE YOU. YOU'RE GOING TO BE MY NEXT STORY:
"THE SHAKESPEARE-SPOUTING CONTRABAND."

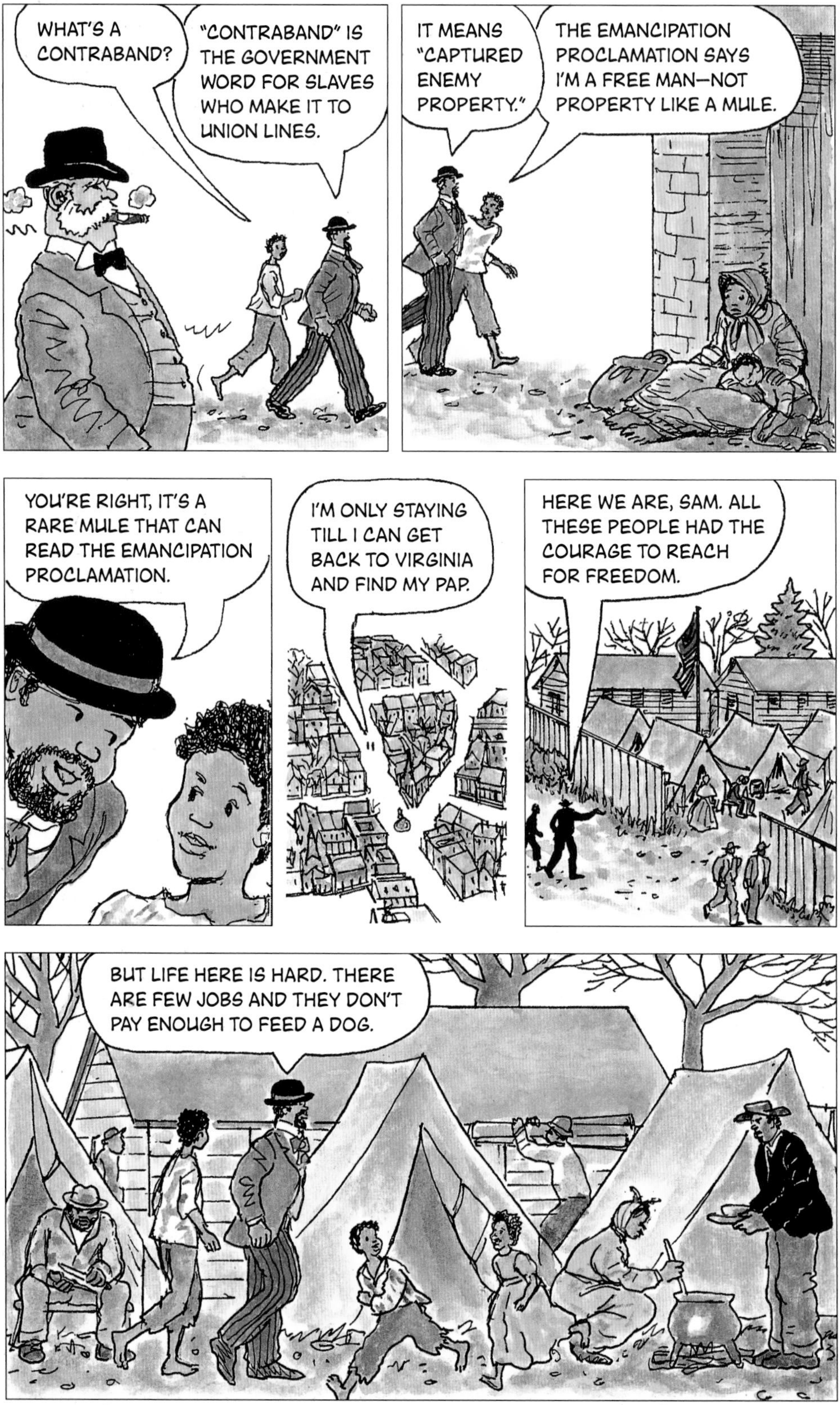
WHAT'S A CONTRABAND?
"CONTRABAND" IS THE GOVERNMENT WORD FOR SLAVES WHO MAKE IT TO UNION LINES.
IT MEANS "CAPTURED ENEMY PROPERTY."
THE EMANCIPATION PROCLAMATION SAYS I'M A FREE MAN—NOT PROPERTY LIKE A MULE.
YOU'RE RIGHT, IT'S A RARE MULE THAT CAN READ THE EMANCIPATION PROCLAMATION.
I'M ONLY STAYING TILL I CAN GET BACK TO VIRGINIA AND FIND MY PAP.
HERE WE ARE, SAM. ALL THESE PEOPLE HAD THE COURAGE TO REACH FOR FREEDOM.
BUT LIFE HERE IS HARD. THERE ARE FEW JOBS AND THEY DON'T PAY ENOUGH TO FEED A DOG.

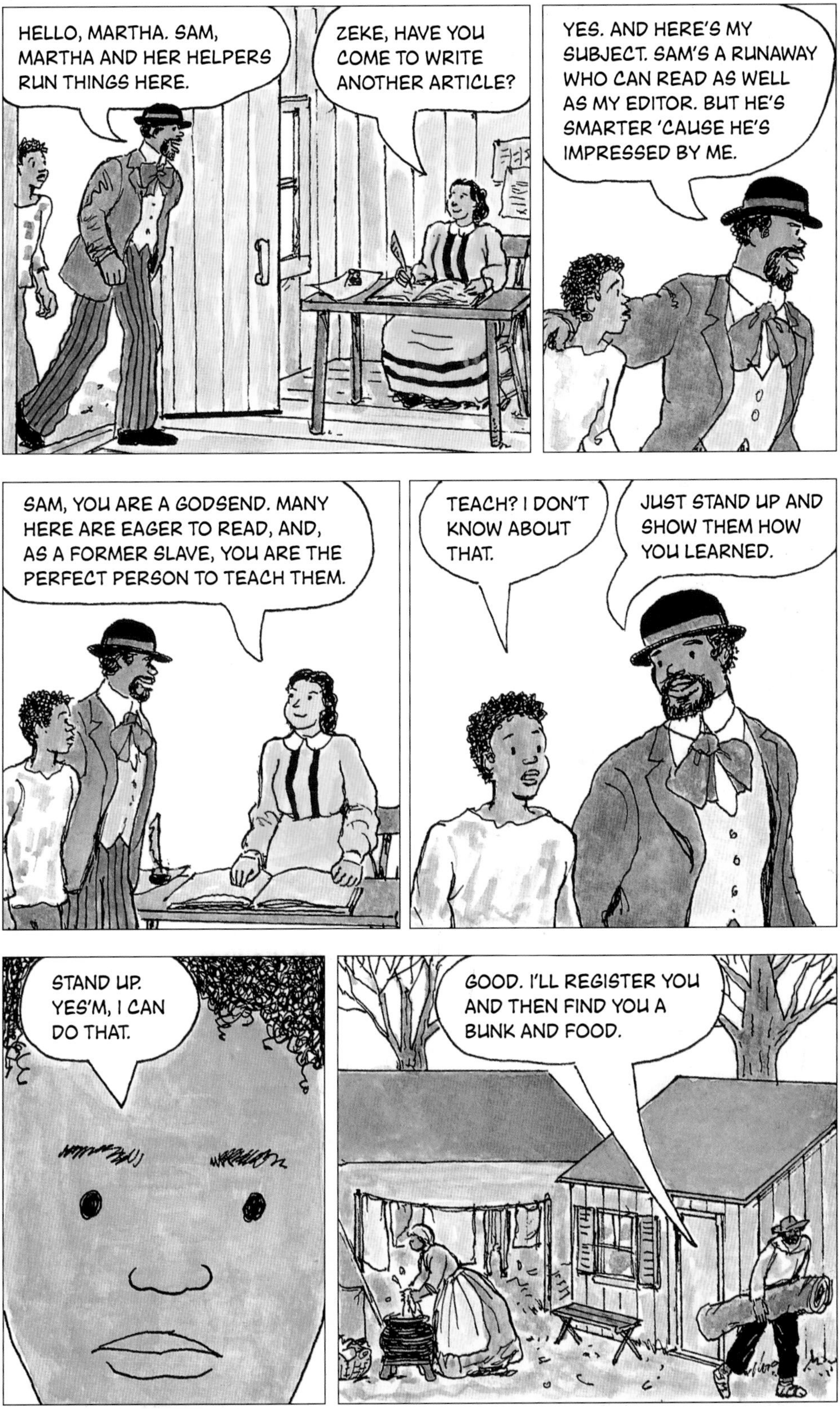
HELLO, MARTHA. SAM, MARTHA AND HER HELPERS RUN THINGS HERE.
ZEKE, HAVE YOU COME TO WRITE ANOTHER ARTICLE?
YES. AND HERE'S MY SUBJECT. SAM'S A RUNAWAY WHO CAN READ AS WELL AS MY EDITOR. BUT HE'S SMARTER 'CAUSE HE'S IMPRESSED BY ME.
SAM, YOU ARE A GODSEND. MANY HERE ARE EAGER TO READ, AND, AS A FORMER SLAVE, YOU ARE THE PERFECT PERSON TO TEACH THEM.
TEACH? I DON'T KNOW ABOUT THAT.
JUST STAND UP AND SHOW THEM HOW YOU LEARNED.
STAND UP. YES'M, I CAN DO THAT.
GOOD. I'LL REGISTER YOU AND THEN FIND YOU A BUNK AND FOOD.

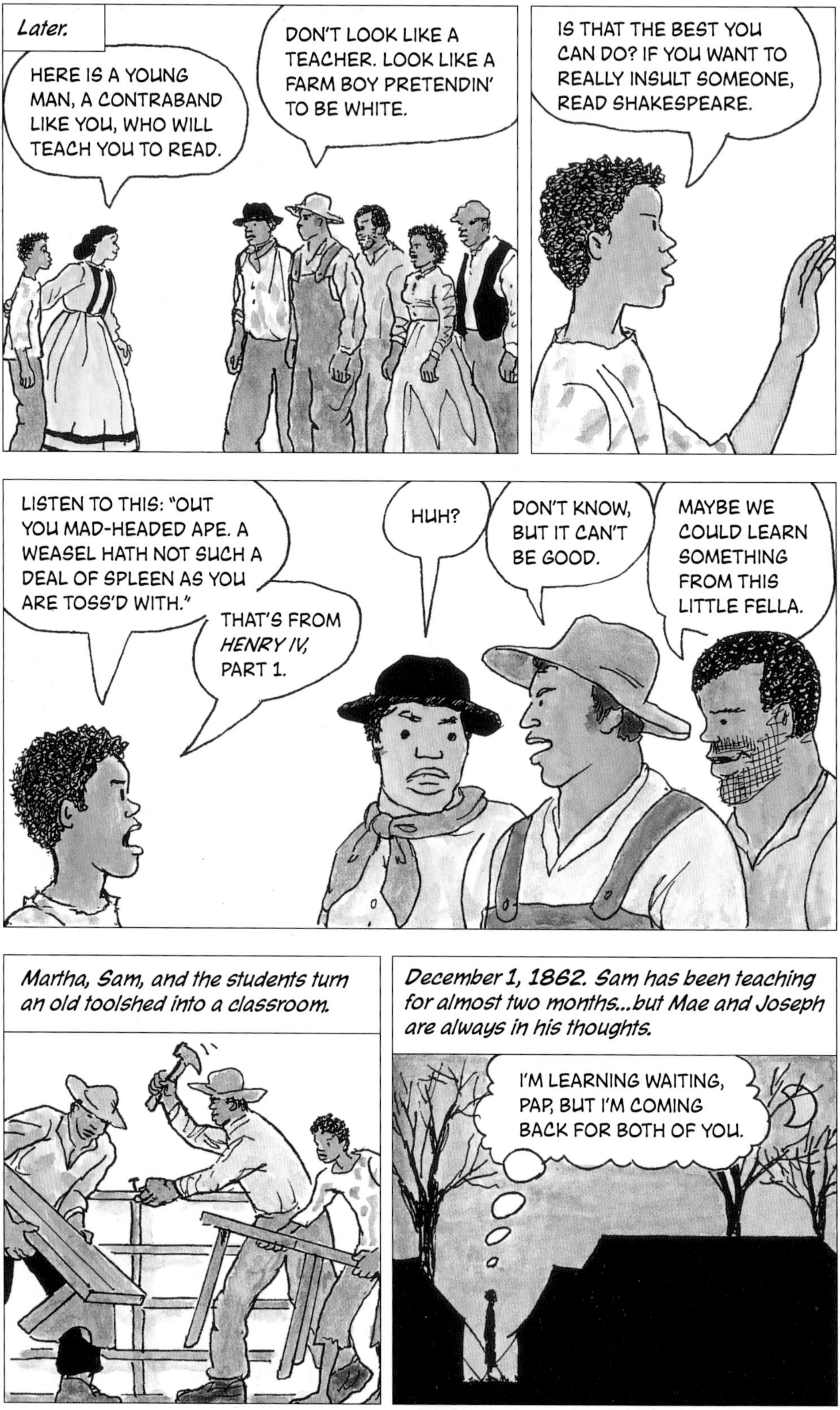
Later.
HERE IS A YOUNG MAN, A CONTRABAND LIKE YOU, WHO WILL TEACH YOU TO READ.
DON'T LOOK LIKE A TEACHER. LOOK LIKE A FARM BOY PRETENDIN' TO BE WHITE.
IS THAT THE BEST YOU CAN DO? IF YOU WANT TO REALLY INSULT SOMEONE, READ SHAKESPEARE.
LISTEN TO THIS: "OUT YOU MAD-HEADED APE. A WEASEL HATH NOT SUCH A DEAL OF SPLEEN AS YOU ARE TOSS'D WITH."
THAT'S FROM *HENRY IV*, PART 1.
HUH?
DON'T KNOW, BUT IT CAN'T BE GOOD.
MAYBE WE COULD LEARN SOMETHING FROM THIS LITTLE FELLA.
Martha, Sam, and the students turn an old toolshed into a classroom.
December 1, 1862. Sam has been teaching for almost two months...but Mae and Joseph are always in his thoughts.
I'M LEARNING WAITING, PAP, BUT I'M COMING BACK FOR BOTH OF YOU.

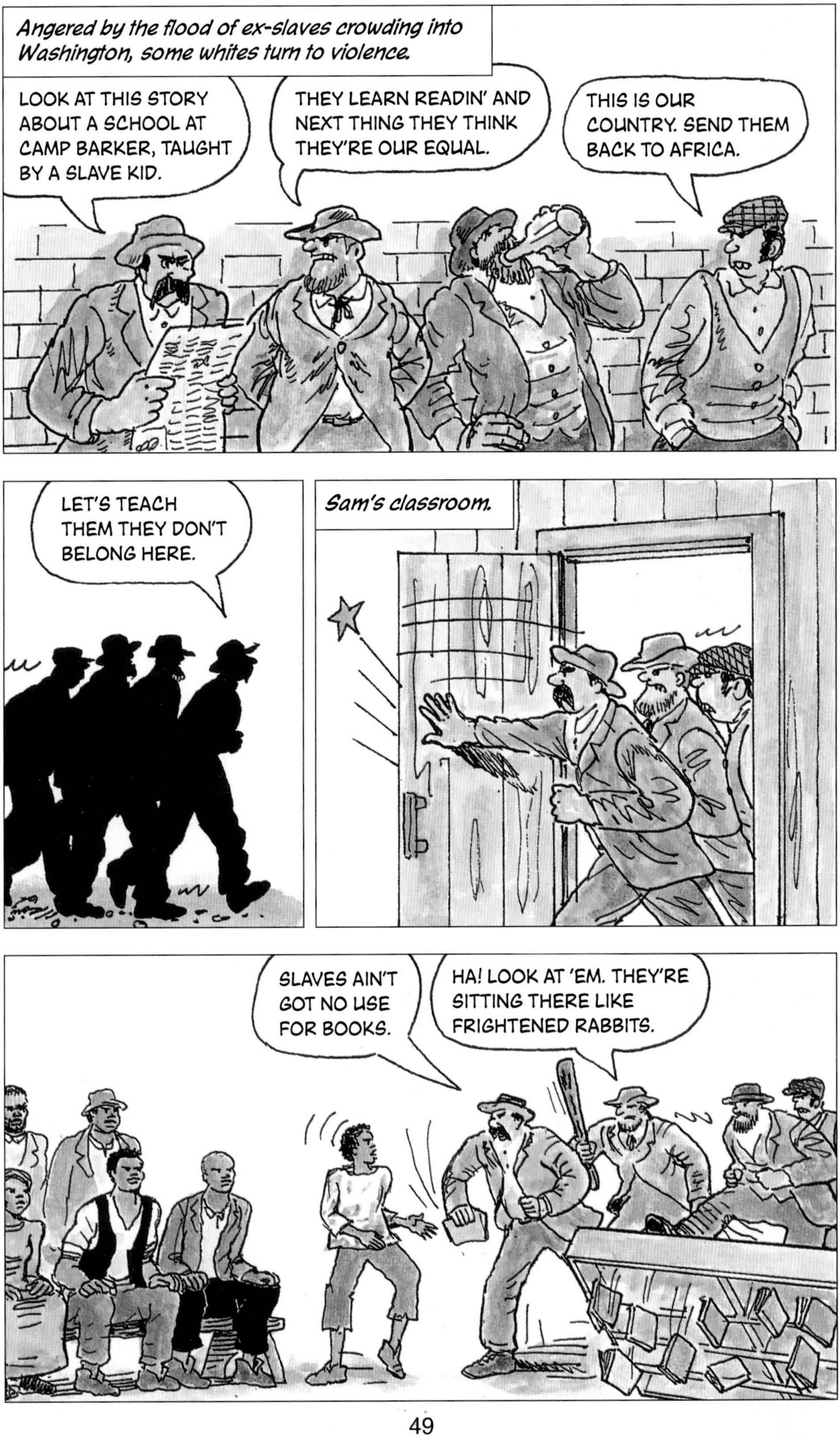
Angered by the flood of ex-slaves crowding into Washington, some whites turn to violence.
LOOK AT THIS STORY ABOUT A SCHOOL AT CAMP BARKER, TAUGHT BY A SLAVE KID.
THEY LEARN READIN' AND NEXT THING THEY THINK THEY'RE OUR EQUAL.
THIS IS OUR COUNTRY. SEND THEM BACK TO AFRICA.
LET'S TEACH THEM THEY DON'T BELONG HERE.
Sam's classroom.
SLAVES AIN'T GOT NO USE FOR BOOKS.
HA! LOOK AT 'EM. THEY'RE SITTING THERE LIKE FRIGHTENED RABBITS.

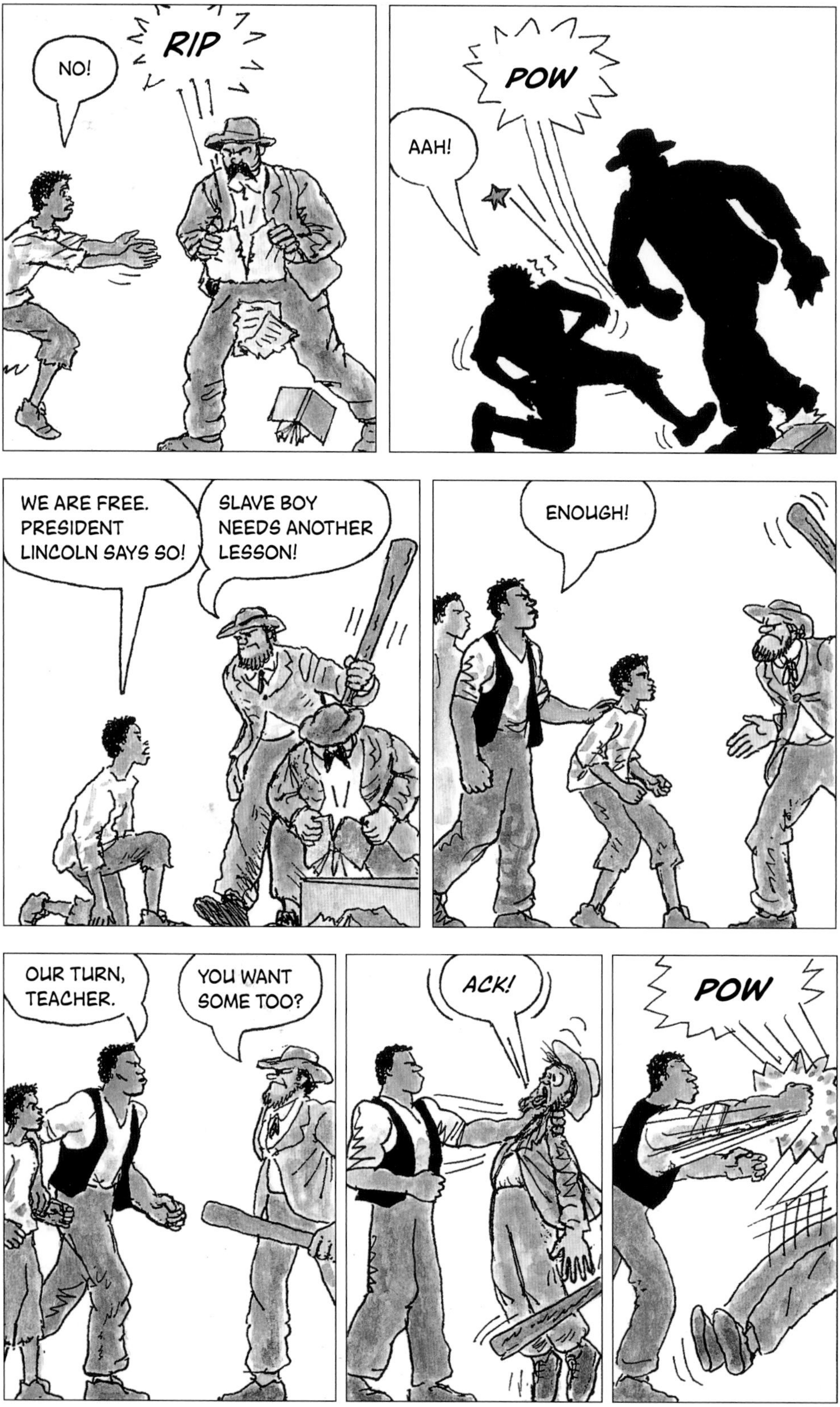
RIP
NO!
POW
AAH!
WE ARE FREE. PRESIDENT LINCOLN SAYS SO!
SLAVE BOY NEEDS ANOTHER LESSON!
ENOUGH!
OUR TURN, TEACHER.
YOU WANT SOME TOO?
ACK!
POW

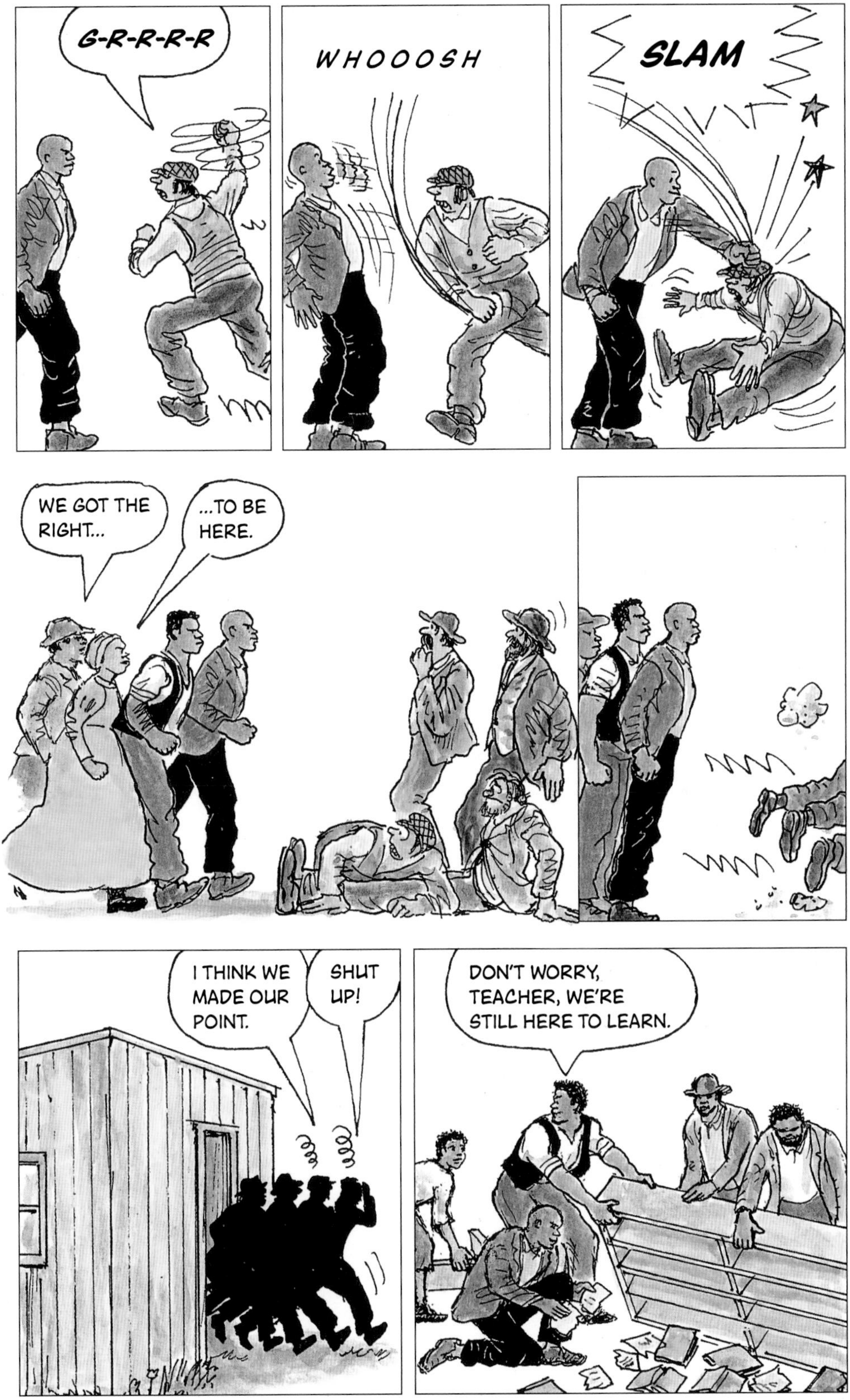
G-R-R-R-R
WHOOOOSH
SLAM
WE GOT THE RIGHT...
...TO BE HERE.
I THINK WE MADE OUR POINT.
SHUT UP!
DON'T WORRY, TEACHER, WE'RE STILL HERE TO LEARN.

CHAPTER 6

The war is draining Southern farms and towns of their able-bodied men. At home, folks must try to survive in a war-battered countryside. It's a situation ready-made for homegrown thieves.

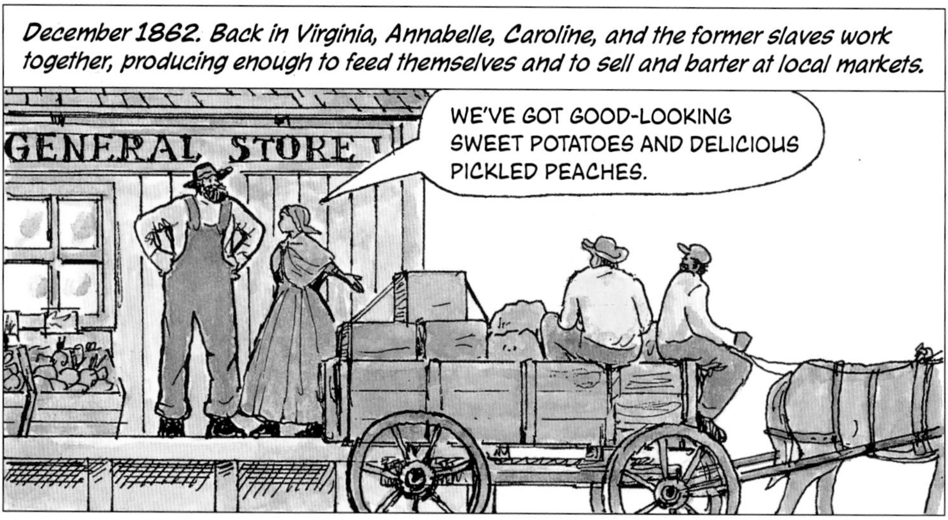
December 1862. Back in Virginia, Annabelle, Caroline, and the former slaves work together, producing enough to feed themselves and to sell and barter at local markets.
GENERAL STORE
WE'VE GOT GOOD-LOOKING SWEET POTATOES AND DELICIOUS PICKLED PEACHES.

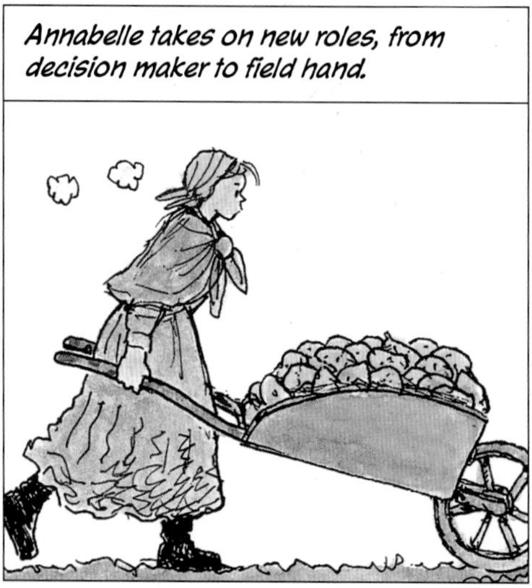
Annabelle takes on new roles, from decision maker to field hand.

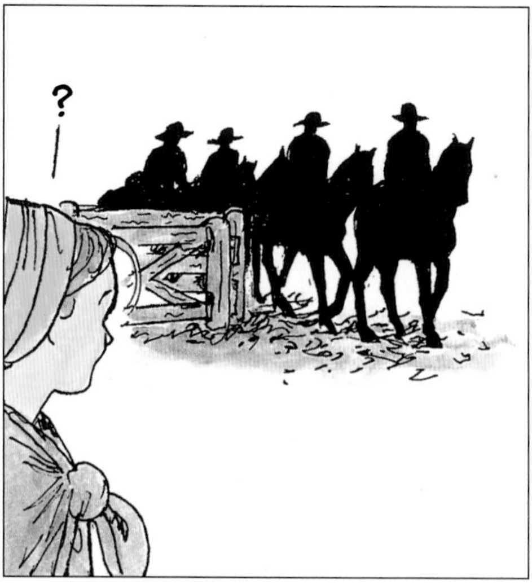
?

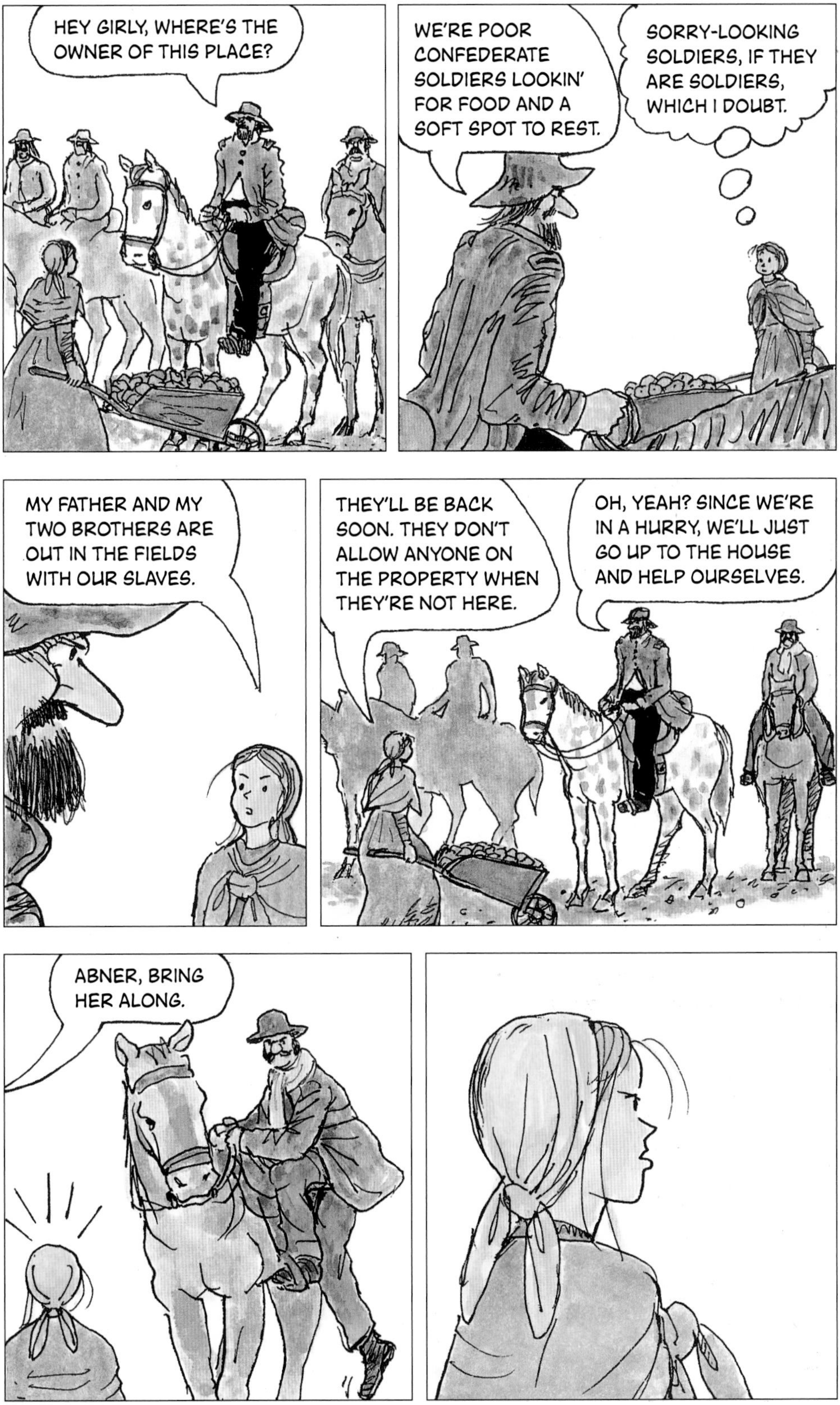

HEY GIRLY, WHERE'S THE OWNER OF THIS PLACE?
WE'RE POOR CONFEDERATE SOLDIERS LOOKIN' FOR FOOD AND A SOFT SPOT TO REST.
SORRY-LOOKING SOLDIERS, IF THEY ARE SOLDIERS, WHICH I DOUBT.
MY FATHER AND MY TWO BROTHERS ARE OUT IN THE FIELDS WITH OUR SLAVES.
THEY'LL BE BACK SOON. THEY DON'T ALLOW ANYONE ON THE PROPERTY WHEN THEY'RE NOT HERE.
OH, YEAH? SINCE WE'RE IN A HURRY, WE'LL JUST GO UP TO THE HOUSE AND HELP OURSELVES.
ABNER, BRING HER ALONG.

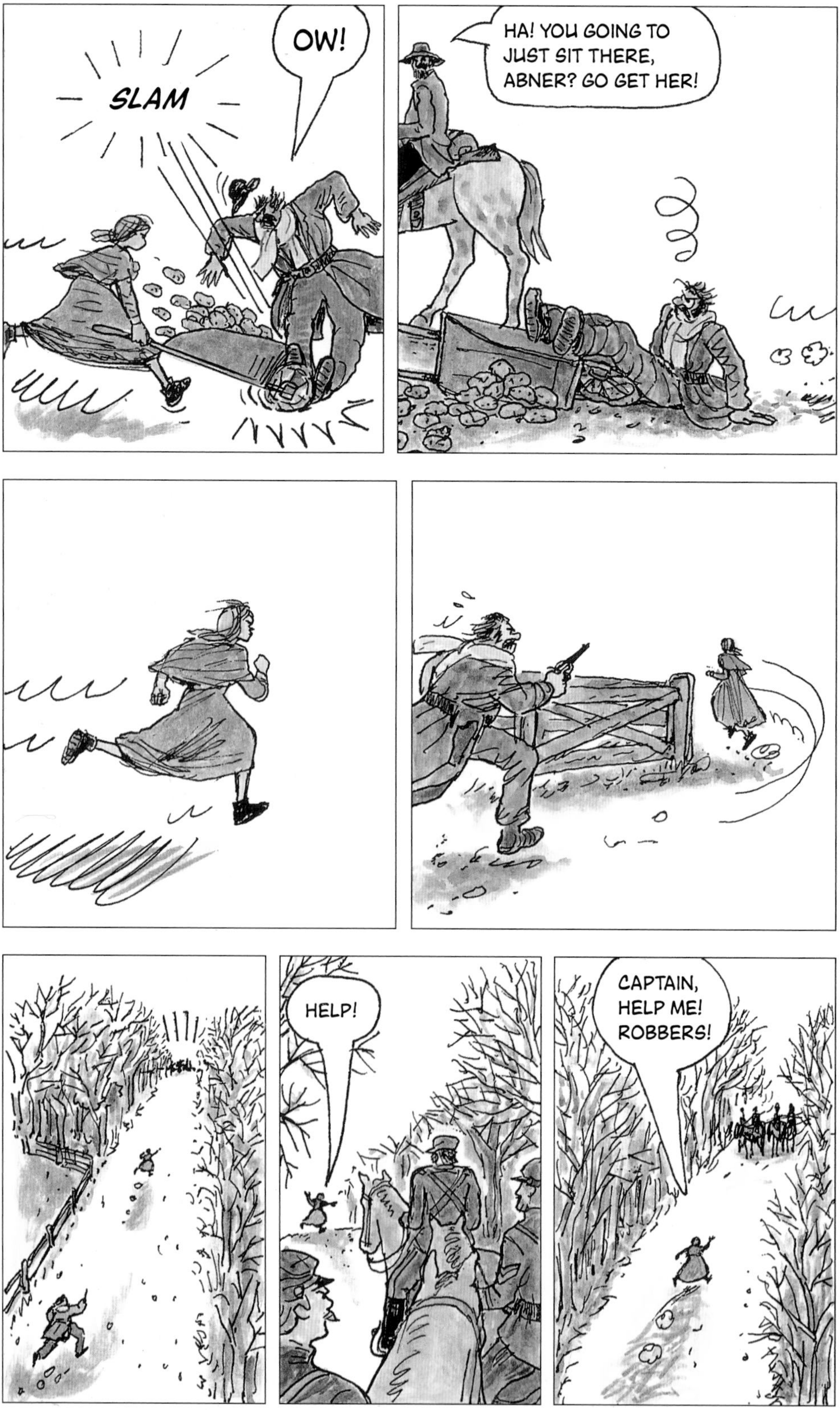
SLAM
OW!
HA! YOU GOING TO JUST SIT THERE, ABNER? GO GET HER!
HELP!
CAPTAIN, HELP ME! ROBBERS!

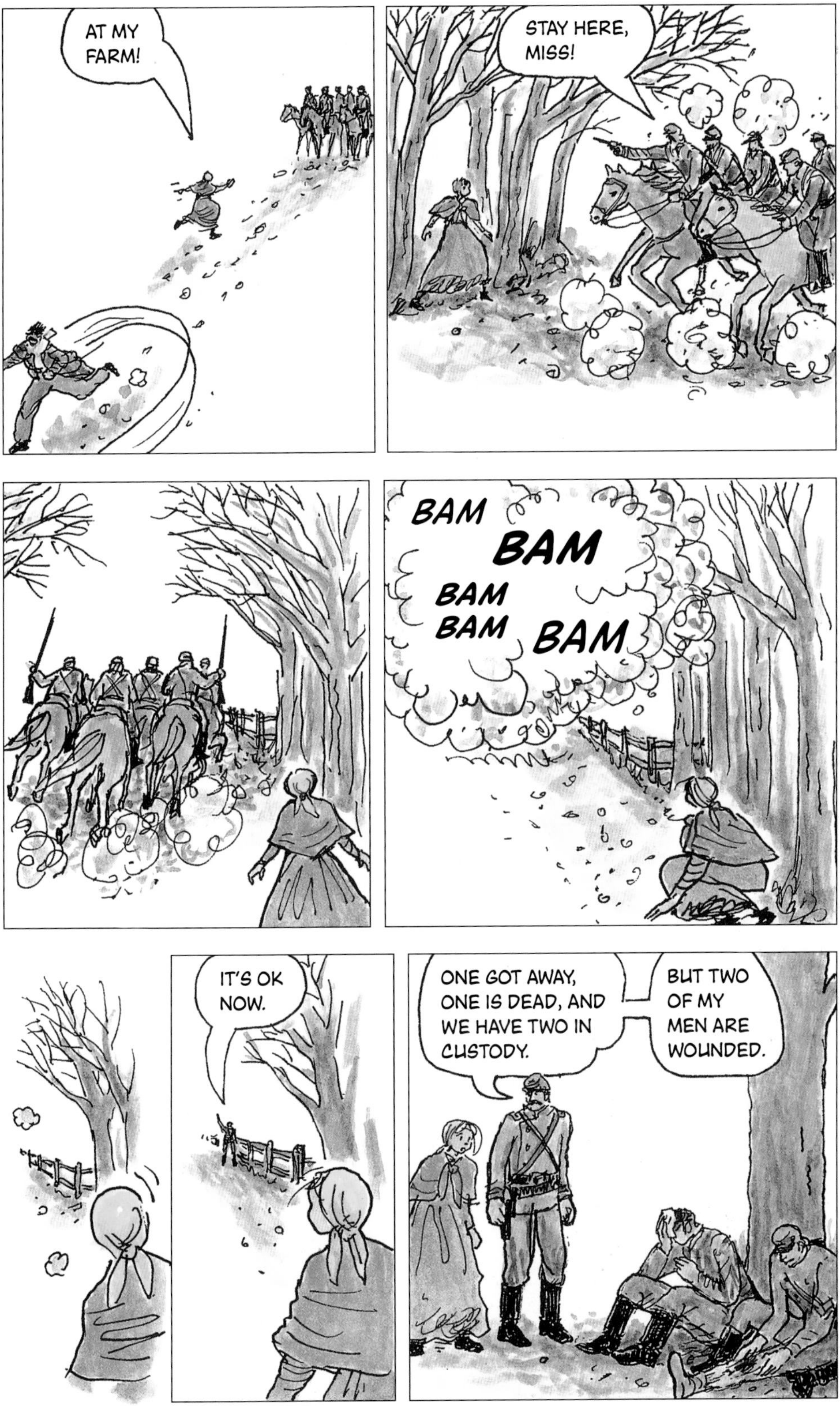
AT MY FARM!
STAY HERE, MISS!
BAM
BAM
BAM
BAM
BAM
IT'S OK NOW.
ONE GOT AWAY, ONE IS DEAD, AND WE HAVE TWO IN CUSTODY.
BUT TWO OF MY MEN ARE WOUNDED.

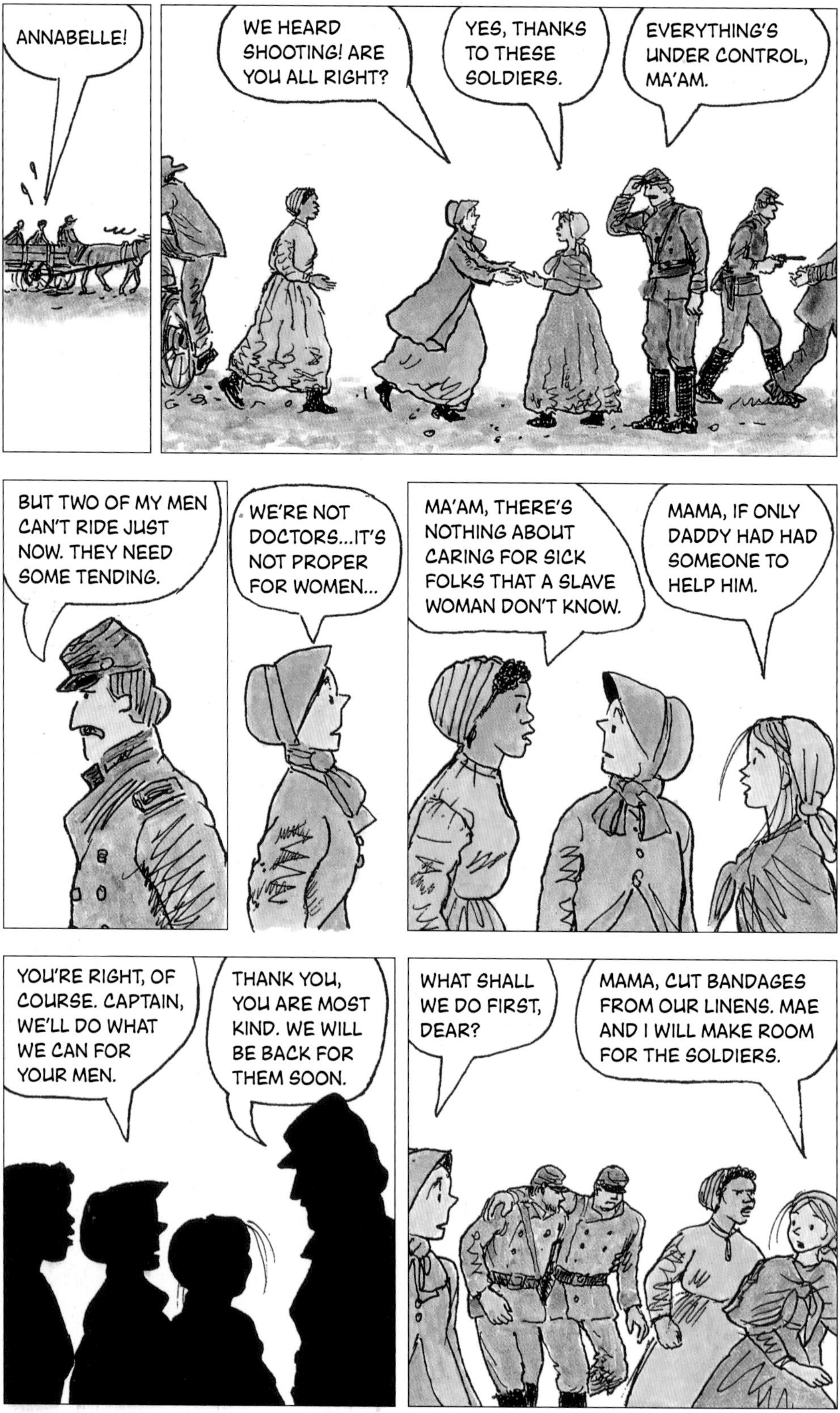
ANNABELLE!
WE HEARD SHOOTING! ARE YOU ALL RIGHT?
YES, THANKS TO THESE SOLDIERS.
EVERYTHING'S UNDER CONTROL, MA'AM.
BUT TWO OF MY MEN CAN'T RIDE JUST NOW. THEY NEED SOME TENDING.
WE'RE NOT DOCTORS...IT'S NOT PROPER FOR WOMEN...
MA'AM, THERE'S NOTHING ABOUT CARING FOR SICK FOLKS THAT A SLAVE WOMAN DON'T KNOW.
MAMA, IF ONLY DADDY HAD HAD SOMEONE TO HELP HIM.
YOU'RE RIGHT, OF COURSE. CAPTAIN, WE'LL DO WHAT WE CAN FOR YOUR MEN.
THANK YOU, YOU ARE MOST KIND. WE WILL BE BACK FOR THEM SOON.
WHAT SHALL WE DO FIRST, DEAR?
MAMA, CUT BANDAGES FROM OUR LINENS. MAE AND I WILL MAKE ROOM FOR THE SOLDIERS.

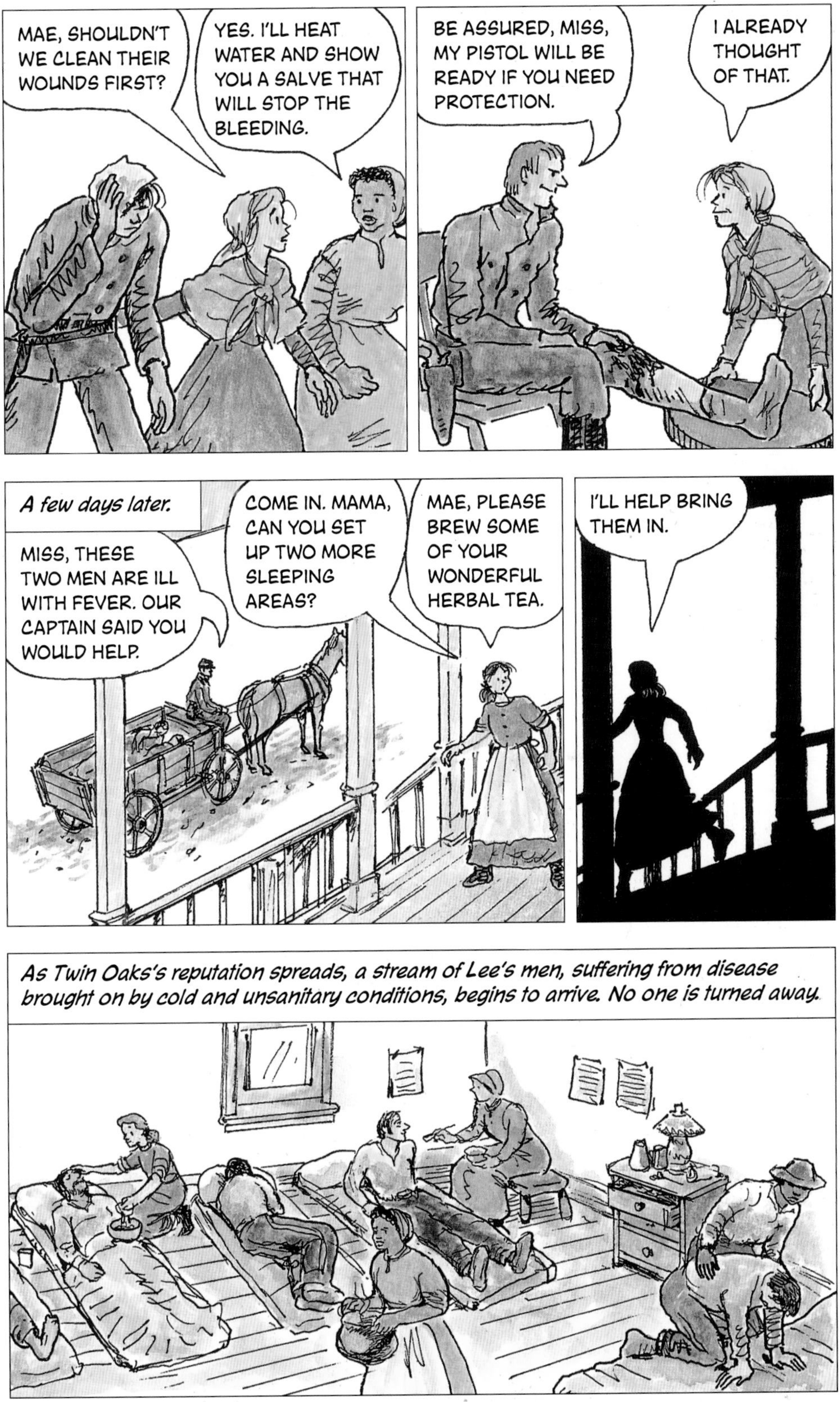
MAE, SHOULDN'T WE CLEAN THEIR WOUNDS FIRST?
YES. I'LL HEAT WATER AND SHOW YOU A SALVE THAT WILL STOP THE BLEEDING.
BE ASSURED, MISS, MY PISTOL WILL BE READY IF YOU NEED PROTECTION.
I ALREADY THOUGHT OF THAT.
A few days later.
MISS, THESE TWO MEN ARE ILL WITH FEVER. OUR CAPTAIN SAID YOU WOULD HELP.
COME IN. MAMA, CAN YOU SET UP TWO MORE SLEEPING AREAS?
MAE, PLEASE BREW SOME OF YOUR WONDERFUL HERBAL TEA.
I'LL HELP BRING THEM IN.
As Twin Oaks's reputation spreads, a stream of Lee's men, suffering from disease brought on by cold and unsanitary conditions, begins to arrive. No one is turned away.

CHAPTER 7

On December 12, 1862, the Union Army attacks across the Rappahannock River at Fredericksburg. The well-protected Confederate Army kills thousands and drives the Union Army back across the river. President Lincoln loses all hope that the war can be resolved quickly.

Cannon fire from the battle at Fredericksburg can be heard as far as Twin Oaks.

BOOM
BAM
BAM
BOOM

DARN THIS LEG—I NEED TO BE WITH MY REGIMENT.

HOLD STILL, OR IT'LL START BLEEDING AGAIN.

Across the road, Annabelle and Mae search for winter herbs for medicines.

BAM
BOOM
BOOM BAM

I FEAR WE WILL SEE MANY WOUNDED SOON.

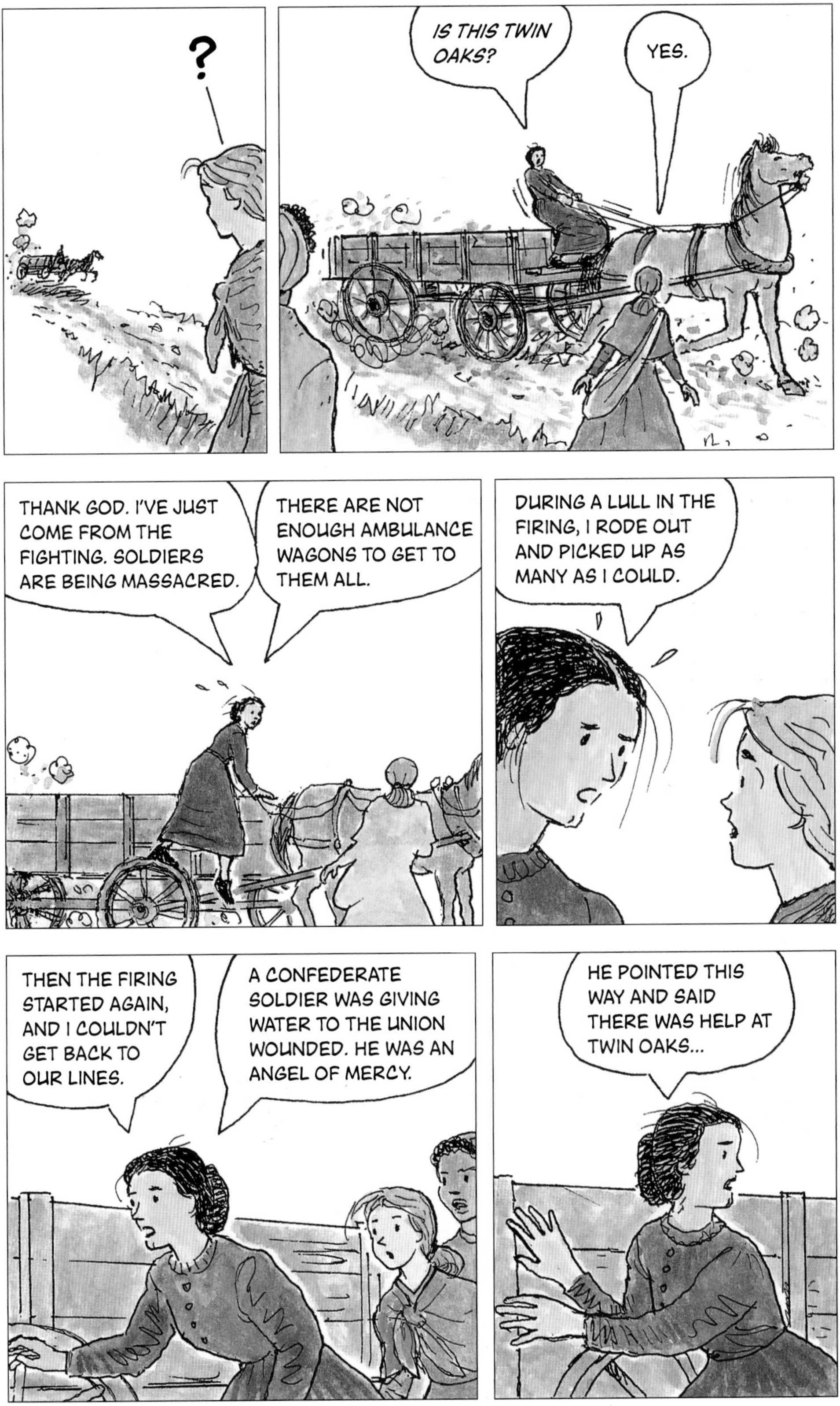
?
IS THIS TWIN OAKS?
YES.
THANK GOD. I'VE JUST COME FROM THE FIGHTING. SOLDIERS ARE BEING MASSACRED.
THERE ARE NOT ENOUGH AMBULANCE WAGONS TO GET TO THEM ALL.
DURING A LULL IN THE FIRING, I RODE OUT AND PICKED UP AS MANY AS I COULD.
THEN THE FIRING STARTED AGAIN, AND I COULDN'T GET BACK TO OUR LINES.
A CONFEDERATE SOLDIER WAS GIVING WATER TO THE UNION WOUNDED. HE WAS AN ANGEL OF MERCY.
HE POINTED THIS WAY AND SAID THERE WAS HELP AT TWIN OAKS...

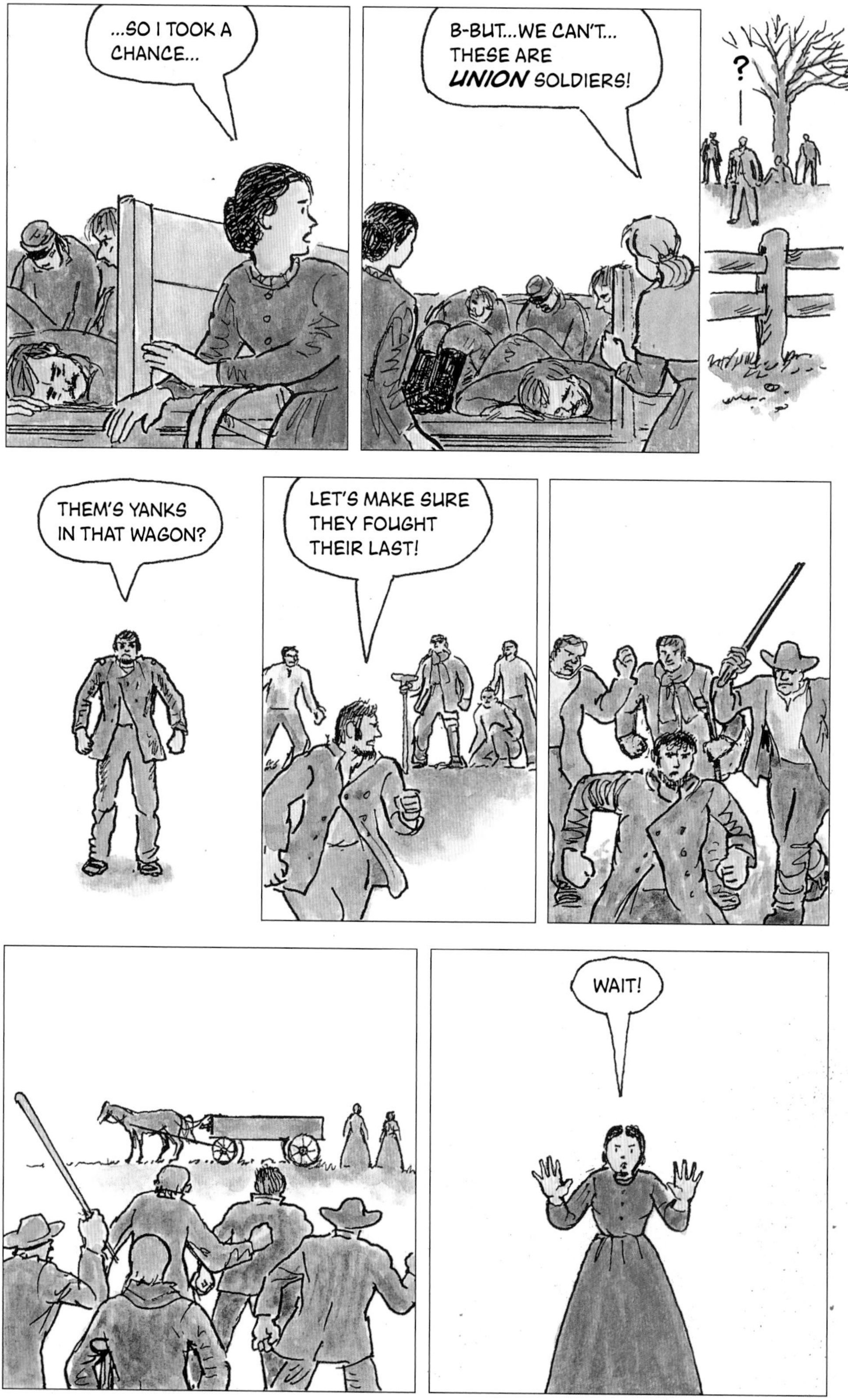
...SO I TOOK A CHANCE...
B-BUT...WE CAN'T... THESE ARE UNION SOLDIERS!
?
THEM'S YANKS IN THAT WAGON?
LET'S MAKE SURE THEY FOUGHT THEIR LAST!
WAIT!

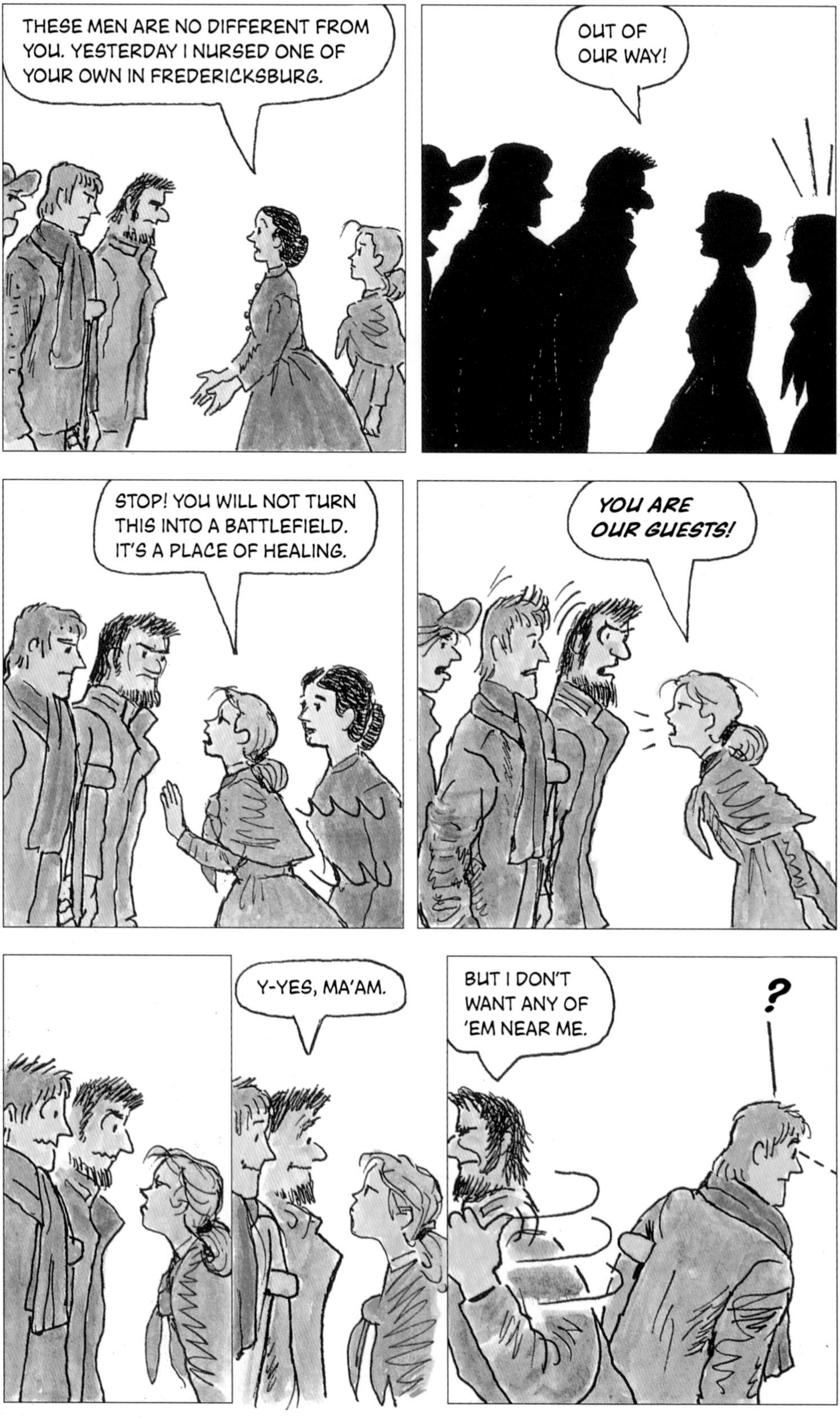
THESE MEN ARE NO DIFFERENT FROM YOU. YESTERDAY I NURSED ONE OF YOUR OWN IN FREDERICKSBURG.
OUT OF OUR WAY!
STOP! YOU WILL NOT TURN THIS INTO A BATTLEFIELD. IT'S A PLACE OF HEALING.
YOU ARE OUR GUESTS!
Y-YES, MA'AM.
BUT I DON'T WANT ANY OF 'EM NEAR ME.
?

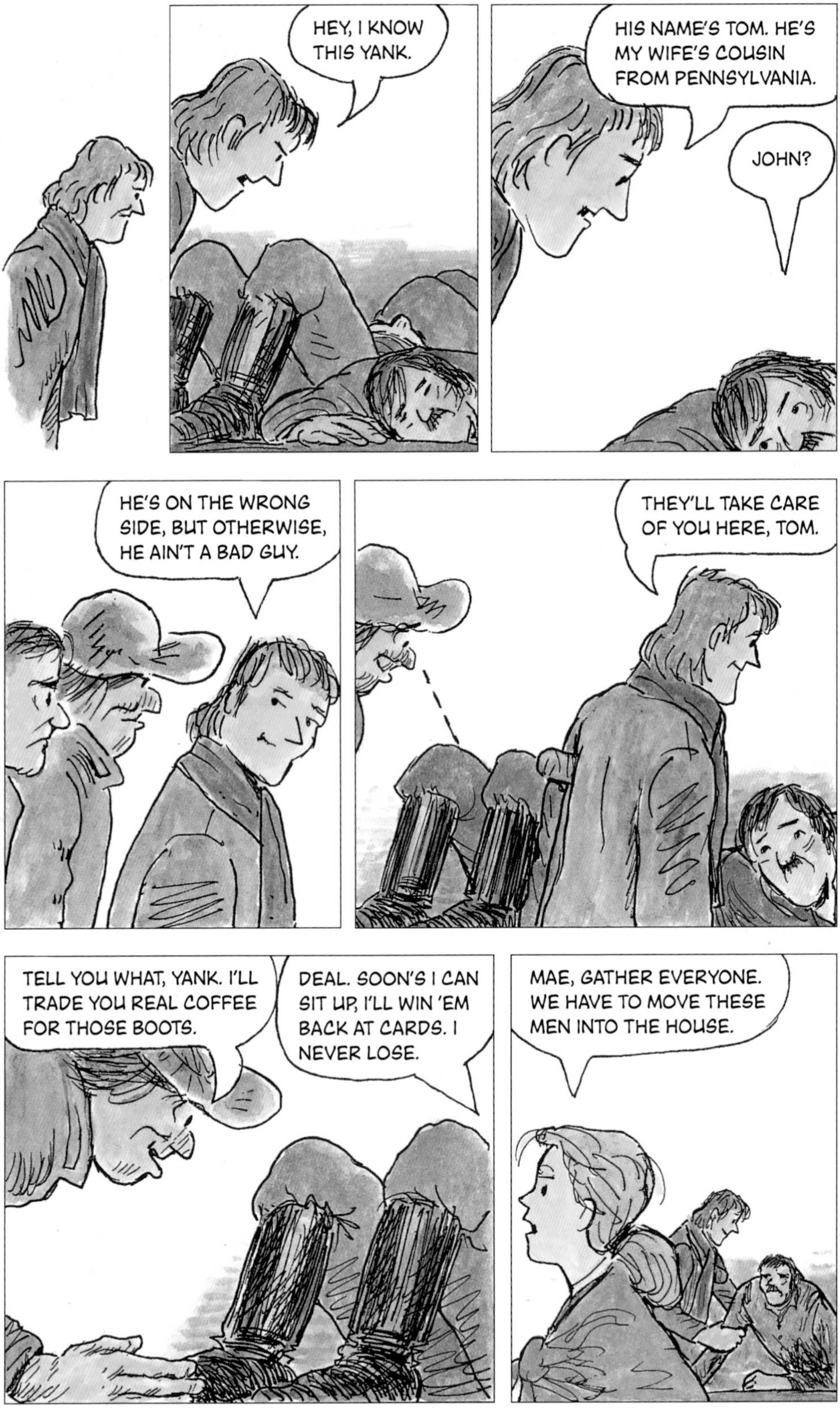
HEY, I KNOW THIS YANK.
HIS NAME'S TOM. HE'S MY WIFE'S COUSIN FROM PENNSYLVANIA.
JOHN?
HE'S ON THE WRONG SIDE, BUT OTHERWISE, HE AIN'T A BAD GUY.
THEY'LL TAKE CARE OF YOU HERE, TOM.
TELL YOU WHAT, YANK. I'LL TRADE YOU REAL COFFEE FOR THOSE BOOTS.
DEAL. SOON'S I CAN SIT UP, I'LL WIN 'EM BACK AT CARDS. I NEVER LOSE.
MAE, GATHER EVERYONE. WE HAVE TO MOVE THESE MEN INTO THE HOUSE.

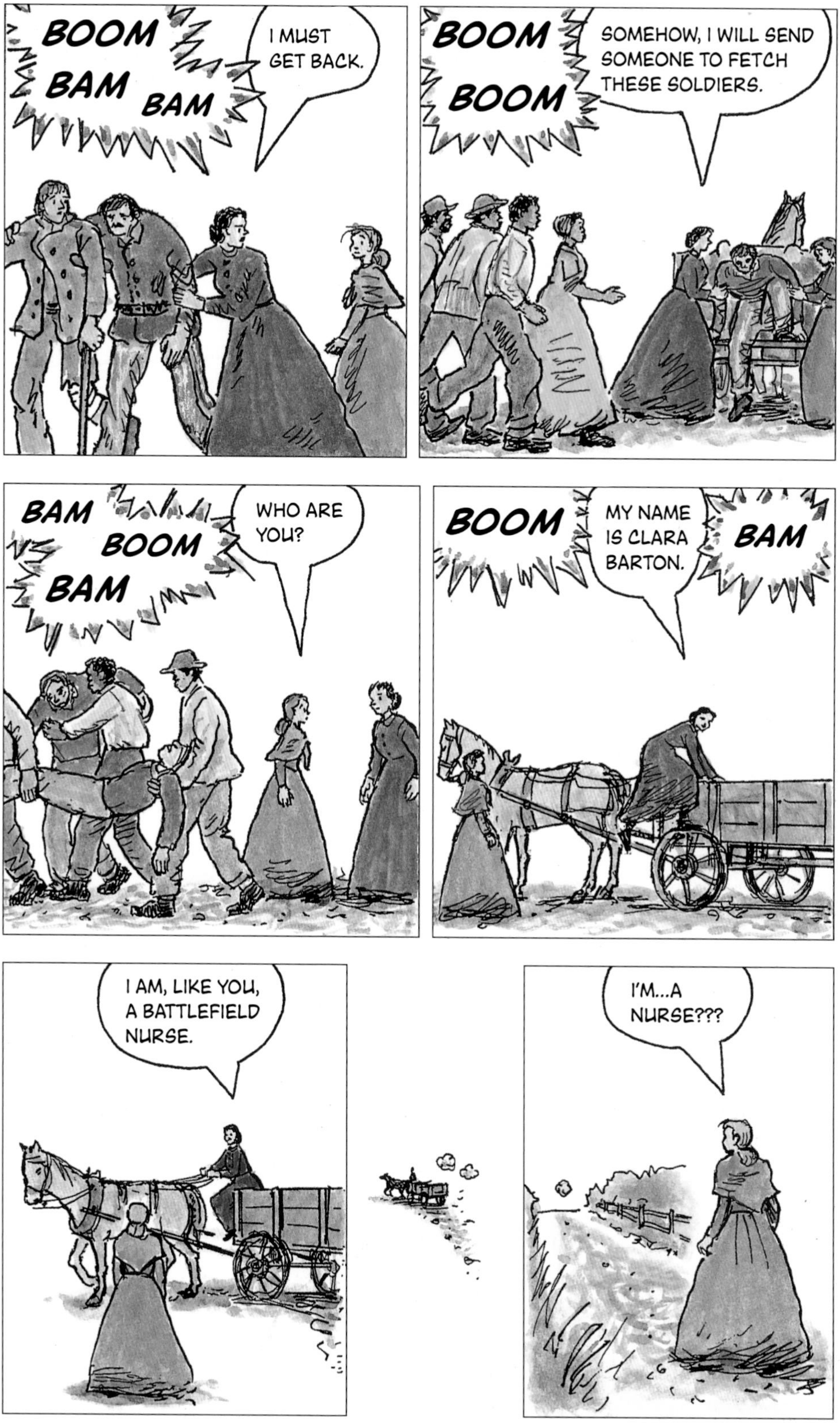
BOOM
BAM
BAM
I MUST GET BACK.
BOOM
BOOM
SOMEHOW, I WILL SEND SOMEONE TO FETCH THESE SOLDIERS.
BAM
BOOM
BAM
WHO ARE YOU?
BOOM
MY NAME IS CLARA BARTON.
BAM
I AM, LIKE YOU, A BATTLEFIELD NURSE.
I'M...A NURSE???

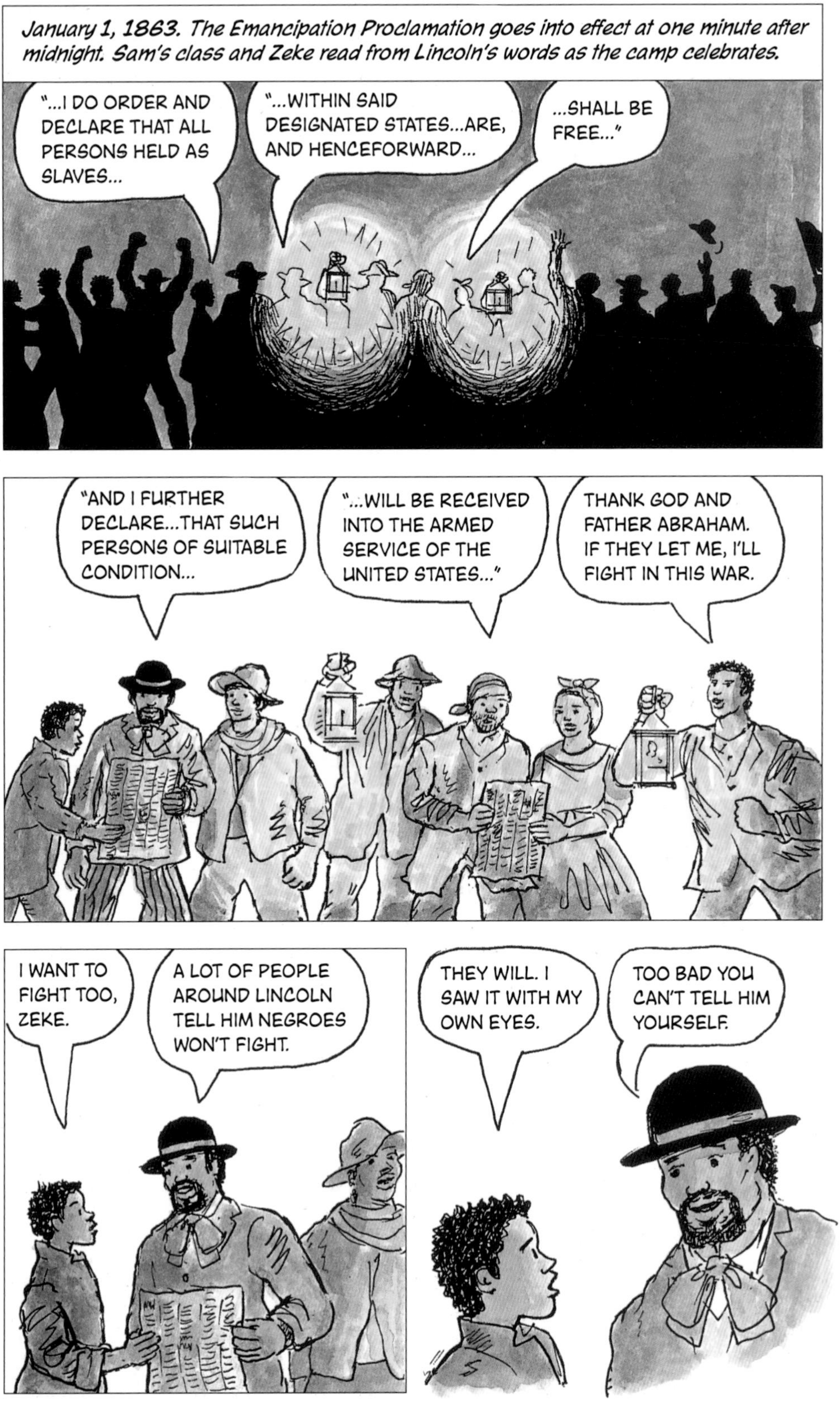
January 1, 1863. The Emancipation Proclamation goes into effect at one minute after midnight. Sam's class and Zeke read from Lincoln's words as the camp celebrates.
"...I DO ORDER AND DECLARE THAT ALL PERSONS HELD AS SLAVES...
"...WITHIN SAID DESIGNATED STATES...ARE, AND HENCEFORWARD...
...SHALL BE FREE..."
"AND I FURTHER DECLARE...THAT SUCH PERSONS OF SUITABLE CONDITION...
"...WILL BE RECEIVED INTO THE ARMED SERVICE OF THE UNITED STATES..."
THANK GOD AND FATHER ABRAHAM. IF THEY LET ME, I'LL FIGHT IN THIS WAR.
I WANT TO FIGHT TOO, ZEKE.
A LOT OF PEOPLE AROUND LINCOLN TELL HIM NEGROES WON'T FIGHT.
THEY WILL. I SAW IT WITH MY OWN EYES.
TOO BAD YOU CAN'T TELL HIM YOURSELF.

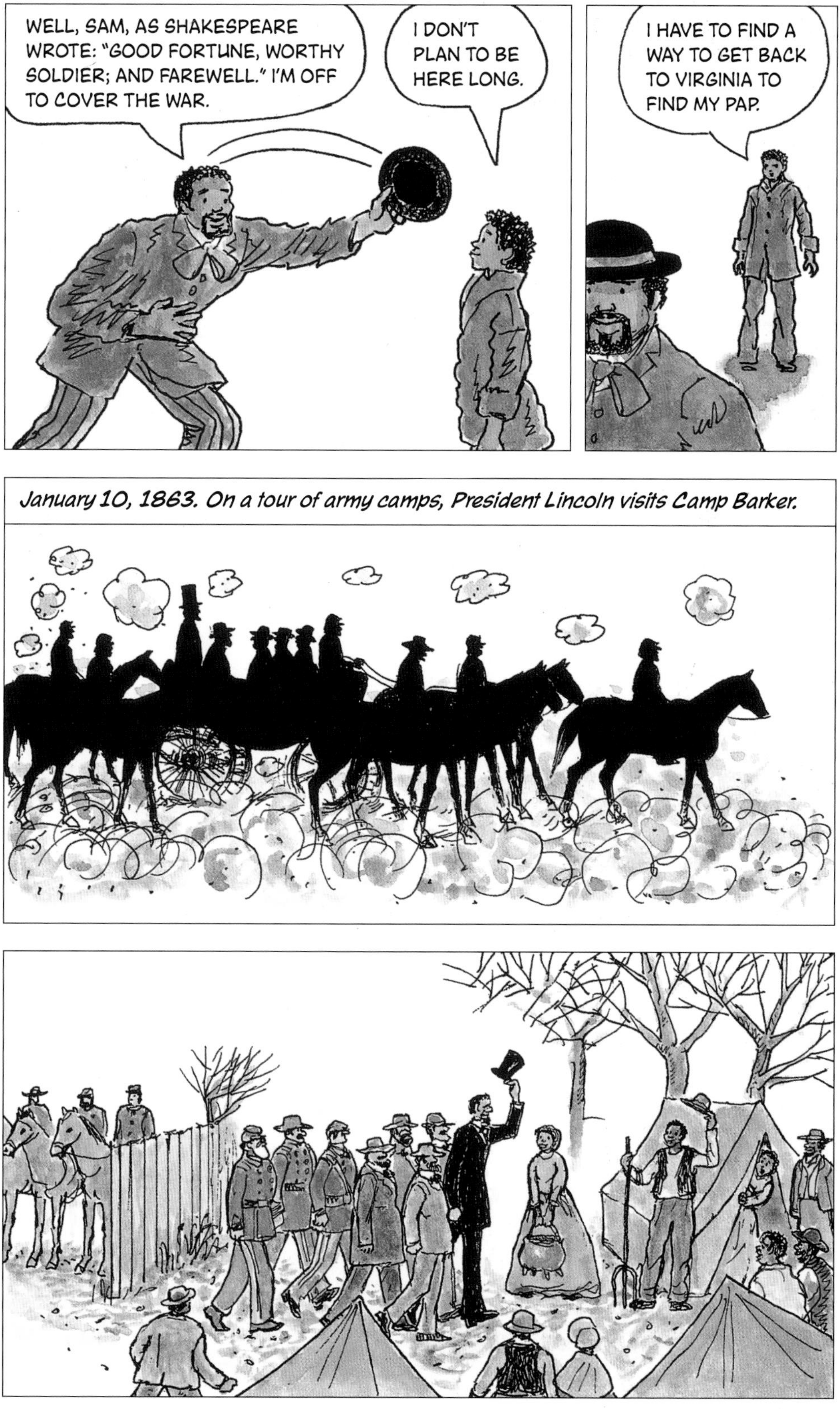
WELL, SAM, AS SHAKESPEARE WROTE: "GOOD FORTUNE, WORTHY SOLDIER; AND FAREWELL." I'M OFF TO COVER THE WAR.
I DON'T PLAN TO BE HERE LONG.
I HAVE TO FIND A WAY TO GET BACK TO VIRGINIA TO FIND MY PAP.
January 10, 1863. On a tour of army camps, President Lincoln visits Camp Barker.

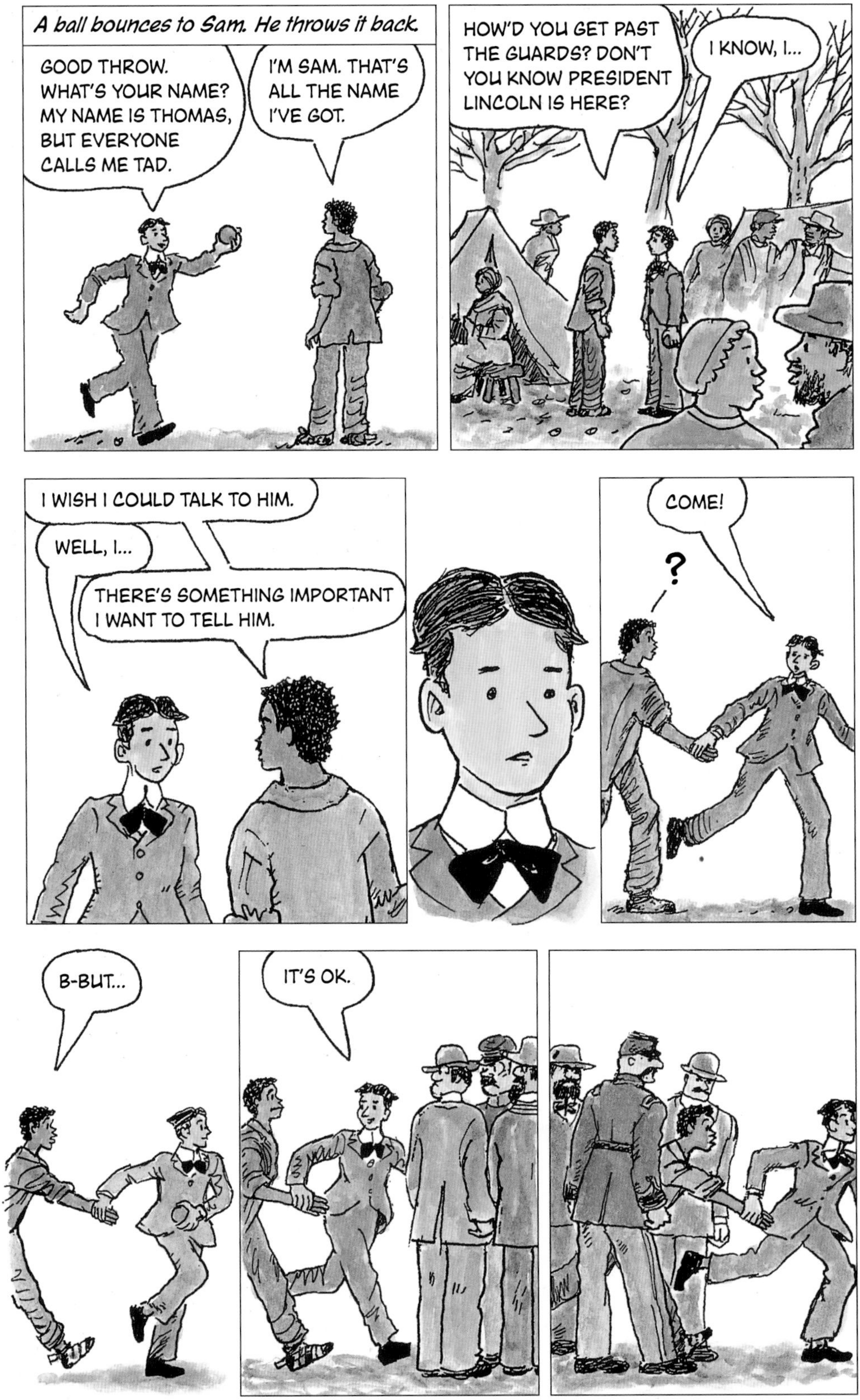
A ball bounces to Sam. He throws it back.
GOOD THROW. WHAT'S YOUR NAME? MY NAME IS THOMAS, BUT EVERYONE CALLS ME TAD.
I'M SAM. THAT'S ALL THE NAME I'VE GOT.
HOW'D YOU GET PAST THE GUARDS? DON'T YOU KNOW PRESIDENT LINCOLN IS HERE?
I KNOW, I...
I WISH I COULD TALK TO HIM.
WELL, I...
THERE'S SOMETHING IMPORTANT I WANT TO TELL HIM.
COME!
?
B-BUT...
IT'S OK.

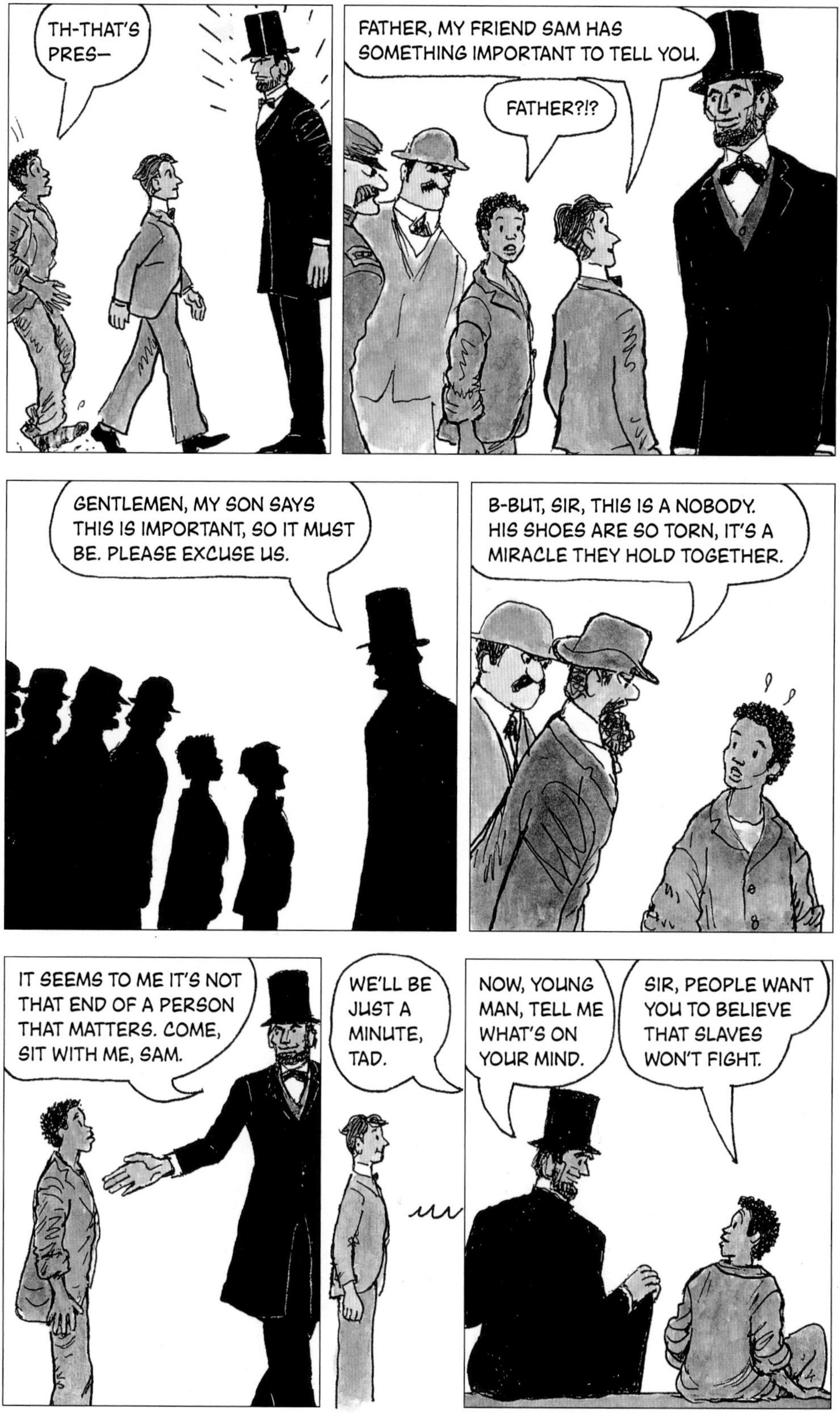
TH-THAT'S PRES–
FATHER, MY FRIEND SAM HAS SOMETHING IMPORTANT TO TELL YOU.
FATHER?!?
GENTLEMEN, MY SON SAYS THIS IS IMPORTANT, SO IT MUST BE. PLEASE EXCUSE US.
B-BUT, SIR, THIS IS A NOBODY. HIS SHOES ARE SO TORN, IT'S A MIRACLE THEY HOLD TOGETHER.
IT SEEMS TO ME IT'S NOT THAT END OF A PERSON THAT MATTERS. COME, SIT WITH ME, SAM.
WE'LL BE JUST A MINUTE, TAD.
NOW, YOUNG MAN, TELL ME WHAT'S ON YOUR MIND.
SIR, PEOPLE WANT YOU TO BELIEVE THAT SLAVES WON'T FIGHT.

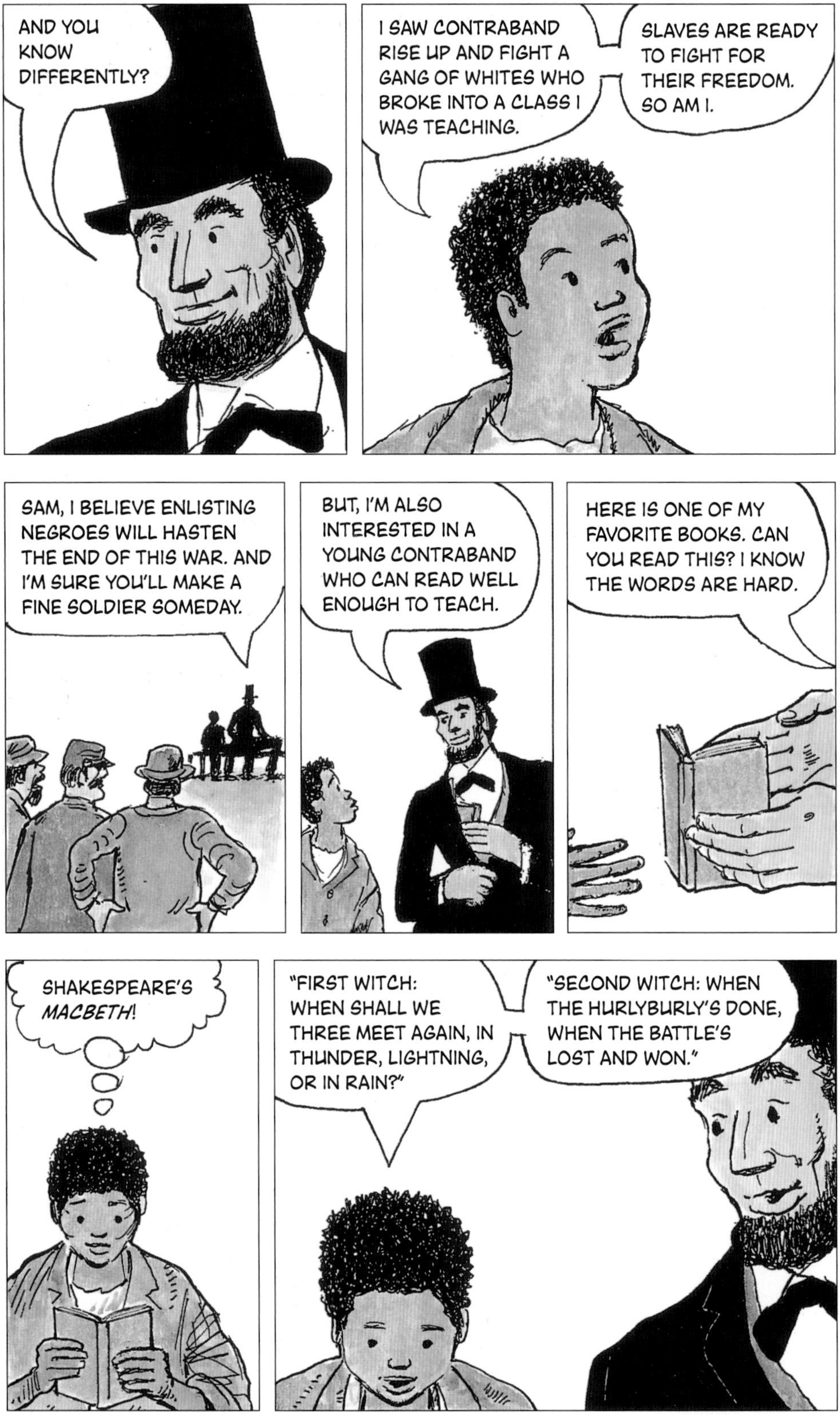
AND YOU KNOW DIFFERENTLY?
I SAW CONTRABAND RISE UP AND FIGHT A GANG OF WHITES WHO BROKE INTO A CLASS I WAS TEACHING.
SLAVES ARE READY TO FIGHT FOR THEIR FREEDOM. SO AM I.
SAM, I BELIEVE ENLISTING NEGROES WILL HASTEN THE END OF THIS WAR. AND I'M SURE YOU'LL MAKE A FINE SOLDIER SOMEDAY.
BUT, I'M ALSO INTERESTED IN A YOUNG CONTRABAND WHO CAN READ WELL ENOUGH TO TEACH.
HERE IS ONE OF MY FAVORITE BOOKS. CAN YOU READ THIS? I KNOW THE WORDS ARE HARD.
SHAKESPEARE'S *MACBETH*!
"FIRST WITCH: WHEN SHALL WE THREE MEET AGAIN, IN THUNDER, LIGHTNING, OR IN RAIN?"
"SECOND WITCH: WHEN THE HURLYBURLY'S DONE, WHEN THE BATTLE'S LOST AND WON."

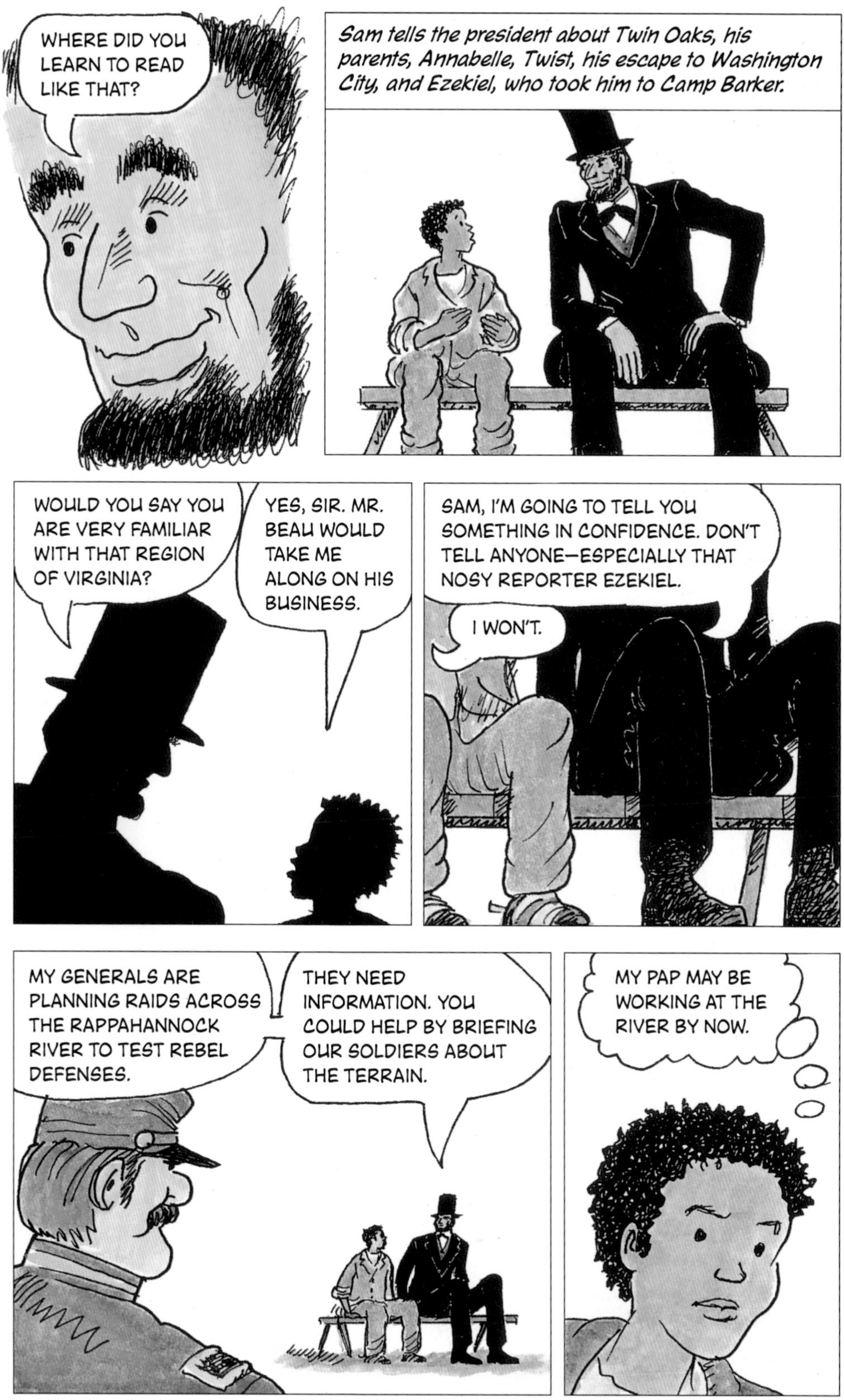
WHERE DID YOU LEARN TO READ LIKE THAT?
Sam tells the president about Twin Oaks, his parents, Annabelle, Twist, his escape to Washington City, and Ezekiel, who took him to Camp Barker.
WOULD YOU SAY YOU ARE VERY FAMILIAR WITH THAT REGION OF VIRGINIA?
YES, SIR. MR. BEAU WOULD TAKE ME ALONG ON HIS BUSINESS.
SAM, I'M GOING TO TELL YOU SOMETHING IN CONFIDENCE. DON'T TELL ANYONE—ESPECIALLY THAT NOSY REPORTER EZEKIEL.
I WON'T.
MY GENERALS ARE PLANNING RAIDS ACROSS THE RAPPAHANNOCK RIVER TO TEST REBEL DEFENSES.
THEY NEED INFORMATION. YOU COULD HELP BY BRIEFING OUR SOLDIERS ABOUT THE TERRAIN.
MY PAP MAY BE WORKING AT THE RIVER BY NOW.

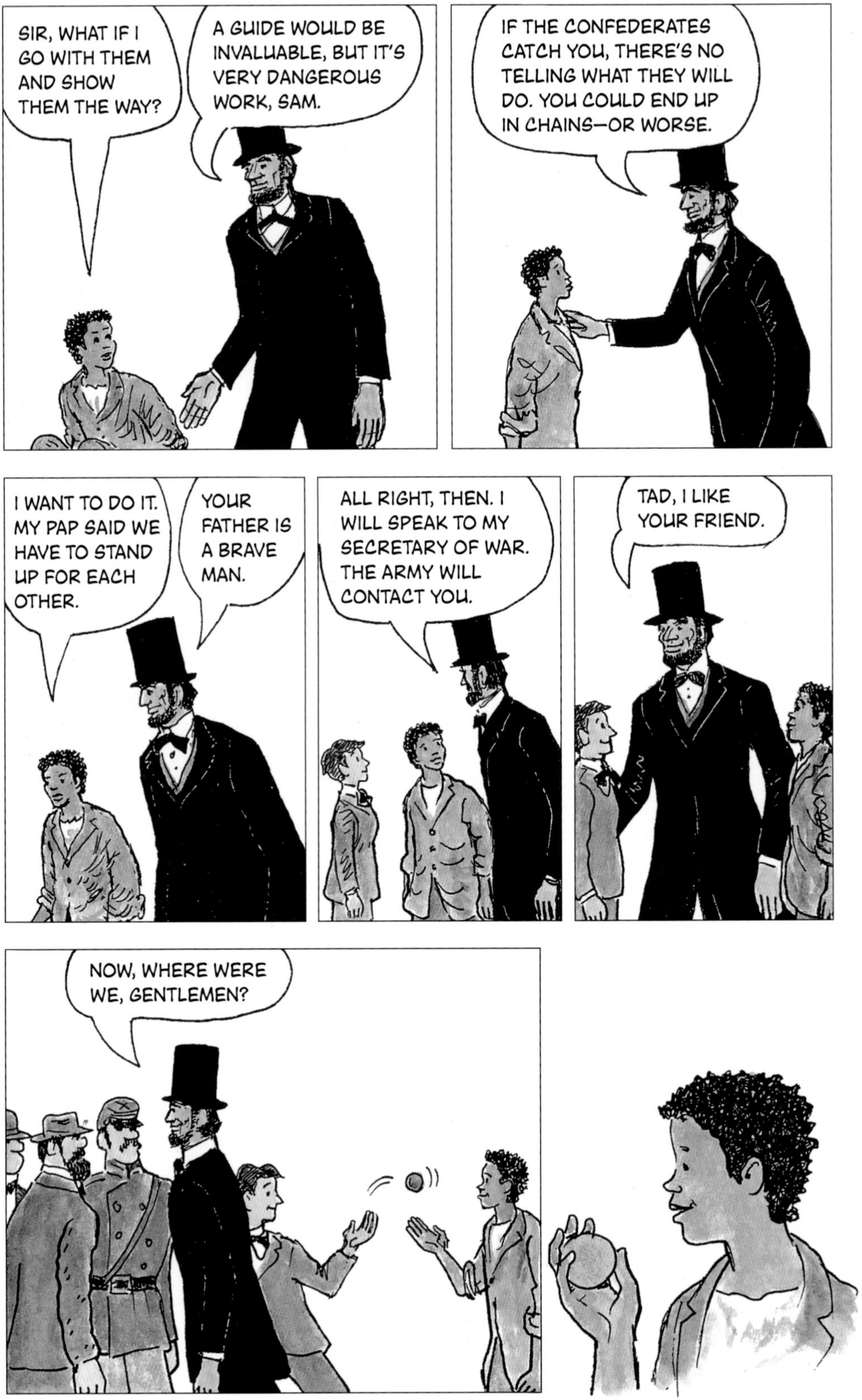
SIR, WHAT IF I GO WITH THEM AND SHOW THEM THE WAY?
A GUIDE WOULD BE INVALUABLE, BUT IT'S VERY DANGEROUS WORK, SAM.
IF THE CONFEDERATES CATCH YOU, THERE'S NO TELLING WHAT THEY WILL DO. YOU COULD END UP IN CHAINS—OR WORSE.
I WANT TO DO IT. MY PAP SAID WE HAVE TO STAND UP FOR EACH OTHER.
YOUR FATHER IS A BRAVE MAN.
ALL RIGHT, THEN. I WILL SPEAK TO MY SECRETARY OF WAR. THE ARMY WILL CONTACT YOU.
TAD, I LIKE YOUR FRIEND.
NOW, WHERE WERE WE, GENTLEMEN?

CHAPTER 8

Early in 1863, the North prepares for a major spring offensive in Virginia. At the same time, both sides wonder if and how the Emancipation Proclamation will affect the course of the war.

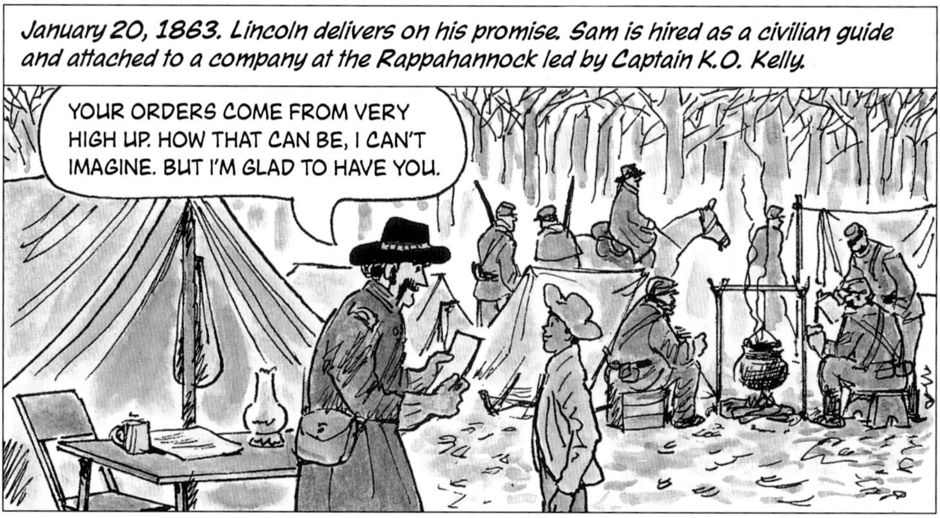
January 20, 1863. Lincoln delivers on his promise. Sam is hired as a civilian guide and attached to a company at the Rappahannock led by Captain K.O. Kelly.
YOUR ORDERS COME FROM VERY HIGH UP. HOW THAT CAN BE, I CAN'T IMAGINE. BUT I'M GLAD TO HAVE YOU.

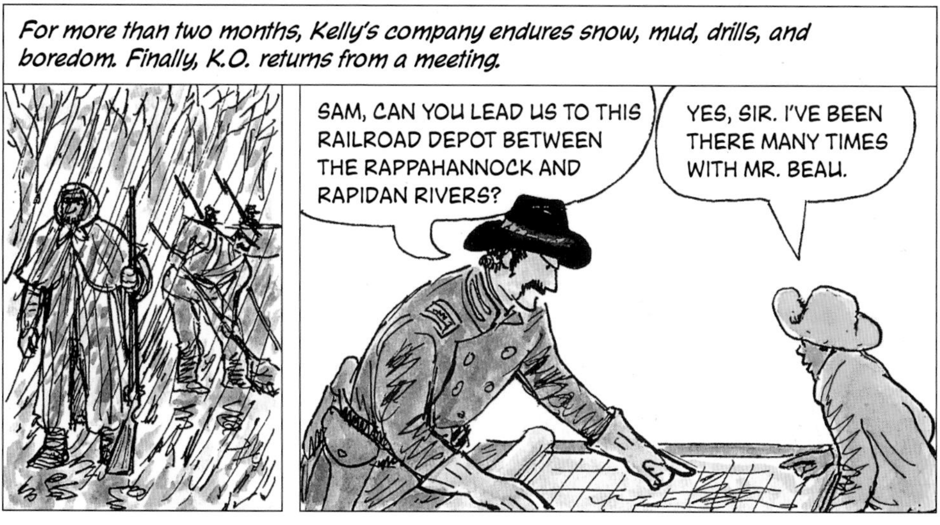
For more than two months, Kelly's company endures snow, mud, drills, and boredom. Finally, K.O. returns from a meeting.
SAM, CAN YOU LEAD US TO THIS RAILROAD DEPOT BETWEEN THE RAPPAHANNOCK AND RAPIDAN RIVERS?
YES, SIR. I'VE BEEN THERE MANY TIMES WITH MR. BEAU.

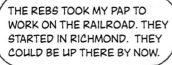

THE REBS TOOK MY PAP TO WORK ON THE RAILROAD. THEY STARTED IN RICHMOND. THEY COULD BE UP THERE BY NOW.

GOOD! THEN YOU HAVE A DOUBLE REASON TO MAKE SURE WE GET THERE SAFELY.

I'M COMING, PAP.

Captain Kelly selects eight of his best men.

IT'S A REBEL SUPPLY DEPOT. IF WE CAN DAMAGE IT, WE'LL GIVE LEE A MAJOR HEADACHE.

WE'LL FORD THE RIVER, AND SAM WILL LEAD US AROUND THE REBEL LEFT FLANK.

WE GOTTA PUT OUR TRUST IN A NEGRO BOY?!?

KNOCK IT OFF, SERGEANT BRAGG. HE KNOWS THESE PARTS; WE DON'T.

TOMORROW NIGHT THERE'S NO MOON, AND WE GO. NOW, LET'S GET READY.

The next night, the men carry muskets, knives, canteens, ammo boxes, biscuits, and matches.

SAM, JUST TAKE A KNIFE AND MATCHES AND GET RID OF ANYTHING THAT SAYS "UNION ARMY."

72

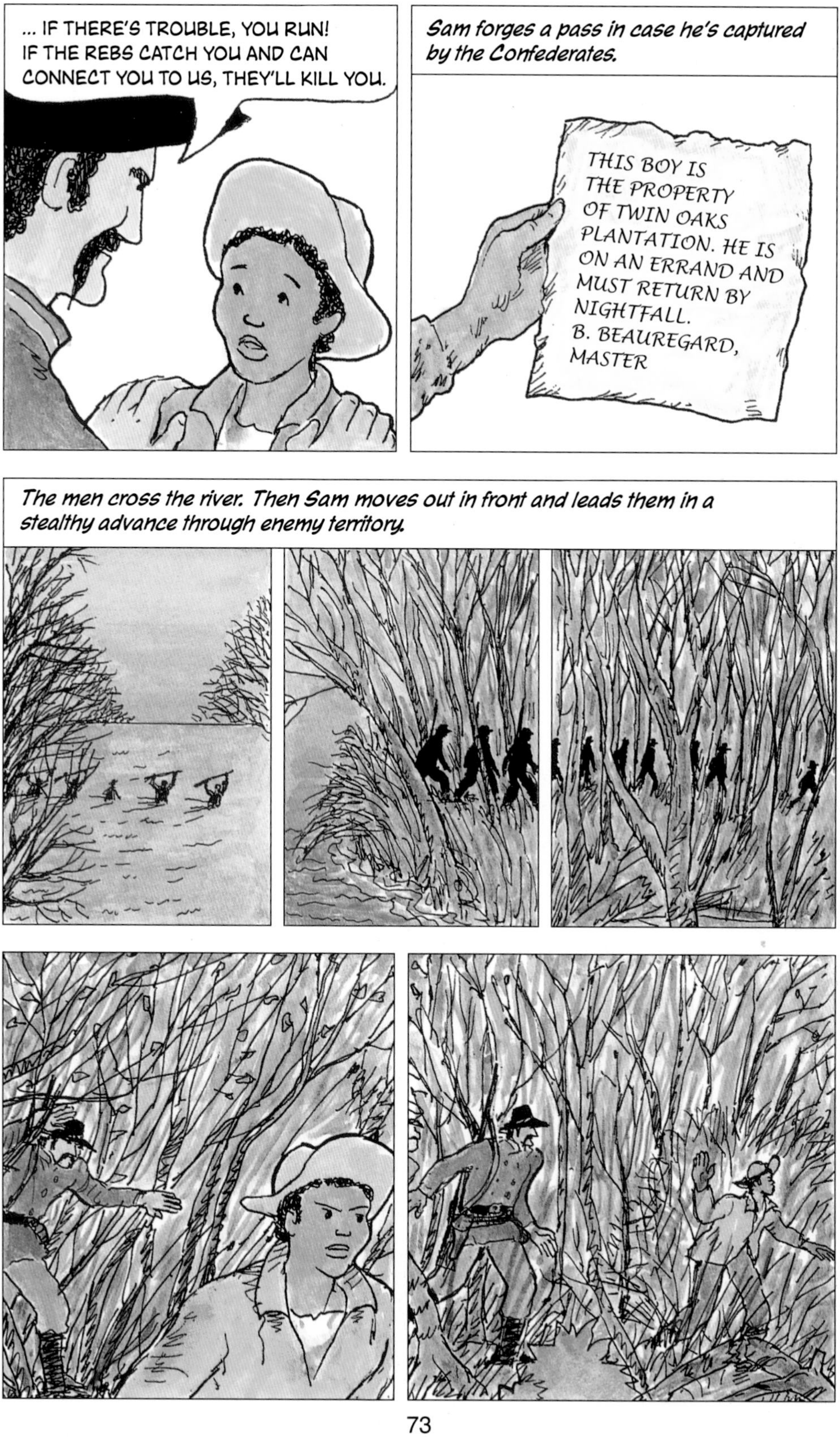

... IF THERE'S TROUBLE, YOU RUN! IF THE REBS CATCH YOU AND CAN CONNECT YOU TO US, THEY'LL KILL YOU.
Sam forges a pass in case he's captured by the Confederates.
THIS BOY IS THE PROPERTY OF TWIN OAKS PLANTATION. HE IS ON AN ERRAND AND MUST RETURN BY NIGHTFALL. B. BEAUREGARD, MASTER
The men cross the river. Then Sam moves out in front and leads them in a stealthy advance through enemy territory.

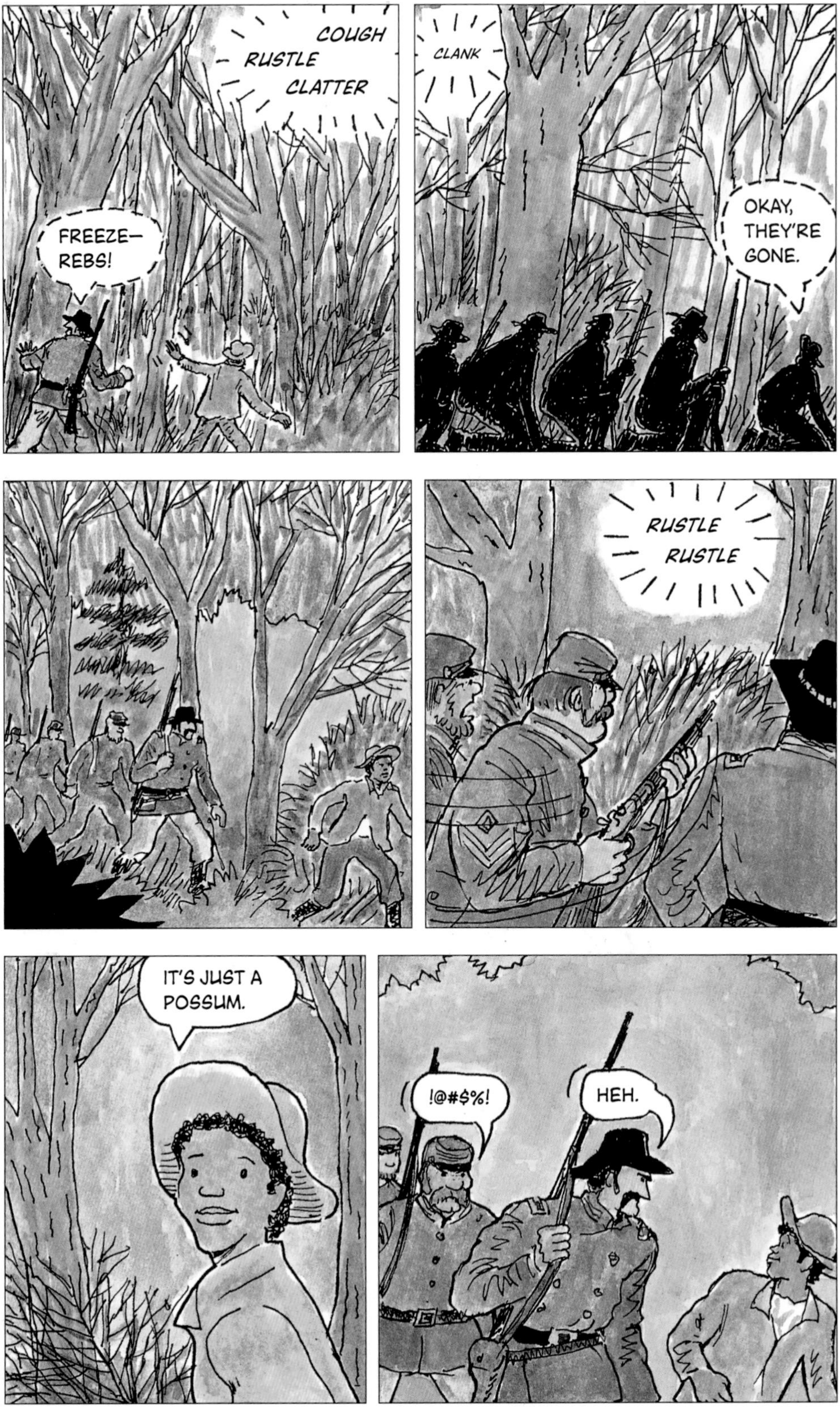
COUGH
RUSTLE
CLATTER
FREEZE—REBS!
CLANK
OKAY, THEY'RE GONE.
RUSTLE
RUSTLE
IT'S JUST A POSSUM.
!@#$%!
HEH.

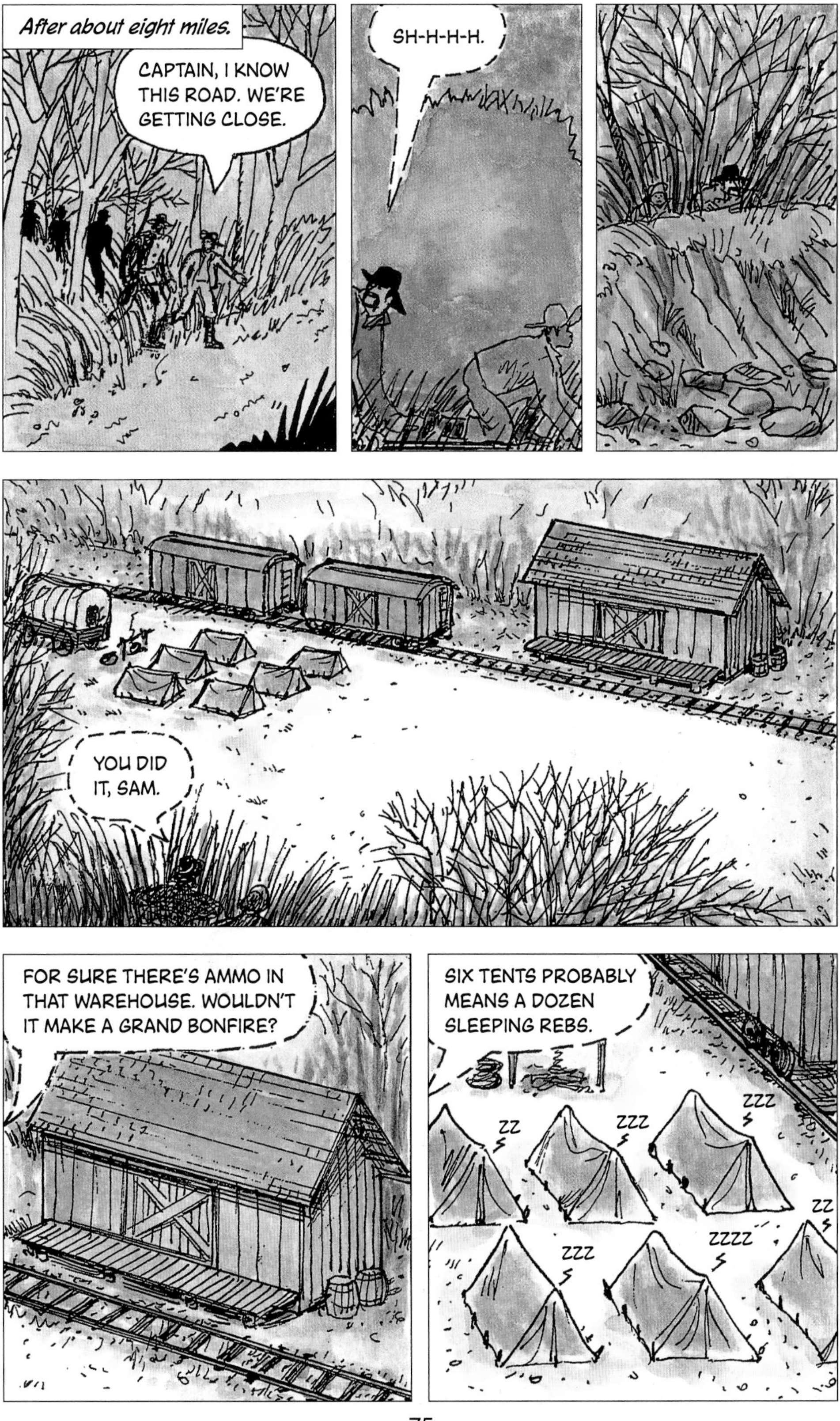
After about eight miles.
CAPTAIN, I KNOW THIS ROAD. WE'RE GETTING CLOSE.
SH-H-H-H.
YOU DID IT, SAM.
FOR SURE THERE'S AMMO IN THAT WAREHOUSE. WOULDN'T IT MAKE A GRAND BONFIRE?
SIX TENTS PROBABLY MEANS A DOZEN SLEEPING REBS.
ZZ
ZZZ
ZZZ
ZZ
ZZZ
ZZZZ

WE'LL HOGTIE 'EM SO THEY DON'T SPOIL OUR FUN.

SERGEANT, TAKE TWO MEN. CIRCLE AROUND AND COME OUT BEHIND THE WAREHOUSE.

SET FIRE TO IT AND GET BACK HERE FAST. BE PREPARED TO BACK US UP.

SAM, GO WITH THEM. SEE THESE CITY BOYS DON'T RUN INTO A FEROCIOUS POSSUM.

ONCE WE SEE A FLAME WE'LL HEAD DOWN TO THE TENTS AND GREET THE REBS WITH OUR MUSKETS.

ZZZZZ

ZZZ

OKAY, GET GOING!

The men plan to circle around, cross over the tracks, and come up behind the warehouse.

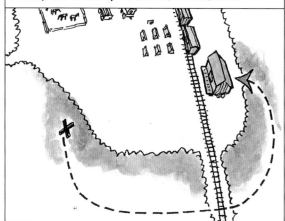

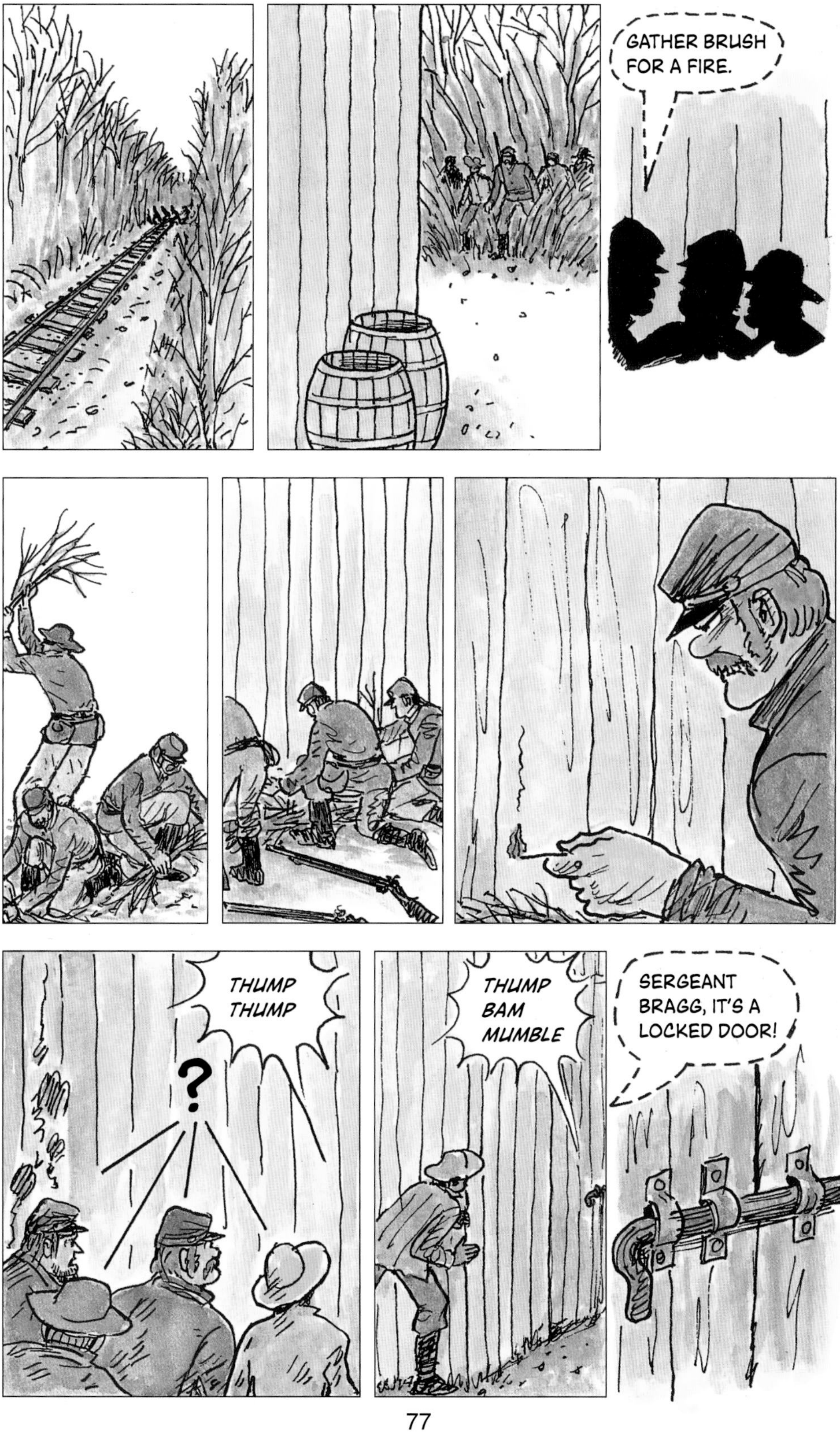
GATHER BRUSH FOR A FIRE.
THUMP THUMP
?
THUMP BAM MUMBLE
SERGEANT BRAGG, IT'S A LOCKED DOOR!

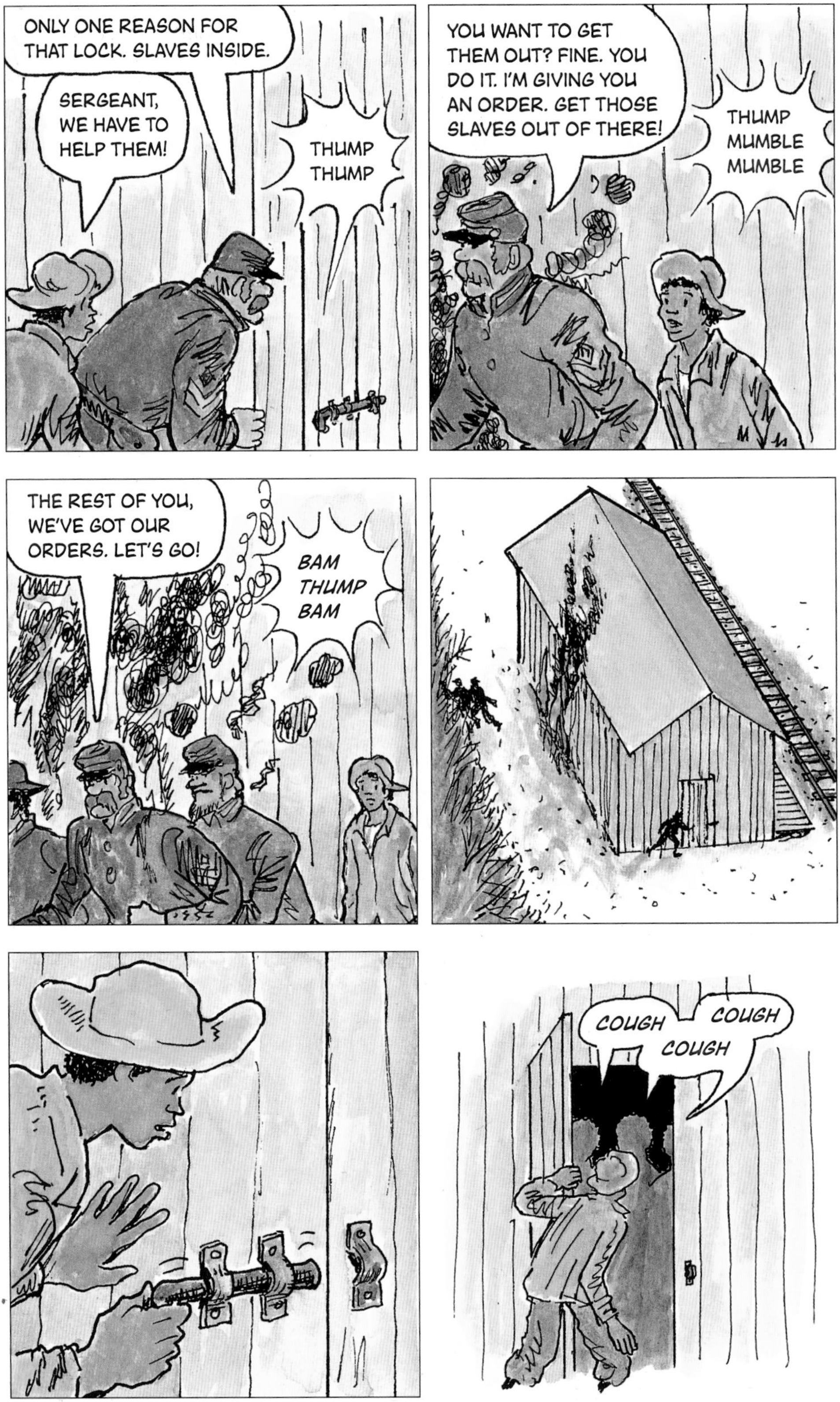
ONLY ONE REASON FOR THAT LOCK. SLAVES INSIDE.
SERGEANT, WE HAVE TO HELP THEM!
THUMP THUMP
YOU WANT TO GET THEM OUT? FINE. YOU DO IT. I'M GIVING YOU AN ORDER. GET THOSE SLAVES OUT OF THERE!
THUMP MUMBLE MUMBLE
THE REST OF YOU, WE'VE GOT OUR ORDERS. LET'S GO!
BAM THUMP BAM
COUGH
COUGH
COUGH

QUICKLY!

PAP?!

SAM?! HOW... *COUGH*

NO QUESTIONS NOW. WE MUST HURRY!

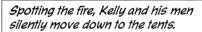

Spotting the fire, Kelly and his men silently move down to the tents.

I SMELL SMOKE!

FIRE! WHOA, *YANKS!*

MORNING, BOYS. DROP THOSE WEAPONS. *NOW!*

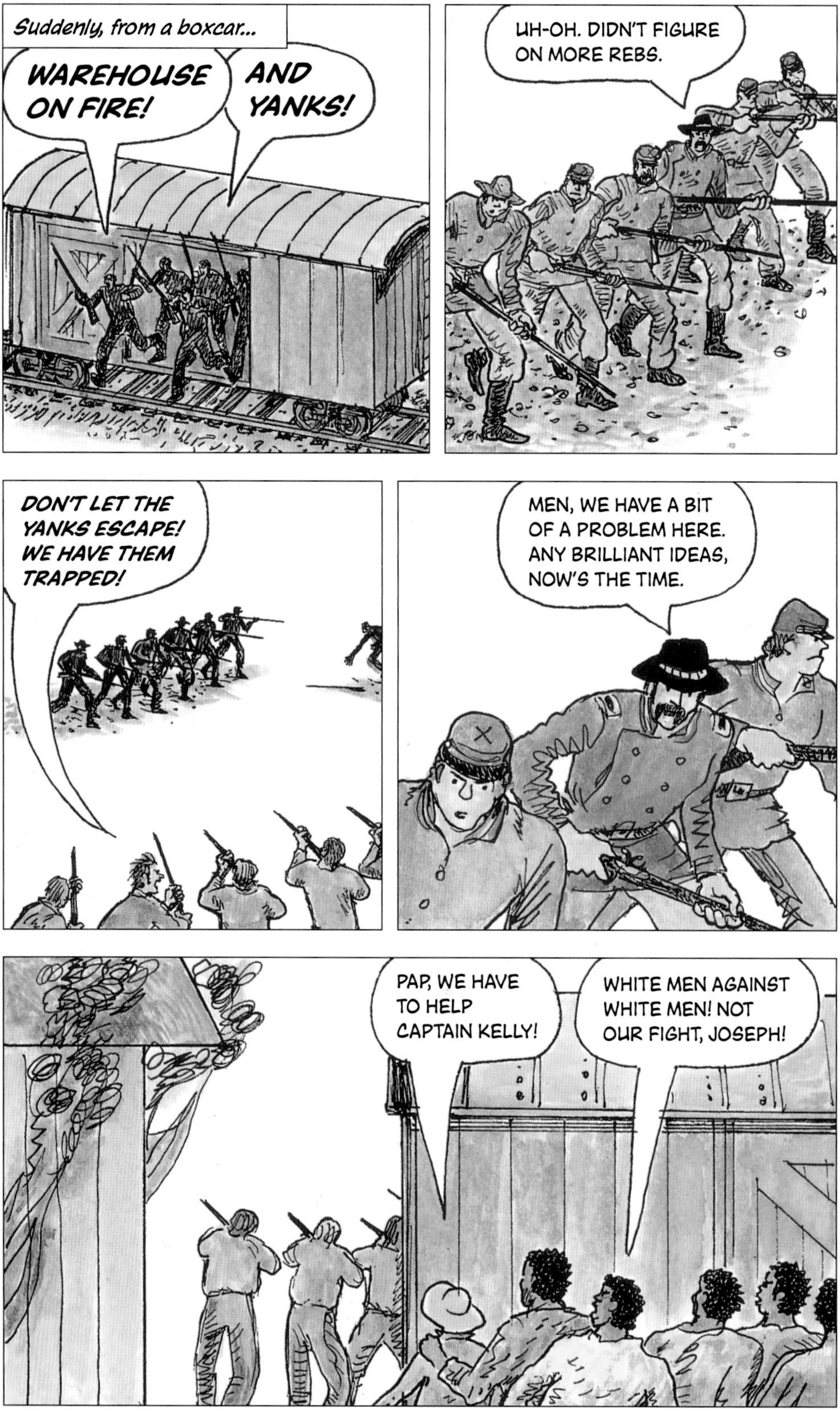
Suddenly, from a boxcar...
WAREHOUSE ON FIRE!
AND YANKS!
UH-OH. DIDN'T FIGURE ON MORE REBS.
DON'T LET THE YANKS ESCAPE! WE HAVE THEM TRAPPED!
MEN, WE HAVE A BIT OF A PROBLEM HERE. ANY BRILLIANT IDEAS, NOW'S THE TIME.
PAP, WE HAVE TO HELP CAPTAIN KELLY!
WHITE MEN AGAINST WHITE MEN! NOT OUR FIGHT, JOSEPH!

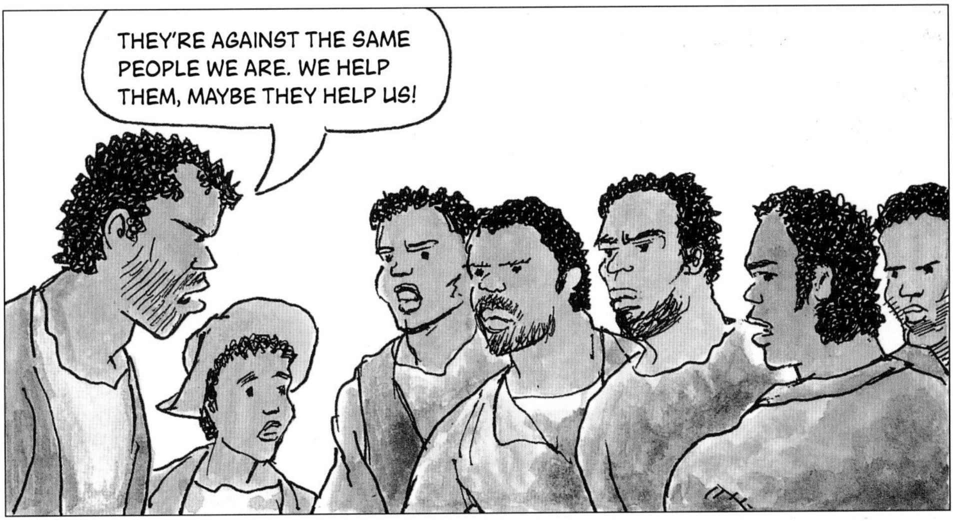
THEY'RE AGAINST THE SAME PEOPLE WE ARE. WE HELP THEM, MAYBE THEY HELP US!

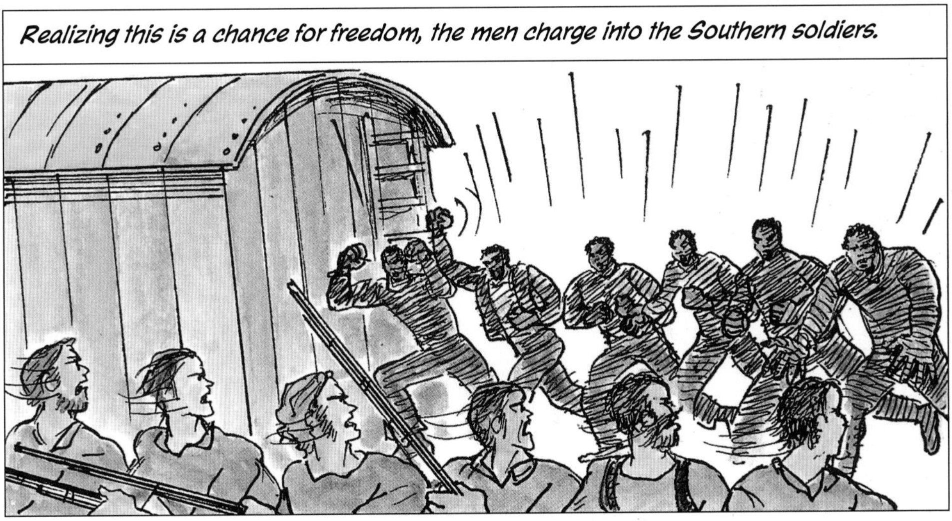
Realizing this is a chance for freedom, the men charge into the Southern soldiers.

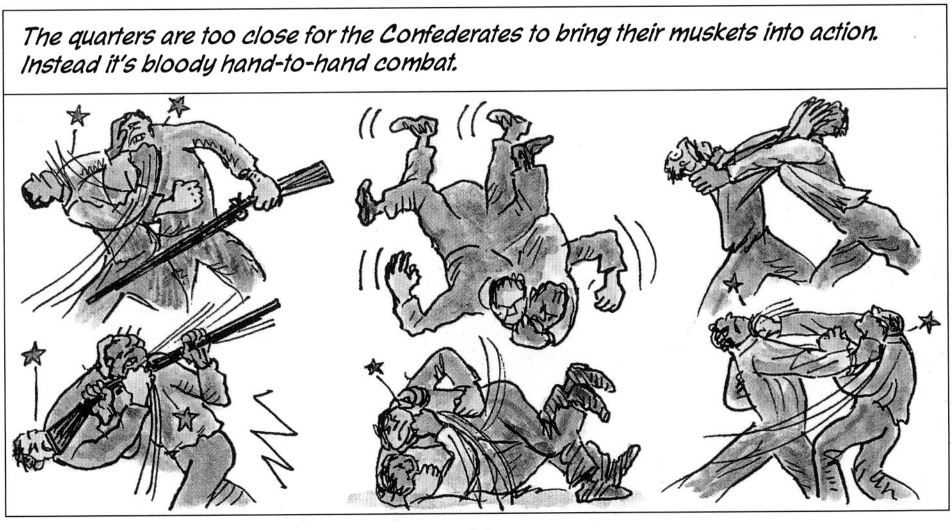
The quarters are too close for the Confederates to bring their muskets into action. Instead it's bloody hand-to-hand combat.

The Confederates are tough, but the freed slaves are relentless in their attack. They beat down their enemy and give Kelly and his men time to regroup.

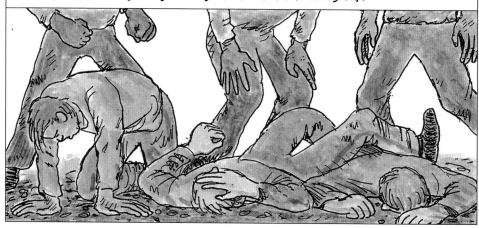

Just then... **BOOM BOOM BOOM**

THERE GOES THE AMMUNITION! THIS IS OUR CHANCE! *SAM, BRING EVERYONE! GET BEHIND US!*

MEN, WITHDRAW IN ORDER! SHOOT ANY REB WHO GOES FOR HIS GUN!

BAM

WHEN WE REACH THE WOODS, *RUN FOR THE RIVER LIKE THE DEVIL HIMSELF IS AFTER YOU!*

RETRIEVE YOUR WEAPONS!

BAM BAM

AGH!

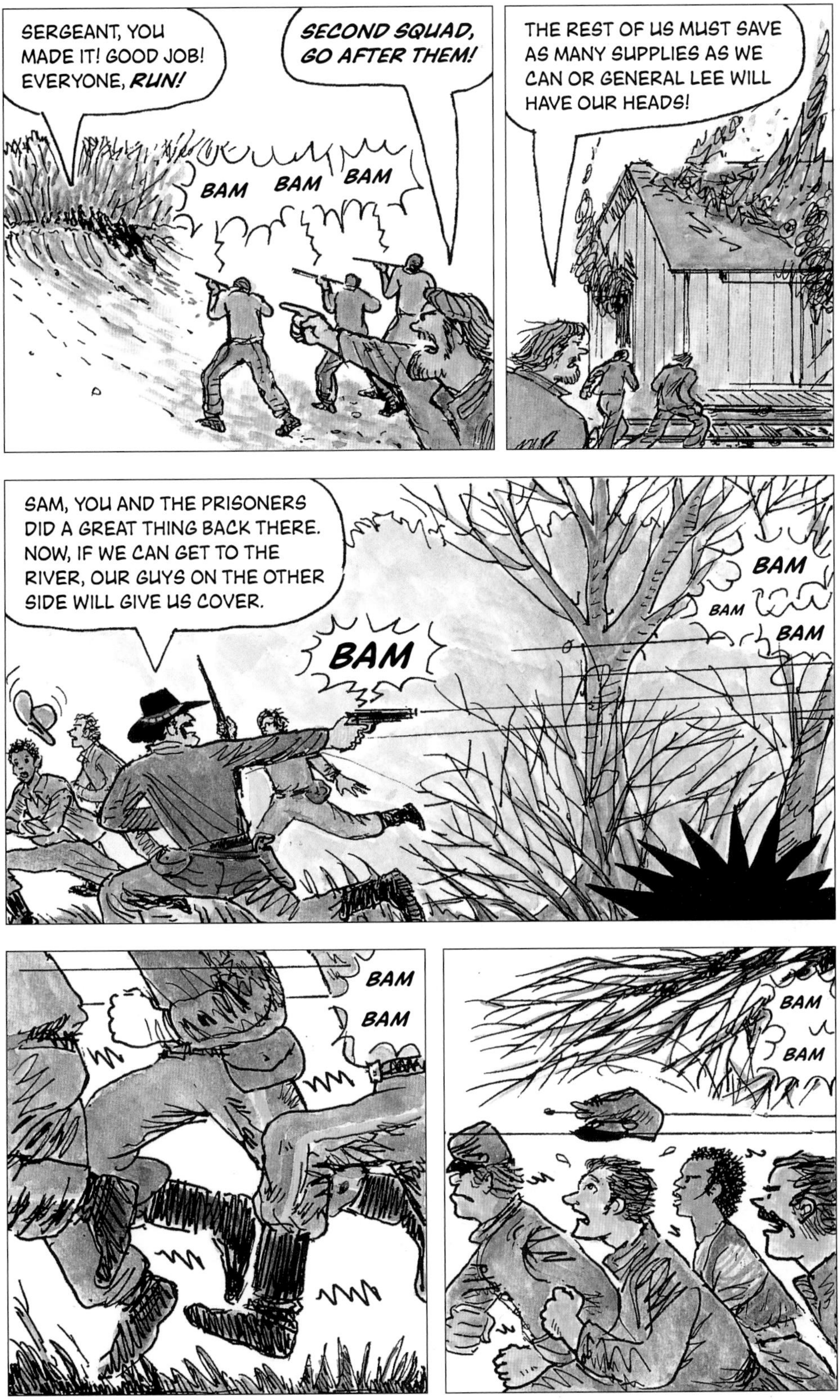
SERGEANT, YOU MADE IT! GOOD JOB! EVERYONE, *RUN!*
SECOND SQUAD, GO AFTER THEM!
BAM BAM BAM
THE REST OF US MUST SAVE AS MANY SUPPLIES AS WE CAN OR GENERAL LEE WILL HAVE OUR HEADS!
SAM, YOU AND THE PRISONERS DID A GREAT THING BACK THERE. NOW, IF WE CAN GET TO THE RIVER, OUR GUYS ON THE OTHER SIDE WILL GIVE US COVER.
BAM
BAM BAM BAM
BAM BAM
BAM BAM

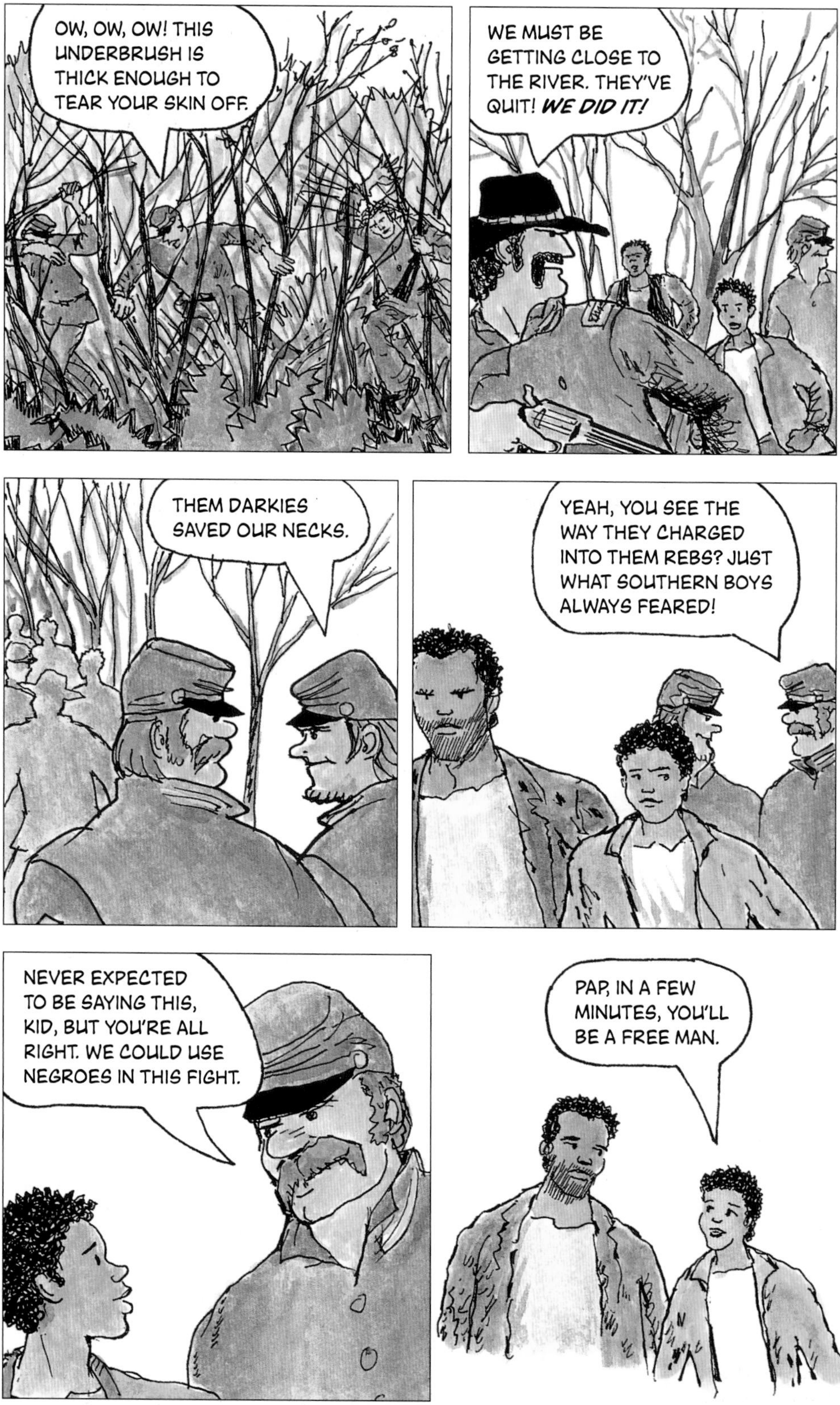
OW, OW, OW! THIS UNDERBRUSH IS THICK ENOUGH TO TEAR YOUR SKIN OFF.
WE MUST BE GETTING CLOSE TO THE RIVER. THEY'VE QUIT! ***WE DID IT!***
THEM DARKIES SAVED OUR NECKS.
YEAH, YOU SEE THE WAY THEY CHARGED INTO THEM REBS? JUST WHAT SOUTHERN BOYS ALWAYS FEARED!
NEVER EXPECTED TO BE SAYING THIS, KID, BUT YOU'RE ALL RIGHT. WE COULD USE NEGROES IN THIS FIGHT.
PAP, IN A FEW MINUTES, YOU'LL BE A FREE MAN.

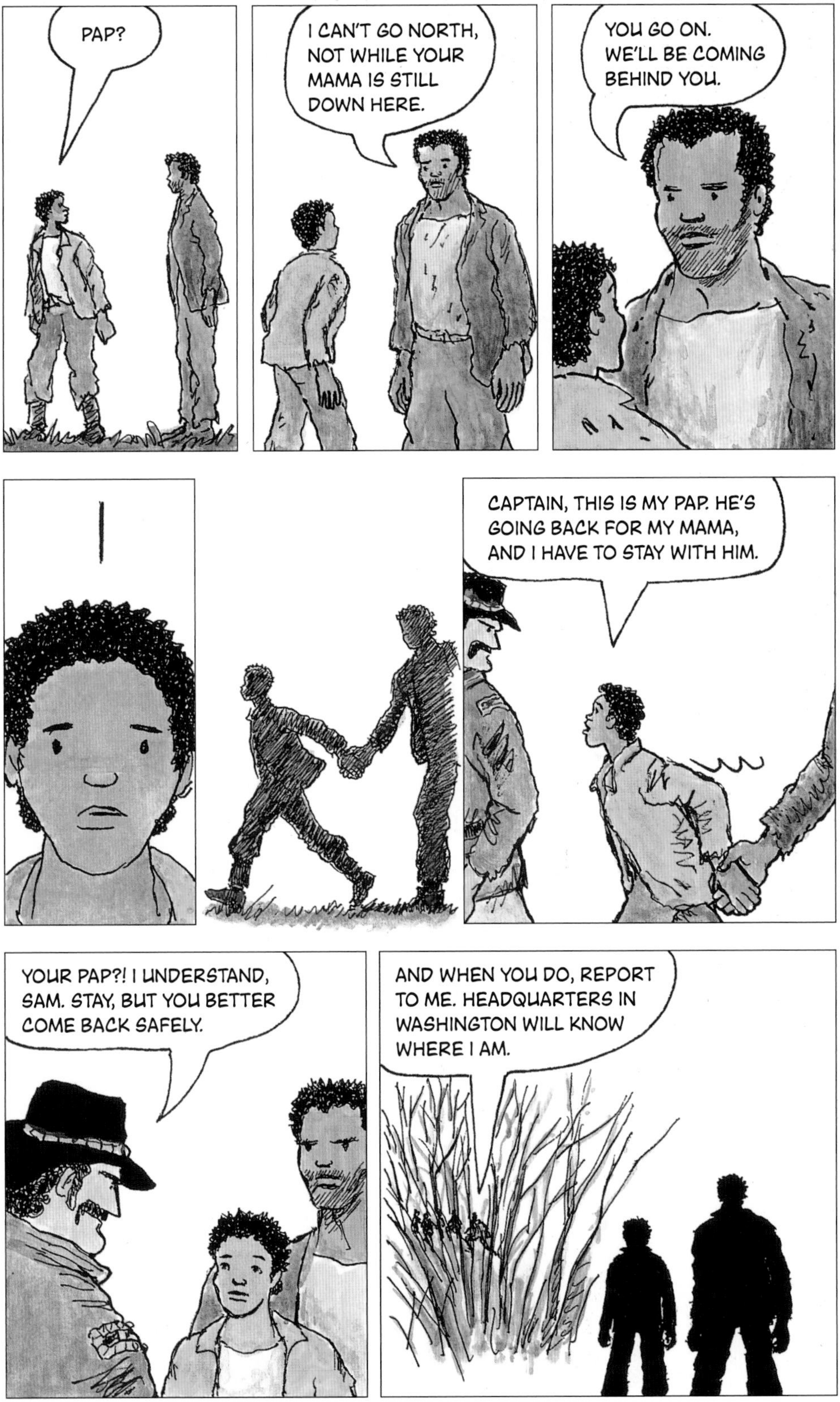
PAP?
I CAN'T GO NORTH, NOT WHILE YOUR MAMA IS STILL DOWN HERE.
YOU GO ON. WE'LL BE COMING BEHIND YOU.
CAPTAIN, THIS IS MY PAP. HE'S GOING BACK FOR MY MAMA, AND I HAVE TO STAY WITH HIM.
YOUR PAP?! I UNDERSTAND, SAM. STAY, BUT YOU BETTER COME BACK SAFELY.
AND WHEN YOU DO, REPORT TO ME. HEADQUARTERS IN WASHINGTON WILL KNOW WHERE I AM.

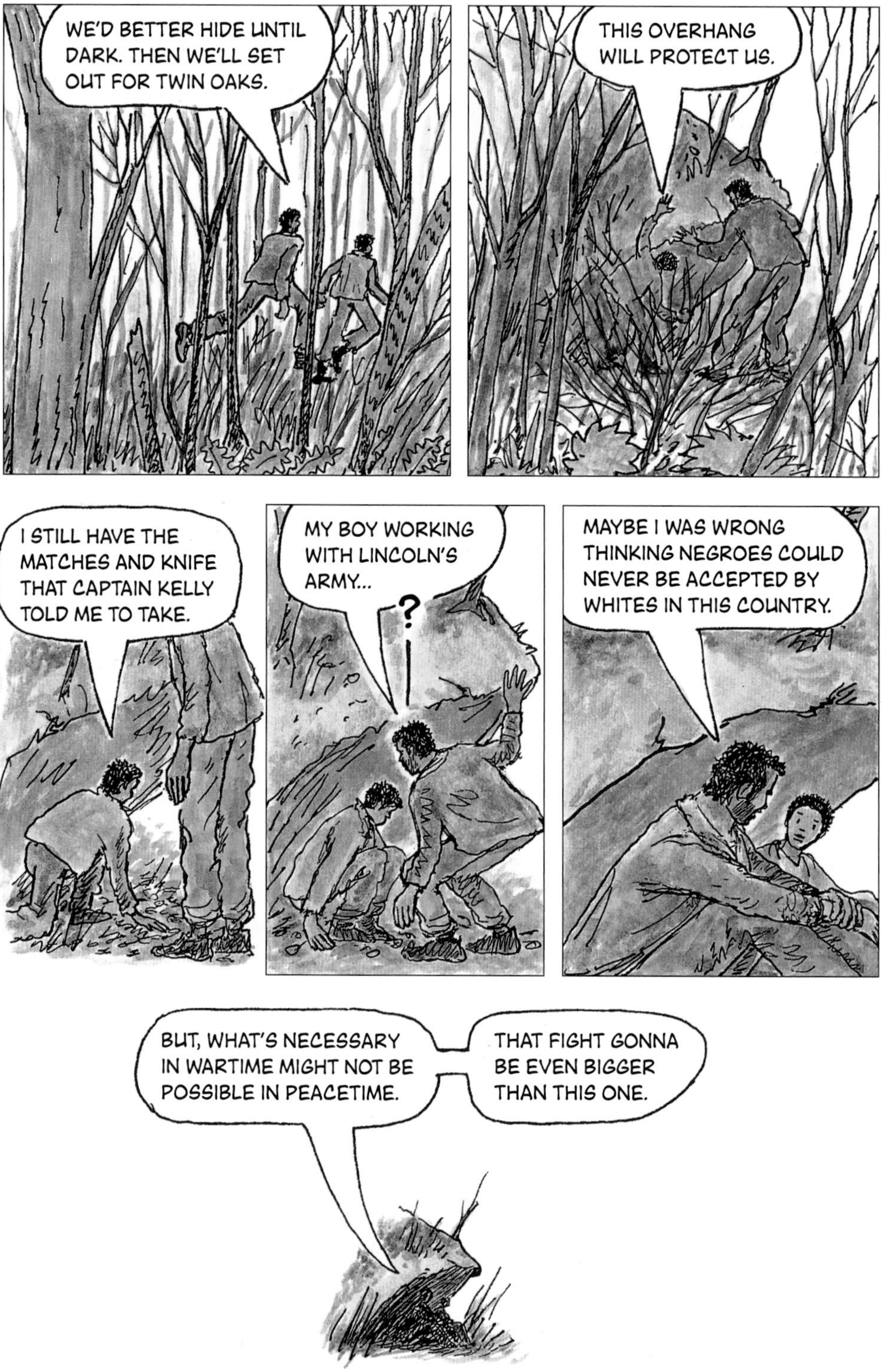
WE'D BETTER HIDE UNTIL DARK. THEN WE'LL SET OUT FOR TWIN OAKS.
THIS OVERHANG WILL PROTECT US.
I STILL HAVE THE MATCHES AND KNIFE THAT CAPTAIN KELLY TOLD ME TO TAKE.
MY BOY WORKING WITH LINCOLN'S ARMY...
?
MAYBE I WAS WRONG THINKING NEGROES COULD NEVER BE ACCEPTED BY WHITES IN THIS COUNTRY.
BUT, WHAT'S NECESSARY IN WARTIME MIGHT NOT BE POSSIBLE IN PEACETIME.
THAT FIGHT GONNA BE EVEN BIGGER THAN THIS ONE.

CHAPTER 9

As the Union Army prepares another attack across the Rappahannock against General Lee, Lee's support in the South remains strong. But the old Southern lifestyle will never return.

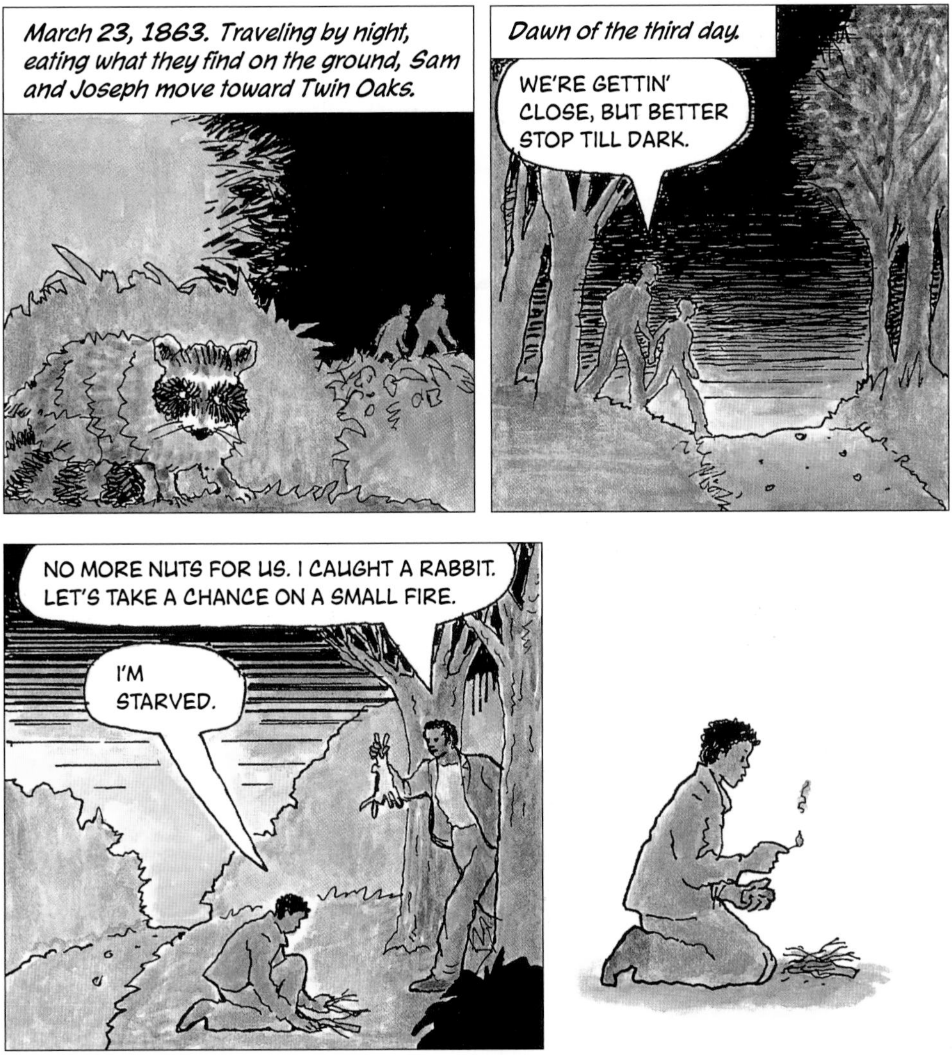
March 23, 1863. Traveling by night, eating what they find on the ground, Sam and Joseph move toward Twin Oaks.
Dawn of the third day.
WE'RE GETTIN' CLOSE, BUT BETTER STOP TILL DARK.
NO MORE NUTS FOR US. I CAUGHT A RABBIT. LET'S TAKE A CHANCE ON A SMALL FIRE.
I'M STARVED.

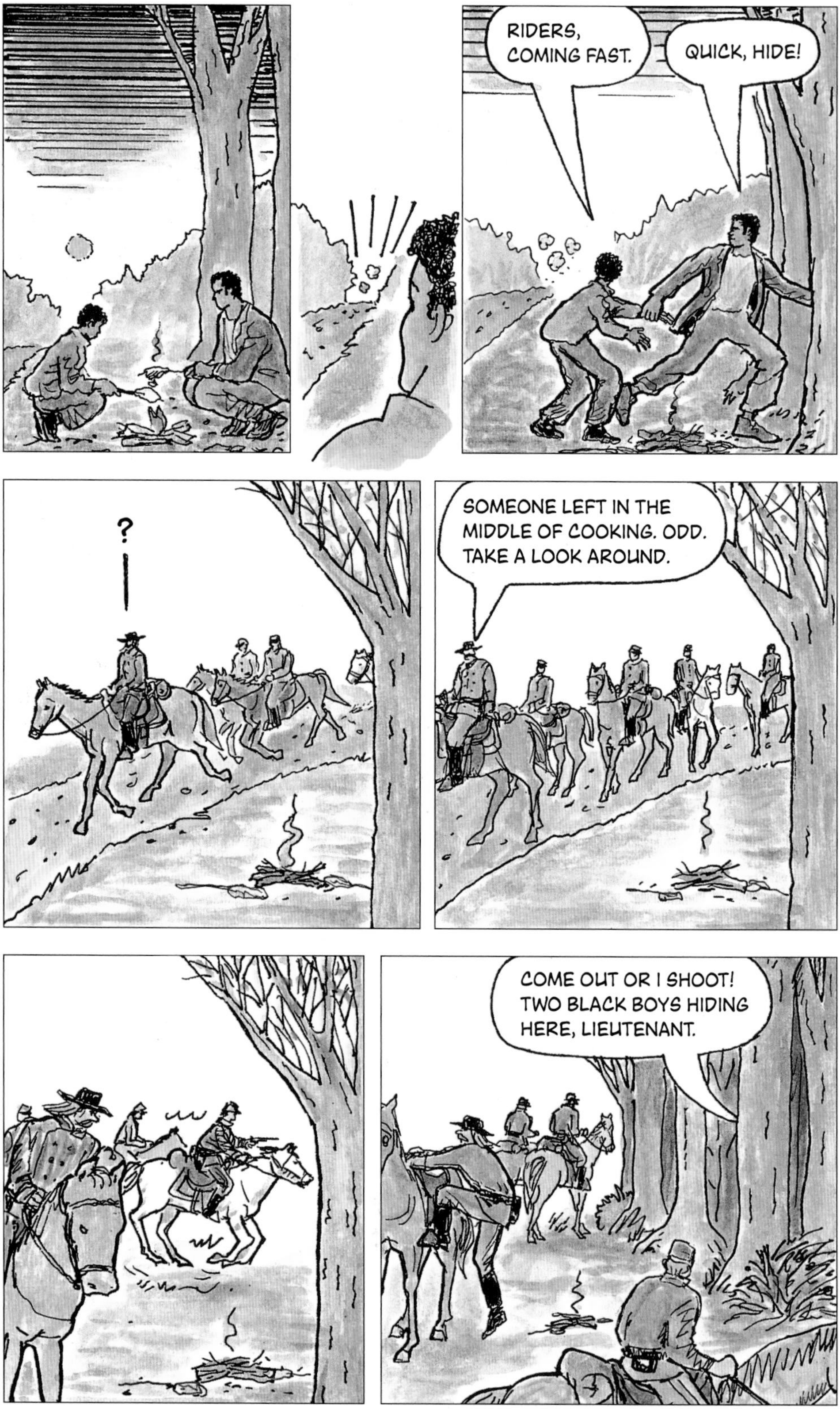
RIDERS, COMING FAST.
QUICK, HIDE!
?
SOMEONE LEFT IN THE MIDDLE OF COOKING. ODD. TAKE A LOOK AROUND.
COME OUT OR I SHOOT! TWO BLACK BOYS HIDING HERE, LIEUTENANT.

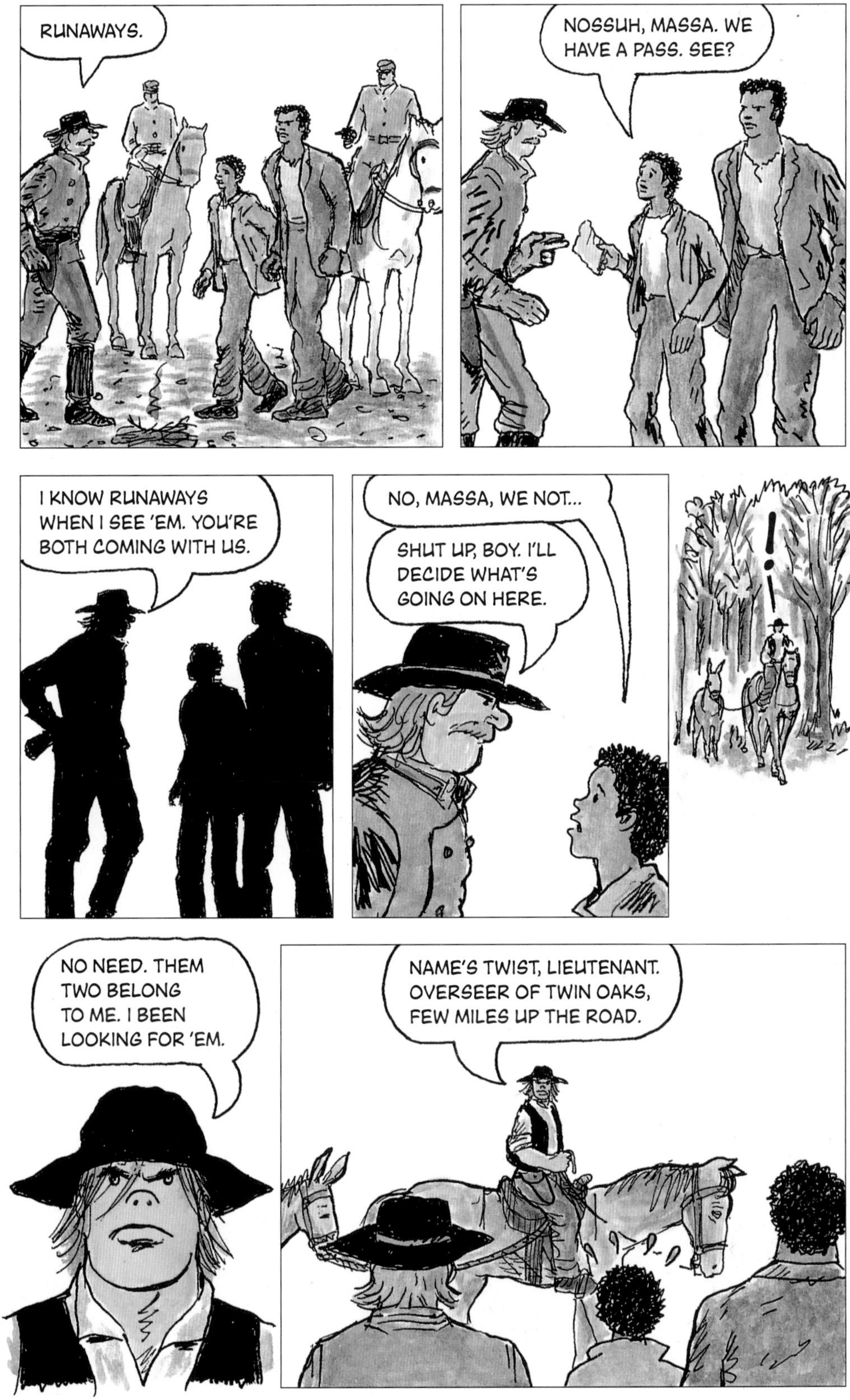
RUNAWAYS.
NOSSUH, MASSA. WE HAVE A PASS. SEE?
I KNOW RUNAWAYS WHEN I SEE 'EM. YOU'RE BOTH COMING WITH US.
NO, MASSA, WE NOT...
SHUT UP, BOY. I'LL DECIDE WHAT'S GOING ON HERE.
!
NO NEED. THEM TWO BELONG TO ME. I BEEN LOOKING FOR 'EM.
NAME'S TWIST, LIEUTENANT. OVERSEER OF TWIN OAKS, FEW MILES UP THE ROAD.

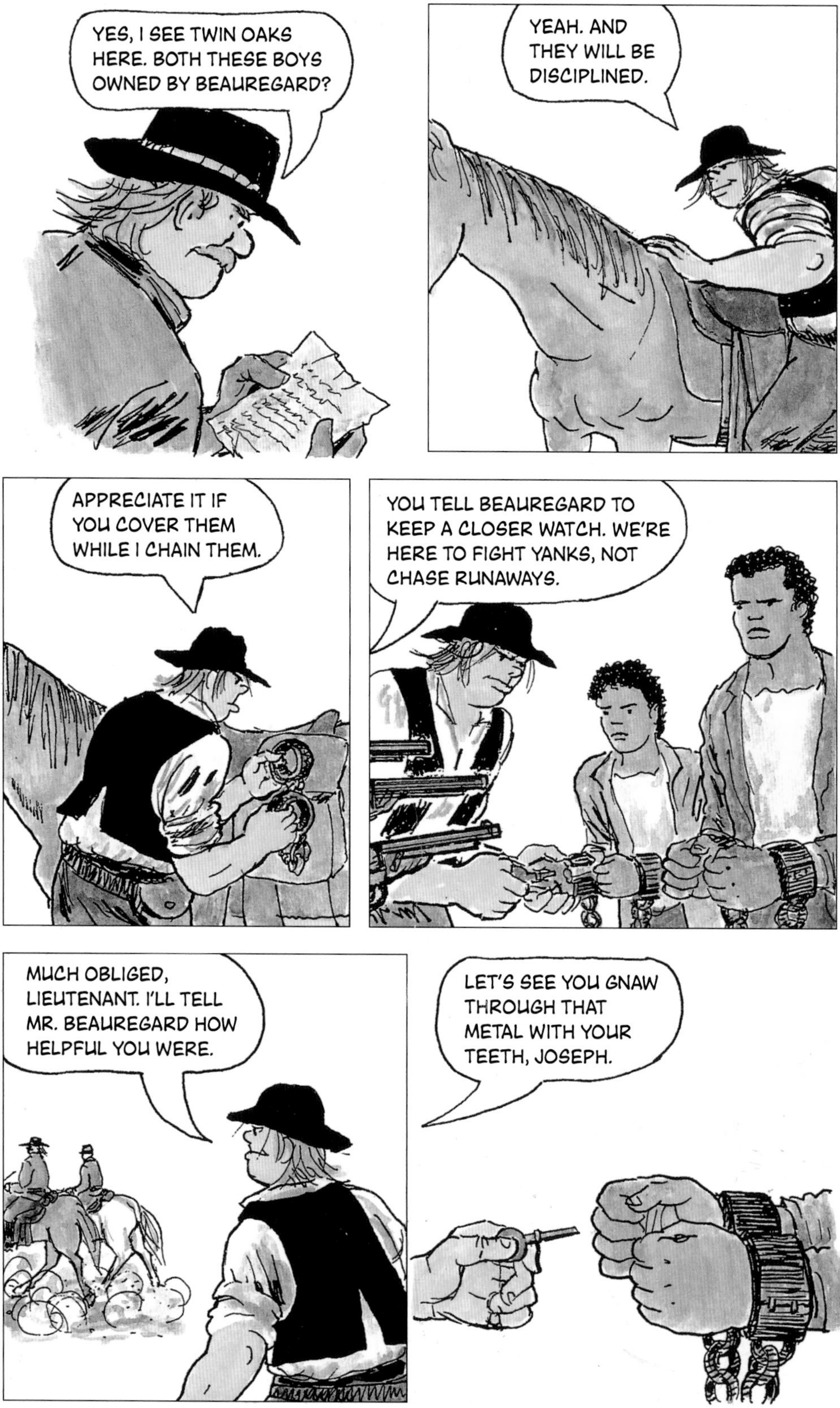
YES, I SEE TWIN OAKS HERE. BOTH THESE BOYS OWNED BY BEAUREGARD?
YEAH. AND THEY WILL BE DISCIPLINED.
APPRECIATE IT IF YOU COVER THEM WHILE I CHAIN THEM.
YOU TELL BEAUREGARD TO KEEP A CLOSER WATCH. WE'RE HERE TO FIGHT YANKS, NOT CHASE RUNAWAYS.
MUCH OBLIGED, LIEUTENANT. I'LL TELL MR. BEAUREGARD HOW HELPFUL YOU WERE.
LET'S SEE YOU GNAW THROUGH THAT METAL WITH YOUR TEETH, JOSEPH.

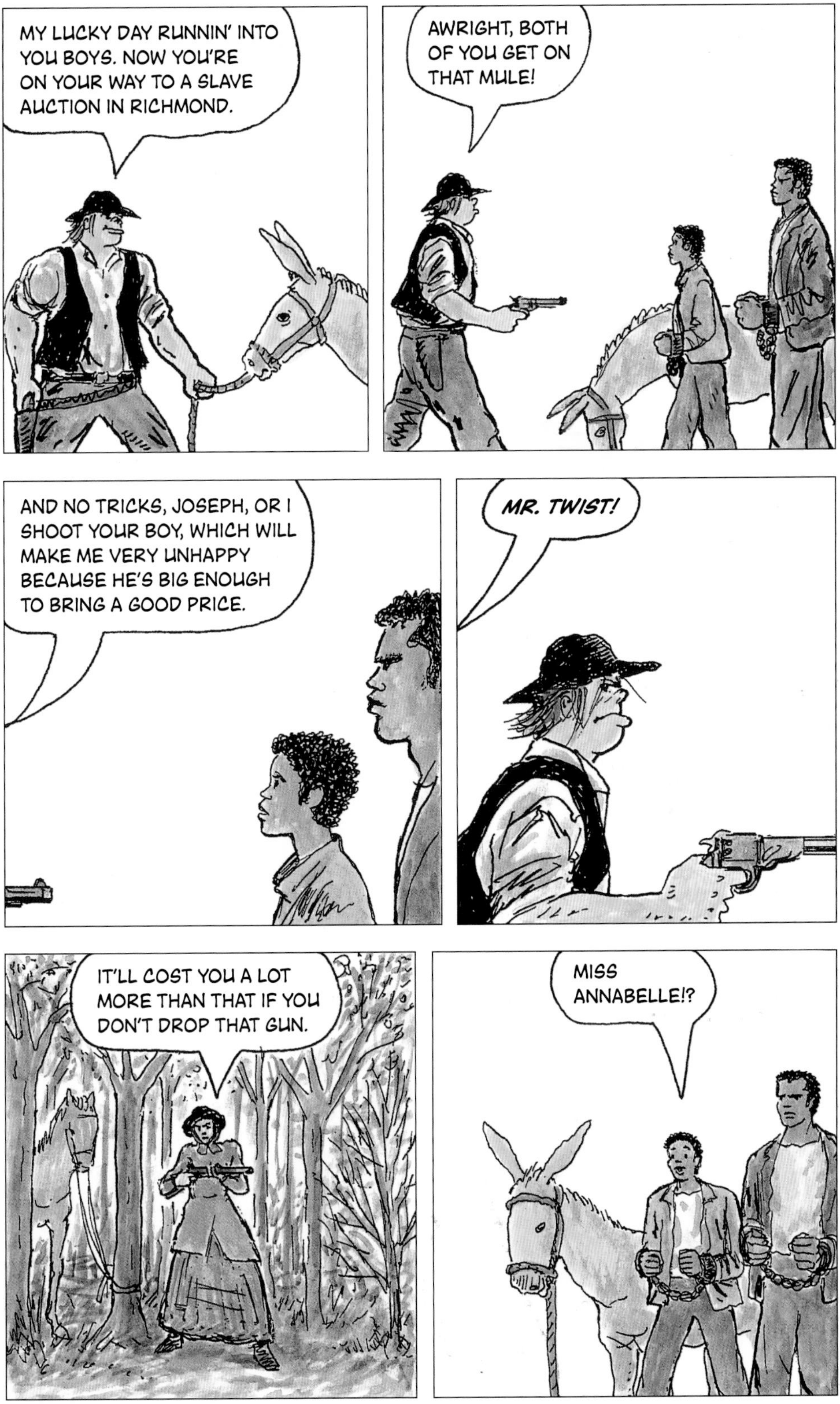
MY LUCKY DAY RUNNIN' INTO YOU BOYS. NOW YOU'RE ON YOUR WAY TO A SLAVE AUCTION IN RICHMOND.
AWRIGHT, BOTH OF YOU GET ON THAT MULE!
AND NO TRICKS, JOSEPH, OR I SHOOT YOUR BOY, WHICH WILL MAKE ME VERY UNHAPPY BECAUSE HE'S BIG ENOUGH TO BRING A GOOD PRICE.
MR. TWIST!
IT'LL COST YOU A LOT MORE THAN THAT IF YOU DON'T DROP THAT GUN.
MISS ANNABELLE!?

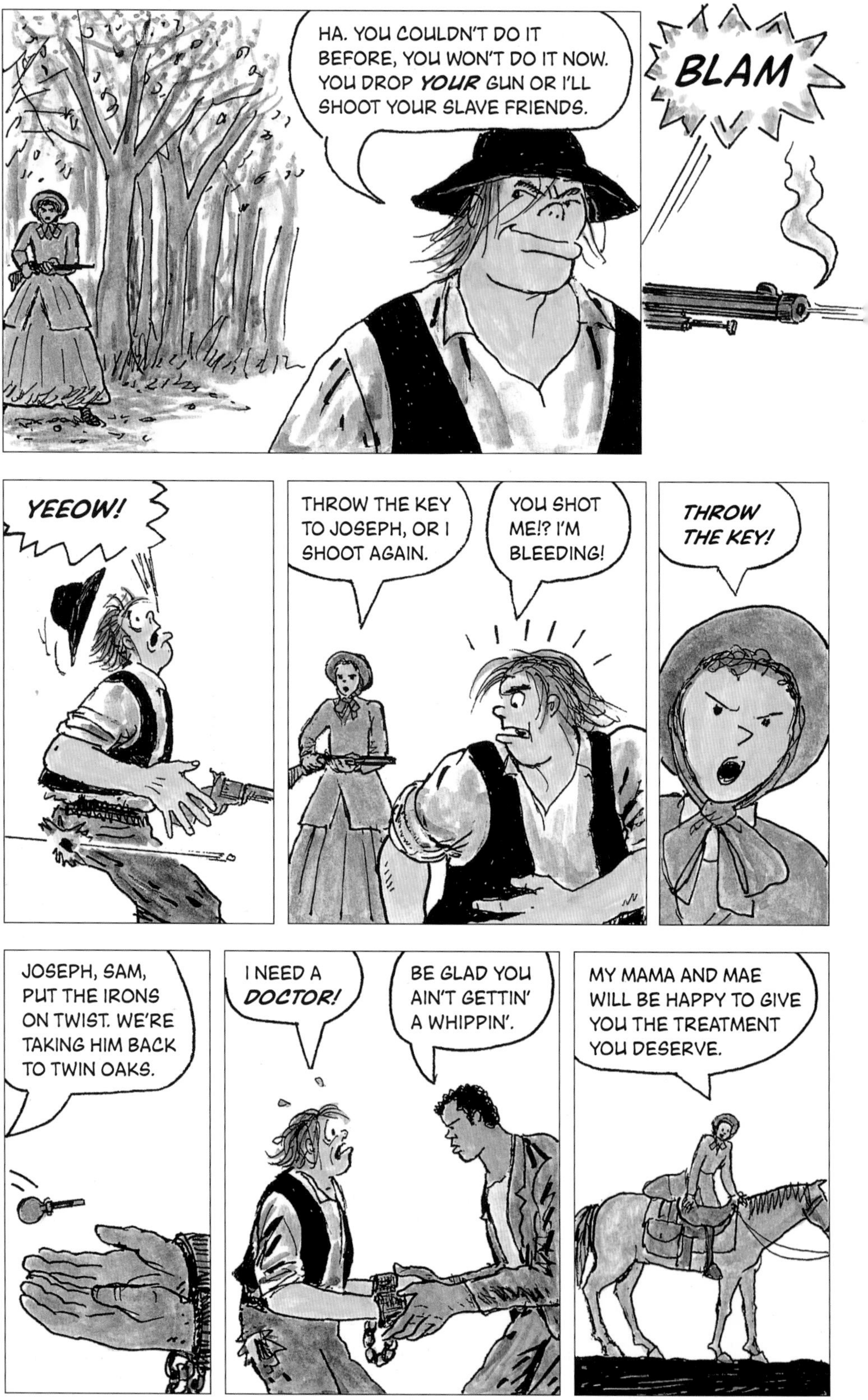
HA. YOU COULDN'T DO IT BEFORE, YOU WON'T DO IT NOW. YOU DROP *YOUR* GUN OR I'LL SHOOT YOUR SLAVE FRIENDS.
BLAM
YEEOW!
THROW THE KEY TO JOSEPH, OR I SHOOT AGAIN.
YOU SHOT ME!? I'M BLEEDING!
THROW THE KEY!
JOSEPH, SAM, PUT THE IRONS ON TWIST. WE'RE TAKING HIM BACK TO TWIN OAKS.
I NEED A *DOCTOR!*
BE GLAD YOU AIN'T GETTIN' A WHIPPIN'.
MY MAMA AND MAE WILL BE HAPPY TO GIVE YOU THE TREATMENT YOU DESERVE.

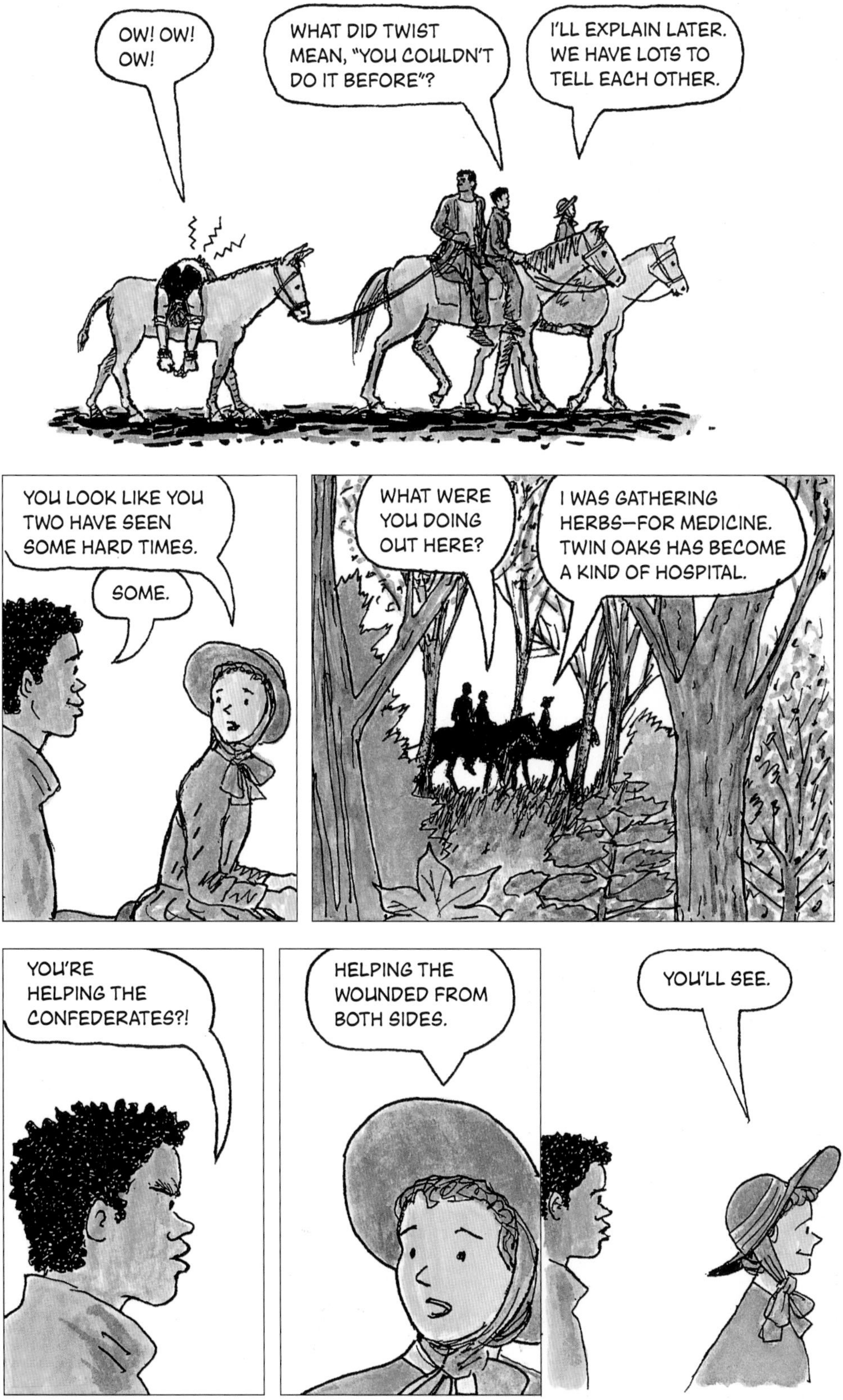
OW! OW! OW!
WHAT DID TWIST MEAN, "YOU COULDN'T DO IT BEFORE"?
I'LL EXPLAIN LATER. WE HAVE LOTS TO TELL EACH OTHER.
YOU LOOK LIKE YOU TWO HAVE SEEN SOME HARD TIMES.
SOME.
WHAT WERE YOU DOING OUT HERE?
I WAS GATHERING HERBS—FOR MEDICINE. TWIN OAKS HAS BECOME A KIND OF HOSPITAL.
YOU'RE HELPING THE CONFEDERATES?!
HELPING THE WOUNDED FROM BOTH SIDES.
YOU'LL SEE.

Twin Oaks.

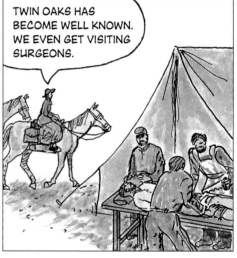

TWIN OAKS HAS BECOME WELL KNOWN. WE EVEN GET VISITING SURGEONS.

WE MAKE OUR OWN SOAP AND KEEP EVERYTHING VERY CLEAN.

WE'RE TOLD MORE MEN GET BETTER HERE THAN IN OTHER HOSPITALS.

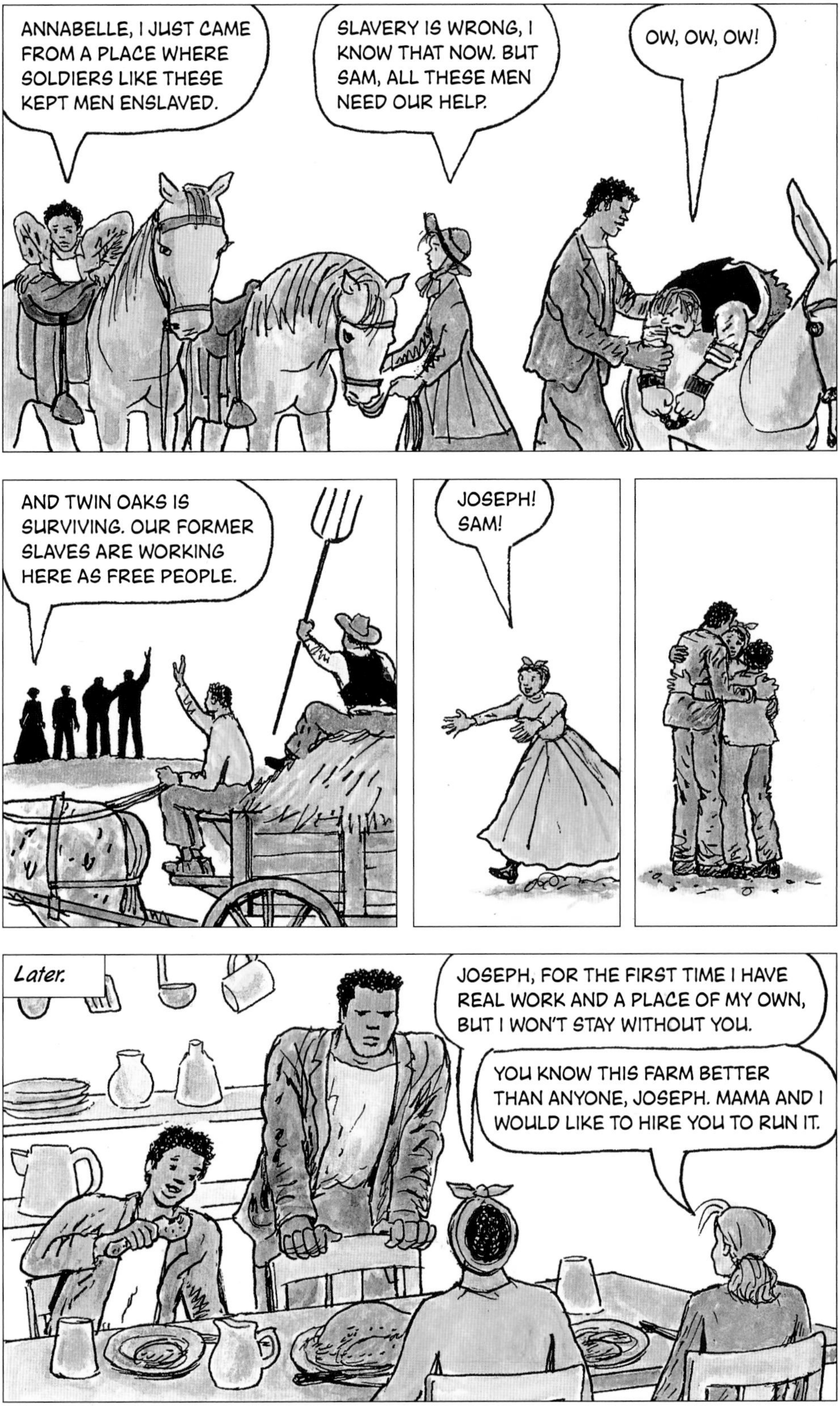
ANNABELLE, I JUST CAME FROM A PLACE WHERE SOLDIERS LIKE THESE KEPT MEN ENSLAVED.
SLAVERY IS WRONG, I KNOW THAT NOW. BUT SAM, ALL THESE MEN NEED OUR HELP.
OW, OW, OW!
AND TWIN OAKS IS SURVIVING. OUR FORMER SLAVES ARE WORKING HERE AS FREE PEOPLE.
JOSEPH! SAM!
Later.
JOSEPH, FOR THE FIRST TIME I HAVE REAL WORK AND A PLACE OF MY OWN, BUT I WON'T STAY WITHOUT YOU.
YOU KNOW THIS FARM BETTER THAN ANYONE, JOSEPH. MAMA AND I WOULD LIKE TO HIRE YOU TO RUN IT.

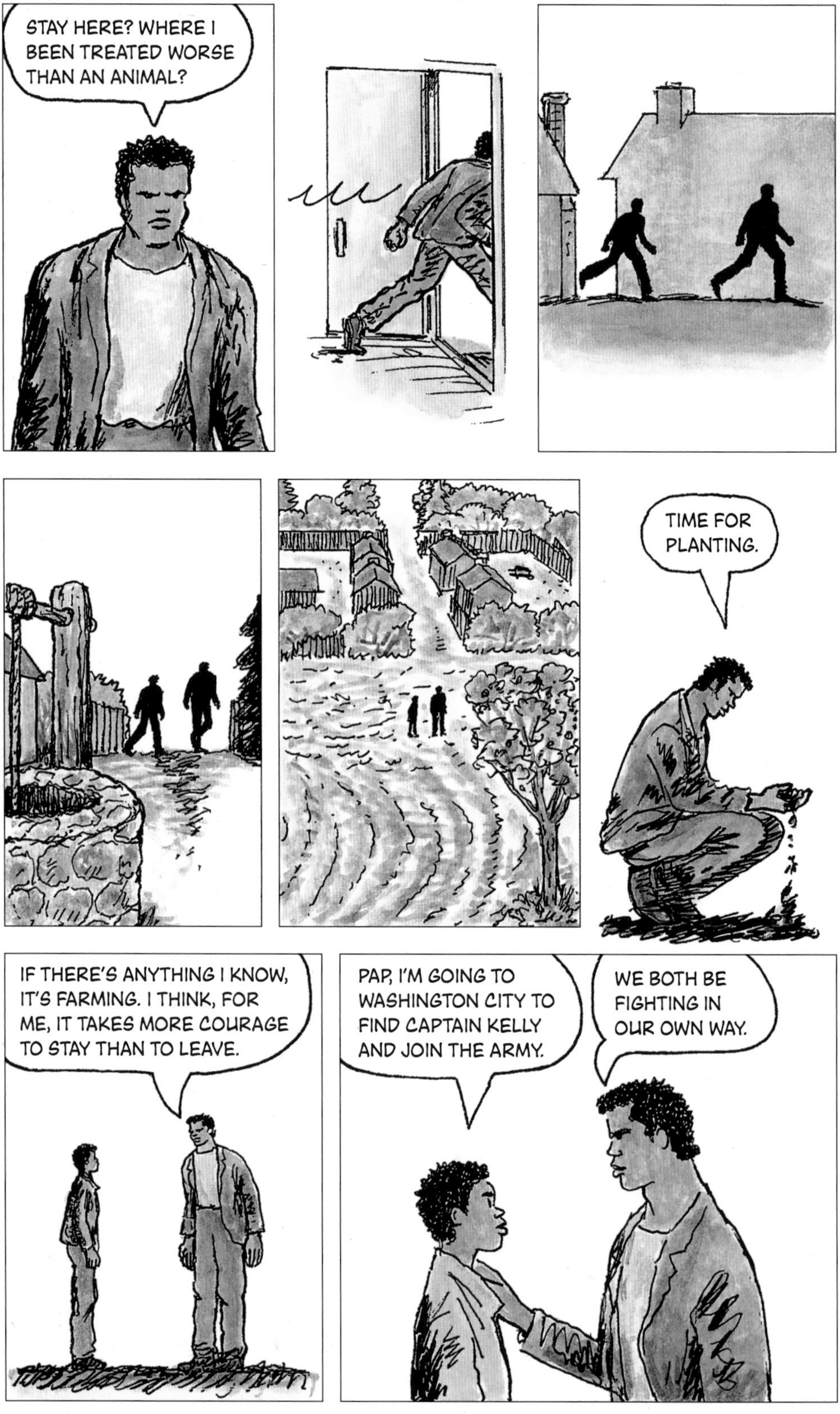
STAY HERE? WHERE I BEEN TREATED WORSE THAN AN ANIMAL?
TIME FOR PLANTING.
IF THERE'S ANYTHING I KNOW, IT'S FARMING. I THINK, FOR ME, IT TAKES MORE COURAGE TO STAY THAN TO LEAVE.
PAP, I'M GOING TO WASHINGTON CITY TO FIND CAPTAIN KELLY AND JOIN THE ARMY.
WE BOTH BE FIGHTING IN OUR OWN WAY.

Later that week, Annabelle speaks with a Confederate officer.

CAPTAIN, I'D LIKE TO TALK TO YOU ABOUT MR. TWIST.

WHISPER WHISPER

EXCELLENT IDEA, MISS.

CONGRATULATIONS, MR. TWIST, YOU'VE JUST VOLUNTEERED TO BE A CONFEDERATE ARMY DITCH DIGGER.

WHAT?!

!@#$%!

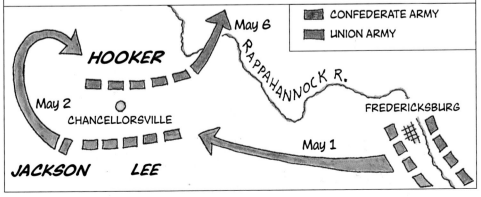

On April 27, the Union offensive, led by General Joseph Hooker, begins. By May 6, with the help of his brilliant general Stonewall Jackson, General Lee has outsmarted Hooker and chased him back across the river. This becomes known as the Battle of Chancellorsville—and Lee's most perfect victory.

May 6

CONFEDERATE ARMY
UNION ARMY

HOOKER

RAPPAHANNOCK R.

May 2

CHANCELLORSVILLE

FREDERICKSBURG

May 1

JACKSON   LEE

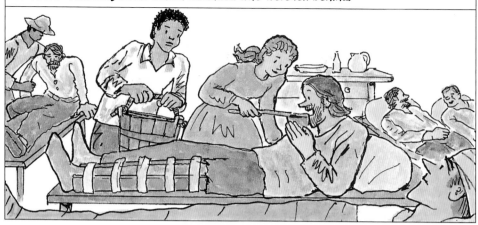

Despite his victory, Lee has lost one-fifth of his army. Twin Oaks is busy tending the wounded—including some Union wounded who were left behind.

I HEAR THAT BOTH ARMIES ARE ON THE MOVE, LEAVING THIS AREA AND HEADING WEST AND NORTH.

SOUNDS LIKE IT'S ALMOST TIME FOR ME TO MAKE MY WAY TO WASHINGTON.

AND YOU WON'T HAVE TO WORRY ABOUT TWIST THIS TIME.

HERE'S SOME WATER.

THANK YOU.

SO, ANNABELLE, I'VE BEEN WONDERING, WHEN YOU SHOT TWIST...

HA! I ALWAYS HIT WHAT I AIM FOR.

CHAPTER 10

As the war continues, the balance of power begins to shift to the North. The Union Army has more men and supplies, and its ranks are growing with the entry of African American soldiers.

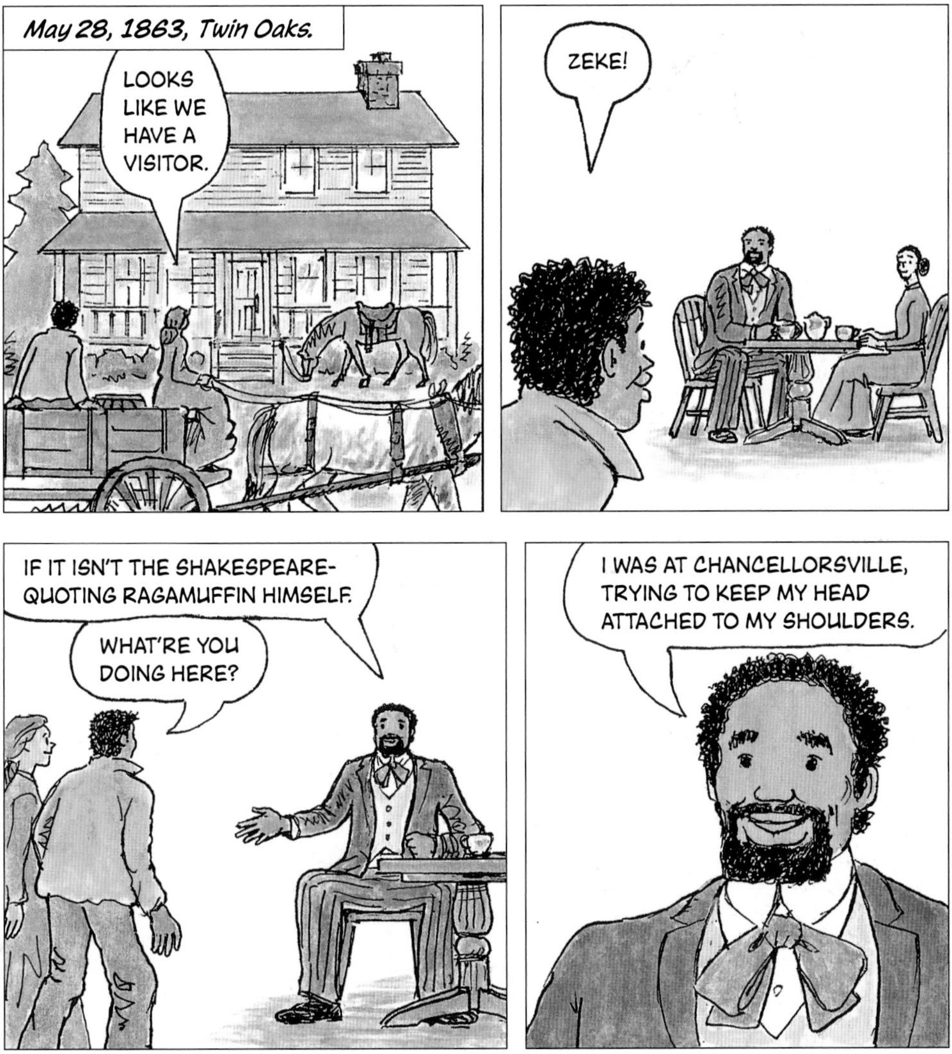
May 28, 1863, Twin Oaks.
LOOKS LIKE WE HAVE A VISITOR.
ZEKE!
IF IT ISN'T THE SHAKESPEARE-QUOTING RAGAMUFFIN HIMSELF.
WHAT'RE YOU DOING HERE?
I WAS AT CHANCELLORSVILLE, TRYING TO KEEP MY HEAD ATTACHED TO MY SHOULDERS.

I WROTE SOMETHING COMPLIMENTARY ABOUT LEE. IT GOT ME BANNED FROM HOOKER'S HEADQUARTERS.

BUT I HAD TO TELL THE TRUTH, DIDN'T I? IT DID GET ME A PASS FROM LEE HIMSELF PROVIDING SAFE PASSAGE THROUGH CONFEDERATE LINES.

IT'S WORKED SO FAR, BUT I DON'T PLAN TO LINGER. VIRGINIA'S NO PLACE FOR NEGROES.

I HEARD ABOUT A PLANTATION HOSPITAL THAT TREATS WOUNDED FROM BOTH SIDES.

WHEN THEY SAID IT WAS CALLED TWIN OAKS, I SAID, THAT'S WHERE THE YOUNG CONTRABAND IS FROM!

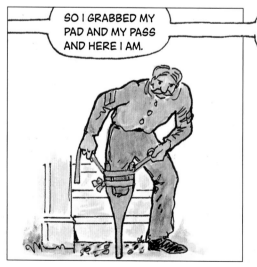

SO I GRABBED MY PAD AND MY PASS AND HERE I AM.

MIZ BEAUREGARD TELLS ME YOU'VE HAD A FEW ADVENTURES SINCE WE LAST MET.

100

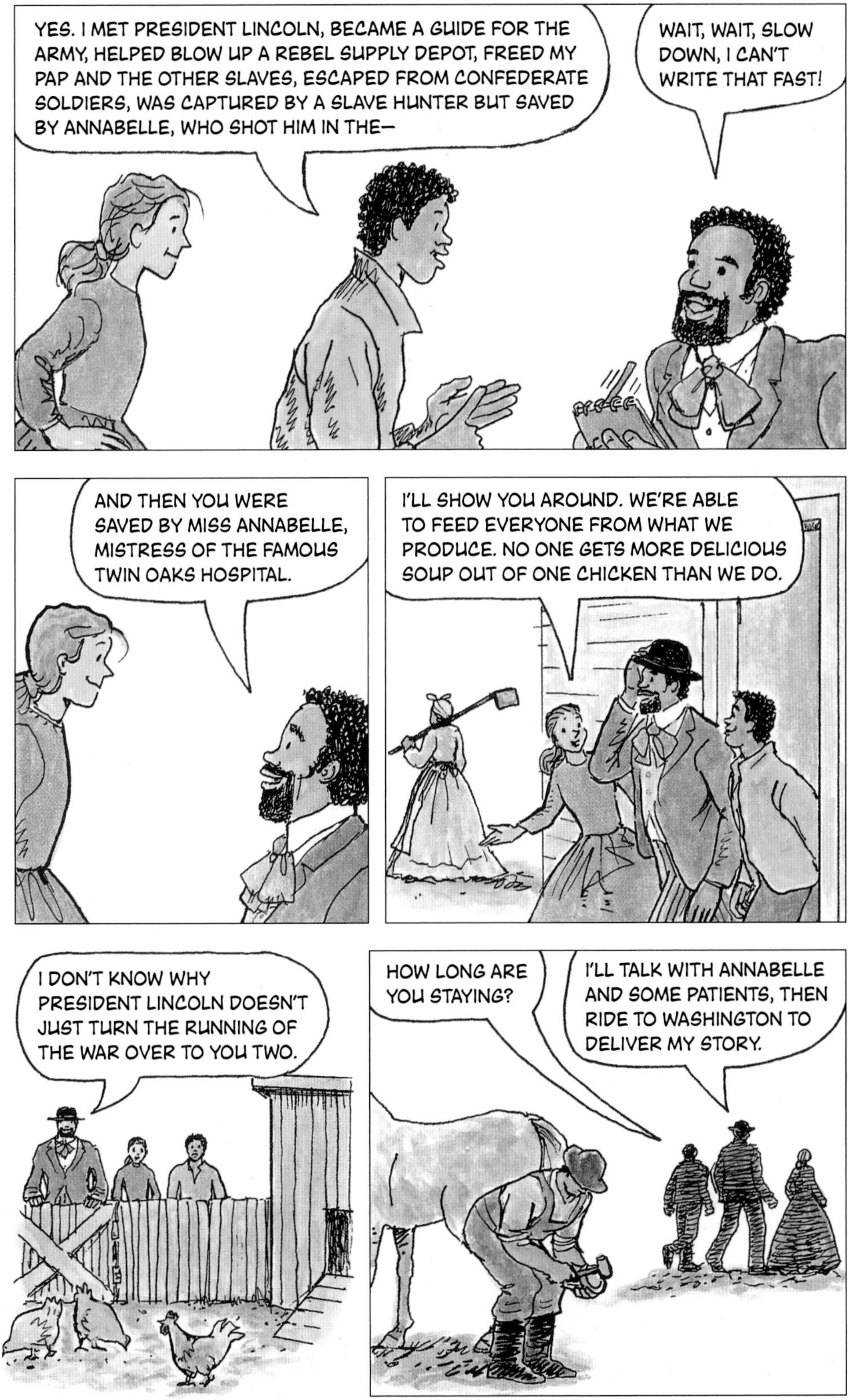
YES. I MET PRESIDENT LINCOLN, BECAME A GUIDE FOR THE ARMY, HELPED BLOW UP A REBEL SUPPLY DEPOT, FREED MY PAP AND THE OTHER SLAVES, ESCAPED FROM CONFEDERATE SOLDIERS, WAS CAPTURED BY A SLAVE HUNTER BUT SAVED BY ANNABELLE, WHO SHOT HIM IN THE—
WAIT, WAIT, SLOW DOWN, I CAN'T WRITE THAT FAST!
AND THEN YOU WERE SAVED BY MISS ANNABELLE, MISTRESS OF THE FAMOUS TWIN OAKS HOSPITAL.
I'LL SHOW YOU AROUND. WE'RE ABLE TO FEED EVERYONE FROM WHAT WE PRODUCE. NO ONE GETS MORE DELICIOUS SOUP OUT OF ONE CHICKEN THAN WE DO.
I DON'T KNOW WHY PRESIDENT LINCOLN DOESN'T JUST TURN THE RUNNING OF THE WAR OVER TO YOU TWO.
HOW LONG ARE YOU STAYING?
I'LL TALK WITH ANNABELLE AND SOME PATIENTS, THEN RIDE TO WASHINGTON TO DELIVER MY STORY.

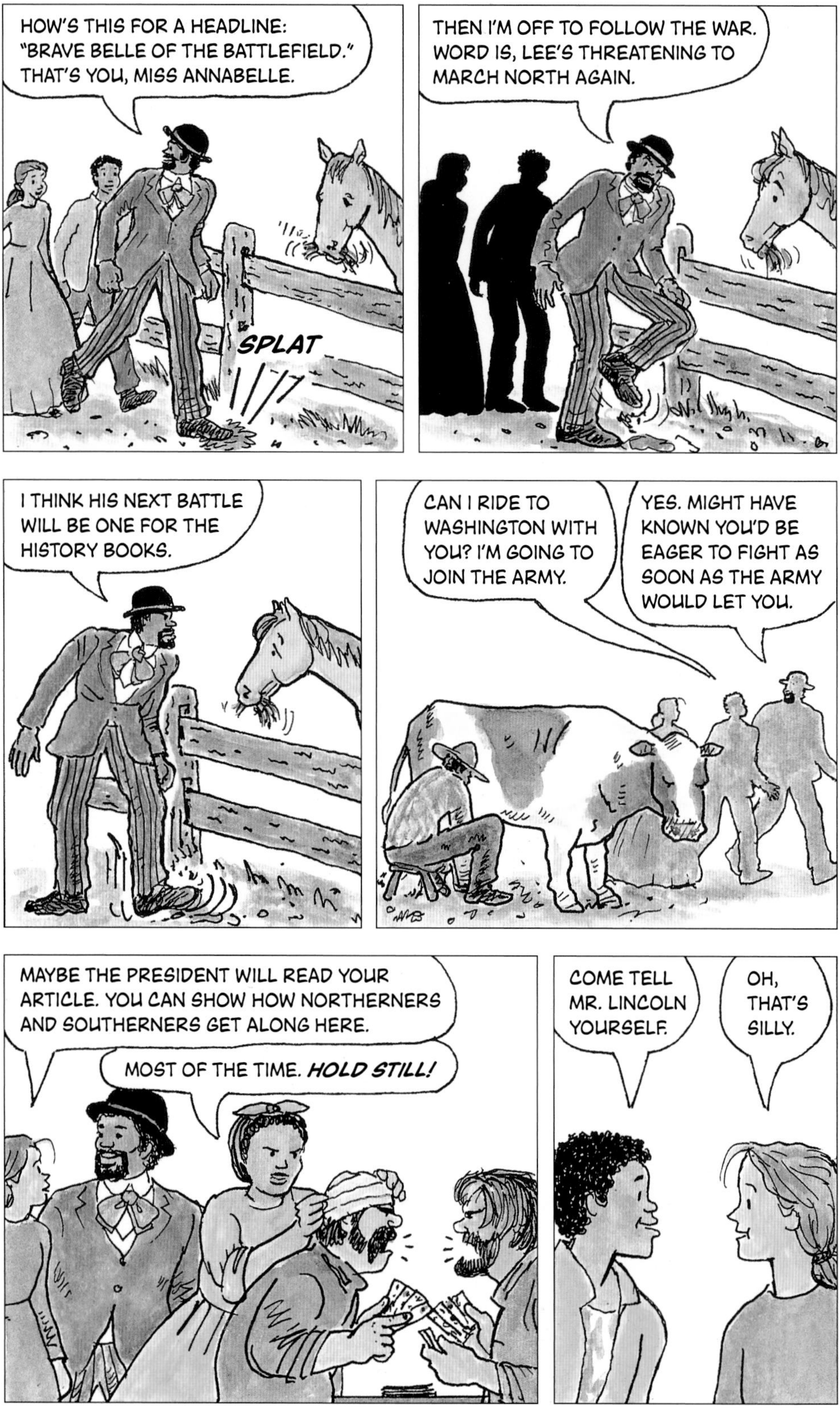
HOW'S THIS FOR A HEADLINE: "BRAVE BELLE OF THE BATTLEFIELD." THAT'S YOU, MISS ANNABELLE.
SPLAT
THEN I'M OFF TO FOLLOW THE WAR. WORD IS, LEE'S THREATENING TO MARCH NORTH AGAIN.
I THINK HIS NEXT BATTLE WILL BE ONE FOR THE HISTORY BOOKS.
CAN I RIDE TO WASHINGTON WITH YOU? I'M GOING TO JOIN THE ARMY.
YES. MIGHT HAVE KNOWN YOU'D BE EAGER TO FIGHT AS SOON AS THE ARMY WOULD LET YOU.
MAYBE THE PRESIDENT WILL READ YOUR ARTICLE. YOU CAN SHOW HOW NORTHERNERS AND SOUTHERNERS GET ALONG HERE.
MOST OF THE TIME. HOLD STILL!
COME TELL MR. LINCOLN YOURSELF.
OH, THAT'S SILLY.

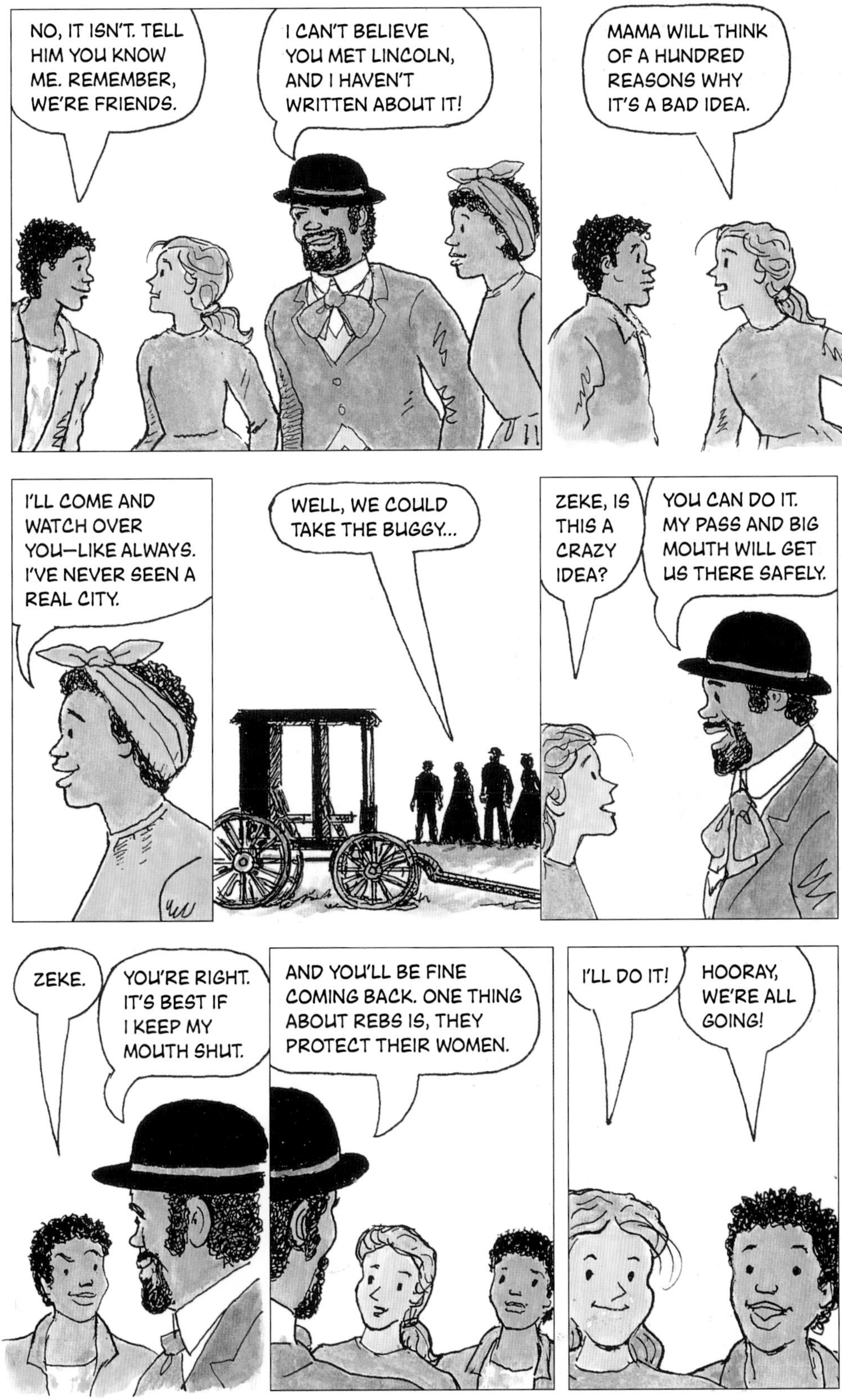
NO, IT ISN'T. TELL HIM YOU KNOW ME. REMEMBER, WE'RE FRIENDS.
I CAN'T BELIEVE YOU MET LINCOLN, AND I HAVEN'T WRITTEN ABOUT IT!
MAMA WILL THINK OF A HUNDRED REASONS WHY IT'S A BAD IDEA.
I'LL COME AND WATCH OVER YOU—LIKE ALWAYS. I'VE NEVER SEEN A REAL CITY.
WELL, WE COULD TAKE THE BUGGY...
ZEKE, IS THIS A CRAZY IDEA?
YOU CAN DO IT. MY PASS AND BIG MOUTH WILL GET US THERE SAFELY.
ZEKE.
YOU'RE RIGHT. IT'S BEST IF I KEEP MY MOUTH SHUT.
AND YOU'LL BE FINE COMING BACK. ONE THING ABOUT REBS IS, THEY PROTECT THEIR WOMEN.
I'LL DO IT!
HOORAY, WE'RE ALL GOING!

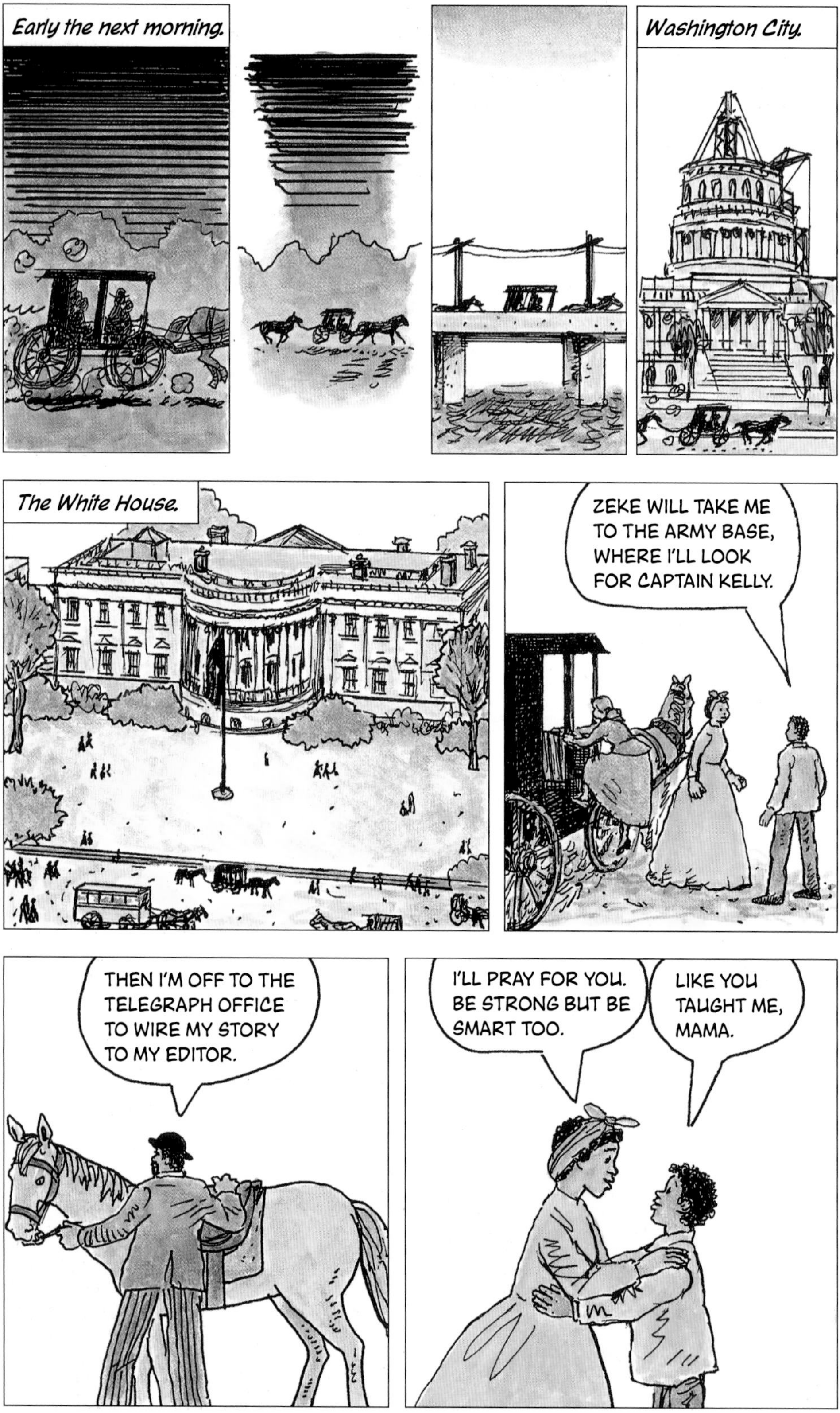
Early the next morning.
Washington City.
The White House.
ZEKE WILL TAKE ME TO THE ARMY BASE, WHERE I'LL LOOK FOR CAPTAIN KELLY.
THEN I'M OFF TO THE TELEGRAPH OFFICE TO WIRE MY STORY TO MY EDITOR.
I'LL PRAY FOR YOU. BE STRONG BUT BE SMART TOO.
LIKE YOU TAUGHT ME, MAMA.

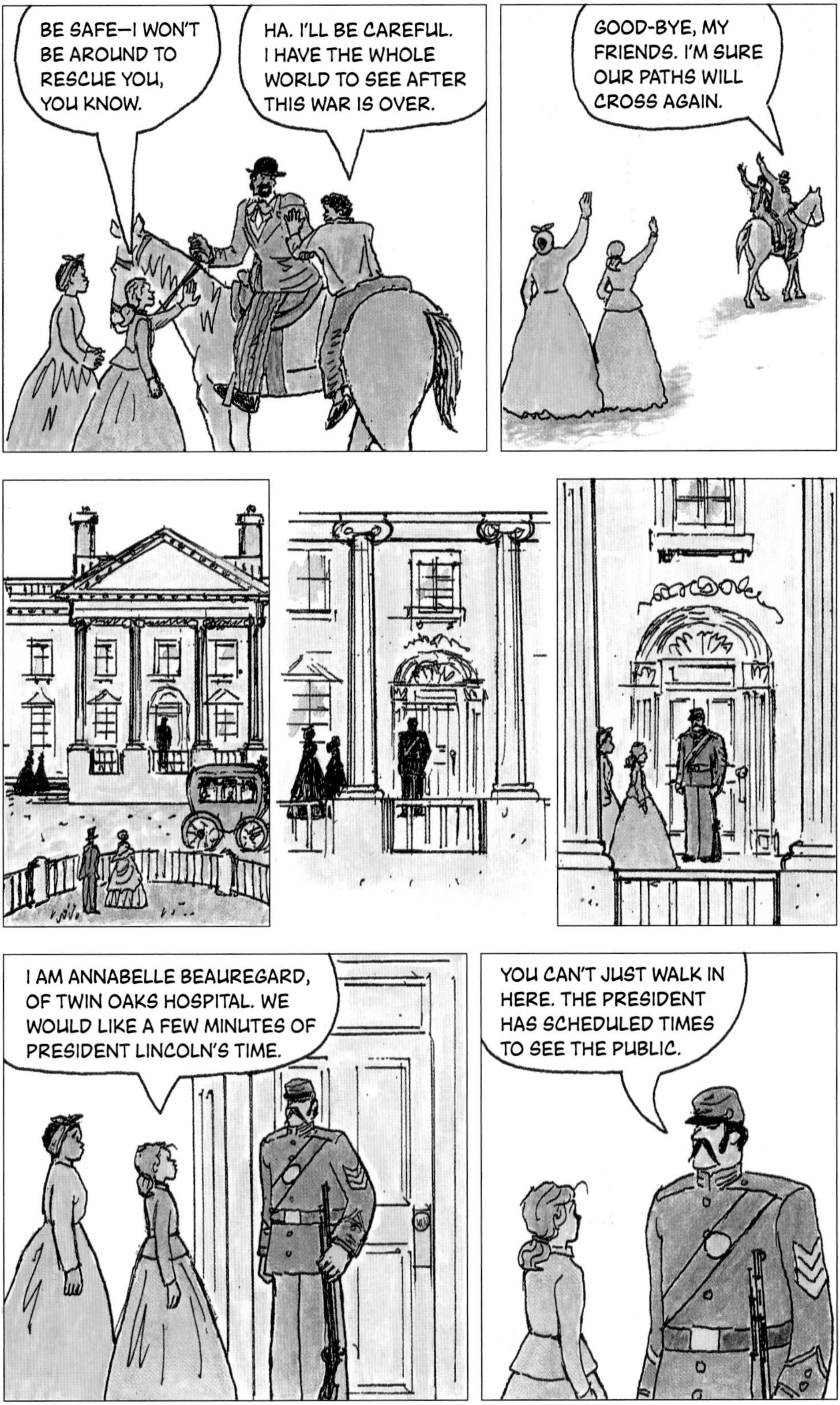
BE SAFE—I WON'T BE AROUND TO RESCUE YOU, YOU KNOW.
HA. I'LL BE CAREFUL. I HAVE THE WHOLE WORLD TO SEE AFTER THIS WAR IS OVER.
GOOD-BYE, MY FRIENDS. I'M SURE OUR PATHS WILL CROSS AGAIN.
I AM ANNABELLE BEAUREGARD, OF TWIN OAKS HOSPITAL. WE WOULD LIKE A FEW MINUTES OF PRESIDENT LINCOLN'S TIME.
YOU CAN'T JUST WALK IN HERE. THE PRESIDENT HAS SCHEDULED TIMES TO SEE THE PUBLIC.

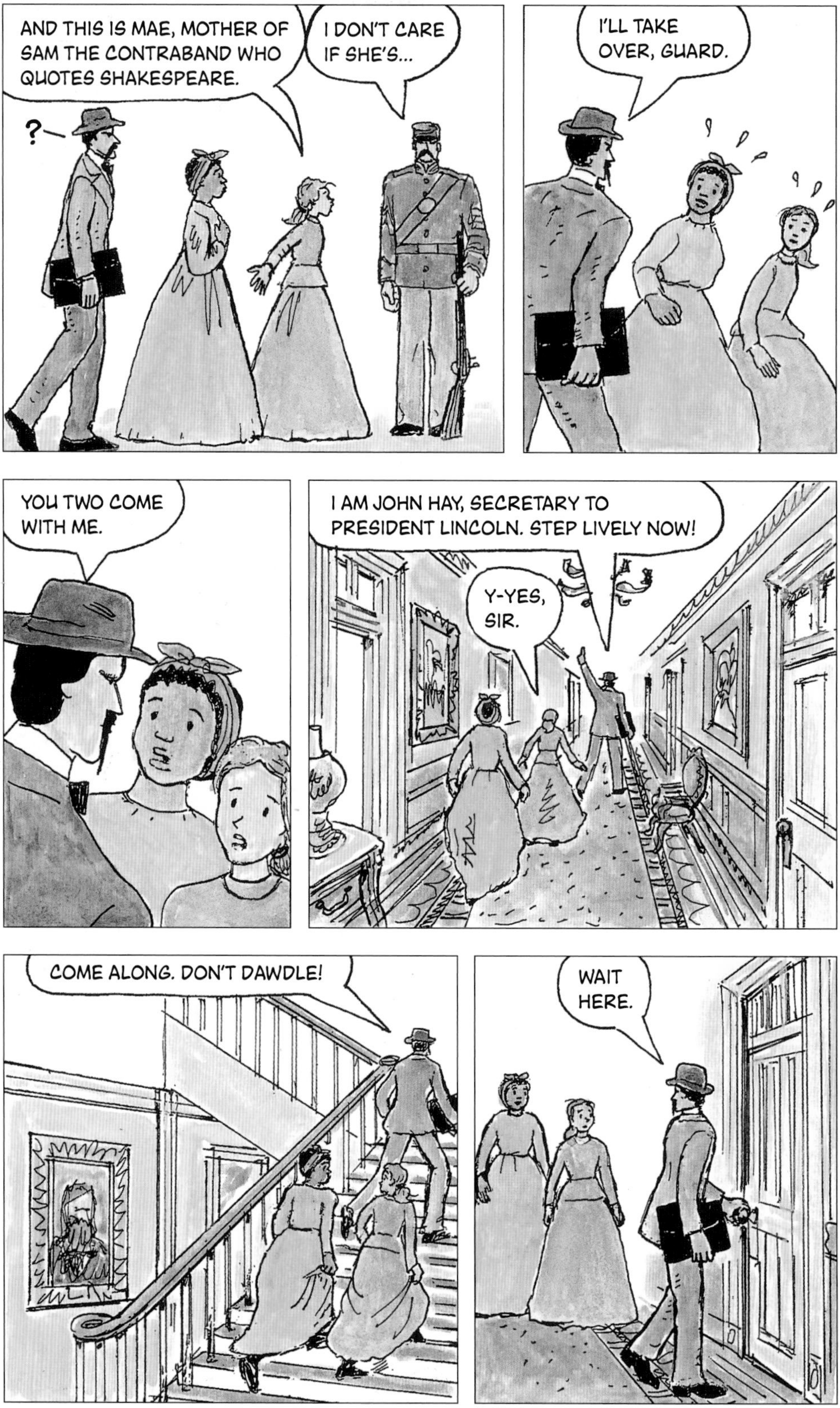
AND THIS IS MAE, MOTHER OF SAM THE CONTRABAND WHO QUOTES SHAKESPEARE.
I DON'T CARE IF SHE'S...
?
I'LL TAKE OVER, GUARD.
YOU TWO COME WITH ME.
I AM JOHN HAY, SECRETARY TO PRESIDENT LINCOLN. STEP LIVELY NOW!
Y-YES, SIR.
COME ALONG. DON'T DAWDLE!
WAIT HERE.

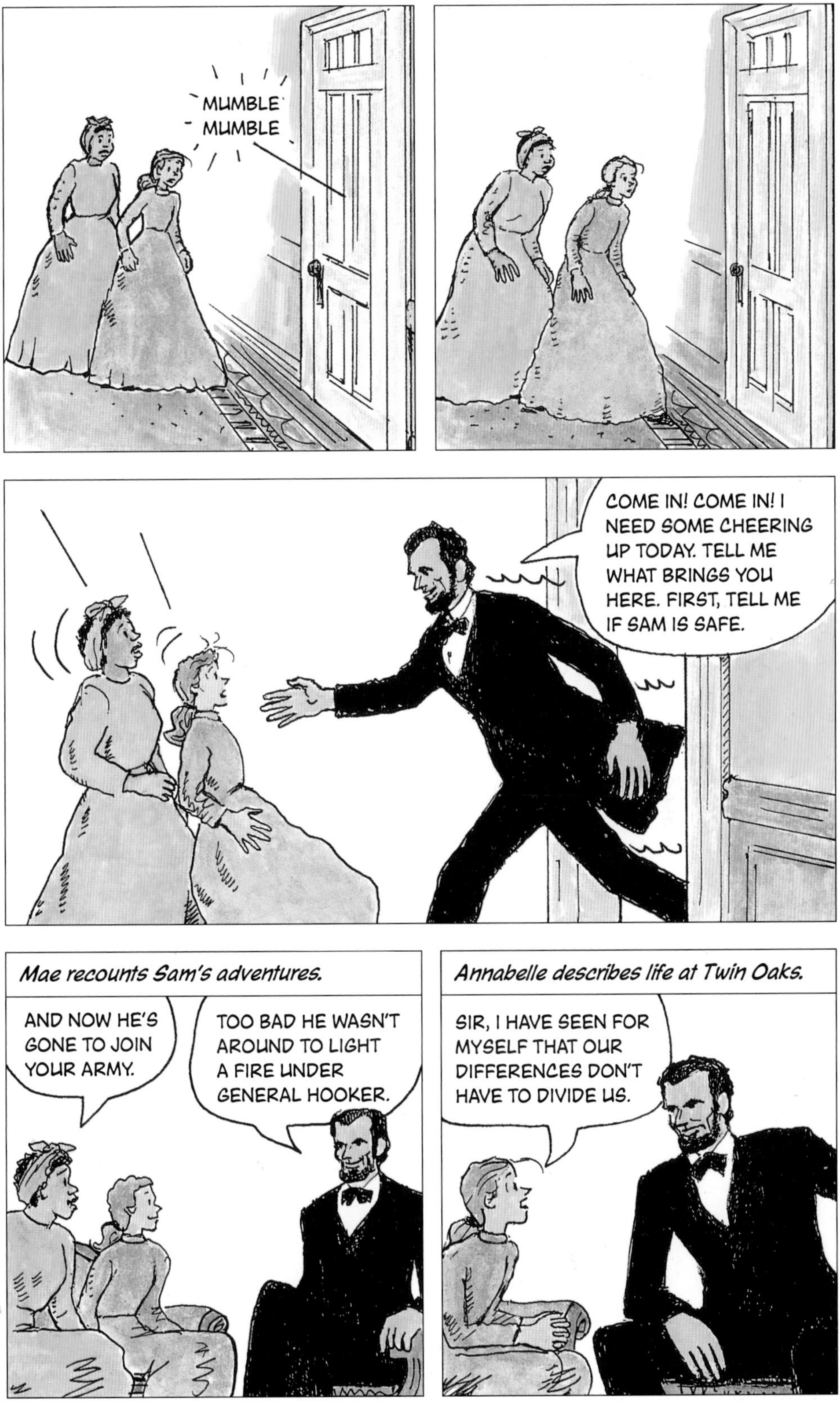
MUMBLE MUMBLE
COME IN! COME IN! I NEED SOME CHEERING UP TODAY. TELL ME WHAT BRINGS YOU HERE. FIRST, TELL ME IF SAM IS SAFE.
Mae recounts Sam's adventures.
AND NOW HE'S GONE TO JOIN YOUR ARMY.
TOO BAD HE WASN'T AROUND TO LIGHT A FIRE UNDER GENERAL HOOKER.
Annabelle describes life at Twin Oaks.
SIR, I HAVE SEEN FOR MYSELF THAT OUR DIFFERENCES DON'T HAVE TO DIVIDE US.

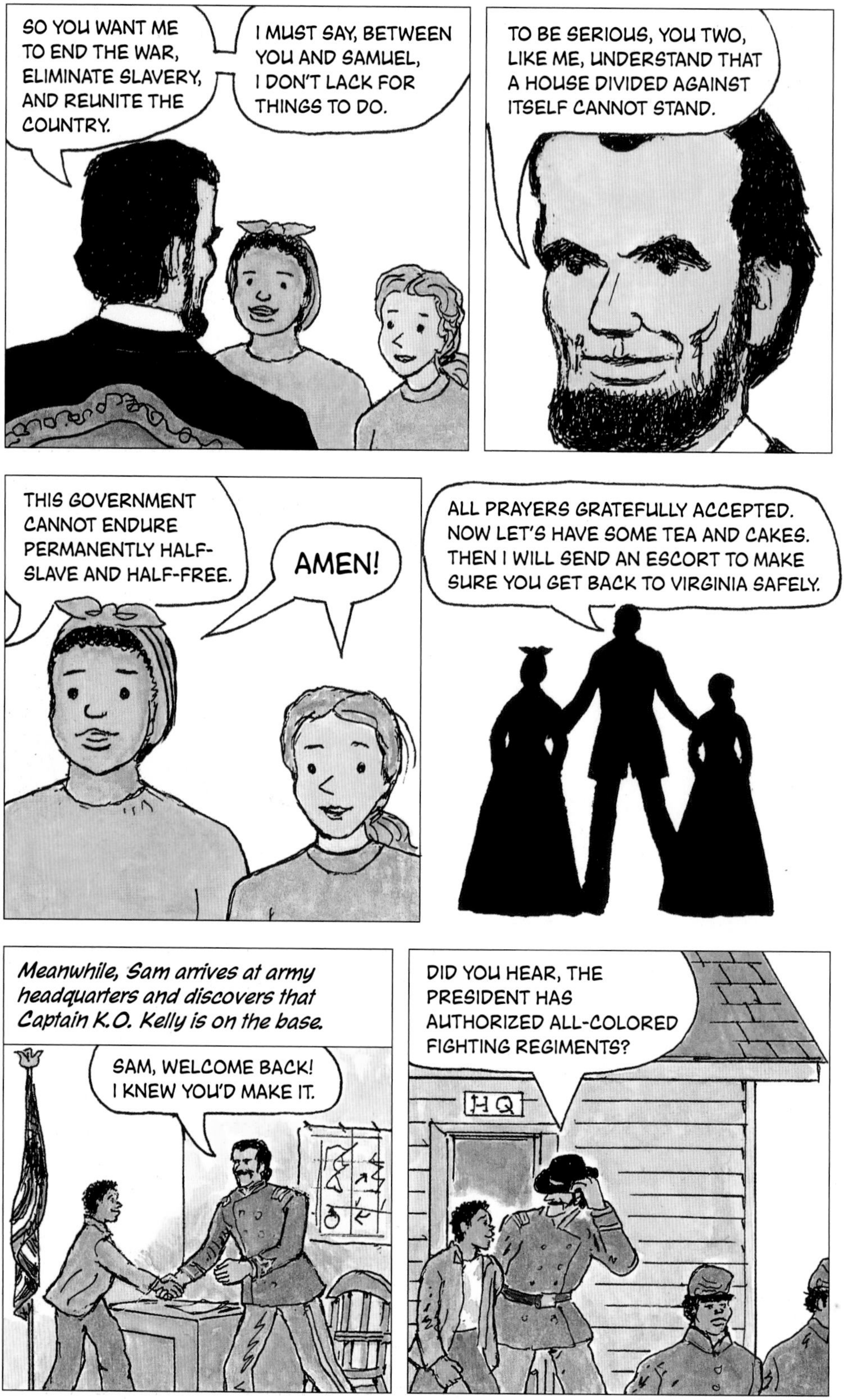
SO YOU WANT ME TO END THE WAR, ELIMINATE SLAVERY, AND REUNITE THE COUNTRY.
I MUST SAY, BETWEEN YOU AND SAMUEL, I DON'T LACK FOR THINGS TO DO.
TO BE SERIOUS, YOU TWO, LIKE ME, UNDERSTAND THAT A HOUSE DIVIDED AGAINST ITSELF CANNOT STAND.
THIS GOVERNMENT CANNOT ENDURE PERMANENTLY HALF-SLAVE AND HALF-FREE.
AMEN!
ALL PRAYERS GRATEFULLY ACCEPTED. NOW LET'S HAVE SOME TEA AND CAKES. THEN I WILL SEND AN ESCORT TO MAKE SURE YOU GET BACK TO VIRGINIA SAFELY.
Meanwhile, Sam arrives at army headquarters and discovers that Captain K.O. Kelly is on the base.
SAM, WELCOME BACK! I KNEW YOU'D MAKE IT.
DID YOU HEAR, THE PRESIDENT HAS AUTHORIZED ALL-COLORED FIGHTING REGIMENTS?
HQ

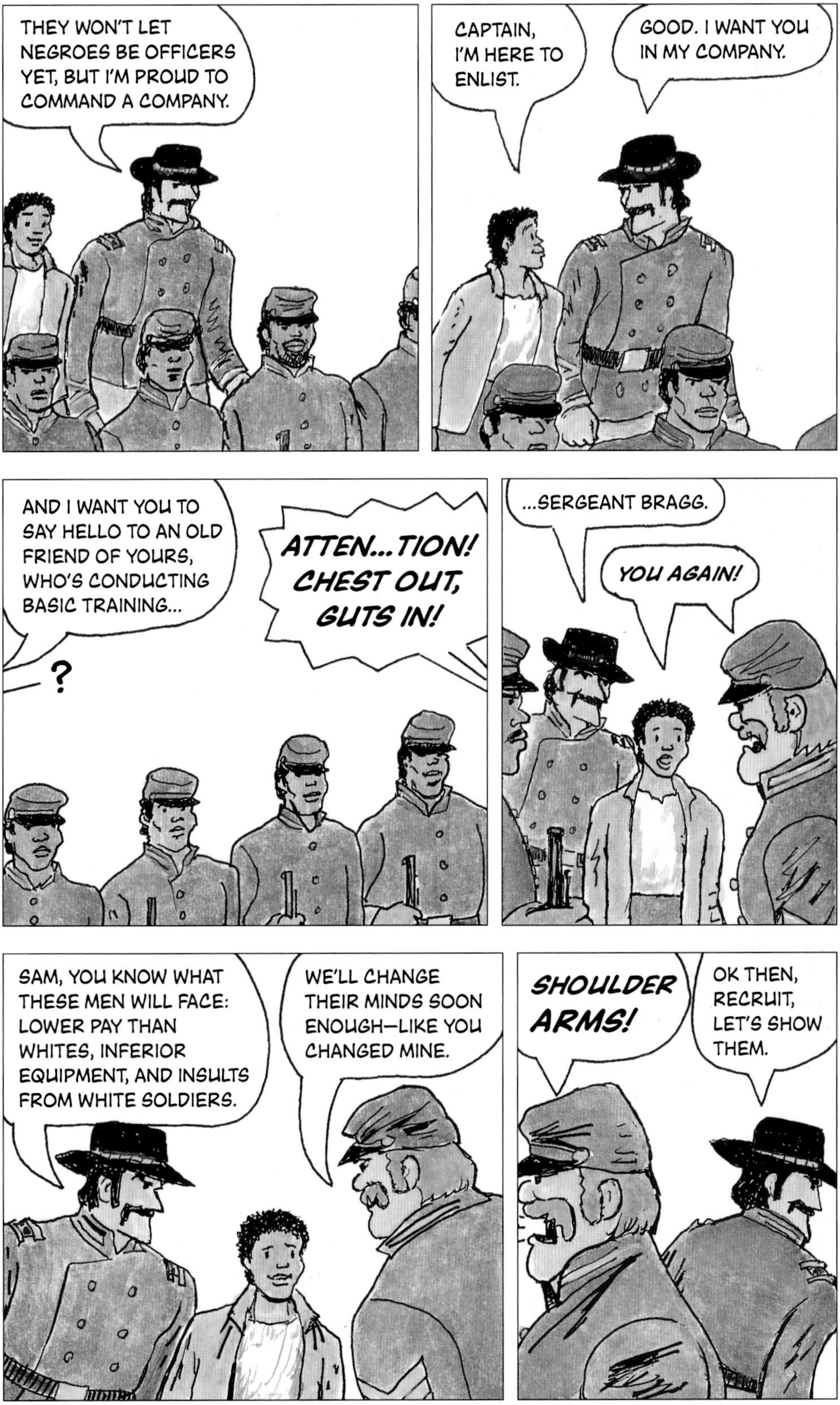
THEY WON'T LET NEGROES BE OFFICERS YET, BUT I'M PROUD TO COMMAND A COMPANY.
CAPTAIN, I'M HERE TO ENLIST.
GOOD. I WANT YOU IN MY COMPANY.
AND I WANT YOU TO SAY HELLO TO AN OLD FRIEND OF YOURS, WHO'S CONDUCTING BASIC TRAINING...
?
ATTEN...TION! CHEST OUT, GUTS IN!
...SERGEANT BRAGG.
YOU AGAIN!
SAM, YOU KNOW WHAT THESE MEN WILL FACE: LOWER PAY THAN WHITES, INFERIOR EQUIPMENT, AND INSULTS FROM WHITE SOLDIERS.
WE'LL CHANGE THEIR MINDS SOON ENOUGH—LIKE YOU CHANGED MINE.
SHOULDER ARMS!
OK THEN, RECRUIT, LET'S SHOW THEM.

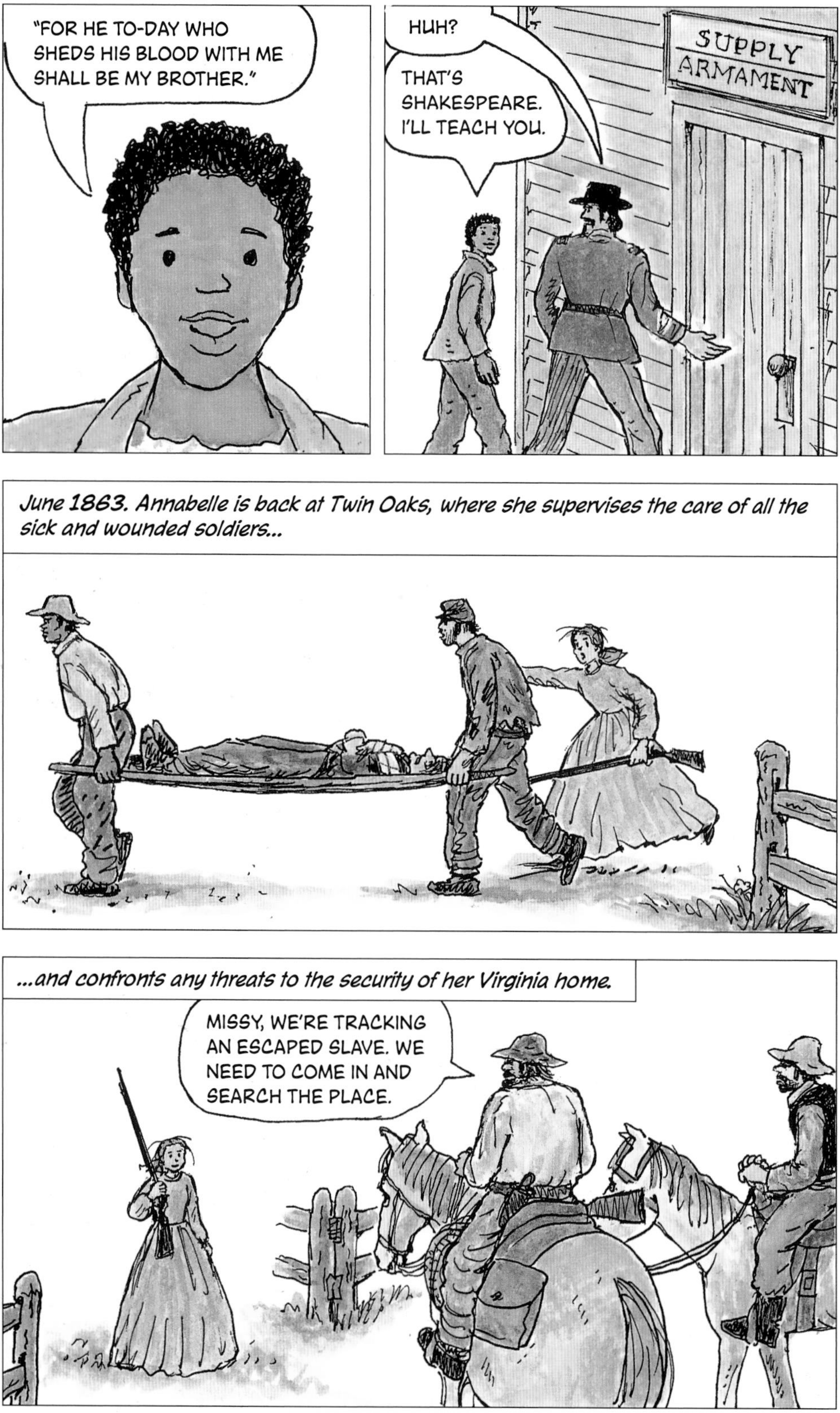
"FOR HE TO-DAY WHO SHEDS HIS BLOOD WITH ME SHALL BE MY BROTHER."
HUH?
THAT'S SHAKESPEARE. I'LL TEACH YOU.
SUPPLY
ARMAMENT
June 1863. Annabelle is back at Twin Oaks, where she supervises the care of all the sick and wounded soldiers...
...and confronts any threats to the security of her Virginia home.
MISSY, WE'RE TRACKING AN ESCAPED SLAVE. WE NEED TO COME IN AND SEARCH THE PLACE.

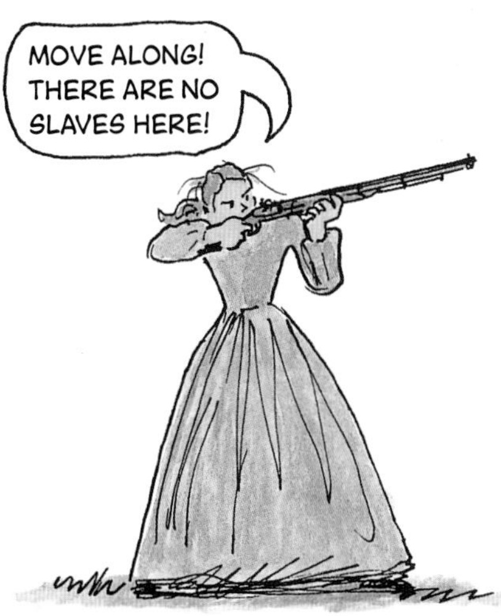
MOVE ALONG! THERE ARE NO SLAVES HERE!

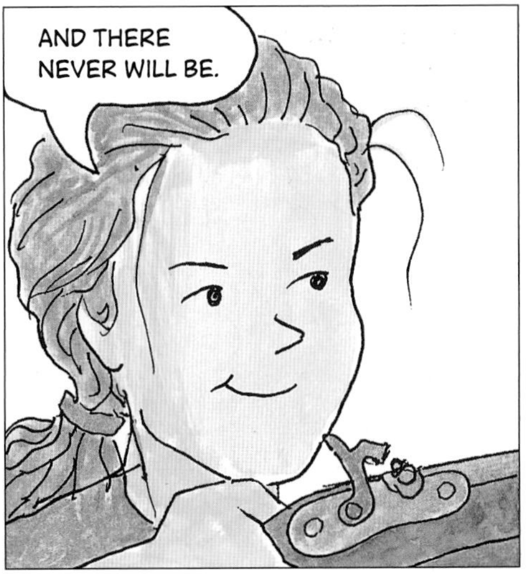
AND THERE NEVER WILL BE.

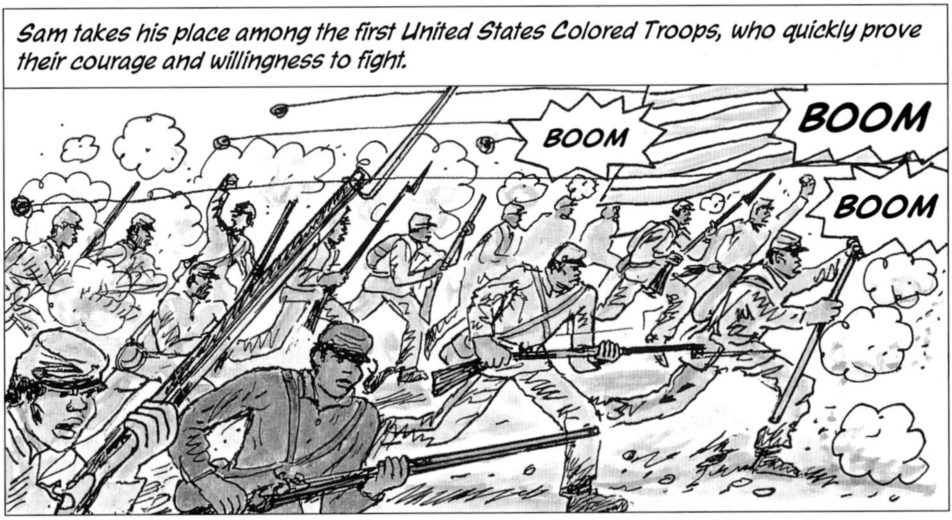
Sam takes his place among the first United States Colored Troops, who quickly prove their courage and willingness to fight.
BOOM
BOOM
BOOM

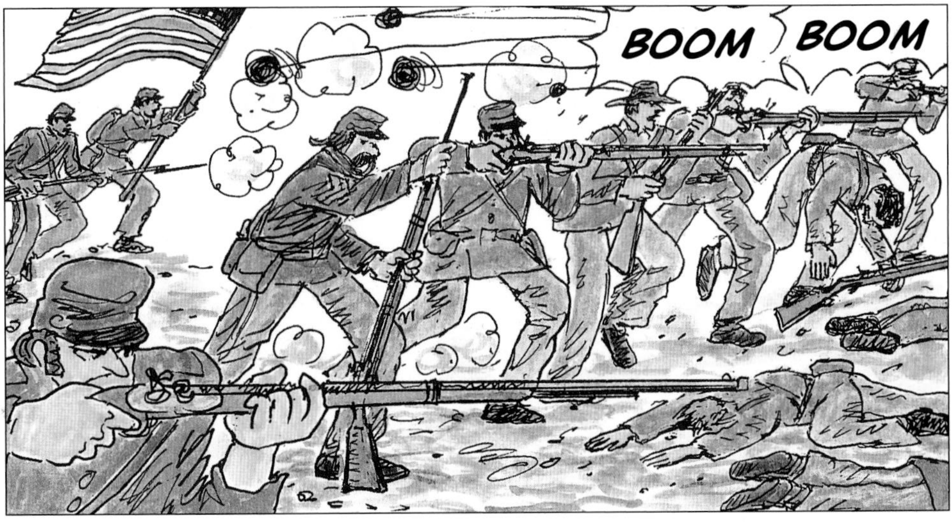
BOOM
BOOM

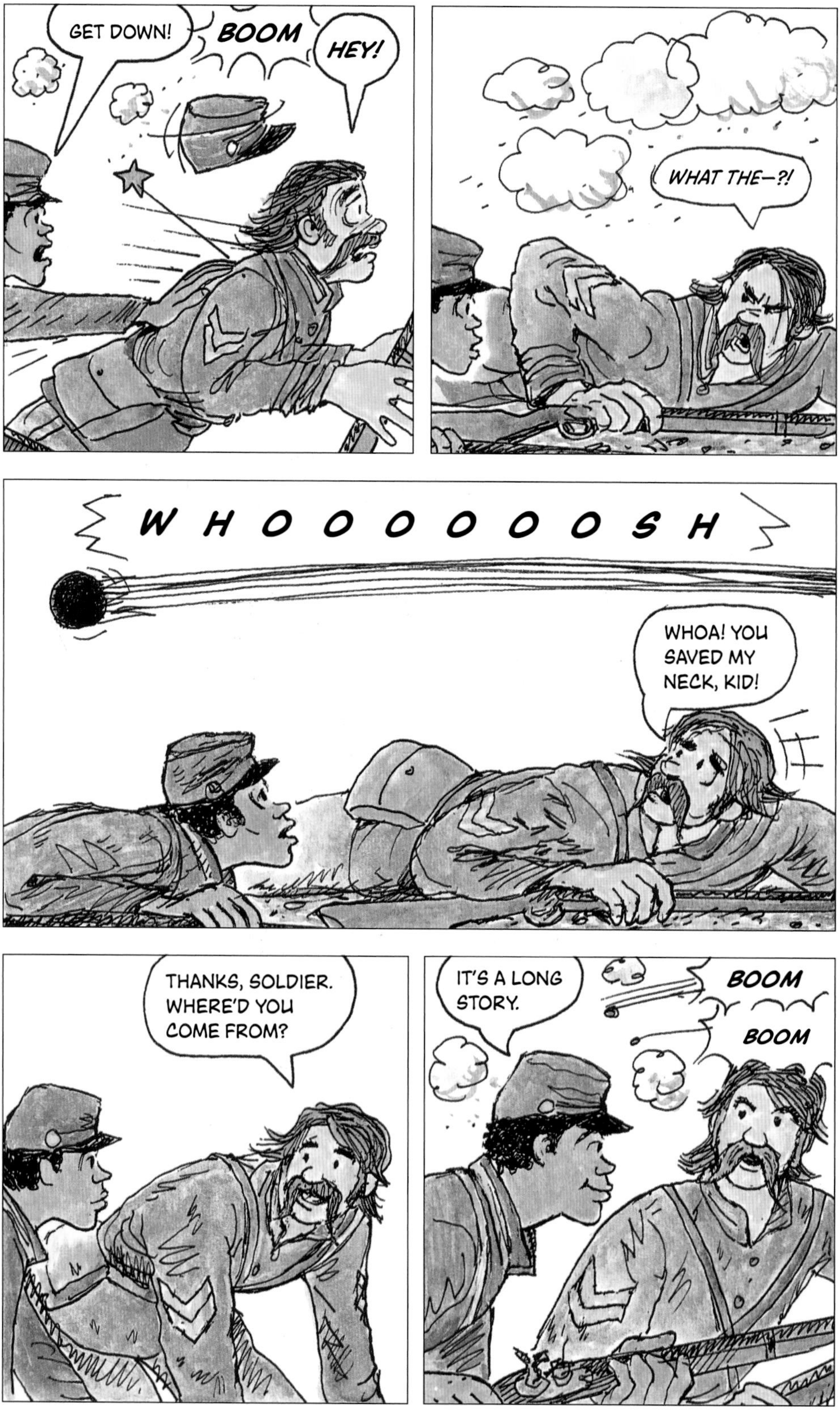
GET DOWN!
BOOM
HEY!
WHAT THE—?!
WHOOOOOOOSH
WHOA! YOU SAVED MY NECK, KID!
THANKS, SOLDIER. WHERE'D YOU COME FROM?
IT'S A LONG STORY.
BOOM
BOOM

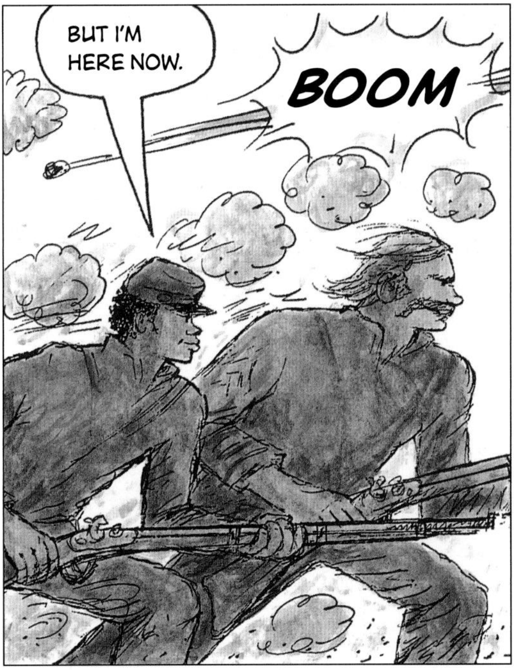
BUT I'M HERE NOW.
BOOM

EPILOGUE

IN WHICH WE LEARN WHAT'S FACT
AND WHAT'S FICTION

CHAPTER 1

Sam, Annabelle, Mae, and Joseph are fictional, but...

* The children of house slaves often did grow up alongside the owner's children on a plantation. Young slaves might work around the plantation house until they were old enough to work in the fields.

* The Bible and the works of Shakespeare were familiar books in Southern homes, so if a slave had the chance and the courage to learn to read (even though it was forbidden), it's possible that they would have read these books.

* Courageous plantation slaves and sympathetic whites *did* help runaway slaves get to freedom.

CHAPTER 2

The actions of the slave hunter and Twist's threat to sell Sam may seem terribly unfair, but...

* Slave hunters did work throughout the South hunting down runaways for reward money. Many turned to trickery—ripping up slaves' identification papers or kidnapping—to grab a profit on the slaves, who had no way to defend themselves.

* One of the greatest punishments slaves suffered was to have their families broken up and family members sold away to distant states.

CHAPTER 3

Sam tells Annabelle, "My father can be free now," but would he really be "free"?

* With the Second Confiscation Act, Union Army officers were no longer obligated to return runaway slaves to their owners. Technically, these runaways were considered captured property, but in reality, upon entering Union territory they were free.

CHAPTER 4

President Lincoln's Emancipation Proclamation declared that slaves in Confederate states were free, but...

*   While Lincoln believed that slavery was wrong, the purpose of the proclamation was really to cause trouble in the South by encouraging more slaves to run. (It said nothing about slaves in the North.) Slavery wasn't officially abolished in the United States until the Thirteenth Amendment to the Constitution was adopted after the war, in December 1865. Nevertheless, despite its limitations, the Emancipation Proclamation seemed to many African Americans the first step toward true freedom, and Lincoln is considered the president who freed the slaves.

CHAPTER 5

Zeke Jefferson didn't really exist, but...

*   The character of Zeke was partially inspired by the real-life Thomas Morris Chester, the only African American reporter for a major newspaper during the Civil War.

*   With the invention of the telegraph—and because the fighting was taking place on our own soil—the Civil War was the first war that could be reported immediately from the battlefield by reporters, artists, and, for the first time, photographers, all of whom competed for "scoops."

The characters Sam meets at Camp Barker are fictional, but...

*   Camp Barker was a real contraband camp, located in northwest Washington City (Washington, DC). Abraham Lincoln was reported to have visited it on his way to his country home outside the city. Today, in the neighborhood of the former Camp Barker stands the African American Civil War Memorial, honoring the African American soldiers who fought for the North during the war.

CHAPTER 6

It may seem unusual that Twin Oaks becomes a hospital, but...

*   Because the fighting ranged everywhere throughout the South and there were so many wounded, private homes were often turned into temporary

hospitals. While it was less common, some hospitals in both the North and the South cared for wounded men from both sides.

* During the Civil War, disease, amputation, and infection killed far more men than bullets did.

CHAPTER 7

Clara Barton never visited the fictional Twin Oaks, but...

* In real life, Clara Barton was the first female nurse to demand to serve on the American battlefields, and she was indeed at the Battle of Fredericksburg. After the war, she went on to establish the American Red Cross.

* Clara Barton talks about a Confederate soldier who risked his life to give water to Union soldiers. There's a statue to this soldier, Sgt. Richard Kirkland, called "The Angel of Marye's Heights," at the Fredericksburg and Spotsylvania National Military Park, in Virginia.

Sam didn't really meet President Lincoln or his son or his bickering advisers at Camp Barker, but...

* Thomas (Tad) was the youngest of Lincoln's four sons. Sadly, Tad died at age eighteen. In fact, only Robert Todd Lincoln, the oldest, made it to adulthood. Edward, the second son, died before his fourth birthday; William (Willie) died at age eleven.

* Unlike many politicians who surround themselves with advisers who agree with them, Lincoln purposely appointed to his cabinet men whose opinions differed from his own—not to mention from one another's.

* It's true that Abraham Lincoln's favorite Shakespeare play was *Macbeth*: "I think nothing equals *Macbeth*," he once said.

CHAPTER 8

Captain K.O. Kelly, Sergeant Bragg, and their mission with Sam are all fictional, but...

* This kind of skirmish may well have happened during the winter of 1862–63 while the Union and Confederate armies were camped on either side of the Rappahannock River.

* At this time (late 1862), African Americans *were* allowed to enlist in the Union Army in noncombat jobs such as cook or scout. But it was extremely dangerous for former slaves to be caught in the South working for the Union. The Confederate Congress stated that any African American soldier or any

white officer commanding black soldiers would be severely punished—or even executed.

Joseph couldn't have known what would happen after the war, but...
* He was right that the struggle for equality would last long after the war was over. The Thirteenth Amendment abolished slavery in 1865, but it took another hundred years before the Civil Rights Act outlawed racial discrimination in 1964. And even though we elected an African American president in 2008, this country still struggles to achieve true equality of the races.

CHAPTER 9

In our fictional story, slaves at Twin Oaks are set free and then hired to work for pay.
* In reality, after the war, plantation owners made deals with former slaves to work their land in return for a share of the profits. The system was called sharecropping—but was almost always an unfair arrangement for the freedmen because the plantation owners rarely passed along any of the profits to the workers.

CHAPTER 10

When Zeke says that he thinks General Lee's next battle "will be one for the history books"...
* He's talking about what will become known as the Battle of Gettysburg, in Pennsylvania—Lee's failed attempt to carry the fight to the North. This was later the site of Lincoln's famous Gettysburg Address, in which he emphasized the importance of equality for all.

Annabelle and Mae didn't really meet with President Lincoln, but...
* It's true that Abraham Lincoln set aside times during the week to speak with ordinary people, who would line up outside the White House for the chance to meet with their president.
* Lincoln really was unhappy with Northern general Joseph Hooker. Although he was known as "Fighting Joe," when he had the advantage over Lee at the Battle of Chancellorsville, Hooker suddenly ordered his troops to retreat and take a defensive position, handing Lee the victory.

• • •

On May 22, 1863, the Bureau of Colored Troops was established. All African American soldiers in the Union Army were now officially designated "U.S. Colored Troops." Despite unequal pay and poor equipment compared to white soldiers, these men fought with courage and tenacity and helped the North win the war. The Civil War continued until April 9, 1865, when Southern general Robert E. Lee surrendered to Union general Ulysses S. Grant at Appomattox Court House, Virginia. Six days later, President Lincoln was assassinated at Ford's Theatre in Washington City, by John Wilkes Booth.

Abraham Lincoln was hated by some, beloved by many, and is now considered one of our greatest presidents. His enduring legacy was to bring about the end of slavery, to hold this country together, and to give us a vision of "a more perfect Union."

ACKNOWLEDGMENTS

It sometimes seemed to us that there are more experts on the Civil War than on any other war in history. We were not among them when we started this project. The following people generously offered their time and their extraordinary knowledge as we researched *Fight for Freedom*. If there are any errors in this book, they are ours.

Will Allison, Pamplin Historical Park, Petersburg, Virginia; Stan Brimberg, Bank Street School, New York City; Spencer R. Crew, George Mason University, and Sandra P. Crew, educator; Rim Gardner, Meadow Farm Museum, Glen Allen, Virginia; John Hennessy, Fredericksburg and Spotsylvania National Military Park, Virginia; Hugh Mercer Apothecary, Fredericksburg, Virginia; Hari Jones, African American Civil War Museum, Washington, DC; Kathleen Lang, Monticello, Charlottesville, Virginia; James A. Percoco, historian and educator; Ron Soodalter, historian; Robert K. Sutton, PhD, National Park Service, Washington, DC; Alex Tillen and Gerry Kester, Frontier Culture Museum, Staunton, Virginia; Yohuru Williams, PhD, Fairfield University, Fairfield, Connecticut.

And the following people helped us in many other ways as we brought the book to fruition: Katie and Matthew Cecconi, Malcolm Liu, Kenneth Mack (map), Margaret Miller (our editor), Marsha Miller, the Milonovich family (Katy, Greg, Megan, Thomas, and Ryan), Gary Morris (our agent), Dr. J. Ronald Rich (neurosurgeon, for enabling Stan to draw without pain), Mariana Serra (graphic design), Richard Shapiro, and Annie Taylor (for fine blacking work on the illustrations).